Folded Birds

samuel leventis

Folded Birds

© 2024 by samuel leventis.

Cover Design by Gráinne Schäfer.

All rights reserved. No part of this book may be reproduced or distributed in any form, or by any means whatsoever, without prior written permission from the author.

The story, all names, characters and incidents portrayed in this book are fictitious. Any resemblance to persons living or dead is entirely coincidental and unintentional.

ISBN-13: 9798323167449

For more, please contact me at: samuel.leventis.books@gmail.com

Contents

The Road...
Greece, 2007

Uncharted Waters
Greece, 1943-1960

San Sto Spiti Sas
Greece, 1962

The Sound Of One Hand Clapping
Japan, 1971

In A City Of High-Rises
Greece / Japan, 1980

Submission
Cambodia / Japan, 1989

...to Mani
Greece, 2007

Check Out
Japan, 1980

Hestia
Greece, 2022

Untested Waters
Austria, 1944

To N, N, and A
everything

Folded Birds

'With a heart unaccustomed to doubting, he never wondered for an instant whether the girl would brave such a storm to keep their rendezvous. He knew nothing of that melancholy and all-too-effective way of passing time by magnifying and complicating his feelings, whether of happiness or uneasiness, through the exercise of imagination.'

– Yukio Mishima,
Shiosai (The Sound of Waves), 1954

'The world is given to me only once, not one existing and one perceived. Subject and object are only one.'

– Erwin Schrödinger,
Mind and Matter, 1958

'Open meeting gate.'

– Sign upon entering Kuonji Temple, Mount Minobu

The Road...

Greece, 2007

1

Diros Caves
19th April 2007

Only when she's back home will she stop to take in what she's done, what she's about to do, here in this land at the edge of the world. Land that almost belonged to her father. But never to her. She has no right to it. She hovers her foot above the brake at a panicked thought – *Do I have the right to be here even now?* – and almost turns back to the airport but she drives on. Her father made his choice. She's making hers.

Even if the land had belonged to her father she could never have belonged to it. Had he chosen to stay then she would simply– not– be. She wouldn't have lived as a local nor would she have arrived today, later in life, as a trespasser. She wouldn't have grown up as a claimed nor a lost daughter, nor would she have been able to speed the national road towards this place nor cycle the mule tracks around it. She wouldn't have borne witness to her father's stories of the golden-lit Hesperides *there* nor would she have been stained by the stardust that has settled on the scorched terrain *here*. Simply she would just– not– be. Unknowing, not existing, nothing at all.

But her father's choices have led to her and to this land and this moment. And now she claims one right to it, that she be allowed to learn its secrets. The land cannot speak but there is a native who can.

That's no practical barrier when he shares her language, although whether he chooses to confess is a different matter.

Alone in the hire car she wishes for company after having kept her recent discovery to herself but all that's around her is strange land and silence. So, although she's ready to talk, to this one man in particular, she isn't sure that she welcomes what he might have to say. She'd like to avoid it in truth. As a psychologist this makes her something of a hypocrite. She's forever reminding patients that confrontation is key, that avoidance is nothing more than instant gratification. She's already booked in for a session on her return; therapists too require professional counsel from time to time and there will be plenty to discuss. Her arrival to the Hellenic mainland. Meeting the man whom she has read so much about in her father's letters. Re-awakening in him a history that he may have resigned to the past.

Learning the truth about what happened to make her father do what he did.

Maybe this is a bad idea but she's committed. Contemplation and morality can come later. She can't turn back now.

She drives with unwavering focus across new ground. She's already travelled far, her destination at the base of the Peloponnese within reach, when she spots the turn-off for Sparta. Its fame has entered the history books and cinemas of her motherland a whole continent away and serves as a stark reminder of where she finds herself, far removed from her ordinary, unremarkable daily living. The tourist in her would be justified to leave the motorway and explore this ancient municipality and its neighbouring byzantine citadel of Mystras, but to visit would be nothing more than misdirection. She glances at the backpack on the passenger seat, its contents so valuable that she's strapped a belt around it, and continues south, resolute that she won't be delayed.

Even so, the city's steadfast army evokes something inside her. Just thirty-two and a life of wanton conformation, like every good Japanese woman, she now shares something of these warriors' hell-bent intractability. Unyielding, impulsive, her seismic act of flying here without telling anyone, not even her husband, has turned her Spartan.

She pulls into a service station following a warning light on the dashboard, the international symbol for low petrol that needs no translation. She doubts the rest of the process will be as simple and is proven right by the attendant who relays something in his incomprehensible language.

"Geia sas," she offers back, pipetting a phrase from the letters and dropping it into this scene.

He's only a teenager and gives a bored expression, uninterested in her greeting.

"Regular," she adds timidly. Another borrowed word, this time from English, which means 'unleaded' back home.

"I don't understand," the boy says, also switching for her sake.

"I want petrol, please."

"Petrelaio?"

She nods.

"Diesel," he says, to confirm.

No. She waves her hand in front of her face, palm outward, to stop him and then looks in the glove compartment for the rental contract.

"Amolyvdi," he says after reading what she can't. "Unleaded. How much?"

She's too afraid to try in any language. She spreads all ten fingers and pushes both hands in the air four times.

"Forty euros?"

She nods, exhausted.

She pays by card then moves to a parking space before going inside the services. She takes a bottle of water from a fridge and places a fifty euro note in front of the cashier who promptly refuses it. She guesses it's because the drink only costs fifty cents and that this is a ludicrous exchange. She uses her card once more.

Back on the road, nausea bubbles low inside her, deeper than ever before. She hopes that the meeting with the man will be easier since he speaks Japanese. She'd attempted to learn some of the local vocabulary but was afforded little time. Flicking through a bilingual dictionary on yesterday's flight, bought on an optimistic whim the day before, she'd landed on a word that resonated more for her than perhaps most students of modern Greek: prosanatolizomai. Despite its gratuitous length the verb has captivated her, comprised of the radicals for 'looking towards' and 'the east' and fused to mean 'to orientate oneself.' She drives on and repeats her newly-acquired word soundlessly – prosanatolizomai, prosanatolizomai – until it drums a rhythm in her head. She'll take this advice and hold off from making any decisions until she has returned home. Until she too has safely re-oriented.

Until then she will meet the man, explain the reason for her presence, and turn stoic as she listens to his justification for what he did to her father. She's already prescribed herself the role of spectator rather than participant, although it's unfair since she's also the instigator. And didn't one of her father's letters share this same sentiment, of the struggle to remain a bystander in the man's life? This gives her a frisson, brings her closer to the author.

It's not too late to about-turn but she's too inquisitive to leave the past to rest, vying for a time capsule that may not want to be uncovered. She can't deny that this excavation is for her own peace of mind even if it's to the detriment of another's. She'll raze the ground and scavenge anyway. She knows this is greed and that it could devastate. Greed always has a cost and despair may be its penalty.

Near the bottom of the land she spots the ocean and pulls over. She imagines what it would be like to flounder out there on a rowboat, battling to gain control of the waves whilst being swept up in them. Her chest tightens, her breath quickens. She needs to compose herself but she can't shake the feeling that after this encounter, sea or land, she'll find herself adrift and flailing. What would she tell a patient? Maybe her only job for now is to stay afloat. Maybe, for today, not capsizing is enough.

Then, after meeting the man, she'll rush to suppress anything that may overwhelm her. Hurriedly, she'll gather up the strands of any exposed, painful discoveries and duly, dully file them into a box labelled something as unproblematic as *Trip to Greece, 2007*, after which she'll seal the lid, only to be opened in therapy or when triggered at an innocuous distance. Perhaps by the wafts of pasticcio from a Mediterranean-themed restaurant in her faraway guarding neighbourhood of Gotanda. Or maybe it will be activated by the glint of azure stitching on a summer kimono, the same hue she saw this morning on the striped flag swelling atop the Acropolis. Even as late as Athens she'd believed that this colour was myth within nature, photo-shopped in, but now that she bears witness to what actually joins sky to sea, here, by the nation's shores, she learns that it truly exists.

This is the land of poetry after all.

Flying away won't numb what mild irritation she's about to rub into an open wound. Pain will follow. She realises that the true meaning of 'out of sight, out of mind' refers not to distance but cognisance. She thinks of her grandmother who would have been proud of her for using a proverb but wonders what she would have made about her travelling here. Either way, this trip deserves a grace period of analysis. It's what she hears the Americans in their shows call closure. She'll take it to therapy where it will be safer to unpack no matter how pretty the wrapping adorning the box.

She turns on the radio for distraction and flicks through the pre-set stations. In between the static there's only a news broadcast that could be describing the end of the world for all she knows and folk music that's unaccompanied by lyrics. She can't decipher the emotion of the piece. If she does bow to visceral emotions in front of the man she can always blame jet-lag; it's currently morning but her body disagrees. Throughout the flight she was restless and relieved to disembark even if that meant navigating the language as well as the land. All she's really had to do though is follow the express-way that's supplanted the mule-ridden tracks since their appearance in the letters half a century ago. GPS and toll-roads; she's grateful for these conveniences but they've left her ahead of schedule.

She feels a swoosh of emetic unease. Maybe it's the mind-boggling heat, maybe fatigue. She ignores a third potential explanation and thinks, most likely it's anticipation. She teaches patients that uncertainty about the future is made up of opportunity, excitement and fear. Today it's chiefly the latter. The whirlpool in her chest counters the fierceness of Charybdis decimating Odysseus's sailors but it isn't enough to deter her.

She joins a winding road, locking herself between the barren Taygetus mountain range and the sun-kissed water. She drives deeper into this middle nail, committing to the second of the Peloponnese's three basal headlands that hook the country's topography into the sea with a grip as unremitting as Athena's brawny owl. The land seems powerful. Severe. Alluring.

This is Mani.

Before this past week, she hadn't heard of this region. That she shares its name, that she too is called Mani, still feels like a coincidence rather than a pointed connection.

Her father had petitioned for this peculiar name. In Japanese it translates as 'gemstone,' as rare and unfathomable a choice as it was common to be called something like Keiko or Yoshiko. Mani might have detested its quirkiness in her youth but she hadn't questioned its origin other than to guess that she was her father's precious jewel. She knew of his interest in Greece but hadn't connected the dots. The clues were in plain sight. There was the framed country-wide map in his office that she'd neglected to scrutinise, noting only its ample ratio of sea to land rather than honing in on its districts. There was his preference for bed-time recitals of the Heroes rather than homespun fairy tales like Momotaro or the star-crossed lovers, Orihime and Hikoboshi. Lastly, and blindly, she'd never questioned why he'd nicknamed her Manishi. Only this week on learning of a place called Mani had she considered the significance. It wasn't just a cutesy moniker; Manishi, literally, 'due west.'

Mani, the place, is where her father's letters have led her, Mani, the woman. She wonders what he would have thought of her belated discovery.

She casts a dewy-eyed impression. The headland is unfathomable, relegating the earlier workable cypress plains and swapping them for steep impenetrable mountains. There are pockets of traditional stone tower houses, some boastful and hardened, others renovated and gleaming. Most have crumbled from abandonment due to the pull of opportune life elsewhere. For a harsh land that offers small salvation, that people chose to settle here at all is remarkable. In hasty research, she'd read that the Maniots held firm not only against the Venetians and the Ottomans but also from the Germans and Italians as they wrangled farther north. Their isolation and mulish reputation enabled them to be the last self-governed region until the unified state of Greece. Obstinacy can be taken one of two ways and she admires the locals rather than considering them unregenerate, not when she lacks their resilience. Not when she pines to be back in Tokyo's incandescence and its cradle of hyperactivity.

From the outset this place shouldn't beset life but life persists in spite of it. Pockets of relief exist when she really looks. There are haphazard bursts of olive trees, pebbled coves that break the dry terrain and a sparsity of clouds to provide momentary shade. Countering the impossibleness of this land is the thing that really makes it enviable: its energy. The electricity is undeniable. She hasn't even stepped onto the ground and can't deny that there's magic. After all, this is the fabled epicentre of the world.

She breaks in Limeni, a picture perfect hotspot of an oasis with its narrow row of hotels and bars. Neat steps cut into the marbled cliff and lead to the crystal water. She could stop and soak up the sun. Do what Japanese women are prone not to and bronze her skin. Dive into the bay and cool her overcooked mind. These are nefarious enticements. She surprises herself with a dredging of nostalgia. She pictures being tucked in bed whilst her father narrated the verse of the Sirens, the temptresses who drew travellers close. From the car window she's presented with the modern day equivalent: a waitress who serves gilded-nectared drinks dripping with condensation. Dry-throated as she may be, she withholds and pulls off.

Farther along there's a junction. An arrow signals Areopoli in one direction and the Spilaio Dirou, the Diros Caves, in another. Her English is adequate, her Greek not even elementary, but together proficient enough to know that she's close. She shouldn't dally but finds herself parking up.

There's nothing much except for a souvenir shop where plates and vases are painted in clichéd motifs of oxidised oranges or peacock-blue hoops surrounding the evil eye. She idles indoors, browsing to escape both the heat and her destination. Without blinking, the owner rises from his chair and kickstarts into a pitch. He points around and gives two prices, the before and after, a time limited offer for a special customer. She waves him off but on the way out he holds up a porcelain chalice. It bears a stem that protrudes through the centre.

"Watch please this Pythagoras cup."

He raises it above a tray and pours water so that the cup is two-thirds full. He takes a sip and refills it but this time to the brim. As the water rises above a marked groove something changes: it floods out from a secret compartment until it has fully drained. It's fun but she smiles politely and leaves empty-handed.

Outside, she considers that this convergence would have been an intervention, the shopkeeper an Olympian god in disguise, if it had occurred millennia earlier. It's not hard to evaluate his interference: he's warning her of greed. But he's too late because she won't be discouraged. At the least he's counselling her to be moderate but there's no middle-ground; between a drought and a flood she'll risk the deluge.

On her arrival to the cave she manoeuvres a final tight descent into the site's car park. The walk down is stunning, the tide even lower turquoise and still. There are a few people loitering. She buys a ticket for the Japanese tour that departs in half an hour's time. She picks out some Greek and American voices but there's no one that resembles her. Soon she's called, in Japanese, to the cave entrance where Greek men organise tourists into bundles and hand them life-vests. To hear her own language is disconcerting where it might otherwise feel comforting because there's just one daily tour in her mother tongue and only one man who operates it.

She clutches the heavy backpack to her chest and approaches. Having expected to delay her reveal, with the man distracted by other non-natives like herself, she's horrified to discover that she's the only one who has signed up. This isn't how it was supposed to be.

She fastens the jacket and is directed inside the dank mouth where plastic boats, sized somewhere between a kayak and a gondola, bob on the subterranean lake. Lights radiate from underwater whilst others are propped behind yellow stalactites that drop the roof to head-height. She watches the group ahead of her gasp as they're unhooked.

An older Greek man calls her towards his boat in perfect Japanese. The tour is due to last forty minutes. She's seized by terror that they'll be together for this long. She's so overwhelmed that her eyes glaze over and she can't focus on his face. She loses her balance. He takes her hand and helps her aboard.

"Konnichiwa. It's just you." He speaks fluently, so unlikely considering his heritage.

She smiles, too choked to reply.

"A private tour. Consider yourself lucky." He looks at her and pauses. She meets his gaze and detects that he too has been caught off guard. He breaks away and acts with indifference. Perhaps he hasn't seen the resemblance.

Despite his age, which she knows for a fact is sixty-two, he's sturdy as he releases the boat from its moorings and pushes off.

"I'm Akis," he says, unaware that she already knows this much. "I can show you the formations that bear a resemblance to animals. People like that. Or I can share facts about the cave's history. Since it's just you, is there anything that you'd like me to focus on?"

"Arigatou. Let me think." She falters as they enter a narrow passage. Her voice is hoarse, the words trapped. She breathes deep and controlled as she's instructed countless patients. "Actually, there is something that I would like to see. A column."

He's already stooped and meets her eyes with a curious, arresting stare. "There are many stacks throughout the cave. Where the ceiling joins the floor."

"There's one that may or may not be complete."

He stops pushing the oars against the wall.

"Ask me my name," she says. She's surprised by her bold request but it's her way of storming past her hesitancy.

The boat makes slow progress until it leaves the tunnel.

Akis doesn't look away from her. Finally, "What's your name?"

"Mani."

The passage gives way to an indoor twinkling expanse. It could appear sinister from the outset, not helped by the shiver that runs the length of her back, but this spot could be romantic in other circumstances. She knows this for a fact because she has read about a kiss that once happened here.

Akis doesn't cast the oars back into the water but instead sits. His mind takes him somewhere else. Probably here, probably forty-five years earlier.

"Mani?" He points to the world beneath. "As in Mani?"

"Okazaki Mani. Haruki, my father, chose the name."

In the last few days, she's role-played this immense moment through to its conclusion. Catastrophic or overly-hopeful, it's been a wasteful guessing game that she berates her patients for playing when, amid every possibility, this isn't how she imagined it, not even close.

"Charupi's daughter?" His eyes mist. He's barely cogent, dissociating to a past that rushes to greet him with ease as if it's been merely biding its time to welcome him back.

Charupi.

She hadn't known of this nickname, not until earlier this week when she discovered the letters.

"Yes," she says. "And–"

She reaches down but pauses. She remembers once more of her youth and being read to in bed. Her father had narrated the myth of Pandora and concluded by offering his own interpretation. He'd been less interested in the hope left in the box, the part most people focused on, and had instead told her to be fearful of what curiosity could unleash. 'A cautionary tale,' he'd said, 'and this my reason for repeating the story so often.'

Perhaps she's about to make the same mistake. Perhaps she's already broken the seal just by being here.

"And I think these belong to you," she continues, despite her father's warning and despite the risk of devastation. She needs to know what happened between the two men to make her father do what he did.

She unlatches the bag and retrieves a thick envelope, certain that Akis knows that inside are her father's letters. Letters that contain intimate details about the two of them, one summer many years ago.

Letters whose pages have yellowed from passing between many hands.

Letters that have travelled a long way.

Uncharted Waters

Greece, 1943-1960

2

Kalavryta
10th December 1943

Three days before the Holocaust of Kalavryta, sixteen-year-old Kurt Neuhold is marched south over the Corinth Canal to enter the farthest reach of European mainland, the Peloponnese.

The young Nazi is stationed overnight on the bay of Xylokastro. Whilst the others in the 117th Jäger Division sleep to escape the war, he has volunteered for night watch.

Greece is dark and resigned. Lame winds can't rouse the tamarisks dotted along the coast. The tide too ebbs with such muted effort that, under the veiled moonlight, the sea resembles an oily battlefield in reprieve. Lone wolves and preying owls pierce the silence. Otherwise, the country understands its part in the occupation and does not speak back.

Kurt's flat-footed gait shoots a needle up his spine with every step along the beach but he forbids himself to wince. Since passing Albania's border some three hundred kilometres ago, he has single-handedly carried a flagpole that bears a swastika and is destined for Ancient Olympia. He hasn't once asked for help despite its weight. Stubbornness has had its price. The December frost has done little to cool him and sweat has rubbed a rash around his collar that stings with every turn of his head. But he won't concede to pain, not when his country requires stoicism on the way to claim the historic site, only right that Olympia is under Austria's ownership. It will be his honour to plant the flag into the ground. He might not have engaged in battle but he's helping to win the war.

"Pain is not the same as suffering," he says to himself, disturbing the quiet with his time-tested mantra. A senior assault leader had offered him this advice back in Salzburg. Later that same day, a grenade had detonated against the officer's hip and the man had died in agony, crying for his mother and lambasting the war. Kurt had watched on appalled, and adopted the line as his own.

Kurt stifles a yawn and reprimands himself; he chose to keep vigil. His mind never strays far from his mother's nor the Führer's approval and, though he's fatigued, he's as amiable as ever. It was only four months ago that he and Jonas were sitting in front of a chalkboard dreaming of serving their country. Even if he envies his best friend and the others who follow the Dinaric Alps through Yugoslavia, a terrain that complements their land-locked country rather than this flat and ugly shoreline, he has walked on without complaint. The Greek Prime Minister may have resisted Mussolini's invasion three years earlier but there's no stopping Hitler. Surety pushes him forward.

But what he can't understand are the mechanisms of the coast. He kicks at the sand and yearns to be back within his alpine slopes. He's lost in the fantasy of reuniting with his mother when he hears the whimpers of injured men.

Two soldiers stumble towards him. Their bloodied faces reveal their predicament: they can't afford discretion over aid.

Kurt raises his gun at the thinner of the two, more of a flight risk compared to the plump one and a more impressive target. But the four-pronged insignia hemmed into their sleeves speaks of their allegiance. He lowers his weapon.

"Where have you come from?"

"Kalavryta," the fatter one manages to say, before choking up.

The other takes over. "In the mountains. The locals fought back."

Kurt hasn't heard of this place but he recognises the infantry number. "Jonas Keller?"

The men cast their eyes down.

Kurt and Jonas were so intoxicated by the draft that neither had begrudged the abrupt end to their academia. Their only disappointment was to be separated, Kurt sent along Dalmatia and wishing instead for his friend's route through the higher altitudes of the Balkan states. He pictures Jonas' face and remembers them play-fighting in the hot springs. He's more determined than ever to hurry this war along so that he can return and tell Elke of her son's heroism. Before that, she deserves requital. Olympia can wait.

He leads the injured men to where the general-major sleeps. They protest that they first merit treatment but the news can't hold and Kurt barks at them in the same cadence as the assault leader that pain is not the same as suffering. The men are older by a few years, they tower above him, and yet his voice cuts them down.

Johann Schreiber is furious at being woken and angrier still on learning what has happened. A new plan is drafted, minded by revenge. So much in war is about power and grandiosity but this concerns retribution alone. At dawn the division turns towards the mountains. Kurt's wish to step back from the sea is granted.

The unit follows a single-toothed train track from its base at Diakopto up to Kalavryta. Kurt's climb is effortless without the weight of the flag, which he will pick up on the return, and yet he's more displeased than ever by the ungodliness of the terrain. The majority of these rocks are sharp and steep and nothing like his silky Gastein Valley. Scarce are the pretty snow-capped peaks from his childhood. He can't fathom that people live in such bleakness. Soulless barbarians.

Greeks.

Ahead of Kalavryta is the Megalo Spilaio, a monastery built into the severe rock-face. The monks pray on even as their buildings are razed. Kurt is the first to shoot.

The Kalavrytans expended their ammunition during the previous advance and this time they surrender without pushback. Schreiber commandeers the central hotel. The locals are deemed a scourge but not a threat and for now are permitted to move about within the town's perimeters. Kurt admires this more wicked choice, a predator toying with its prey rather than going straight for the kill. In turn, and in despair, the Kalavrytans have no option but to go about their daily rituals with pained denial.

Yet soon after their encampment Kurt self-quarantines. He tries to shake off an unsettling feeling but with no success. Kalavryta confuses him. It's a beautiful place set in a mountain basin and not unlike the makeup of his own village. The air reminds him of home, fresh and fragrant with pines. The angles are similar, the surrounding hills sloping and inviting. They impress happy memories. This isn't the dusty Greece that he's witnessed up till now.

When he does go outside he watches children as they chase one another in a courtyard. He stares on at their game for longer than he should and even laughs at one point. The more he attempts to disentangle their innocence the more his thoughts become knotted.

"You are the enemy," he forces himself to say about them.

He senses a pair of eyes trained on him. He turns around as a shadow melts from the far corner of the pharmacy. He's almost certain that someone has been following him since his arrival. He tries to catch up but doesn't know the back streets and his tail eludes him.

He can't sleep that night, thinking of when Jonas and he were younger, dunking one another under the thermal baths. He wonders if the Kalavrytans know how fortunate they are to have scenery that rivals home. How can he blame them when he would defend Bad Hofgastein? He corrects himself. Their situations aren't alike. He struggles to remember why.

We shouldn't be here.

The assault leader's screams penetrate Kurt's sleep.

This wasteful war.

He wakes in terror. His body is wet despite the frigid night. The man's proclamations had then landed on deaf ears but they play on like a stuck record.

He sits on the edge of the bed and brings Jonas' death to mind. It renews his hatred of the people here. They speak a different language so there's no way of finding out who murdered his friend. It's easier to hold them all accountable. He opens the window for air but stops short of looking out at the stunning pre-dawn vista.

By the afternoon of the second day he's grown restless from the lack of news. The room offers only the assault leader for company so he walks Kalavryta's periphery. New snow brings with it a handsomeness. He's staring into the distance when he trips on the icy cornerstone of a house.

The landing winds him. A girl his age rushes over. He wants to shoo her away but she holds a finger to his mouth. He doesn't expect a prisoner to be so brash. Her finger brushes his bottom lip. He hasn't been touched by anyone since bidding adieu to his mother so he allows it.

Before she darts off, the girl speaks an instruction that he can't decipher but understands from the tone that he's to remain on the step. The frozen ground numbs his sore buttock anyway. She hurries back with a glass of spring water and wets a cloth before giving him the rest to drink. The water is cool and heavy with minerals that transport him to the Alps. The girl is too busy tending to his graze to notice his damp eyes.

Kurt remains supine to her as she dabs his hip where it weeps through the torn fabric. She soaks up his blood.

He reasons that she's been his shadow. He blushes to think that she's seen him with his guard down. Gazing at the landscape, petting dogs, laughing alongside children.

She's hunched over so that they're at head-height. Other soldiers are holed up or patrolling elsewhere with no one to catch sight of his subservience. It's fortuitous really. The fall might have been an accident but this is a dereliction.

She's pretty now that he examines her. Not classically beautiful like the Austrian girls back home. Dark, a wide nose, skin like milky coffee, and thick hair that shapes her head like an almond. Broader than his classmates. A Greek all the same. But, not brutish.

"Danke," he says.

The girl meets his eyes, their faces barely separated. She mutters his peculiar syllables before catching sight of his red-raw neck. She pulls his shirt away to inspect it. Kurt can't contain his nervelessness any longer and yelps like a child delayed after an accident when back in the presence of a parent. A held breath will break when it runs out of air.

His word takes shape on her lips once more as she retains it to memory. She holds out her hands but Kurt thinks of Jonas and the imminent revenge. Her efforts to charm him are pointless, her attempts to memorise something from his mother tongue wasteful. He lifts himself up.

She beckons for him to follow. He should turn and let their paths diverge but she stands with her hands on her hips. It's hard to refuse when hers is an unremitting persistence. Besides, she'll only trail him if he says no.

He lets her take the lead.

"Danke," she says with a heavy dose of derision.

They walk in single file, him enough paces behind that he can veer off if spotted. She stops at the last of the moss-covered cottages and checks before waving him in.

The smell of last night's log fire makes him nostalgic. Vials of liquids and pills are cluttered between dried-out laurel garlands and mountain herbs. Her actions are confident as she readies an ointment. For a while he stands ill at ease before he limps over to a chair. He considers the unlikelihood of this encounter, that their lives have entwined through the offer of water.

No sooner has he sat down than she wrangles words at him and he shoots up onto his feet. She acts out the removal of his trousers. He freezes and she sighs and turns away. Under her counsel he seems to be devoid of choice. He takes off his shoes, unbuckles his belt and shimmies out of the pair. He sits with his legs clasped together. A Nazi should be impenetrable to criticism but he hasn't been able to change his underwear for days. He pulls his shirt low to afford what little propriety remains.

He coughs to attract her attention and she sets to work on his leg, giving no heed to his nakedness. She also unbuttons the top of his shirt and drapes a fresh towel where the skin has worn. The medicine stings. After she finishes she trains her eyes on the trousers. Kurt can read her expression: skin might heal on its own but material is a passive player. This isn't her concern. He's ready to re-dress and end the encounter.

"Danke." He's brusque, using the only word in their shared arsenal.

"Danke danke danke," she spits back, dismissing his haste.

He frowns. He won't tolerate being humiliated. His gun is on the table. She follows his gaze. Indifferent, she takes the trousers and begins to sew.

Kurt's father died young and his mother has had nothing of interest to say about him since. He's only learnt about intimacy through snippets of his friends' parents. It isn't unlike this moment. He can see the appeal.

The girl returns the pair but he can't stand to dress, not because of pain but of manifest arousal. If anything, it's the fantasy of a consummate relationship that has caused his penis to become attentive. For years erections seemed to be ever-present but they've mostly disappeared since firing his first gun. Any time he's grown hard recently an image of the assault leader's gaping waist has turned him flaccid in seconds.

She sees the rise from under his shirt. She places the trousers on the table and strokes his cheeks teasingly, copying with precision how he petted the strays nearby. So she was his shadow. He wishes that he could ask why.

She holds out her hands and, this time, Kurt lets her take his weight as he joins her. She unpins her dress which falls to the floor. She unbuttons the rest of his shirt and kisses his neck above where it has started to scab. All the while he doesn't know what to do. His arms hang by his side. She envelops his body as she pulls in towards him. His fingers take life and clutch her taut skin. His penis pushes against her hipbone, begging to be freed from the restrictive underwear. There's no rush. Nothing good waits for either of them outside.

"Kurt," he says afterwards, pointing at himself as they dress.

"Stavroula."

He smiles. "Danke, Stavroula."

Back at the hotel he learns what will befall the Kalavrytans the next morning. He nods accordingly and takes to his room. He lies on the bed and toys with the patched fabric, poking a hole until the mend gives way. He can't sleep. Another soldier is happy to be relieved of night duty.

Kurt walks far and dreams of escape.

At daybreak he takes part in the massacre of every man his age and older. These Kalavrytans are taken from the school building where they have been rounded up and led to a field. Within minutes the male population has all but been exterminated. The women and children are left behind, locked in the school which is set alight. Though Kurt engages in every part of the genocide, the gunshots and crackling fire aren't loud enough to drown out the assault leader's words. *Pain is not the same as suffering.*

But what he experiences surpasses matters of the body or the mind. His heart has clogged with tar. He should have listened to the assault leader in his final throes of life, where the greater truths were revealed, but he has left it too late to learn the danger of words. Instead words have become commands and commands wretchedness.

Fumes billow from every crack of the school. The flames cause a high window to shatter. Kurt vomits. Soldiers laugh. He hurries to where the doors are chained shut and shoots three times before hitting the lock. He clears the way and shouts for the women to leave.

His eyes are too blurry from smoke and panic to see who is who. Friend or foe no longer makes sense—

A gun goes off.

Only after Kurt drops to the ground does he realise that the bullet has passed through his chest. And it's only when Johann

Schreiber stands above him that he can take in the general-major's look of disgust. Schreiber creases a smile. This second expression chills Kurt even more but he's powerless to do anything but listen.

"You have served your country well. Because of you these women will endure a lifetime of grief."

Kurt is horrified by how his actions have been twisted by the words. It isn't what he intended but it's how it'll be portrayed. This is the version that Sophie Neuhold will hear.

It was simpler in the cottage with Stavroula, safe in the confines of just being able to thank one another. He hopes that she's managed to run far. Even if she were here to see him dying he wouldn't blame her for not rushing forward and tending to him a second time. He wouldn't expect that of her. He turns his head but her shadow has slipped away.

He would like to think that she's too distant by now to have heard Schreiber. At any rate she wouldn't have been able to translate his words. He's glad of that much. He only wishes that his mother should equally not understand the account that will come to her. But, sharing his language, of course she will. Delayed, maybe, but the story will arrive in time.

3

Outside Kalavryta
13th December 1943

The knock comes after nightfall and breaks the standstill of a twilight during which no Kalavrytan can sleep. These insufferable hours in which it's too dark, too early and too hopeless for anyone to peer through their window and learn what a third day under the Nazis might bring.

Leonidas Asteriakos and his daughter, Stavroula, are sitting by the fireplace staring at the logs that burn with sluggishness when they hear the person make himself known. It's not unexpected that someone would come for them but the rap against the wood is cautiously quiet. It seems weak for a reckoning.

Leonidas wouldn't have predicted such an hour but, given his weariness, it's almost a relief to be done with the uncertainty. To him, that the Germans are nearby but out of sight is the beginning of a bed bug infestation; perhaps none has yet bitten but to know of their presence makes a mattress uncomfortable and sleep impossible.

Dread clings inside the house overpowering the smell of pungent balms. Stavroula's expression has been distant these past hours. Leonidas assumes that it's exhaustion mixed with apprehension but she's alert now and goes to answer.

He holds up his hand, to not only silence her but to stall her. The wrong decision could prove fatal.

He's already furious with himself for not having fled but he hadn't been able to leave his community behind. As their doctor he has treated them for two decades and a state of war doesn't mean a hiatus for the indisposed. He's learnt that the mind and body are linked not only in all things corporeal but psychical, and to abandon his patients, to neither tend to them nor console them, is outside of his code of ethics. Despite this he has fantasised about escape. The best bet was the subterranean lakes in the nearby Kastria Cave, a place to hold out from soldiers and hypothermia. There is somewhere more remote, and far from here, but it's out of the question.

With the person at the door it may be too late.

Leonidas tries to stand but his legs don't follow. He massages his thighs to get the blood flowing but they don't return to life. Perhaps his body portends the visitor's news.

He's witnessed plenty of death across his career but it's usually timely or expected from encroaching symptoms. With war, death has been blunt. Neither he nor Stavroula took part in the first defence but they treated the wounds of the men who had. Stefanos Kostakos was one of the casualties. The boy was hardly older than Stavroula, herself still a child in Leonidas' eyes. It confuses his timeline to see her taking charge of the injured, her proficiency shunting her forward a decade from the vision of his babe of six to a sixteen-year-old woman.

She speaks up now. "It might be one of your patients."

It's a reasonable supposition but, except for the onset of labour, being called on at this time of night is never good news. He could settle it easily but fear holds him back. He wants to ask his daughter to take charge once more, to decide for him, but it isn't fair; she shouldn't be accountable for what is his responsibility. He wishes that he could ask for a consensus from his philosophy club.

Twice a week, as if set in stone, five men had gathered in the kafeneio and thrashed out an ethical dilemma. Typically, these issues were sourced locally but so obscured to protect confidentiality that the content became foggy with confusion or too theoretical for the men to be passionate about any one stance. The most recent meeting was a sombre affair, held before the Nazis arrived a second time. The men wanted to celebrate the pushback but they also knew that a cog had been kicked into motion. The resistance of Kalavryta was anything but guaranteed. Their new quandary came naturally and profoundly: to stay or go.

Nikos the Carpenter had killed several of the Germans in the first wave and wouldn't abandon the town. In an unusual turn of events, Nikos the Beekeeper, who usually provoked him, agreed. Adonis, twenty years the others' senior at sixty-years-old, with an untameable wiry beard and anything but his mythological namesake, called for them to move to the mountains. The preservation of life, he argued, warranted more than obstinacy. Leonidas, foremost a carer, would follow whatever the group decided. Stefanos' father, Giannis, cut through. 'I won't leave my son. If I'm buried alongside him then so be it.'

They'd turned to their favourite paradox. Even in the mountains the Greeks fancied themselves an educated breed and a physicist named Schrödinger had given them the solution for such stand-offs. It frustrated them that he was an Austrian but they couldn't deny his genius. In his experiment a cat was shut in a box with radioactive material and would surely die from poisoning. And yet until the box was opened the cat was both alive and dead. The men agreed to leave the box untampered with; to both stay and go, pacifyingly, viable. As with many of their conundrums the debate was adjourned if not resolved.

Another knock.

"Hello?" Stavroula calls out.

Leonidas shushes his gutsy daughter. It's strange though. It's barely audible but he swears that he can hear the girl's name carry across the wind. He shakes his head. The Nazis wouldn't whisper. They're brasher than that. They'd come down on Kalavryta with such intensity that he'd worried that their roar would disturb the higher reaches of snow, an excessive strike bestowing an avalanche on his already incapacitated town.

What had followed were two long days of house visits and apportioning out his supply. His advice fell short of what each patient asked of him: 'What should we do?' Outside of a terminal prognosis, a doctor's next worst answer is 'I don't know' but incertitude is all that he's had to offer. If anything he'd been experimenting with each appointment to fine-tune what he could say to Stavroula, delaying his return in case the dreaded question was asked of him once more. He'd reunited with her this evening, again empty-handed and defeated, and now someone has come for them.

The tapping becomes hurried. Unremitting.

Leonidas crosses to the door whilst his daughter grips her chair. He reaches for the handle, pleading to god that someone is hunched over with food poisoning or has sprained an ankle. Anything but the unordinary. He pictures the cat locked in the box and waits a few seconds. Stavroula meets his eyes and nods, forcing his hand.

The blonde soldier is babyish but the inhumane uniform is designed to sit heavy and age him. Leonidas has witnessed enough clenched teeth and quivering jaws to know which stems from the cold and which depicts fright. It's evident that the grim-looking boy is scared. Leonidas smells something familiar. He has learnt the acrid scents of sepsis and fever but where he works soon becomes permeated with his own concoctions. It seems curious that his doorway has the distinct odour of aloe, camomile and rosemary. The boy steps past him before he has a chance to make the connection.

"Stavroula."

The boy isn't just addressing Leonidas' daughter but conveying something intimate. The accent is thick. The tone lands incorrectly at the beginning of the word. Her name carries meaning though it has been altered, perhaps more so to hear it spoken on a foreign tongue.

She joins them as the boy continues in his incomprehensible language. Betrayed by their lack of understanding, he thrusts coats into their hands. Stavroula dresses but Leonidas can't move. He isn't ready to leave the house. There are too many mementos. Prized possessions that help better than any drug. A photograph of Marika. The brush that became her sole pleasure whilst cancer ran through her body, the disease ridding her of feeling human outside of this tender act of having her hair stroked. The list goes on. All these items amassed in her thirty short years of life. Their ten, even shorter years together.

He won't be coming back any time soon. He can't choose so he can't leave. Everything here matters.

Stavroula guides his arms into the sleeves before nudging him into the night. He turns back towards the house but the soldier ushers him forward. Despite the forcefulness he means him no harm, Leonidas is sure of that much.

Stavroula follows with a lit branch.

"Nein."

The word sounds so much like their affirmative 'nai' but it's clear from the tone that it holds the opposite. She throws it back into the fire. Leonidas guesses that it will smother to ash long before they can return, far too late to stoke life back into the hearth.

The three move towards the treeline. They pass Nikos the beekeeper's house where Leonidas shunts as if to sidestep and rouse him. The Nazi wags a finger. No one else can come. Leonidas' feet walk him away from everyone he has known. What would the philosophy club make of his departure? He knows the answer. Solidarity has lost to self-preservation.

He smells the mixture again and doesn't need to wonder why he's being saved. He's been so invested in the lives of others that he's missed whatever occurred under his nose. He's perplexed by how Stavroula had learnt of the wound but not by how she could treat a Nazi. Moral quandaries don't exist in medicine. Either Leonidas gives people what they need or he's doing them a disservice. He recalls Adonis walking off after hearing his take on treating an enemy just as he would an ally. It was a long time ago, when Nazis were elsewhere and a second war inconceivable, but his persuasion had stoked overpowering emotions in the others. His friends had berated him. How could he make congruent the wish to offer his adversaries care when it strengthened the hands that would quash him?

Fortunately he's never been confronted by such an event but his daughter apparently has. And now they're being smuggled away. The boy's lack of allegiance makes little sense. Perhaps not. The cold reaches Leonidas' head and stops his thoughts from spiralling towards nauseating explanations. The frost has never been such a mercy.

The snow conceals their escape. The soft crunch underfoot mutes their tread. Leonidas' shoes aren't built to withstand an endured temperature and the wet leaks through to his socks. He considers turning back to dress in more layers but already the village is behind him. He thinks, of all things, of the sea and himself on an ocean liner, cutting a cord to leave behind a raft full of dejected people, hapless and adrift, so that he can weather the storm. Within his freedom will be his punishment.

Considering it a safe distance, the boy stops. He exhales billowy puffs of air but his shallow breath is not from the cold. There's no better medicine for anxiety than a glass of tsipouro. Medical treatment might be one thing but even if Leonidas carried a bottle of the alcohol he would keep it to himself. This is no predicament; he could never share a drink with a German. Leonidas wants to hate the boy but he is only young and foolish and where he was born happenstance. The war has left them all as mere players, pawns with the same dread and geography the only determining factor on which side of the board they'd landed.

Stavroula stands in front of the Nazi and places her hand on his shoulder. "Danke, Kurt."

Leonidas is constantly in reverence of his daughter but now he's disquieted. The boy's language has invaded, the infestation begun.

No more is spoken before Kurt leaves; even if they shared a mother tongue there are no words for what any of them have yet to find past daybreak.

The father and daughter continue deep into the trees to where they can no longer see Kalavryta and Kalavryta can no longer see them. The forest is so dense that they don't realise when it turns to morning. They huddle against a pile of snow-capped branches that serves as a wind break.

Leonidas has drifted off when he hears a crackling fire. He stretches his body to embrace its warmth but his legs are stiff and remind him of his situation. As his senses return he understands the noise as gunshots, innumerable and cataclysmic. He doesn't look at Stavroula. The sound continues. It shakes birds free of their perches and black squirrels out of hibernation. The number of shots is astounding. He doesn't want to count but there's nothing to distract him. The explosions far outnumber the townsfolk. Stavroula cries silent tears that stop halfway down her face, the freeze building them up like a used candle. He wants to brush them away but his fingers have set in a crooked position and any attempt will be unintentionally blunt. It isn't long until the stillness is reinstated and he can smell a rotten burning. The sky blackens with a tearing thick smoke. Ashy snow begins to fall.

As with the preceding hours, Leonidas is unable to find the words to soften any of this. He only knows how to prepare people for death, not to offer condolences. He's a man of little conversation at the best of times. His craft has taught him to favour abruptness; being everyone's confidante has kept his position tenable in a tight-knit town. He's been privy to the unfairness of the world: the pious afflicted with chronic pain, the good dying young, the undeserved faced with misery. But he's struggled to believe that it's all just base physiology. Leonidas, to his shame as a man of science, holds true to superstition. He believes that the evil eye can cause headaches just by glancing at another with envy. He will never admit it but this guides his actions more than any virtuosity of being a physician.

He considers where they can go now that they can't go back. He still can't fathom turning to his village at the base of the Peloponnese. He can't bear to return to the place that he abandoned.

There, in Vatheia, he'd learnt medicine from his father and yet neither of them had been able to revive his mother after her lungs choked with seawater. The young Leonidas had dragged her from the freak rip-tide but there was nothing to be done and he swore that he wouldn't be faced with anything like it again. In Kalavryta a broken leg in the winter is par for the course but the snow melts in its own time and there is never more than a puddle an inch or two deep. The seasons meld into another without tempestuous changes or the beckoning of a beach trip with threats that lay under seemingly kind waves. The mountains fit his temperament. Never looking at the ocean again would be too soon. He's been minded to leave it that way but now that *here* is no longer an option he has to reconsider where could be *there*.

He's been thankful, in a contorted way, for what happened to make him leave Vatheia. There would be no Marika. No Stavroula. He tries to summon his wife's face but the frost intervenes. He stands to shake life into his joints, ready to march back and retrieve her photograph, but Stavroula tugs at his jacket and pulls him to the ground. She's right. For now it's too dangerous to return but it's also unsafe to move off whilst it's light. In the absence of these options, staying put in the sub-zero winter is the most sensible thing to do. The only chamber of a gun not poised to go off just yet.

Come sundown they trek to where wild thicket and tall pines shroud them. The snow tears at them and offers them silent passage. They continue on past morning. Hunger pangs are dulled by the cold. The farther they go the more certain it is that they've evaded death.

His daughter finally speaks. "Baba?"

"Yes, Stavroula mou?"

"I'm sorry."

He doesn't comprehend. If it wasn't for her then they wouldn't be here. Unless what transpired between her and the boy went beyond some bandages. Because why else would an act of such little tenderness have amounted to the boy helping them abscond?

"What's done is done." He won't ask for clarification. He's too cowardly to confirm that it's not true in the event that it is.

They walk without direction, their sole purpose to create more distance. Leonidas becomes increasingly paranoid about a disturbing, potential consequence: that his daughter could be carrying the Nazi's wicked seed. He can't reconcile that whilst death has only just befallen Kalavryta perhaps his nation is already being replaced.

Stavroula looks like him and has inherited little from her mother. It was that way with him and his own parents. He concludes that the blonde boy will donate more of his appearance to any baby. Stavroula might argue that the soldier is good but no Greek child can resemble one of them. The philosophy club will—

He mourns his friends' assumed executions. If any of them are still alive then they should rightfully shun him and his offspring.

"Stavroula," he finally nerves himself to ask.

"Yes, Baba?"

"That boy?"

The two words are enough because she turns away.

It's so unlikely but he can't take any chances. A light-haired child will raise questions. He needs a place to shelter Stavroula. War happens on roads and in cities and he doesn't imagine that they can truly be left alone but an isolated, hard-to-reach village should be of no one's concern.

The deepest part of the Mani peninsula is cut off from civilisation. It has the reputation as a place of fierce resistance. Perhaps Leonidas was greedy in expecting to thrive away from there. He should have seen his luck in Marika and Stavroula and taken them years ago.

The distance seems unfathomable and to tell Stavroula that they'll finish their walk at the lowest point of the Peloponnese merely speaks of the impossibility of such a thing. For the time being he tells her only that they're heading south to where spring will arrive sooner.

He allows himself a moment to think of the weeks ahead, mounted with parched and starved desolation, as the two of them march towards the barren coast. To a hamlet where they can take refuge. Any semblance of their shoes will be long gone. The skin on their soles will be toughened and scarred. But however he tries to distract himself his thoughts don't stray far from the colour of any supposed child's hair. Desperate, he makes an appeal to both science and god, imploring the former to shun its irrefutability and then, silently, he begs the latter for mercy.

4

The Path to Mani
14th January 1944

Weariness has consumed Stavroula across four gruelling weeks but, this far into the trek and with her father not allowing her to rest anywhere longer than a single night, she's buoyed by the promise that they'll soon reach the edge of land. At least she wants to believe this, acting on faith alone that they've expended the length of the Peloponnese. That there's a place waiting for her. A house by the sea. Four walls and a bed. Somewhere she can call home.

She's learnt how incomprehensibly large the world is. That a single footstep can feel like a minute, an hour like a day, a week a year. She's tired of perpetual forested ascents and yearns for the ocean simply to know that she can't walk any farther.

But the water as a destination unsettles her. Nothing since fleeing has made any sense but strangest of all is that her father has bypassed the towns and villages for the sea.

During her childhood she and her mother would take the odontotos train to spend their days at Diakopto, ducking under the warm waves and burying one another in the sand. Her life was small, these beach trips the only time that she broke free. The sound of gulls was absent in Kalavryta and she greeted the birds each time she went to the coast, tracing their paths with envy as they soared impossible lengths across the gulf to Mount Parnassus. She imagined sprouting wings and flying above the entirety of her country. Other escapes: building a raft, swimming the breadth of the channel, or sneaking aboard one of the liners that carried along the Corinthian Gulf and through to the other side of the canal. Instead she always returned to her father who she missed after these short hours; her happiest times were by the sea largely because she would later be swept up in his arms. He always refused to join them with a tremor in his voice whilst citing too much work, but he would wait at the station craning over the track in desperation to see them safe, and unwilling to let go of their hands as they walked the main arcade home.

That channel had formed in a shallow depression, still and ankle-deep and painlessly warm. There was no need for Stavroula to brace before entering to her hips. Her father came at everything with doctor-speak and said that cold water immersion was linked to the kidney line. She hadn't been allowed to test out the hypothesis in the winter months but now, even in the depths of January, when they hit the shore she'll run straight in and let the water take her weight. Anything but walk another step on dry land.

The final journey to the beach was on her ninth birthday, as unsuspecting a day as any other except that her mother had flagged easily. Stavroula had tried to ignore this decline for months but on the train back she overheard women discussing her mother's fate with unabashed crudity, that if Leonidas was such a good doctor how could the cancer have progressed this far? There was an awkward moment when she stood to reveal that she was within earshot. Her mother hustled her along the carriage but Stavroula didn't care for the explanation that they'd all lost their husbands and were bitter about the world, and instead glowered in their direction as she cursed them with the evil eye.

She tended to her mother over the next year, the two of them forever rescheduling a return to the beach, and then devoted herself to shadowing her father. She kept away from the railway, a painful reminder that even if she had the desire to be elsewhere she had no one to accompany her. She was intrigued when outsiders arrived, usually bringing grains or vegetables grown in lower climes, but they all disappeared without much impact. Then the war drew near and she wished only for stasis.

Like it or not she's now been forced upon the world.

She's struggled for the entirety of the walk, pleading with her father to settle at any one of the villages, but all that he's allowed them are abandoned shepherd huts, lucky if they find discarded cereals, preserved rusks or jarred spoon sweets which have become so sickly in their absence that despite her hunger she can't manage more than a few bites. She sips from alcohol but only enough to burn her throat.

There's no sign of the war as they cross Taygetus' difficult peaks. The stopovers break the cold, where she and her father can fashion blankets into extra layers, but she craves a proper bed or for someone to tell them that they can turn back. Her father is resolute that they won't dip into even the outskirts of residential areas. His argument alternates between the villages not being safe and that the two of them aren't beggars. She disagrees with the second part when that is exactly what they've become. What she doesn't do is tell him that they need to protect her baby. She can't risk hearing that he doesn't care.

Bloating, tenderness, needing to urinate often, it's a month into their crossing that her pregnancy begins to show. She's terrified to tell her father. When she does he merely grunts that he's aware and directs her forward.

When they near the chestnut-laced vineyards of Kastorio and he once again directs her on a wide berth she sits on the ground and cries.

Her father crouches in front of her and confesses his fears. "This is not about protecting or punishing you. It's because I'm afraid. I can't bear to hear any news of what has happened."

But that night he mutters two words in his sleep. "The shame."

Stavroula wants to believe that this is about leaving his patients to the Nazis but it's because she's carrying one of them.

Their strength dwindles. Leonidas is winded by any path that isn't flat or downhill whilst she has become thin-boned and faint and with an agitation that she swears is the baby wrestling her to return it to its father.

Another mordant week passes, their advance so gradual that the features on the horizon remain fixed, when she begins to vomit. There's no bump to her stomach but her father concurs that they require more than just shelter in a dilapidated house. He re-orients them. In the distance is a city. He tells her that it's Sparti.

She has never known him to leave Kalavryta so it's astonishing that he assuredly directs them to a guest-house under the cover of darkness. There seems to be no Nazi intrusion here and she figures that the name of the fierce warriors has carried across millennia to deter even a modern-day militia. Her father instructs her to take in the city right now because she will do nothing more than enter and leave. Unlike home, Sparti is gridded, flat and low and set away from the mountains. There are myriad shops. She's desperate to see them come alive and thinks of breaking free from her curfew but she won't disappoint her father. Not again.

Her father knocks on the door. She wants to hide; it's been so long since speaking to anyone that his misgivings have burrowed under her skin.

It takes a while for the woman who answers to place him. "Leonidas?"

"It's the beard, isn't it?" His joke falls flat. However this woman knew him, his gaunt figure has robbed his spirit.

The stranger turns to her. "Stavroula? My goodness."

She ushers them in and gives her name. Astymelosia. It means nothing to Stavroula.

The woman sends her to a bathroom. Stavroula holds her ear to the door but the conversation is muffled. They'll only stop if she emerges. She savours the hot water, soaking for longer than is respectable when intruding on a stranger in the middle of the night. Only, this woman isn't that.

She swaps with her father and nurses a cup of sideritis mountain tea. Astymelosia warms fasolada soup and fries sausages that give off the scent of oranges, unflurried in the task as if a midnight feast is anything but out of the ordinary. Stavroula has so many questions but remains tongue-tied. She instead offers to help with the meal but is pleased to be directed to remain sitting. She never wants to stand again.

"I'm sorry we arrived late. My father refused to enter Sparti before the sun set. Even then he held back for some hours."

"He's a wise man to tread carefully. I cannot imagine how cold you have been."

Stavroula hasn't let herself believe that they'd survive. She hasn't wished to tempt fate.

"It's miraculous," she answers, deeming it safe to now say. She doesn't know what else to add because any more might risk a rush of catharsis, undignified in front of a stranger.

Astymelosia breaks up squares of feta. Stavroula guesses that she's the same age as her father although betrayed by wrinkles that suggest a hard life.

"Actually there has been no fighting here. I'm sorry about Kalavryta. It was a charming place."

"You heard what happened?"

"Only what your father told me."

"But you've been?"

"Once. My husband had an infection and Leonidas saved his life. He gave us ten more years together. You were just a baby."

"I'm sorry for your loss."

"I'm not sure Michalis would have wanted to see this world. With no guests for months and my son defending Greece, this house has been too quiet."

"It will be over soon."

"I'm sure you're right. I must sound like a bitter old woman."

Stavroula shakes her head but Astymelosia has turned away.

"Did you meet my mother?"

"She was beautiful like you."

"Everyone says I look like my father. It's the nose." Stavroula flares her nostrils to emphasise its largeness and laughs for the first time in a month.

Astymelosia disagrees. "You have her eyes."

Leonidas makes his presence known and the women stop talking. Stavroula and her father eat greedily. She looks at him with a new lease of admiration. He isn't boastful and so she was unaware that his reach had cast so far. She loathed his hard exterior on the route here, detested his indifference as they walked, but she forgives him. Even good men exhaust their compassion from time to time.

She sleeps well but panics when she wakes to find him absent. She remembers, she has her own room and no rush to plough on or fend off the frost from grappling at her feet. She pushes herself into the mattress until the sunlight treads a line across the room and meets her face. Her body embraces this treat by giving her a reprieve from vomiting. She worries about a miscarriage but puts her hand to her stomach and knows that the baby is simply enjoying the break.

Outside her door are a set of folded clothes including a pair of shoes that fit snug but are in good condition. Downstairs she thanks Astymelosia.

"Where's my father?"

"He'll be back soon. He's on an errand."

"I should join him."

"He asked that you don't leave."

They aren't under house arrest and it isn't as if danger lurks outside. "Why is only he allowed to explore? Do you know where he went?"

Astymelosia nods. "This is my son's guest-house. I'm managing it whilst he's away. He's thirty-six but I still remember how it was to be pregnant."

"You can tell?"

"The way you touch your stomach and how your cheeks remain rosy whilst the rest of you is faded out."

Stavroula is impressed and then relieved to share her pregnancy with someone willing to talk about it.

Astymelosia giggles to herself. "You aren't showing. Your father told me."

"So you can't tell?"

"No, but I was a midwife so perhaps I can talk you through what will come."

"That's why my father brought us here?" Stavroula wells up. Despite any reservations about the legitimacy of the child, his love for her has overpowered any shame.

"And that's why he went out now. May I?"

Stavroula lets Astymelosia inspect her even if she can't offer certainty about the baby's health. The woman soon moves on from her belly and stares at her face. Stavroula doesn't need to be told that she's lost colour. "I'm just tired."

"Your baby is strong. Given its start with the cold there was every likelihood that it would die but it has clung onto life."

"He. He's a boy. Akis."

"Akis?

"Short for Apostolis."

"Very well. He's robbing you of your health. You'll need plenty of rest."

"He'll be fine?"

"I'm talking about you." She sighs. "I remember as if it was yesterday. You love him more than you thought possible."

"I do. But my father's disappointed."

"Your father will become a grandfather and that will change everything. I'll convince him to stay a while longer."

"Do you know where we're going?"

Astymelosia tuts. "Ach ston diaolo. Why he seems to keep you in the dark I don't understand. To the sea. To where he was born."

"He was born in Kalavryta." She works it through. "Although he's been here before."

"That's a conversation for the two of you. Before I forget. I want you to have something. It was my son's. I kept nothing from his infancy except for this."

40

Astymelosia presents her with a knitted red hat, impossibly small and perfect.

"That's too precious."

"Nonsense. What use is it here? What would it keep warm? One of my ears?"

"Thank you. I'm sorry he's far away. I'm sure he'll return soon."

"You'll make me cry. Everything we can discuss is likely to bring on tears so let's make you breakfast. You must be starving."

Stavroula eats eggs and bread and watches Astymelosia bind the hat to the lining of her coat. As she pieces together what she has learnt she can hear the woman sniffle. She wants to comfort her. She runs through every topic in her head but Astymelosia is correct: whether it's about the past where sadness lies or the future where uncertainty lurks or right now when any haven is soon to be ruptured with them again on the move, there's nothing innocuous that can be said.

Close to the next daybreak, affording Stavroula one more sleep, her father leads her out of Sparti. They are rested and in fresh, hardier clothes. This time there are no roads to avoid, the region south of the city undisturbed. Stavroula has never seen a place so wild. She doubts that there's anyone left but the two of them.

They keep to the middle of the three peninsulas. The land awakens something in her father that she hasn't witnessed before. He becomes animated, walking lighter and detailing the geography as if his youth was put on hold and is now re-emerging. At first she only sees barren wasteland until he reveals its hidden secrets. He shows her how to manage the mule tracks without losing her footing, how the mountains are no longer covered in conifers but desolate and red, and he points at lonely olive trees that prosper in the arid landscape. He evidently loves this place. She wants to ask what made him leave but she doesn't dare interrupt his flow.

She's never seen the architecture before, of isolated tower houses built of grey stone. Some are upright but many have toppled.

"Earthquakes?" she asks.

"Cannonballs."

"From pirates? Real pirates?"

"And clans. This land is bloody-minded and so are its people. For centuries there was such infighting that no one could trust his neighbour. But they come together to defend themselves from outsiders, unbreakable when they need to be."

"What will they think of us entering their land?"

"We aren't trespassers. I was born here and so we have a claim. This is Mani and we are Maniots." He sighs towards the stark land and rubs the wet from his eyes.

This isn't easy territory and she's glad to have an insider's advantage even if her father's explanation leaves her rattled. If he abandoned this place will there be such a convivial welcome?

Her fears don't have long to manifest. After one more day the sea sneaks up on her. She doesn't notice the washed-out blue of the horizon until the sun glints on its surface. It's no longer just dusty land but the finish line that she's prayed for. By now her feet are sturdy and her skin buffered by the elements. She can walk double the length if her father remains by her side. It was her accident that initially saved them but it's his formidable nature that has kept them alive.

She wants to rejoice but can't escape the nausea that circles like an eagle vying for her corpse. She hasn't let on just how shivery she is. Bed-rest will solve her malaise, as Astymelosia insisted.

The cliff too springs up on them without fanfare from where it's a plummet to the pebbled beach below. Unlike the level sand in the north, Mani is formed of dimensions far more brutal, and yet the water is more exquisite, a cloak of sapphire and emerald that outstrips any dream.

Everything here is a marvel, hard but astonishing. Over the final hours of their journey, Stavroula and her father pass clusters of stone towers until a larger hamlet takes shape ahead of them. It's by no means as big as Kalavryta. More like a fairy-tale kingdom than a modern-day settlement, built for kings and queens defending their castle from dragons.

Stavroula finds herself walking alone. She retraces her steps to where her father has stopped. One of his tears falls onto the impermeable ground. She takes his hand and squeezes it.

5

Vatheia
3rd July 1944

At the southernmost point of continental Greece stands a fortified constellation of stone towers that for centuries has defied, among others, the Ottomans and the inhospitable microclimate. If the arid Mediterranean is the epicentre of the ancient world, Vatheia is where god's finger touched the earth. Life has blossomed outwards and left a scorched place of barrenness and hardship. Still, there's a beauty to the forlorn land. There has to be for the Vatheians to call it home. Its people are proud, shunning roads, electricity and arable land. They survive with cunning and modesty. Gallantry too. Each of the families has competed at one time or another for the grandest of the forty grey monoliths, the distance between them at arm's length when times are civil but unfathomably farther when turning on one another.

The hamlet is high on a mound with views across the Messenian Gulf, a coastline of jagged cliffs and countless bays. Anyone playing backgammon at one of the low tables in the plateia, the public square set around an ancient oak tree at the lip of the village, is treated to a perfect seascape. Stepped wedges trace natural contours to the water's edge, leaving a subdued palette of stalwart wildflowers and abrasive low shrubs, patches of watermelons and pumpkins, and abundant but worthless prickly pear cactuses whose fruits are covered in microscopic spindles and are too bothersome to pick.

There's a snug haphazardness to Vatheia. Every tower shares its courtyard's walls with another. The cobblestoned alleys are a confusing labyrinth but even in the most overlooked recesses there's no privacy: two people bearing a grudge cannot avoid one another, what a neighbour buys at the grocery store is public knowledge, and who is absent from church services is everyone's business.

Perhaps it was once at the heart of creation but Vatheia is now so forsaken that the locals retain an affinity to the god Ares who is said to have walked these parts; to them their village might as well have been built on the next planet along to Earth, on Ares itself, desiccated and burnt red.

The population has reluctantly aged, with the latest war stealing its youth. The fighting has otherwise passed Vatheia with the exception of lessening the already rare boat deliveries until the villagers have learnt self-sustainability like never before. And now two strangers amble towards their knoll. The news spreads fast and neighbours join arms in coalesced preparation.

Petzechroula Tzanetakis, an Asteriakos until marriage, and who knows nothing of the world beyond here, is the first to spot them. She has forever romanticised her village and never more so than from a vantage point along the cliff where she walks daily. Despite almost fifty years of this drill the panorama leaves her breathless.

Vatheia might appear fossilised but the world has not been so kind as to have preserved the people inside. Petzechroula often fantasises about a moat and a raised drawbridge but it's too late. The war took her son to the Battle of Pindus and stripped her of her spirit. She's been reduced from thriving to simply enduring. It's a mercy that her near-deaf husband no longer joins her on these strolls because, although he can just about hear her, she's run out of things to say. She's tired of lamenting her brother who fled in their adolescence and she can no longer seek reassurance about her son. At least from Tassos' last letter, the army had seen his potential and trucked him from Metsovo to the safer confines of command offices, somewhere, maybe Cairo?

Everything is as muted and one-tone as the stone towers. That is until Leonidas walks right into her path. She recognises her brother from a distance, his gait the same as decades earlier. The girl with him could be her niece. It's not Tassos but the advent is almost a sweet.

She has grieved Leonidas under the furious belief that she would never see him again but there are no more seconds to waste. Grievances carry through Maniot blood but so does kinship and she throws her arms around him as if animosity can vaporize like smoke.

She doesn't acknowledge the girl at first, a spectre that needs time to become opaque, but simply leads them to the house as others come to gawk. Some of the more cognisant residents recognise Leonidas as the doctor's son who broke away before the older Asteriakos died and Petzechroula became orphaned.

She forgets any lesson in humility. "This is my brother and niece," she shouts with plume. She pushes the girl to the front of their small parade despite not having confirmed this or learning her name.

"Tyresia! Tyresia!" She yells so loud that it stuns the already overwrought arrivals. Yet the women who gather don't blink. Instead they too shout this name through the side-passages, sending a chain across Vatheia until a man shouts her name back.

Tyresia! Petzechroula!

This is how communication between the couple has always been.

Tyresias isn't fully deaf but his inattention tips him into being that way. The problem is congenital. There isn't a more interesting story, no swashbuckling pirates nor cannon-fire, and so it has always been someone screaming his name. His mother, his friends, his teacher, the priest, and now not only his wife but the entire community. Everyone is so used to his name carrying across the ether that it's a strange day to not hear it, especially if it doesn't come in the late afternoon when Petzechroula has readied his meal. The locals can't set their watch by this call but it gives a completeness to their routine and has even become a local saying: 'A cockerel for breakfast and Tyresias for bed.' The world might change beyond Mani's borders but everything here stays the same.

Tyresias greets his brother-in-law with a kiss on each cheek. They were already close as children. They have since become family.

"My friend," Leonidas says, regressing to the needed volume. "So this is who you married. For your sins." He slaps Tyresias' arm.

"Don't tell Petzechroula but your wife looks better than mine. I'm joking. Half joking."

Petzechroula scoffs.

He turns to the girl and introduces himself. "Tyresias."

Stavroula smiles and gives her name.

"My incredible daughter," adds Leonidas.

Petzechroula keeps the thought to herself that the girl's frame might fit her adolescent years but her face is gaunt and her stoop round-shouldered. Still, she has a niece. Tassos has a cousin. Their family has doubled in an instant. Miracles do happen.

The four leave the crowd and enter a house where Petzechroula instructs Leonidas and Stavroula that they will stay with them. They can have the attic and Tassos' floor beneath that. They will have to climb through hatches but it will be their own space, cramped but warm from the cracked floorboards through which heat can rise.

"I'm afraid I haven't tidied," she says though the place is spotless. "I'll make tea first."

"Tsipouro," Tyresias insists.

Leonidas stops Stavroula after a few sips, proclaiming that she is underage.

The explanation doesn't convince Petzechroula who has always seen through his lies. Whatever caused their arrival, the girl has been dragged through hell. If she's old enough to be hauled here then she's old enough to drink. Petzechroula catches her eye. The girl looks away.

They fill in the erratic family tree that mostly speaks of loss: Petzechroula and Leonidas' father, Leonidas' wife, and all of Tyresias' family. There are few additional branches: Tassos in his late twenties and the younger Stavroula. There's a skirted mention of Kalavryta. Petzechroula gasps. She'd heard about the mass killings and is relieved that she didn't know it was where they'd been living. She thinks of how to bring Tassos back. The war has swept up her son but in one of the world's twisted acts it has reunited the rest of her family.

It's only later, too pent up to sleep, when it dawns on her that there will be one more addition to the family. How they escaped Kalavryta has not been made clear but she assumes that the pregnancy formed part of the equation.

They're here now and that's what matters.

Six months on and Petzechroula and Stavroula have become inseparable, making up for lost time and piecing in the other's blotted history. The girl is amiable and has a quiet resoluteness, assimilating fast and taking on the local dialect with plenty of gumption. She embraces Vatheian life and handles herself against the men more coquettish than those she knew in Kalavryta.

But whilst her spirit grows, her body doesn't recover. Her illness plateaus for a while, dormant until the first signs of spring when it begins to flake away at her. Hours of activity shorten as the sun clings to the sky longer. Leonidas' condition has been the reverse; a shave and a few sleeps and he's as fit as ever. And yet he continues to disappear for whole days, unable to shake whatever trauma clings to him like a December shadow.

Stavroula wants to fly but weakness keeps her grounded. Her stomach grows and her breasts heave but her skin is pale and her balance slipshod. Her matchstick legs solidify Petzechroula's belief in miracles: how could these frail limbs have travelled a thousand kilometres if not carried along by god?

Petzechroula brushes away the cobwebs of her father's medical equipment and tells her brother to snap out of whatever fugue he is in. Leonidas tells her in confidence that hypothermia has likely weakened Stavroula's immunity. Petzechroula has found tinted yellow liquid on the girl's bedsheets and underwear, traces of amniotic fluid which Leonidas passes off as nothing, but she can tell from his face that they are in fact heart-rending. He acts like Samson after his hair has been cut and declares himself defeated. Bed rest, the warming sun, thawing baths, his suggestions are amateurish.

"I don't know how to save her," he says.

"Try harder," Petzechroula demands, but her bossiness is to no avail.

She becomes Stavroula's constant carer. She treats the girl like a china doll but the baby saps nutrients from within. She can't prove it but it's as if Stavroula is allowing this to happen.

Where the women argue most regards trips to the bay beneath Vatheia. It's too steep, too far and too cold. Stavroula is defiant. She wants to invoke memories of her mother.

"You really are a Maniot," Petzechroula says after conceding.

Sometimes a fever dream carries on at the shore and Stavroula addresses her as Marika. Then the girl dizzies by the village lofty above them. She doesn't understand why there's no train station an easy walk across the sand.

In the last months of pregnancy, walking to the beach is nigh on impossible but today Stavroula has insisted that they go one final time before the birth. They shuffle down the slope and sit on the sand together. Petzechroula has no idea how they will broach the climb back.

"Akis is kicking. He wants to be in the water." Stavroula is certain it's a boy whilst Petzechroula thinks the lack of a pointed belly means a girl. The one thing they never discuss is the child's father.

"Will you promise me something, Theia?" Stavroula asks her aunt. "My father refuses to go near the sea. Don't allow my son to be swayed by his fears."

"Tell the child yourself."

"Maybe when Tassos returns he can teach him to swim."

"Teach him yourself."

An elevated voice: "Let's teach him now."

Petzechroula begs her to hold back but Stavroula has already dragged herself off the towel. The girl pulls her towards the water where they dip their toes and shriek at the freezing temperature. Petzechroula only pretends to complain. There's laughter once more in Vatheia.

Since Stavroula arrived there have been sparse boat deliveries. Eventually Petzechroula managed to send a letter with Tassos' name on it and an address so vague that she could only hope that it would somehow find its way to him. She wants the cousins to meet. She's sure that the news of an extended family might persuade him to hurry along the war, as if one boy can turn the tide in a global fight.

She pictures him gaily diving in the sea. She has already decided that he can do with his life whatever he wishes, as long as he comes back to her. She will dote on him and never complain. He can become a drunk like old Petros Gerakeas, foggy like her brother, or absent-minded like her husband. She would prefer him to be studious but that matters less than having him alive. It's a mother's prerogative for her child to enter one of the professions required for a family to survive in Greece: a doctor or an architect or a lawyer or a bureaucrat. With Leonidas returned and Tyresias having restored the tower house with his own hands she dreams of Tassos pursuing one of the latter two occupations, but she will forever hold her tongue and just smile at his presence.

All he'd wanted to do before his conscription was collect rocks and break them apart in search of fossils. An archaeologist, Petzechroula would say, liking that it sounded impressive even if unserviceable. Then he would shatter her hopes as bluntly as he would one of his stones by correcting her: he wanted to be a geologist. He passed his days counting the limestone layers in cliff-faces or returning from the sea bed with pebbles that he swore had pigments he'd never seen. To Petzechroula each was brown. Now she would delight in receiving a murky rock from him. She would marvel at it and treasure it and not object if he did that and nothing else.

She picks up a stone but it's unsightly, bespattered with grimy kelp, and drops it as quickly.

For the time being she has a new child to look after but it comes with a heavy burden on her conscience. Her niece only appeared because of a genocide. She seeks penance every time her mind turns to the atrocity in Kalavryta because it has benefited her. She begs god's forgiveness each Sunday but can't tell Papas Giantakos. Neither can she divulge it to her friends should they too not understand. When they're alone she mutters the confession to her husband. She tells him that it took a village to be exterminated for her family to return to its nest. She can't resolve the lopsidedness of this but, grateful that he can't hear her, she kisses him on his forehead and allows him to remain ignorant of her woe. There's momentary relief in speaking it out loud. Perhaps it's the same lightness that Tassos used to describe after free-diving in weightless exuberance.

Stavroula kicks her feet in the water and the cold returns Petzechroula to the present.

The girl trembles and reaches for her aunt's shoulder.

"Let's get you into bed and warm up those dainty toes."

Stavroula laughs. Her feet might be petite but they're unruly since the trek. Toe nails have blackened or fallen off. "They're so rough they could be used to start a fire."

"They'll be fresh out of the box soon enough but not if you keep thrashing about in the ocean."

"One more minute. I'm so happy I met you, theia."

"As am I."

"Don't be mad at my father."

Petzechroula does blame him. She and Stavroula would have died unaware of the other had it not been for the war. She sours her lips. "I wish we'd met sooner. That's all."

"It was far and difficult. If he told me about you I would have sprinted and tripped at the first hurdle."

"You're here now where you belong."

"Look over there," the girl says. "What do you see?"

Petzechroula turns to the horizon. "Nothing. Just water."

"Exactly. But nothingness amounts to so much. That's what it was like going over the mountains. The world is so big and I saw so little of it. I want Akis to travel far."

Petzechroula silently disagrees. Stavroula can't understand the pain of having a child out of reach. Not so far, she thinks, at least not until the war is behind us.

Stavroula stands tall and shouts across the sea. "Danke!"

"That word. What does it mean?"

"It means whatever you want it to. Maybe it'll meet the ears of a far away nation and they'll recognise it. Try it."

"Danke?"

"Yes."

"Danke."

"Louder."

"Danke!"

Stavroula giggles and joins in. Then she screams the names of her aunt and uncle. "Petzechroula! Tyresia!" The ritual the village plays in helping direct the couple towards one another, the communal game of hot and cold, is one of her favourite things.

Petzechroula is pleased to hear her laugh. She sometimes calls her husband even when she doesn't need to. She joins in now, the two of them shouting his name. It spreads like ripples.

It's fortunate that they draw attention to themselves because moments later Stavroula faints. Men point Tyresias towards the descent so that he can help carry the girl to the house. Petzechroula looks back at the spot where she was spread out; where her hips were has turned a deeper shade than the sand around it.

A message goes out to find Stavroula's father. He has been useless during the pregnancy but Petzechroula will force him to deliver his grandchild. She will beat him if she has to, even if afterwards he's so aggrieved that he leaves again.

He rushes to the house and works hard whilst the rest of Vatheia gathers outside. There are nearly two hundred residents and each has a tender story about Stavroula in her short time there. She's one of them. Father Giantakos leads a petition.

Only Petzechroula stays by her brother's side, mopping her niece's brow. Once the baby is born she hopes that Leonidas will overcome whatever has plagued him. She adds it to her list of silent prayers, comforted by the priest's muffled voice outside.

There's a pungent, metallic smell. Petzechroula looks down and sees a lot of blood. If Leonidas is panicked then he doesn't show it but he reaches for more cloths and instruments than should be required.

Stavroula whispers for her coat in between bouts of breathlessness. Petzechroula fetches it and wraps it around the shivering girl. Leonidas stands from his crouched position and squeezes his daughter's hand. "I love you," he says. The words terrify Petzechroula.

He returns to where the baby is egressing and instructs Stavroula to push, but it's his hands that do all the work. He turns to his sister. "I can't stop it."

"Stop it," she instructs, throwing his words back at him. "You're doing great my darling girl."

Stavroula grapples with the lining of the coat but all of the colour has faded from her. She gasps for air and makes a choking sound before stopping breathing altogether.

Leonidas hurries the delivery as fast as he can. He cuts the cord and passes his grandchild to Petzechroula. He works on resuscitating his daughter but to no avail. The baby cries, orphaned at its first breath.

"Look," Petzechroula says to Stavroula calmly, wanting nothing more than to wail and lament her niece in the wild Maniot way. She has never shown such restraint, as if this conventional volume could coax the girl back to life. "You were right. It's a boy."

She wraps the baby in a blanket. His head is covered in light brown hair, blonder than any newborn Vatheia has seen. Leonidas toys with the blonde tufts and lulls the boy to sleep.

Petzechroula switches the coat with a sheet that covers Stavroula's whole body. She notices what Stavroula was trying to show her. Bunched red fabric is sewn to the lining. She breaks off the hat and forms it into its conical shape. She brings it over to where her brother cradles the baby.

"Isn't he beautiful," he says. "An Asteriakos through and through."

"Put the hat on him. He'll catch a cold."

"Not yet. His hair shouldn't be covered." Tears fill Leonidas' eyes. "I was a fool. I thought it would matter."

Petzechroula doesn't follow but she recognises that something inside him has lifted. She steps outside to give the grandfather and grandson space and to tell the community the wonderful and devastating news.

6

Diros Caves
3rd July 1958

Across his fourteen years, Akis Asteriakos has had a cherished upbringing, raised by his grandfather and great aunt and uncle. He knows nothing beyond his placid village despite growing up through a civil war. He's dismissive of the industrial boom in Athens that might as well be occurring on another planet. In Vatheia nothing happens. Every morning he visits Petzechroula's chickens and greets them the same way: "Sit on your eggs." It makes him laugh to see them take no notice, this favourite expression of his for holding firm not only fitting but reassuring.

Change is for politicians and city-dwellers. There are still no roads into Mani. Ships are rare and hiking paths lined by scratchy wildflowers. Some routes are impenetrable depending on the season. It suits him fine. He has everything he needs: his family, friends that make the small classroom tolerable, a village full of familiar faces, and a sea in which to cool off.

He rarely wonders about his father, a man who travelled through and had a love affair with his mother. To Akis this man is as foregone as her. He asks Petzechroula about the past but she only answers if he accompanies her to church. There she says that Stavroula had Moses beat, that she delivered a precious treasure within the chosen land, so precious is he in fact that the entire Jewish diaspora has nothing on him.

The only person he loves more is his grandfather, Leonidas, the postman of Mani. Akis accompanies him often on the twice-weekly delivery runs. The baby blue row-boat, the two of them, and alternating sides of the peninsula. There's little money in the work but they don't need much. Now that Akis is older and stronger, and his grandfather tired, he frequently takes the oars. When they pull into the bays it's Akis who jumps into the shallows, runs to the villages and is back in a quarter of the time it would take his grandfather. But there's nothing better than returning to Vatheia at the end of the day. Distributing parcels and letters along the coast reminds him that nowhere else compares.

The village is his playground, safe and familiar and constant. The only thing that he doesn't mind cutting into his tidy life are the summertime visits from his older cousin, Tassos, who lectures in Athens. They spend these weeks together challenging one another to deeper dives. Akis practises year round and is now as proficient.

During those evenings, Tassos tells them about the technological and architectural advances in the capital, impossible to imagine had he not brought photographs. The city is shooting upwards and the Acropolis is disappearing from previous vantage points. But no amount of cinemas, sports pitches or kiosks has swayed Akis to visit.

'Where's the beach? How can I run along those streets barefoot? Why does everyone look so miserable?'

Tassos answers that the photographs can't capture the vibrancy. Petzechroula claps her hands and suggests that he may be teaching in a university but his cousin has him there. Leonidas chimes in that Akis is free to be wherever he wants and that he can do whatever he puts his mind to. Tyresias sits back and says nothing, perhaps unable to follow the conversation or just pleased to have them all together.

Today Tassos will arrive ahead of his scheduled visit, passing through with geology students before the semester ends. He's pushing for a professorship, and leading students on excursions is the sort of add-on that the university looks at favourably.

Petzechroula is delighted for this bonus. She misses him but never complains about his absence even if every so often she picks up a pebble at the beach and grumbles, 'There are rocks here.'

She's been lucky following a renewed interest in the nearby Diros Caves. Second to Vatheia, it's Akis' best-loved part of the coastline, a hard-to-reach bay, the sea a satiny blue lined by white pebbles. When he doesn't have school and his grandfather doesn't have work Akis goes there to swim and usually has the place to himself because, even if researchers come to take samples from the flooded caves, they don't stay for long. Tassos once brought with him a set of postcards of countries from around the world including a place called Cambodia. In the photograph the beach was alluring but busy. Diros is better because there are no tourists.

Tassos' boat docks at Vatheia and he allows the rowdy students an hour-long break, in part to marvel at the village but mostly because his mother would kill him if he denied her the chance to fuss. The house is too small for the group of twenty so they sit in the plateia. Akis watches from a distance at the camaraderie between the students. He's agreed to go with them to the caves but is now unsure. They are only a few years older but the boys are broadened out, confident in open shirts, whilst the girls wear high-ridged shorts that on their arrival Petzechroula deplored as immodest.

One boy swats at a fly before sweeping his floppy hair from his face. Others laugh at him as he battles on with the bug.

Akis stares from behind the oak tree, timid and feeling like his wings have been clipped.

Tassos jostles him forward and puts him in a headlock before messing up his light mop. "This is my cousin, Aki. It's his birthday."

Akis breaks free and brushes his hair. People sing to him and cheer. He grimaces throughout.

"My name is Apostolis." It's the first time since birth that he or anyone has used his full name.

There's an awkward silence across the square until the students turn back to their smaller groups. Tassos and Petzechroula look at one another amused. It only peeves Akis more and he walks off kicking stones until he reaches his bicycle, a busted-up thing that nonetheless works. His grandfather took it a while back from the post office in Gytheio in lieu of payment. He continues along the slope that winds down to the beach and waits on the boat. He'll cycle the bumpy path back from the caves whilst the others carry on to Areopoli.

The fly-swatting student boards and snickers at the state of the bicycle.

"What?" Akis asks.

"Huh?"

"You're laughing at me."

"I wasn't."

Akis holds his position. "You were."

"I was telling Marina about something else."

"On three, you and Marina both tell me the joke."

A few people stop to watch the altercation. The older boy's expression sours. He's about to retort when Tassos appears.

"Anything wrong, Theodoros?"

"All good here." He takes another boy's arm and drags him to the bow. He barely makes distance before he laughs again.

"What's going on, Aki? Sorry, Apostolis?"

"Nothing."

Akis regrets coming. He throws imaginary breadcrumbs towards the gulls that follow the boat.

Tassos details the history of the caves to the students who want to listen. Akis looks past them to where Theodoros sits alone, one knee up to his chest, smoking and staring out to sea. His profile is striking. Akis remembers his smirk and can think of nothing better than pushing him overboard and wiping it off his face.

Theodoros takes a sketchpad from his bag and begins to draw. He stares back and forth from the landscape. Akis is too far away to see the result.

His mood improves as they near Diros because the group are awed by this spot that belongs to him. He enjoys the reverence on their faces. The Laconian Gulf spans from the lighthouse at Cape

Tainaron in the south, where it's said to hold an entrance to Hades, to the lower villages of Limeni and the steep reaches towards Areopoli and Sparti in the north, but nowhere is more arresting than here.

They dock at Diros and one of the girls moans that they've been given no time to swim. Akis pulls off his top and jumps in. The students look on enviously. Tassos allows them fifteen minutes. Afterwards they trek the one hundred metres uphill that feel ten times this under the midday sun. They enter the cave mouth, a long slit within the cliff-face that resembles the jaw of a rabid dog.

Akis has been inside plenty of times but it always seems like he's seeing something different to his cousin. It's a stupefying site no doubt but Tassos breaks the charm by giving technical names to the formations that have spanned millions of years. The caves became water-logged during an earthquake one thousand years earlier. Now it requires long-boats to navigate farther. The glow of the students' torches hits hundreds of stalactites. One boy accidentally drops his light into the water. He reaches for it but the pool is icy and he pulls back in shock. The nearest people crane over the edge to see the light sink low, illuminating stalagmites that rise to impressive heights.

The first time he'd led a group Tassos had allowed them to row to the wider chamber. Someone had lost an oar and others screamed that they'd be stranded. It was a Herculean effort to have everyone back so it was the last time to bother. Besides, so few of the passages had been explored that it would be easy to get lost. Akis occasionally hears tales of men who have gone in search of riches and never returned so he has no desire to voyage farther in. The unsettling echoes of the drips and the columns that resemble monsters lurking in the shadows keep him at bay.

Tassos lectures the students, fussing over intricate details. It bores Akis and he steps out into the sun. He returns to the beach, strips to his shorts and runs over the hot stones towards the sea. He wants nothing more than for Tassos to join him. He looks up from the surface wistfully and is surprised to see Theodoros sitting in the shade. The boy is staring back at him. Drawing him.

Akis swims towards land and throws on his top despite dripping wet. He marches over. "What are you doing?"

Theodoros turns the page towards him. He's drawn the bay in abstract purposeful lines that capture its ruggedness. Akis is absent. Somehow that bothers him more.

"Sit. I'll draw you."

Akis sops onto the stones. "Why?"

"Why not?"

He's never had anyone draw him before. He sits and combs his fingers through his hair.

"Don't. It looks good as it is."

Akis has to stop himself. He tries to place what's making him uncomfortable. Maybe it's that he's being judged. He glowers but Theodoros laughs at his change of expression.

"I'll call it *The Pugnacious Boy Of Vatheia.*"

Akis doesn't know what that means but he won't give him the satisfaction of asking. He blushes each time that Theodoros inspects his face.

"Do you go to school?" the older boy asks.

"I'm top out of the six of us."

"Good on you."

"How many were at yours?"

"Two hundred."

"Oh."

"Do you study French?" Theodoros doesn't wait for an answer. "I've forgotten most of it now but it's good to be grounded in multiple languages, you know?"

Akis is being disparaged. He remembers himself. "I don't need anything but Greek."

He goes to stretch back and claim the land as his. Theodoros tuts and keeps him upright.

The group is nowhere to be seen. Akis grows impatient. He cricks his neck and is admonished again.

Theodoros sighs. "If you were a few years older and not related to my lecturer."

Akis doesn't know what he's on about but is embarrassed all the same. Theodoros is worldly and talented. Perhaps Tassos was right. This is the gain of living in Athens.

He can't sit any longer and rises to leave.

"I'm not done yet."

Akis shrugs.

"Want to see it at least?"

Theodoros turns the sheet over. Akis is flattered. He's captured his best features. So many of his aunt's friends grab his cheeks and call him cute and their crown but he's never been looked on as handsome.

"Wow."

"My model made it easy. Want it?"

Akis reaches out to take the paper but retracts his hand. If it's so good then why doesn't Theodoros want to keep it? He's swooped in, been indifferent to the caves, and belittled him. Now he'll leave without thinking twice about him, this day trip from the city soon to be forgotten.

Akis will never be able to look at the drawing without feeling discarded. He senses that he's about to cry, and runs.

He grabs his bicycle and pushes it to the top of the cliff without looking back. It's only halfway to Vatheia when he realises that he hasn't said goodbye to Tassos.

7

Vatheia
3rd July 1960

After Leonidas helps to drag the boat onto the sand, he waits for his grandson to look away before stealing a much-needed deep breath. Akis has rowed nearly every delivery this past year but today, on his sixteenth birthday, Leonidas took up the oars as a present: for him to sit back and laugh at his tired grandfather who'd wanted to recreate their past. It was also a self-appointed test that Leonidas has barely passed.

Their deliveries cover the east side of the peninsula to Gytheio on Mondays and a second run to Kardymili, originally on Thursdays but changed to Saturdays so that Akis could work and attend school. Now that the academic year is not only done but his classroom days are finished in their entirety the schedule doesn't much matter. Not that Akis cared about any clashes, intent on taking over the postman role when his grandfather retires. Nikolaos Christakos has been Vatheia's only teacher for a decade, a stuffy man in a stuffier room tucked away at the back of the church, and has done little to inspire him. Any attempt to wrangle enthusiasm out of Nikolaos has only made him double down in his belief that rote learning is the prescribed method.

Leonidas has taken it upon himself to teach Akis arithmetic, science and Ancient Greek. The boy flourishes in the latter, a natural polyglot, but comes unstuck with the lack of opportunity. Some English and French slip into the Greek vocabulary, Akis particularly keen to learn French a few years back, but no one knows either well enough to help him. He's been invited to stay with Tassos in Athens where he can have his pick of teachers but no amount of encouragement to study under his cousin's guardianship has been fruitful. Each suggestion is shut down or fought off. Akis is insistent that life outside of Vatheia isn't for him even if he's seen little else. There's no offer attractive enough to sway him from a life traversing the coastline.

Leonidas supports this choice as he would any other. The boy is headstrong like Stavroula. She'd wanted to follow his career into medicine. He takes pride in having inspired both of them. But that was a lifetime ago and even if he wasn't a humble man he still cannot of course share this fact with his grandson.

Akis secures the boat as Leonidas stands back, grateful to be relieved of the heavy lifting. The boy is tireless in and out of the water. He glows when he swims and manoeuvres the boat as if the sea travels through the oars and into him. He is also fearless, a trait that has passed down through generations of the women he's never met: Stavroula and Marika and Leonidas' mother. Despite that each summer the boy's hair bleaches blonder than any of his classmates, any thoughts that Leonidas had of his grandson being anything other than Asteriakos blood are long forgotten.

Except for questions about his parents and his frustration at the scant answers, Akis hasn't inherited his mother's curiosity, at his happiest the closer he is to Vatheia. She'd wanted to break free of her small world and Leonidas has since accepted that Akis should set his sights wider, this small chick folded into his clasp no longer needing protection and yet when he releases his hand the bird has no interest in taking flight. Stavroula died on the cusp of seventeen, less than a year older than Akis is now. What would she say about his decision to stay and deliver post? A life unfulfilled or one of embracing love?

Familiar voices pitch in.

Leonidas has never been able to liberate himself from the musings of his friends from his kafeneio days. Sometimes this chorus is a faded hum but other times it comes on like tinnitus, reverberating as if the last philosophy club was only yesterday. He swats at the air as Giannis laments his own son's cut-off youth.

"Are you feeling alright, Pappou?"

"Just some annoying flies."

Akis loves the peacefulness of the sea, the two of them in lulling silence or gentle chat, but he doesn't know how crowded the boat can get. The men, rowdy in their sixties, sit just above centre of Leonidas' eyes and bicker almost daily. Some err on the side of Akis staying whilst others argue for him to leave. Adonis chimes in with a final, cutting remark: there's a village much farther north in the midst of being restored whose abandoned train route needs a driver.

"Ready old man?"

Leonidas brings the meeting to a close and massages his sore forearms; mental exertion plagued his career as a doctor but he's never known physical burn-out like this.

"Go ahead. I might sit and watch the sun go down."

"Petzechroula will be frantic. She's planning a surprise meal."

"Do you have your expression ready?"

Akis pulls an exaggerated look of shock, causing Leonidas to laugh. It winds him again.

"No rush," Akis says. With limitless stamina he runs into the surf. His body is tanned and athletic. In the last year he's begun to resemble a young man.

Time plays a trick on Leonidas and for a moment he thinks that he can chase him. He was once fit like that but now needs days of stasis to recover enough to get back on the water. Sometimes the idea that he walked the length of the Peloponnese seems impossible, as if that body belonged to another.

Kalavryta was so long ago that he often convinces himself that it never happened. He leaves it that way, with Akis knowing nothing about his other heritage. The philosophy club thinks differently, as does Petzechroula, but Leonidas makes her swear not to tell. Ganged up on, he nonetheless knows that this is best. No good will come of Akis learning about his father. His hair is dark enough and his features heavy enough to pass as fully Greek. He's taller than the rest of them but that could be a generational thing or a consequence of Petzechroula force-feeding him. He is Greek. He doesn't need others thinking that he's anything less. But, firm as he is, Leonidas isn't able to settle the other men's consternation. Rowing might exhaust him but it also spares him at the end of each day, too spent to listen to any one of a number of soliloquies before he passes out stone cold.

He leans against the boat's upturned hull and watches Akis' leisurely strokes.

He'd wanted to forsake his own identity on the return to Vatheia. For a while he'd carried on treating people but being unable to save Stavroula was the culmination of a career too gruelling to continue forward. In the end he took on an apprentice, a young man who returned from the war with a leg full of shrapnel but a surprisingly clear head. Yiannis Mavromichalis learnt apace and within a few years was so trusted by the Vatheians that Leonidas consulted from a distance. When the call for 'Giatre' now sounds out across the village it is no longer him that anyone has in mind.

Stepping away entirely required something that would physically distance himself. News came from Gytheio that the postman had died. Leonidas had taken Tyresias' boat and rowed there immediately. He was nearing fifty but, considering the back-breaking work and poor salary, no one else wanted the job. It was hilarious to Petzechroula that her brother, who had shunned the sea, found himself knitted to it.

He regrets not accompanying Marika and Stavroula to the beach even once so he couldn't have disappointed Akis too. He's lived through so many tragedies and missed opportunities that he'd never expected that simply to sit with his grandson on a boat could bring so much joy. Despite the rowdiness of his critics he hopes that they'd be proud of him.

As Akis grew he wanted nothing more than to be out on the water listening to stories of Maniots and Spartans, ancient legends and the clan battles that also sounded like a thing of lore. He'd evaded any fighting but the war had depleted the country's spirit and the civil war that followed knocked it to its feet once more, a tower house dismantled and its shell bulldozed and any reconstruction insufferably slow. Akis has innocence on his side, especially if he holds back, and so Leonidas is agreeable to the boy's decision to take over the family business.

Family business, Leonidas hears the men repeat with derision. But there's some truth to it seeing as he's delivered mail for over a decade. He throws his hand into the breeze to bat off the men before they cast semantics his way.

"To hell with you all," he says, relieved that Akis is too far out to hear.

When Akis was born the village wanted to celebrate him, a cheerful note on a wretched exchange. He was kept indoors for forty days and then taken to the church to be blessed. Being guided by superstition was the least that the family could do. Akis has lived a charmed life ever since but eventually roads will unite Mani with the mainland and a postman wrestling with a boat will become redundant. He has half a century of work ahead of him but Leonidas doubts that delivery vans will wait that long. What then? Perhaps the boy's confidence with the sea can be reimagined into a profitable shipping position. That reassures him.

He calls Akis to return to the beach but the idea of climbing the slope rattles him. He lifts himself up but his calves give way and he falls back humiliated.

Akis joins him. He shakes his hair and wets his grandfather.

Leonidas pretends to be annoyed. "Ela, my crown."

"You have to stop calling me that."

"Why? You're only sixteen."

"I'm a man."

"What does that make me? A poky mule ready for the slaughterhouse?"

"Grandfathers are meant to be old. Anyway look at what you can do."

Leonidas sighs. "I know what it's like to be your age but you don't know what it's like to be mine."

"I know, I know."

Leonidas has a sudden desire to tell Akis everything but the impulse passes as always. It's his last vestige of protecting him. A birthday present that he can't disclose.

"It's going to be a beautiful sunset," Akis says.

"Not if Petzechroula starts screaming."

"Let me dry here for a minute."

"It's your funeral." Leonidas is relieved by the suggestion but plays it off with indifference; Akis is likely delaying for his benefit.

"Aki-mou, how would you like to do the deliveries on your own for a few days? I have some business to take care of. Don't give me that look. Just say yes."

Akis smiles, setting up the same joke that they've shared for years. "I can row the entire length with one hand tied behind my back."

"Then you will row in circles. Promise me something."

"Anything, Pappou."

"The world is full of virtuous people but don't let them sway you. Their truth is not yours."

Akis rolls his eyes. "You're talking in code. Or you've finally lost it."

"Listen to me. There will be days when you have to make choices that tear you in half. Your heart will say one thing and your head will say another."

"You told me both are important."

"I did."

"So how can I choose one over the other?"

"A worthy game of tug of war has two fierce competitors. Reason will dictate the prudent route but the heart will lead you to paradise."

"I'm already in paradise."

"No," he says firmly, surprising Akis. "Paradise is an ever-challenging place. You cannot sit idle and expect the ground to cultivate fruit."

Akis looks at him as if he has turned delirious. "Why are you telling me this now?"

"A man does not plant trees for his own shade. Come, before Petzechroula brings the tower down. Then we'd seriously be kicked out of Eden."

Leonidas is grateful that Akis takes his arm and they amble back at a turtle's pace.

Petzechroula has prepared the birthday boy's favourite dishes: fried sage lalagia, pork in lemon, and pancakes with carob honey from beans that Tyresias has ground. It's a feast considering the pitiful stock typically afforded to them. They eat and laugh and sing and after drinking wine fermented from quinces Petzechroula drags Akis onto his feet and they dance.

Later that night, some hours after the four of them have played cards under the stars, Leonidas dies in his sleep.

It's as peaceful as death can be. In his dream he's welcomed back into the fold of the philosophy club. The men are excited for his opinions but are mostly impatient to share theirs. But there will be an eternity for these meetings and he instead excuses himself to catch a long-overdue train towards the shore.

Akis is the only person to not feature in his passing and yet Leonidas isn't alarmed, having fallen asleep comforted by his grandson's fortitude. Reassured that the boy is capable of weathering any storm that could, and undoubtedly would, come his way.

Even in a settled bay like Vatheia.

San Sto Spiti Sas

Greece, 1962

8

Athens
20th June 1962

Haruki wanted to screw up the letter and toss it from the aeroplane's window, his words lost to the world below.

His writing was childish, his thoughts scattered. He'd embellished the pages with superfluous adjectives, flipped between introspection and the third person, and given his grandfather the cutesy moniker 'Jiji' whilst suffixing honorifics to the end of every verb. He hated what he'd written: *You asked me to document this summer so that I might work out what I want to study, that this will give me a* – he'd tried to recall the character for 'revelation' but the altitude had dulled his mind – *chance to decide*. During endless hours in the sky he'd made little headway. At least it was offset by the distance covered, with whole countries skipped or reduced to identically-drab landing strips as the plane refuelled on the route from Tokyo to Athens.

His penmanship was also poor, scrawled up to the end, but that wasn't really his fault. Just as his sister's stomach hadn't settled, just as his mother hadn't stopped snapping her fingers at air hostesses to fetch sick-bags, and just as his father had been oblivious throughout, glued to the porthole and desperate to disembark rather than forgo the rock formations lost to the contrails, not one of the four

Okazakis had grown accustomed to the hum of the engine nor the shaking of the plane.

The assignment was a promise to his jiji. Over the next two months Haruki was expected to tie himself to the mast of a sinking ship, namely, what to study at university and more specifically whether to enrol in his father's or grandfather's discipline. An impossible choice when he wanted neither.

It had been his mother's idea for him to follow into Waseda and cement a family tradition. Ever since, the two men had routinely sat him down and argued that their domain mattered more, jostling to win a competition that to Haruki seemed little more than egotistical. They couldn't have chosen more distinct fields. His father lectured within the geology department, chipping away at minerals shaped over millennia, whilst his grandfather had been professor emeritus of ethology, monitoring the effects of subtle but precarious climate deviations on snow monkeys until his retirement. Haruki envied their passion but both options left him cold.

He couldn't see any worth in the summer-long exercise but would do it anyway, fed up with hearing about his so-called 'wayward insubordination' when he was otherwise a top student.

He switched to the book his father had lent him. The novella *Shiosai* with its minimalist cover of a sunrise, a few strokes of the sea under a rising sun, was incongruous with Toshihiro Okazaki's usual boring articles about bedrock, and yet it was as heavily dog-eared. The plot surprised Haruki, not only that Yukio Mishima rarely wrote light romance but that his father had enjoyed it. He begrudged the words that flowed when his own were awkward. He copied a random sentence, exchanging the nouns for his situation. It read not only stunted but stolen.

A flight attendant checked the cabin ahead of the final descent.

Haruki had a burst of inspiration: *I'm the first of my classmates to fly across the world but I haven't enjoyed the view from up here. I sound ungrateful but let me explain what leaves me unresponsive: Jiji, your pursuit is like rowing the Pacific and expecting to understand the vastness of the ocean by scrutinising each wave, whilst Otou-san's is like these flights, as far removed from civilisation as his geological ages. Neither reveals much about the world. I would rather something graspable, like a train ride or cycling cross country–*

He groaned at the failed analogy. There was no middle-ground, no discipline that bridged the animal kingdom to minerals. He scribbled out the lines that could never reach his jiji. He couldn't write the one thing he wanted. He'd tried to tell them once but his grandfather had clutched his chest as if words could be so savage.

Haruki caught his father peering at the crossed-out sentences.

"Excited?" his father asked him, with a level of enthusiasm that hadn't been dampened by the interminable journey.

"I guess."

"Your friends will be jealous. And think of all the stories you'll have for Jiji."

Haruki shrugged. He'd had other plans for the summer. Vying with Yuki for their grandfather's attention as he raced them through the hydrangea paths around Kamakura or spoilt them with grilled dango skewers at temple stalls, all the while pointing out cormorants in flight or koi ponds in which carp and turtles lived in harmony.

Then his father had announced that he'd been invited to explore a cave in southern Greece and they would need to obtain passports. Haruki had been horrified. It was his last summer of freedom before the one sparking his move to university, the last before he was too old to be coddled. There were caves in Japan, plenty close to Tokyo no less, but it was final: the trip was green-lit.

It was late night when they took a taxi to the hotel. Haruki was rattled as they crossed Athens. The city was underdeveloped compared to Tokyo's neon explosion. Even the glow of the Parthenon was dulled by the dust particles in the air. He would reserve judgement about the Peloponnese until he had seen it. He was told that the sea was more spectacular than in Kamakura where the sand was muddy and the waves foamed with debris. He didn't care. Though he was only sixteen he felt nostalgia for something that had barely passed. He pined for the beaches near his grandfather's summer residence on the Shonan coast. In the distance was Oshima where his jiji had promised to take him on his return. There they would eat freshly-caught fish and bathe in onsen alongside macaques. Haruki couldn't wait even if it was an offer laden with a certain condition.

He was the first awake the next morning. The crack in the curtain suggested daylight but it was too dim to read or write. He didn't want to disturb the others so he dressed in the dark and wandered the hotel with its unintelligible signs until he found breakfast being served on the rooftop. He was treated to a more favourable view of the Acropolis set back from pastel-coloured houses lining its slopes. A waiter offered him a menu but it was in Greek. He sat there subdued until the man returned with an orange juice and a flaky pastry.

"Spanakopita," the waiter said. The word was long and alien and didn't reveal anything about its contents.

Haruki took a bite. It was filled with spinach and something pungent that he hadn't tasted before. It turned his stomach.

Guests at other tables peeked at him with all the curiosity of an exhibition in a travelling circus. He distracted himself with *Shiosai* until the waiter refilled his cup and pointed at the title. Haruki read it aloud. After the man left, Haruki tucked the book under the table.

He wondered how he would fare this summer. He'd learnt Russian at school due to the country's proximity but it had no value here. His father had searched for an interpreter but no one was bilingual, and the question of how he and his counterpart would communicate had been answered with a vague response: they would get by in elementary English.

Haruki listened to car horns and peddlers erratic and brash until his father approached alongside a Greek man with thick stubble.

"Haruki-kun, this is Doctor Anastasios Tzanetakis."

"Tassos," the man corrected him.

"Okazaki Haruki," Haruki said, slipping into the home-grown manner of giving the family name first. He bowed as Tassos reached out a hand. Tassos switched to a bow and Haruki blushed at the mix-up. At least he wasn't expected to kiss him on each cheek as he'd seen between two people reuniting at the airport.

The men sat and traced a path over a map of the country. When his father stole away to look at the Parthenon, Tassos asked Haruki a question. He responded with a blank stare.

Toshihiro translated. "Want to learn some Greek?"

Haruki nodded.

"Nai," said Tassos, holding up a thumb. He turned it upside-down. "Ochi."

They practised everyday phrases through mimes and repetition until Haruki had built a small repertoire that settled his stomach.

His mother had skipped breakfast, holding out in the room supposedly on account of Yuki's nausea, and met them in the hotel's foyer from where Tassos guided them through the city.

They walked across the Constitution Square, where people drank coffees in front of the Parliament, and then they dodged electric trolleybuses ahead of Plaka's marble-paved arcades. Megumi shuffled Yuki wherever there was shade despite holding a parasol above them. Seven years stood between Haruki and his sister and she was drawn to ice cream parlours whilst he stuck by Tassos' side and continued the lesson, spelling out the lettering on shopfronts. He recognised Π and Σ from mathematics and it wasn't long until he could point at every letter that formed Tassos' name. The alphabet seemed simple, nothing like the thousands of kanji he'd memorised on top of its two supplementary alphabets. If it wasn't for the absurd length of Greek words he'd swap his language for this one in a heartbeat.

They made a courtesy call at the Japanese Embassy after the Director had organised visas for them. It had opened two years earlier at the same time as its counterpart in Tokyo. Haruki watched his mother breathe easier at the familiarity of removing her shoes and being offered a cup of ocha.

Athens was a village next to Tokyo but everything had historic importance. Tassos directed them through the ancient Agora, the centre of philosophy, and then on an effortful hike up the Pnyx, the birthplace of democracy. The hill that sided the Acropolis gave them a vista of the city which stretched from the sea in one direction to mountain ranges in every other. Haruki was more captivated by the gasps of the others than the view itself.

By then they were parched and Tassos passed around a bottle of water. Haruki took a sip and handed the bottle to his mother but she refused.

"A samurai uses a toothpick even when he has not eaten," she said in Japanese but to no one in particular.

Tassos asked for a translation but Megumi brushed it aside.

Haruki rolled his eyes at her attempted snobbery. She liked to drop sayings into conversations at an inordinate rate, the more convoluted the better. He'd noticed her habit gain momentum recently, especially when his friends' parents came to the house.

Yuki complained that she was tired. Tassos lifted her onto his shoulders and she signalled him onwards to the steep stairs to the Parthenon. Toshihiro thanked him in both of their languages. Megumi scowled behind them, incensed that Yuki was exposed to the sun, but Toshihiro was fixated on Tassos' stories and she was reticent to interrupt. She pulled the parasol closer to her but everything was marble and the sun reflected onto her face from all angles. Haruki was more engrossed in his mismatched parents than the ruins, unable to believe they'd ever been affectionate, any love that they might have shared as derelict as the site.

After, they broke at a cloistered square on lower ground where old men played board games and younger groups chatted over a clear spirit, each round accompanied by a different platter.

"Tsipouro," Tassos said, having seen Haruki staring. He asked Toshihiro for permission before calling over a waiter.

Haruki assumed that the alcohol would taste like saké but it was strong and unrefined and he pulled a face that made Tassos laugh and pat him on the back.

The square centred on a Byzantine church covered in decayed sandstone and a Cyrillic script. Saints were painted onto the walls, their faces flat and worn, their thumbs and forefingers curled. Green parrots flitted between the eaves. Yuki chased one that dared to swoop low and peck at breadcrumbs but it darted off before Haruki could inspect the blue under its wings and report its shadings to Jiji. His father would favour the immovable church and his grandfather the shorter-lived birds but neither captivated him.

The family lagged. Summer in Japan was humid and heavy whilst Greece's dry heat was scalding. Tassos suggested a taxi but Toshihiro rallied them to walk to the hotel where they hid from the sun for the rest of the day. Haruki's nose had turned a bright red that soothed under the bathroom's cold tap.

Tassos met them again in the evening and recommended a takeaway souvlaki. Haruki devoured it whilst his mother squirmed at the lack of plates. Toshihiro found a stoop for himself and Yuki. They ate messily as the sauce fell from the pitta wraps and coated their hands.

It was late but not dark as they continued along the olive-lined Panathenaic Way. Stray cats slunk across marbled stairwells whilst dogs picked at fallen scraps outside tavernas. Men with thick beards and oval eyes acted differently to those back home, catcalling one another without reservation. Haruki and his sister followed militantly behind their mother. Elsewhere women skipped with their children.

They came to the Herodeion, the amphitheatre at the rear of the Acropolis, and entered under its mammoth yellow-stone arch. Tassos had treated them to seats with an outstanding view of the stage. The marble benches had retained the heat of the day and Yuki rested her head on her mother's lap and was asleep before the first scene. Megumi was usually strict but allowed her to sleep through.

Just as the sky seemed to be in no rush to turn to night, audience members were in no hurry to stop gossiping and settle down. It was some time after the play started when the stars came out.

Haruki was locked out of the language and the style. He hadn't loved accompanying his grandfather to kabuki but the costumes were colourful and the performances animated. This had soldiers standing around giving lengthy monologues about, from what he'd been told, a retelling of the Tyrannides and the two lovers Harmodius and Aristogeiton, both of them men. This point concerned Megumi but since Tassos had gifted them the tickets it would have been ruder to refuse. Haruki looked around at the five-thousand-strong audience who didn't seem to find the relationship problematic.

Haruki adored the setting despite the tedium. The preservation of the columns was more in line with his father's sphere of interest so he debated whether to mention it to his grandfather. He spotted birds perched high but he had no desire to chronicle them either. As with earlier in the day, the reactions of others was much more arresting. One man in particular intrigued him. He sat on the same row with the bench curved enough so that his profile was in view. He was a little older than Haruki and was lost in the play. His face spoke more about the events than anything happening on stage. He smiled and cried. His eyes widened in wonderment. Fearful intakes of breath. Reverent taut temples.

During the interval Haruki spied him pecking a second man on the lips. At one point it seemed as if he'd locked onto Haruki's gaze – Haruki froze – but he looked away as suddenly, just a general glance in this direction. Haruki continued to watch him through the second act, missing the brutal ending and the actors taking a bow. He couldn't stop returning to him even when his mother tutted. He'd never seen someone so taken in a moment. He desperately wanted to know how it was to see the world through his eyes.

He felt a rush of excitement. On his first day he'd learnt what he wanted to study. Men. People. He wanted to understand them.

His heart soared long after losing the man in the crowd. He wanted to hug him, kiss him on both cheeks, or even the lips, because he'd painted for him a future.

Haruki had a second, invigorating brainwave. Perhaps studying humans was the bridge that would satisfy his family; flitting animals at one end of the spectrum and rocks weighed down by inactivity at the other, humans existed in the middle living in emotion.

"What did you think?" his father asked him in the taxi on the way back to the hotel.

"It was great. The characters fought for what they believed." He proceeded carefully. "Do any of your colleagues study this?"

"Theatre?"

"Human behaviour."

"Yes. In the anthropology department."

"Is it not psychology? Sociology?" He needed to know for sure.

His mother turned to him from the front seat. Her consternation made him queasy.

His father was less suspicious. "The play had quite an effect on you. It's too late to work it out now. Perhaps we could think about it in the morning?"

"Thank you," Haruki said. But his mind continued to make strides as he lay awake in his bed. He didn't want to forget the man's face. He wanted to uncover its secrets. He was sure that he could study it forever.

9

Piraeus to Vatheia
22nd June 1962

No sooner had Haruki adjusted to the city than he and his family and Tassos headed for the harbour. It was a squeeze in the taxi. His mother had loaded their suitcases not only with clothes, accessories, and workbooks for Yuki but with seaweed, miso, matcha and other non-perishables that would cloak the taste of anything foreign.

One case was reserved for gifts. Megumi knew only that they would stay with Tassos' family. She hadn't been told ages or genders and so she'd brought a little of everything, from dolls to obi sashes and from cutesy-packaged corn snacks to a woodblock print.

She'd also packed for each member of the family a wardrobe that ran the gamut of formality. Haruki couldn't understand what was needed to pass a summer under the scorching sun except for a shirt and swimwear. Around them Greeks were in one-toned suits and dresses, many only had a single outfit that they wore every day. There was nothing to match his cut-off jinbei shorts and definitely nothing like his sister's yukata with its vibrant fireworks embroidered into the fabric. His mother reminded him that they were ambassadors of Japan and couldn't show up their country. 'Mune wo haru,' she had told him in Tokyo when he'd seen the amount of clothes. Spread your chest.

Tassos had also brought plenty of bags filled with fresh produce for his own mother. Haruki was enamoured with him; rather than just his father's colleague, he had fast become the family's lifeline in all things practical and negotiable.

Piraeus was a bustling offshoot that resembled Yokohama's trading port. Foot passengers boarded ferries for the islands although these tourist operations were dwarfed by ocean liners at this crossroad from east to west.

The sea was a dusty grey, oil-slicked and stagnant, but as the boat chugged through the Saronic Islands the water became silky and inviting. Haruki stood on the deck and watched as the mainland turned sparser. In the distance, cars zipped past Eleusis and Corinth. Tassos explained that the winding roads towards Epidaurus and Sparti were barely fit for purpose. The Vatheians, he continued, lived even farther south within the mule tracks, a point of stubbornness in fending off modernity but one that came with the cost of estrangement.

"Will we be the first Japanese there?" Haruki asked.

Tassos laughed following Toshihiro's translation.

"Except for around the Embassy you're the first everywhere."

The Athenians had already kept a suspicious berth and Haruki grew perturbed at what the villagers would think. Given his own island mentality, growing up in the insular Japan, he'd held that it was outsiders who brought threat. It was easy to buy into this sentiment when on the sanctimonious side of the equation but not now that he had crossed over as one of the agitators.

Tassos noticed his unease. "Don't worry," he told him, using a newly acquired phrase. But Haruki couldn't escape the dread and under the guise of the wind he retreated to the salon.

His mother and sister were near the toilets, with Yuki as disposed to motion sickness on the sea. They were playing a game of snap with animal pictures. Haruki distracted himself by writing about the previous night but already the theatre felt like a dream, his revelation less momentous. A group of women pried at his efforts, marvelling at the script. He shot his mother a look of needing help but she returned to the cards, unable or unwilling to intervene. The most courageous woman spoke up and Haruki understood one of her words. "Nai, Iaponezika," he replied. It was Japanese that he was writing. He was caught between politeness and not wanting to draw attention to himself but his answer charmed them and invited further inspection. He handed them one of the pages and steeled himself during their coos over its exoticness. The characters might have been nothing but a quirk to them and yet they spoke of his future. He stood to leave, refusing to take back the sheet that was now, redundantly, theirs.

He moved to a quiet corner and picked up his book so that he could return to Japan. He'd studied excerpts of Mishima's works at school. The author depicted a brutal world through political analogies but this story was an anomaly. Sweet and unthreatening, it told of a young fisherman and a pearl diver falling in love on an island west of Tokyo. Their first meeting was accidental and charming. Haruki envied the mutual attraction. He'd kissed a few girls but nothing beyond that.

The boat made a brief stop on Spetses, a circular island that catered to the wealthy. Women wrapped scarves as headdresses whilst men swung keys on chains to draw attention to themselves. Tassos ordered grilled octopus that wasn't so different from home. He reminded them that Vatheia was nothing like this.

Whilst waiting to re-board, Haruki and his sister sat between two yachts and wiggled their toes to attract black nibbling fish. Soon the island cluster was behind them. Up ahead the southern mainland appeared like a wasteland. Haruki had camped at the base of Mount Fuji where the volcanic soil allowed for pears and grapes but here the plains seemed inhospitable to anything.

The ferry arrived at the end of the land and followed the coastline back north, stopping and starting with such frequency that it was evening by the time they docked. They would carry on tomorrow in a chartered boat. Gytheio was a moderate town with three parallel levels of colourful houses. It had been a wearing day, the journey more punishing than walking the blistering city, and

Haruki was pleased to stretch his legs along the harbour after the sun had set.

They reached Vatheia by mid-morning, home for the next two months. The village was unlike anything Haruki had seen with its grey towers at a height above sea level that he hadn't expected. For all the good of Tassos' map it hadn't revealed the coves, cliffs and grander elevations of the Peloponnese, on paper all of it flat and unrealised.

Between them they managed the suitcases in one go, with Yuki riding on Tassos' shoulders and Megumi unimpressed behind them. Haruki carried Tassos' bags. Around him the air was filled with hot spice and oregano.

A stout woman appeared from the top of the slope. "Tyresia!"

Tassos embraced his mother. She was introduced as Petzechroula and welcomed them with an onslaught of foreign phrases. At random intervals, breaking her sentences, she screamed the word again. Close by, but out of view, others called the same thing. Soon a man with bushy eyebrows shuffled towards them. His name preceded him.

Vatheia was both dainty and a relic, its breadth over before it began. It took up no more space than a cul de sac in one of Tokyo's back streets, the total number of inhabitants here likely no greater than the occupants of an apartment block there. There were noticeable absences: no electricity wires overhead, no hawkers, and no traffic other than bicycles left unchained against walls.

People peered through slitted windows. Petzechroula, with no time for restraint, beckoned her neighbours forward. If her guests were to be goggled at then it should be unabashed.

Nowhere in Greece except for the Embassy had Haruki been expected to take off his shoes before stepping inside. Entering the tower was no different. It seemed unfit to host all seven of them. A kitchen, chairs around a table, and a fireplace took up the ground floor. There was a farmyard smell that permeated the air overpowering the wafts of herbal tea from a steaming pot. Chickens clucked from nearby. Haruki assumed that Petzechroula and Tyresias barely noticed in the way that his grandfather had desensitised to the stale cages of his laboratory rats. Yuki followed the smell of the livestock to a curtain but Megumi stopped her, her own nose turned up above a laboured smile.

Haruki spotted a hatch in the corner of the room. Back in Athens Tassos had suggested that he and Toshihiro go to Vatheia whilst the others remain in comfort. Haruki's father had refused. Outside of Tassos' comprehension he'd told his family that not one of them would complain about whatever awaited them; the more humble the better, and a good reminder of the privilege that came with their wealth. Haruki's mother had nodded along. She would hear nothing of them being divided. He wondered if she might have reconsidered had she known about this vertical living.

His curiosity was satisfied when Tyresias climbed up through the trapdoor, matching Jiji's age but with the agility of one of the goats that scaled the surrounding bluffs. The three Tzanetakis' would sleep on the floor above the communal area. Megumi and Toshihiro were given the next floor up and their children the attic. Haruki followed his father who bounded up the ladders. He assumed that his mother would be on the first boat to Athens; he turned to capture this moment but she was right behind him.

"Gou ni itte wa," she said to him, with a self-gratified look. When entering the village, obey the village.

They formed a chain to move the suitcases. Haruki felt bad that Tassos would be sharing with his parents. He was sure that his own parents had also noticed but no one said a thing.

Downstairs again, Petzechroula took Megumi's hand and asked her incomprehensible questions about how the kitchen compared to Tokyo. Petzechroula didn't mind that she couldn't understand, used to Tyresias' deafness and just pleased to have an audience. Haruki watched his mother freeze. According to his grandfather, a snared animal held limp to endure the least harm. He'd only known his mother as a fierce tiger but she was a cub in Petzechroula's jaw.

"San sto spiti sas," said Petzechroula. From the way she directed them to squeeze around the table on the assortment of borrowed chairs her words didn't need a translation. Tassos gave it anyway, to make themselves at home. Much of what he brought was shared rather than saved. Petzechroula encouraged them to eat, the food to be stabbed at with forks or picked with fingers. There were cured meats that required solid chewing, floury pancakes that tasted of nothing and olives that were talked about in Japan as being the fruit of the Mediterranean but were slimier than Haruki had imagined. He didn't know what to do with the stone and held it in his mouth until he saw Tyresias drop one onto his plate. The more he tried the more he appreciated their tang.

Petzechroula poured them mountain tea; nothing tasted close to anything from Japan but this wasn't dissimilar to sencha. Megumi's pleasure at the chance discovery soured when Tassos poured syrup into his cup. She was even more aggrieved when Toshihiro copied him.

Tyresias asked everyone for their names but to be spoken at force. It was strange for Haruki to hear Tassos shorten his father's name to Toshi for ease. The only time he heard this was between his father's oldest friends in bathhouses or when jeering at him when losing at Go. At home everything was formal. Not only did Haruki and Yuki refer to their parents as Okaa-san and Otou-san, Mother and Father, but these were the names that they used on one another. Now they were simply Toshi and Megumi.

Yuki jumped in with her name. Petzechroula grabbed the spirited girl's cheek.

"Takoyaki," Yuki said, before rounding her thumb and forefinger over each cheek and squeezing them into fatty lumps.

A series of translations revealed this as fried octopus balls. Through Tassos, Petzechroula asked Megumi to share the recipe. She nodded but Haruki knew that she'd never cooked them. She never made anything, delegating all of the household chores to their maid.

Haruki was the last to introduce himself. He thought that he'd said his name loudly enough but Tyresias turned to his wife.

"Charupi?"

"Haruki."

"Charupi!"

It was too late. The others repeated the word with a flurry of excitement. Yuki lapped up the mistake and joined in.

"Charupi, Charupi."

Petzechroula pushed the jar of honey towards him, then grabbed a bag of light brown flour from a cupboard. Tassos went outside and returned with a mauve string bean pulled from a tree, its colour as deep as a moonless night.

"Inago-goma," said Megumi. The locust bean.

For the rest of the meal Haruki was addressed with the name given to the carob tree by everyone but his mother. He kept quiet, unable to join in on the joke that seemed to be at his expense even though he knew it wasn't. He envied Yuki and his father for assimilating with little effort and hated that he fell in line with his mother.

In an attempt to relax he thanked his hosts. "Efharisto poly."

Petzechroula threw up her hands in delight. According to her, if the translations were correct, he was a good boy and a clever boy.

Tassos was interrogated by his own parents until Toshihiro rescued him by turning the conversation towards the caves. Haruki thought that he'd heard Petzechroula say 'Aki' a lot, the word meaning autumn in Japanese, but it must have been a coincidence.

By the end of the meal it was too late to trek to the caves so Haruki and his sister were given the rest of the day to explore Vatheia. The school would remain open for another two weeks and Megumi had asked that Yuki be enrolled. The girl whined but it was no use, she would make friends and experience something that the rest of the family couldn't. For now she focused her efforts on convincing Haruki to take her to the beach.

He wanted to watch Tassos interact with the old couple having decided that the man was a good enough subject if he was going to study human behaviour. Over lunch he'd formulated a plan for his university admission. He would detail how parent-child interactions differed between his own race and the Greeks, one unimpassioned and at arms length and the other loose and expressive.

Yuki promised that she wouldn't call him Charupi and so the sea beckoned. Once they were on their way she reverted to the new name.

The beach was theirs alone. It was quite a distance to come for a swim but there was no denying the water's splendour. His mother had asked him to be vigilant so he kept a watchful eye as Yuki splashed around whilst he dried on the sand and fine-tuned his project. He needed to find someone as captivating as the theatregoer. In the absence of anyone else Tassos was a fine candidate. He also needed to ask his father again for the correct discipline; Haruki guessed it was psychology but wanted to be sure. The stronger his convictions the easier it would be to convince them.

He was so lost in this thought, dragging the characters for 'psychology' through the sand, that he didn't notice the approaching row-boat. He only looked up when the man jumped into the shallows and up to his ankles.

He had his back to Haruki and wore a loose shirt that was tucked into a pair of shorts rolled above his shins. He slung a burlap sack over his shoulder.

"Geia sas," he greeted Yuki in a deep voice.

The girl waved in return.

Haruki caught sight of his face and was surprised that he was younger than he'd first thought. They were around the same age but the boy was muscular and tanned from a life of toil rather than one sat behind a desk. He was even more handsome than the man two nights ago.

"Geia sas," the boy said again, this time addressing him.

Haruki knew from Tassos to reply in kind but he could only gawp. The boy was bemused and continued onto Vatheia.

Yuki wanted to leave soon after but Haruki couldn't avoid missing him somewhere in the village and forced her to wait. She moaned that she was thirsty but it wasn't long until the boy bounded down the slope, his bag fuller than before.

"Geia sas," said Haruki, his words not so loud.
The Greek boy pushed the boat out.
"Geia sas!" Haruki shouted with more force.

This second time, the boy turned to him, tipped his head mannerly but uninterested and carried on his way.

10

Vatheia
24th June 1962

Stupid locust bean Charupi.

Yuki pulled the blanket from her face and cursed her brother for letting in the sun. "Baka! Close the shutters."

"Ssh, you'll wake the others." Charupi's face was gloomy in the bright light.

Yuki groaned and threw her head back onto the pillow. Why had she been dealt such an irritating brother? It was unfair. She would soon be called downstairs for school whist he had a summer with no responsibilities. So what if he had to choose a degree?

"Just pick something and go to the beach," she said from under the cover. "Or think about it on the beach."

"I already know what I'm studying."

"Good. Then go back to bed."

Yuki didn't care to ask. He would go to Waseda unaware of how lucky he was. All that was expected of her was to raise a family. She had bigger plans than that. She knew exactly what she wanted to do and she was only nine.

She'd worked it out years ago even if no one had bothered to ask. She would be one of the women who wrapped gifts in a department store. Mitsukoshi, if she had a choice, where there was a section dedicated solely to cotton and silk furoshiki. She admired the workers who selected the perfect sizes and patterns and folded the cloths with precision. Each completed present was a thing of beauty, better than whatever was hidden within. Yuki loved these women with their nifty fingers and the foresight to manipulate packages, conjuring breath into a thing previously lifeless.

Her mother would never hear of it. There was no way an Okazaki would be allowed to work an unskilled job. Yuki disagreed with this accusation; there was more skill in a single wrapping than in any of her father or grandfather's lectures, bored the few times she'd been forced to sit at the back folding paper until the hours passed.

It was even more unfair that Charupi would go to the caves whilst she would be imprisoned. It was either the classroom or the kitchen and that was an unjust destiny. She would have preferred another summer on Kamakura's black and gummy sand and not having to share with her moody brother.

She remembered the thing that her father said about time zones, that the hour was different. She couldn't make sense of it but if it was light here then it was dark there. Or something like that. It made her even more homesick. It didn't matter how beautiful the sea was if she had no one to splash about with or demonstrate her cartwheels to. Charupi didn't count, thinking he was grown up by speaking Greek and writing stuffy letters. She'd snuck a look at one yesterday. She couldn't read all of the characters but got the boring gist of it.

Her mother called her through the hatch to get dressed. Using the cue that the others were awake, Charupi descended the ladder without bothering to wish her luck.

She put on her uniform, a pleated sailor outfit with its navy collar and knee-high socks. It should have been stored away, exchanged for floral swimsuits and her evening yukata, adorned in red lanterns, a safer colour after last year's disaster with her white robe ruined by the oily drips of yakitori skewers. Yuki felt even farther from home at the thought of food peddlers wheeling carts with roasted corn. She salivated at the idea of steamed squids, their alien faces imprinted into flattened wafers. She missed the commotion, the littered waterline, the squeals of swimmers in the cold water. She'd been promised a village fete tonight but there would be no one for her to laugh with, plus school again the next morning.

In the kitchen Petzechroula marvelled at her uniform before taking away her uwabaki slippers and storing them on a ledge. There was no need to change shoes at the school. Megumi stood from her cup of mountain tea to walk her along the road but Petzechroula waved her down and took Yuki herself.

The school was less than a minute away through a courtyard shared with the church. It was built with grey stones like the other tower houses but resembled a barn inside. Yuki counted twelve chairs. Her school had a few hundred students and the class register lasted a couple of minutes. And to think that she'd been worried for months about being unable to answer that she was present.

The teacher was lanky with thinning grey hair. He wore dusty trousers and a jacket that reminded her of the librarian in her father's research department. She bowed, he frowned back. Petzechroula said something in a firm tone and pointed Yuki to a seat at the front. She kissed her on the forehead before leaving.

Some children ran in, then a few more until there were seven others. They varied in height with Yuki somewhere in the middle. There was no uniform, the others in simple tattered clothes. They gawped and giggled and she blushed redder with each arrival. She wrapped her hands around her neck to hide the ribbon that hung from her collar.

Her teachers would call on her when they wanted someone to give the correct answer but here the man glazed over her. All the while seven pairs of eyes burnt into the back of her head amidst mumbles that would set the others off laughing.

She didn't understand anything written on the chalkboard. The lesson could have been about history or science or whatever and she wouldn't have known. She couldn't even hear the breaks between words. Charupi was better at languages. He'd glided through kanji classes. She was about six hundred characters in, confused many and still had another thousand to go. Even if she learnt a few Greek words what use would they be? English, Russian, German and French had invaded her language with their loan words, orenji and ikura and arbeito and pan, but Greek had made no impact. This was pointless. She grew angry to think of her brother under the sun.

Her eyes followed the slither of light that came in through the doorway. She day-dreamt about the beach, about the weeks stretched in front of her, and mostly how she was missing the Tanabata matsuri along the coast in Hiratsuka with its night-time parade under colourful streamers. She surprised herself that she could conjure so strongly the smell of ayu sweetfish, salted and grilled whole. It was so vivid. The charcoal smell, the crackling fire, the warmth of the flame.

It wasn't just her imagination. The classroom erupted into raucousness. She swung around to see a younger boy cooking a fish on a makeshift grill by his feet. Smoke filled the air. The teacher shouted. The children belly-laughed.

The boy winked at her before being chased out of the room.

She couldn't believe what was happening. It was audacious. The most exciting thing in her school was when older girls were sent home for rolling their skirts too high.

The commotion settled as the teacher stamped out the fire and discarded the fish but the smell lingered and he dismissed them. The others ran off leaving her behind. She caught the teacher's resigned expression. He closed his book and walked out too.

She wanted to tell her family. It might make them think twice about the classes. Then again maybe she wanted to keep coming if it was like this. She couldn't wait to repeat what had happened to her friends, revised to make her seem less alone.

If she went to the house her mother would only give her a workbook, squared rather than lined to focus on the spacing and sizing of her kanji. She could listen for her classmates but she would only watch them from a distance. She wandered the streets, passing strangers who stared at her like a landed alien, and followed the slope to the bay. Her brother's gaze was fixed on the sea.

"Hey, Charupi."

"Don't call me that."

"I thought you were going to the caves."

"Tomorrow. Tassos volunteered to help set up the square. Why are you here?"

"Okaa said I could join you."

"I thought you had school?"

Yuki told him about the fish. He didn't react even though she laughed throughout. "What are you doing anyway?"

"Nothing."

"I thought you'd decided on your future."

"You can stay here but don't annoy me."

Yuki dug a hole in the sand. Slyly she covered one of his hands in the process but when he noticed he shook his fingers free with only a half-formed snarl.

"Let's swim."

"You're in your uniform."

"Help me with cartwheels then."

"I said don't annoy me."

"You're no fun any more."

She walked away. She expected her brother to apologise but when she turned around he was lost in the far-off waves.

She ended up back in the classroom, deciding it was better to be alone than in the company of people who didn't want her. She'd never normally take things from a teacher but she needed something to settle her frustration. She swiped a sheet of crumpled newspaper from the desk, tore off a perfect square and smoothed it until it lay flat. Origami helped whenever she was sad, eased by the neat lines. She could change a fold and end up going on weird and wonderful diversions. She role-played one of the women wrapping gifts for a living.

Her fingers worked on autopilot to form a crane, the bird replicated across classrooms since poor Sadako-chan in Hiroshima. She ironed out its wings and nipped the beak so that it creased in two whilst the tail tapered to a point. She and her friends could make one hundred in a single break. They would string them in a vertical line, their uniformity broken only by their colours. Her crane did nothing to brighten up the empty classroom and it wouldn't raise her spirit to make more. She accepted defeat and returned to the house.

She needn't have worried about an interrogation because everyone was busy preparing for the evening. There were few causes for a panigiri with hardly any marriages or births in the ageing Vatheia and, as the square saw little action outside of the Feast of Saint Nikon at the end of November or the country-wide Dekapentaugoustos celebration of the Virgin Mary in August, the Vatheians were treating the Okazakis' arrival as an excuse.

Women were crowded into Petzechroula's kitchen chopping cucumbers into matchsticks and stirring them into minced garlic and gloopy yogurt. Yuki thought that the combination looked revolting but, when no one was looking, Petzechroula instructed her to dip her finger in. Her eyebrows shot up with delight. She'd never tasted something so sharp and creamy and delicious. She couldn't wait to try everything else.

Her mother was preparing a wakame salad from dried kelp that had survived the flight. Yuki didn't know what the other women were saying behind her mother's back but she noted the ridicule.

"What is it?" her mother asked as she approached.

"It looks delicious." Yuki went to taste some but her mother swatted away her hand.

"If you have nothing better to do, find your brother and tell him to help you practise your kanji."

"OK," she answered, with no intention of doing that. She went to leave.

"Yuki-chan."

"Yes, Okaa-san?"

"Don't get enticed by the sweetness of their food," she said in the language that only the two of them could understand. "They might have a soft-shell turtle but we have the moon."

Yuki carried onto the square where long tables were being erected. A hog was in the early stages of being roasted above a spit. Tassos waved but was called to hang lanterns. She wandered back to the house, climbed to the top and hid until evening.

Charupi sulked on his return and read his book until it was time to get ready. He put on the silk hakama that had been bought for his graduation and not yet worn. Even if he was an idiot he looked handsome in the Prussian blue robe. Megumi dictated that they all dress in their smartest clothes so that the villagers could admire the traditional Japanese designs. Yuki's kimono was light but elegant and, downstairs, she twirled for Petzechroula and forgot for a moment that her classmates would probably scoff. Her mother wore similar to her, her own kimono nightingale green with woven gold streaks that portrayed a sun-trapped scene and was good enough to be modelled by the Emperor's wife.

Yuki's wooden sandals hit against the stone tiles of the plateia as if a horse was approaching but the musicians drowned out her arrival and none of the children noticed. There were already more people present than Vatheia could hold. Tyresias led her and her family to a reserved table by the edge of the hill. An overhead branch was lined with lanterns and gave a glow that carried past the sunset as if fireworks were exploding just above her eyeline.

The musicians played a hand drum, a lyre, a flute, and a guitar that was smaller than any she had seen. The strumming sounded across the square as women danced in a circle, their hands linked and their feet following in a rhythmic procession like an upbeat version of her o-bon festival of the dead.

Tassos poured her some yellow-green wine although distilled down until it lost its colour. Husks of bread and dips including the one that she'd craved all afternoon were set out on the table. Tyresias brought over a platter of meat. Petzechroula urged them to fill their plates.

The women dispersed from the floor and one of the band began to sing as if he was grieving. A man took to the centre and danced on his own to the mournful song. Across the square, people greeted one another with open arms. At a far table the children sucked on red lollipops. Occasionally one of them would look over at her, turn to the others and say something before the rest glanced her way. The girls had loose mops whilst her hair was pinned tight. She toyed with a clip, struggling to release some strands, but her mother pulled her hand away.

Her brother stared past the crowd, his eyes vacant just like on the beach.

"Are you homesick, Charupi?"

"Don't call me that. No. Why?"

"It looks like you're miserable. Do you want to leave?"

"I'm fine here."

"Don't you miss Jiji? I do. This place is strange."

"Okay."

Okay? Yuki burnt red at his dismissal. She wanted to stab him with a fork just to get a proper reaction.

He continued to shift his gaze between each path leading into the square and remained dour even when the music sped towards something upbeat.

Petzechroula stood and grabbed Megumi's hand who was unable to refuse. They joined a growing circle of women. Every so often one woman would break free and dance more complicated steps on her own until she reconnected the string of dancers into a chain. Yuki had never seen her mother dance like this and thought it an amazing sight. She elbowed her brother but he threw back his head in a way that she'd never seen him do before.

After the women completed another revolution, Petzechroula beckoned for her to join them. Yuki slid in between her and her mother and tried to keep up. Each time she learnt the routine it changed; either they switched direction or narrowed the circle to pull in tight at the centre. She was sure that her classmates had noticed but her head was light from the wine and free from embarrassment she continued to dance.

After the song ended she returned to the table where her father and Tassos were talking about the excursion the next morning. She begged to go but was outright refused once more. She was promised plenty of trips throughout the rest of the summer. She sulked as she picked at scraps of pork and wished for the night to end even though people were only just turning up.

She felt a tap on her shoulder. She was surprised that it was a boy from the classroom, the one that had cheered the loudest at his friend with the fish. They stared at one another until he held out her paper crane. It was distorted, the sheet opened under inspection and put back incorrectly. The bird had been given new seams and forced into resembling its original shape. She would have been sad to see its delicate folds ruined if it wasn't for the curiosity of him approaching.

He addressed Tyresias. There was no way that the deaf man could have heard above the noise but he winked and pointed her towards the table where the other children were waiting.

She followed the boy slowly, worried that she was walking into a trap. Two girls made space for her in the middle of the bench. In front of where she sat was a wad of paper. Everyone watched expectantly.

She handed out the sheets and demonstrated with clarity and precision how each of them could make their own bird. She was a natural teacher and leant over to help when someone became stuck or missed a step. With enough patience soon everyone had a decent version. An older boy handed her one of the sugar-spun lollies shaped like a rooster. Some of the girls wanted to start again whilst a few of the younger children thrust their birds through the air and made whooshing noises.

But the boy who brought her over cradled his crane in his palm and stared at it with incredulity as if its existence was the most magical thing to ever happen.

11

Diros Caves
25th June 1962

Haruki thrust open the shutters to a day already in bloom. For the second morning running Yuki shouted at him to close them but he ignored her. He didn't care. The music had carried on late into the night and hours after he'd turned in he could still hear it. Now he'd overslept and possibly missed the boy again.

He'd found his subject. But only if luck was on his side and their paths crossed more over the summer. What better person than someone his age? He would not only detail a Greek's life but one that ran in parallel with his.

The party had been entertaining but he couldn't enjoy himself whilst wondering why he hadn't shown. Neither the fried loukoumades soaked in carob honey nor the sight of his mother being dragged around the dance floor had lifted his spirits.

There was nothing to suggest that the boy would row into the bay today. The worst thing was if theirs had been a chance meeting. A one-off, unrepeated event. Perhaps he had no business coming back.

Later, Haruki would rifle through the presents his mother had yet to distribute. He'd seen her pack a daruma for someone who might appreciate the blank-faced wish doll. He would claim the papier-mâché figurine as his own, inking in one of its eyes whilst desiring to see the boy again. He would fill in the second pupil when his wish came true. Before that, today was the much-awaited trip to the cave and he couldn't back out. He didn't share his father's excitement, especially now that he had sworn off geology from his future. He would have preferred to return to his post on the beach but knew better than to protest.

He closed his eyes. He could see the boy's face but it was fading fast. He conjured the memory: the assured honeyed voice, the heft of the bag as it slapped against his shoulder, ankles sturdy in the seabed. The description was too feeble for an essay. And what could he say about the boy's character beyond his appearance?

Haruki guessed from the silence that everyone was asleep so he succumbed to Yuki's protests and went back to bed. He read but took in nothing and kept returning to the top of the page. In the scene, Shinji ran around the island carrying out chores for the lighthouse-keeper. Haruki pictured him as the boy in the row-boat. Frustrated by his obsession he flicked through the opening chapters for a portrait to break the spell but he could only find that Shinji was tall, well-built and burnt by the sun. Haruki's mind filled in the rest with the Greek boy. He cursed the author's sparsity. Imagination was a privilege of fiction whilst his anthropological study required precision. He needed to work out what made his new subject so fascinating that he should be able to explain it to others. He needed to get close to the boy and scrutinise him.

He began a new letter about what made him stand out but could only think of trite adjectives that applied to all Greek men. His jiji could single out identical-looking snow monkeys by the way they played whilst his father had such an expert eye for rocks that he could pour out a pile and describe one so accurately that Haruki knew for certain which it was. Its proportions and its shape, its lean and hue, the emotion of it, the way it caught the light, its imperfections, its history. So many fine details that spoke of how his father attended to his work. Haruki had to learn more about the boy and size him up. It was his duty if he was to be a man of science.

Despite their hangovers, Toshihiro and Tassos gathered themselves and with Haruki started off for the cave. In a sharp turnaround Yuki was not only unbothered to be left behind but excited for school. Megumi had no interest in going anywhere and would stay to do laundry that necessitated the manual beating of their clothes. Haruki found this a funnier prospect than her dancing or eating with her fingers. What would be the breaking point for someone so prim? He considered changing his study to her. It wasn't a terrible back-up.

Tassos had a row-boat but wanted to show them hamlets farther inland and so they went by bicycle. The smallest was rusted with bent spokes but it suited Haruki. The men circled the dirtied plateia where Petzechroula bossed around sluggish women before they left for Diros.

There was no shade as they followed the coast west along a goat-path that was bumpy and overgrown with poppies and ferns. They passed the turn-off for Gerolimenas, a village built on a cove, and stopped halfway to drink water by a cluster of tower houses. Tassos pointed out features and exchanged Greek words for their Japanese counterparts but at no point did the languages converge. It took another hour to cycle to the quaint settlement above the cave. From there a road widened and carried on to Areopoli but they turned onto a slope that dropped sharply towards the sea. Haruki was drawn in by the welcoming bay. He took his feet off the pedals and picked up speed. Tassos hollered at him to stop from carrying onto the white-pebbled beach and directed him instead to the cave mouth partway down. The men entered but Haruki dawdled, not ready to let go of the water.

His eyes adjusted to the darkness after he ventured inside. It looked like every complex he'd visited across Japan. The same dampness, the same mustard-coloured stalactites. He joined his father who was up ahead angling a torch at the flooded cavern to reveal thousands of stalagmites rising to the surface.

For a moment Haruki shared his wonderment. Once, he had escorted his grandfather to an izakaya pub modelled on a Parisian salon. There were emerald frilled light-shades, velvet chairs and candles wedged into wine bottles that melted down and set as waterfalls of wax. Diros' formations reminded him of that, only here it was nature's doing.

Tassos pointed out fossils and tools that had been excavated, proof that an ancient tribe had called this place home. There were weeks ahead to explore. To measure and hypothesise and look on in awe. But Toshihiro was impatient and clambered into one of the two long-boats.

Tassos unhitched it once Haruki was safely inside and rowed them through a crevice barely big enough for them to fit. Their torches lit the way as everything behind them returned to the void. Haruki dipped his hand into the cold water and caused a ripple with little power to it. He knew some Greek mythology, the most famous being the story of the Minotaur in the labyrinth and the calculated strategy to exit but, rather than using a reel of string, here they could only rely on Tassos' familiarity. The other tale he remembered was Heracles' descent into Hades to kidnap Cerberus. He pushed that image even farther from his mind.

Tassos rowed on, ducking when the roof near-on met the water and all of them having to lean to the side to avoid a stalactite that obstructed the way. Water dripped without a melody and reminded Haruki of a bamboo feature in his mother's garden.

They came to a chamber which Tassos flooded in light. It was as wide as the junior baseball field opposite Haruki's school. Haruki looked back. Already their passage was cloaked in darkness. His thoughts returned to the land of the dead, with this place as devoid of life. His mother couldn't learn about this or he'd never be allowed to come again.

Any of his apprehension was offset by his father's eagerness as Tassos veered them into a new but indistinguishable tunnel. They moored along a deep ledge that was raised from the water. Haruki crept across to the far wall and, though cautious, he skidded. He reached out but the rock-face was slimy. He found his balance but by then the men were ahead of him and hadn't noticed.

When he drew closer he saw that they were inspecting an incomplete stack that was marginally unfinished, a stalactite above a stalagmite with the merest of gaps. Bigger than one of Yuki's origami sheets but smaller than her little finger. Haruki was more fascinated by the men's interaction: the way their bodies leant towards one another and the shallow, pitched excitement of their speech.

Tassos retraced their route with ease but Toshihiro wasn't ready to leave, wanting to examine erosion marks along the water line. Haruki excused himself outside where the air was less dense but the heat was insufferable. He sat within the shade of the entrance and understood why a community had found solace inside the cave before it had flooded. The others wouldn't be hurrying out any time soon so he followed the path towards the beach that was more cut off than Vatheia's. He removed his shoes and stripped down to his underwear. The pebbles scorched his soles as he ran into the sea and ducked under the surface.

Refreshed, he hopped over to his pile of clothes and spread out his shirt so that he could lie back. His mother would be doubly mad that he'd gone from a lake threatening hypothermia to exposing himself to the sun's rays. It would be fun for Yuki to go on the boat ride but he could imagine his mother's growing displeasure with each passing second.

The heat became intolerable. He dressed and was ready to return to the cave when a small boat crossed the bay. Halfway it changed course towards him. His heart pounded on realising who was rowing. He failed to smooth his hair that was full of sea salt as the boat drew near.

Close to the surf the Greek boy locked the oars into place, jumped from the boat and bounded towards him. His breath was unstrained despite having rowed under the immense sun.

"Geia sas."

"Geia sas."

The boy seemed confused. He scanned the scenery for Haruki's method of transport. Haruki pointed at the cave but the bicycles were hidden from view. He mimicked pedalling. The boy restrained a smile brought on by the charade.

Haruki remembered the word for his father. "Pateras. And Tassos Tzanetakis."

The boy pointed at himself. "Akis."

"Haruki."

Akis shook his head as if this was wrong. "Charupi," he said, correcting him.

Haruki blushed. So the boy had heard about him. He spotted the burlap sack inside the hull. Akis followed his gaze and fetched it. Inside were letters and parcels that Haruki assumed were addressed to villagers along the coast. Akis seemed too young to be a postman.

Haruki pointed at the pile and then to the village above them. "For Diros?"

Akis shook his head.

There was so much Haruki wanted to ask. How old was he? Where did he live? Where was he last night? And if he had no post for the small commune then why had he stopped?

Akis led him to the edge of the bay. Haruki had never felt such heart-stopping delirium. Perhaps it was how his father felt when entering a cave or what his grandfather experienced in the presence of a new species.

Akis was good-looking like he remembered. Tall and with the lightest shade of hair he'd seen on a Greek. His shirt was unbuttoned low. Haruki noticed a small crest of hair between his pecs, manly unlike his bare pigeon-chest. He tried to undo his top button but his hands were clumsy and Akis caught him and grinned an effortless, unbelievable smile that made Haruki want to grab his cheeks and fix them in place but also made him want to look away in humiliated comparison.

Akis crouched by the cliff and ran his finger through the slither of sand. He drew an elongated curve and made a dent near the bottom of the map's outline. "Diros."

"Yes, here in Mani," Haruki answered in broken Greek.

Akis looked up at him impressed.

Haruki made a second, lower mark. "Vatheia."

Akis traced a continuous line that followed the coast, dipping in and out at various points where he delivered post. There were nine stops in total.

"How often?"

Akis stared at him, baffled by the language change. Haruki drew the seven kanji that represented the days of the week in a row. He circled today's. It was two days ago that Akis had come to Vatheia and he circled that one too.

Akis crossed out today and circled tomorrow.

Tuesdays and Saturdays. Today was? Haruki didn't know.

Akis studied the pictograms.

"Kanji. Iaponezika." Haruki wanted to explain that the characters were drawn from natural elements. He made a basic line drawing of the moon above today's kanji (月) and added the sun (日) for the day before. Tuesday was the symbol for fire (火) and Wednesday was water (水) both of which were easy enough to mimic, much to Akis' ongoing fascination. Thursday's (木) was the most obvious, closely resembling a tree, at which point Akis clapped his hands.

Sixth was the kanji for gold (金) given it was the payday at the end of the week although maybe not applicable to Akis. Haruki acted it out anyway by pretending to insert money into a slot. Akis pulled coins from his pocket in acknowledgement. Haruki concluded the series with Saturday and the character for soil (土) which represented a rest day but this definitely wasn't true for the delivery boy. For this he grabbed a handful of sand and let it run through his fingers.

Akis said something that he didn't understand. The Greek boy then pretended to row after which he wagged his finger back and forth between the boat and them.

"Nai," Haruki said despite not following.

"Good." Akis circled the kanji for Wednesday, the day after tomorrow. "Sti Vatheia stis deka." He opened his bag and filed through the envelopes until he found an address with the number ten on it.

If Haruki was right then this was an instruction to join him on the boat in two days at that hour. He clenched his jaw and nodded. It was all he could do to stop himself from bursting with joy.

"It was good to meet you," said Akis.

"You too," Haruki replied, never more grateful for Tassos' stock phrases.

He watched Akis row away until he was out of sight. He played back the interaction and only then remembered his mission to study him. He had plenty to write about.

"Stis deka," he repeated to himself, the phrase too precious to risk being forgotten. He too wanted to preserve the conversation in the sand and cherish it like one of his father's fossils. In the impossibility of that he wiped it out with his foot. It could belong to no one else.

The men emerged from the cave and called to him. He hurried up the slope to meet them. His father prattled on about the things he'd seen and eventually asked if he'd been alright left alone for so long. Haruki answered only that he'd swum.

On the way back he cycled close to Tassos and asked to be taught the Greek numbers. Tassos obliged but only added to the list when he could repeat the previous numbers with accuracy. Haruki memorised them fast, eager to hurry it along.

His heart soared when he arrived at ten.

12

Vatheia to Estia
27th June 1962

Snoring carried through the tower house. Yuki covered her head with a pillow to drown out the noise whereas Haruki was less bothered. He'd been awake for hours. He played back the conversation with Akis and wished away the hours until they would meet again. Finally the day was here.

Since Diros, nervous excitement had taken hold and he'd been too fevered to sleep. The night had dragged on, as had the previous day throughout which he'd attempted to distract himself by writing, reading or practising the Greek days of the week with Tassos. He'd even searched for Yuki and found her on the beach playing with her classmates, but they'd snubbed him as he approached and mocked him as he retreated.

He imagined what Akis had planned. It wasn't a delivery day but they would go somewhere. He was apprehensive about being asked to take the oars. The closest he'd come to rowing was on a swan-shaped pleasure boat around Lake Kawaguchi but even that was foot-pedalled. He lay in bed trying to picture the boy's grip and turned his hands to simulate the movement.

A rooster brought the village to life but there were still plenty of hours ahead of ten. Already the Tzanetakis household had fallen into a routine. Toshihiro and Tassos ate breakfast and set off early, wanting to beat the sun before it bore down on them. For the second day in a row Haruki asked to be excused under the pretence that he wanted to plough on with the book. Neither man was affronted; his father even suggested it was better this way, preferable to the pressure of him wanting to return sooner than they'd like.

Megumi fetched water from a communal well whilst Petzechroula and Yuki went to the bakery to buy a carob loaf. The girl wore casual clothes following a compromise that her uniform could be packed away if she didn't complain about attending school. A double win, and she played along accordingly. Tyresias sliced the bread and made coffee for the others before joining his friends at the kafeneio. Haruki watched on at the alchemy as Tyresias spooned ground beans and water into copper pots and then placed them onto a tray of sand that sat above an open flame where, instantly, the coffee boiled.

Haruki liked the first sips but anything more was bitter and sludgy. "Thank you for the coffee."

"You're welcome, Charupi-mou."

"Today is Wednesday. I'm sixteen." He was happy to be understood but it was all he knew and it made him sound like a child.

"Bravo."

He stopped himself from asking Tyresias' age. He only knew the numbers up to twenty anyway. The conversation stunted, revealing just how little he could manage, and he drank on in silence.

Haruki was the only one to have a permanent fixture at the table. Everyone else busied themselves with housework, studying or socialising. He bided his time but couldn't contain himself past nine. He took his book to the beach where he sought out shade and watched the horizon without once looking at the pages. Restless, he studied the shadow of the novel as it moved across the sand. He'd fashioned sundials at a summer camp but the gradual shift of the silhouette without markers gave nothing away. In the heat, and from a lack of sleep, he drifted off.

He was nudged awake by a hand on his shoulder. "Charupi?"

Akis stood above him. The sun was behind his head and, when he moved a fraction, Haruki was blinded by the glare.

Haruki rubbed his eyes but the sun spots remained.

"I'm sorry," said Akis.

Haruki stood and swallowed a yawn. "It doesn't matter, I'm fine, let's go," he replied, burning through the sentences he knew.

Akis picked up the forgotten book. He flicked through the pages and marvelled at the print. He logged the character for 'tree' and showed it to Haruki.

It formed a compound with other characters and gave a different meaning but Haruki didn't want to spoil his excitement. "Thursday," he said in Greek, confirming Akis' find but more to show off the newest addition to his vocabulary.

Akis searched on and became frustrated.

Today's symbol, Haruki guessed. "Wednesday?"

"Yes, Wednesday. Water."

Haruki turned a few pages and found the character but again in a different context. It satisfied Akis and he handed back the book.

Haruki wished that he could describe more than just stand-alone kanji. He wanted to tell him about the plot. He wanted to share that the setting reminded him of here and the protagonist of him. He wished that he could ask the boy about the books he had read and the songs he had heard and the places he had been and all the things that he thought about them.

Akis led him to the boat. Haruki waded through the water and climbed in to face him. He was exhilarated as they rowed away.

They carried on for a while without speaking but there were only so many times that Haruki could look towards the sea instead of in Akis' direction. Each time he planted his eyes on him Akis was looking back. They smiled and broke away.

"How old are you?" Haruki asked.

"Seventeen."

"I'm sixteen." They were so close in age considering how differently they carried themselves. Haruki wasn't any more slight than his classmates but against Akis he seemed like a child.

Akis followed the coastline until Vatheia disappeared. Haruki relaxed. Somehow, compared to being with Tassos and his father in the cave, he felt safer out here in the deep with a stranger and with no one knowing his whereabouts. It would give his mother a heart attack but if she didn't ask then he wouldn't need to lie.

He sat with his father's book on his lap doing his best to protect it from the splashes caused by the oars. Akis noticed and placed it in the empty sack before rowing on. His hand brushed Haruki's thigh in the process. He didn't apologise.

Haruki thought back to Petzechroula kissing Yuki's head, the dancers holding hands, the friends reuniting at the airport, and the men embracing at the theatre. Holding distance was a Japanese convention. He envied the unabashedness of the Greeks. He'd never been kissed goodnight by his mother and would never dream of hugging his friends. He wondered if they missed him. If he was honest he didn't miss them. They'd been grouped under the expectation that rich families banded together but he'd always thought it pathetic that this was a consequence of status rather than of shared pursuits. He assumed that their friendships would fizzle out as he started afresh at university with people that wanted to spend time with him without knowing that he was an Okazaki. It was a relief that Akis didn't–

His spirit plunged. Someone in Vatheia had told Akis to befriend him.

He hid his indignation as his mind spiralled. It explained why the boy had known to call him Charupi and why he'd been so forward with the invitation. Akis was not his pet project. He was Akis'.

His mood darkened and his body became heavy as if he could sink the boat with the weight of the revelation. So what if he was a hypocrite, cocksure in expecting to use Akis as a case study without being tricked himself? His experiment had spoiled. His father's and grandfather's fields side-stepped knotted human complexity whilst his own brought risk. It was good to be reminded of this early on. Maybe he could offer the anecdote at an admissions interview as a lesson in humility.

"Ola kala?" Akis asked him.

His annoyance must have become transparent. Haruki forced his brow to relax but his mouth was dry and instead of answering he merely nodded. He snuck glances at Akis, peeved that he could feign tranquility when the trip was little more than a chore. Haruki would be civil for the rest of the day but would refuse further play dates.

Akis pointed out life around them and helped to build up his word bank. Clouds, oars, the bag, sweat. Haruki gave the Japanese equivalents but felt justified to occasionally lie by saying something different. A ripple became a yawn, a seagull a fool. If the day was a sham then what did it matter? At least his vocabulary would grow. He might as well take something and punish Akis in return.

The postboy loosened his grip and leant back so that they bobbed on the water. He closed his eyes and lifted his head up to the sun. "Eftychia."

"What does it mean?"

Akis waved his hands to include the entire scene.

Haruki didn't grasp the concept but was too dejected to care. It was unfair to have a babysitter forced on him, invalidating his excitement in the build-up. He wanted to abandon the boat and hide in the attic until the flight to Tokyo. Back to where life was simple and minded only with grades and credentials. Where joy was limited to narrow parameters. Take his grandfather's summer residence, a place for relaxation but also somewhere to hone the mindfulness of calligraphy and zazen. Or holidays to Yamanashi that were primarily for his father to collect geological samples from the ice caves within Aokigahara Forest. His mother had only agreed to Greece under a veil of education, moulding it into a person-building, resume-expanding opportunity.

"Fish," said Akis. A school passed close to the surface. He thumbed the waves and they dispersed.

He rowed them towards a small cut-off bay. Despite Haruki's mood it was the most picturesque so far. Diros and Vatheia's remoteness paled in comparison. There was a dash of sand in front of a slim woods. The bay was cradled on three sides by insurmountable cliffs with protrusions where birds nested and with a height that rivalled the Acropolis. There was no way in but the sea.

The only other thing that stood out was the bare bones of a house nestled between two trees. There was no roof and not one wall was fully completed. The front was stacked with large stones but there were gaps where windows should have been. A canvas tent was pinned away from the floor. Nearby, Akis had dug a well to take advantage of the run-off of water.

"Spiti mou spitaki mou."

Haruki knew these words well enough to spell out the sentiment of 'my house my little house,' as insincere as it was.

He crossed the beach to the structure. He'd never seen anything like it. Even in its early stage it was alluring. He only wished that Akis' invitation had been genuine. The boy added a second phrase that Petzechroula had also said, for Haruki to make himself at home. He had to give it to him: he was a good actor.

The foundations were broad as if a tower house had been designed on its side. The intention was clear: there was no need to build upwards because there would be no neighbours. Stones were piled high and ready to be bonded to the walls. Unless they'd fallen from the cliff Akis must have lugged them by boat. It was an arduous task that required tenacity. No one could just claim land in Tokyo where everywhere was prime space but here no one would fight Akis for the bay. Haruki guessed that he lived alone. He felt a wave of sadness but didn't know how to convey it.

He stepped through the doorway and crossed dividing lines. Rooms were spacious and raised off the ground. Clothes were piled in one corner and a gas burner occupied another. Akis followed close behind, his face full of pride. Outside, the skeleton of a terrace ran the length for unspoilt views of the sea. Somehow it was easy to picture the house in its finished state.

A makeshift sign leant against a wall, not yet ready to be nailed into place. Haruki could read some of the painted letters. "Es–"

"Estia."

Haruki pointed to both of them in turn. "Haruki Okazaki. Akis Estia?"

Akis tutted. He started an explanation but pursed his lips.

"Father? Mother?" Haruki wondered aloud.

The boy ummed before landing on something. "Dias. Poseidonas. Athena. Artemis."

Haruki recognised the names. Estia must have been one of the Olympians. He liked the serenity of the syllables. He was jealous that Akis had found a place that was so peaceful. But he couldn't ignore that there was no electricity. No shops and no offices nor trains. There wasn't even a road. In bad weather he would be stranded.

Akis walked them to the side of the house where weighty pumpkins and watermelons sat on the ground. Lemon trees sprouted in their infancy and would need years before producing fruit. A clothes line was pulled tight between two trees but instead of laundry octopuses were flopped over the rope and dried under the sun.

Mani was a starved place but Akis had found shelter and food and water, even if it was primitive and made the tower in Vatheia look modern. Haruki blushed at the extravagance of his mansion in Aoyama that overlooked the famous ginkgo trees. But he was also in awe. School had taught him nothing about survival except for how to get ahead in society. In the wilds, away from a city, he would die, the only question was whether malnutrition or hypothermia would reach him first.

He was desperate to understand Akis' situation. "Your parents?"

Akis gave an over-exaggerated shake of his head.

"I'm sorry."

"You?"

Haruki knelt on the sand and drew a family tree. He connected himself and Yuki to their parents and grandfather. He looked to Akis to draw his own lineage and confirm what he assumed. The boy stared at an untouched piece of sand but didn't move. "Japan?" he asked instead.

"Tokyo."

"Show me."

Haruki carved a map of the country and marked the capital.

Akis held out his hands and widened and narrowed the distance as if playing an accordion.

"Tokyo and Athens?" Haruki knew the populations because of Tassos and wrote the answers: *1,800,000* for Athens and next to Tokyo he scrawled *11,000,000*.

Akis creased his eyes as if Haruki had made a mistake and then he laughed.

"Estia," he said and etched a solitary line in the sand.

Haruki had been brought here out of obligation but he crossed out the single digit and wrote *2*.

"Come." Akis directed him to a pile of logs and picked up a saw.

Haruki had misread this day more than he'd first thought. He'd actually been recruited as free labour. There was no first aid kit let alone a hospital. Sheepishly, petrified, he took the saw as Akis showed him a cut plank whose size needed to be replicated dozens of times. Haruki grappled with the tool and turned red, unable to make a decent groove. Akis demonstrated how to work with the grain to allow for cleaner cuts before going off to roughcast one of the walls.

After a while Haruki began to enjoy the hypnotic routine, more satisfied with each finished piece, each better executed than the last. Even if the invitation was insincere he was glad that he could use it for his case study. Whatever the reason for Akis' isolation it would make for a commendable report. But he didn't know how to get around contaminating the project with his presence. The least he could do was to disallow emotions to get in the way. He blushed with the memory of drawing a two in place of Akis' lonesome digit.

The longer he was there the more they built a shared language, and the more he relaxed the more impossible it was to deny that it wasn't just as fun for Akis as it was for him. Whatever had caused the boy to base himself here had been guided by a need for seclusion. To bring him had to mean something. Or maybe it didn't mean anything. He was fed up with trying to figure it out.

He leant the saw against the stack and wiped his brow. He crossed over to the shoreline and lay on the sand. He smiled in response to the honest work he had done, happy to be for the first time in his life physically rather than mentally tired.

Akis joined him. He turned onto his side and raised himself up on his elbow so that he towered above him. He'd barely broken a sweat but a strand of hair clung to his forehead.

"Thank you," he said to Haruki as he stared down at him.

Haruki struggled to catch his breath.

The boy fell away and landed heavily. "Eftychia," he said for a second time followed by a contented sigh.

"Eftychia," Haruki echoed. This time he understood. Happiness.

Akis spoke on whilst remaining on his back. His upbeat tone was infectious. Haruki didn't understand any of it but guessed that he was talking about his plans for the house. He caught the word for 'cold' and wondered how Akis would fare in the winter. Resources were scarce and carting them here was slow-going. There was a fire pit in the sand that contained smouldering logs. There was also a rough structure of a fireplace but it was unlikely to be finished in time. This jump into the future, with him long gone, left him melancholic.

Akis got up and wiped the sand from his hands. He stripped down to his shorts and jogged into the sea. Haruki sat up and watched Akis' toned body as it gleamed under the sun. For the sake of his report it was a requisite to stare, describing his physicality a necessary part of the documentation.

Akis shouted that he should join him before diving under the surface. He came up for air and rubbed his eyes to see that Haruki was still on the beach. He splashed his hands in the water and grew tired of waiting. He stiffened like a board and fell backwards, disappearing once more.

Haruki had spent his life going to sento. He had no issue with nudity, first with his family and then, after he reached mid-adolescence, entering the public baths alongside his father and his friends. Boys and men of all builds washed and soaked next to one another. Older men had pot bellies whose yellow skin turned lobster-red in the hottest tubs whilst the young were still lean. They sported hair around their calves and genitals but were otherwise smooth and slight.

Inner city baths were backed by mosaics of Mount Fuji and cranes flying overhead whereas the countryside offered plush onsen that overlooked gardens or valleys. Their aesthetic pleasure revitalised not only the body but the mind. In the spring dewy leaves dripped like chimes, the summer heard cicadas hum like a mindful vibration, the red of the autumn maple leaves allowed for quiet contemplation, whilst the winter snow offered a purity to the nakedness of the bodies and the land.

Haruki had forever been unafraid of nudity but even though he could retain his shorts with Akis he felt exposed. His body revealed a life free from manual labour. He was under-toned. His skin was sensitive to the Icarian sun and his tapered chest told of his privilege. But it would be more awkward to sit it out. When Akis front-crawled through the water he hurriedly stripped and swam out to a depth where he couldn't stand.

Akis was delighted. They fell into a game of splashing and tumbling and scrapping with one another, reverting to youthfulness and not needing any words to have fun. Haruki was too busy lost in the pleasure and too busy staying afloat for his brain to worry about the sincerity of the invitation or his physique under the surface of the waves, and any remnants of his foolish notions were left behind on the shore.

13

Vatheia
12th July 1962

Neither of them could have predicted a summer filled with such unbridled happiness. Akis' peaceful existence traipsing the coastline and building the house was already satisfying enough but the last two weeks were bettered not only by Haruki's second pair of hands but his company. As for Haruki, any expectation that he would be biding the days until his return to Japan had been proven wrong. He was having the best time of his life.

The only downside were the interminable days when Akis delivered post and Haruki was consumed with boredom and the ever-lurking dread that the summer could not stretch on forever. Some nights, nursing the blisters that had formed on his hands, he considered whether it would have been better if he had never come at all. His grandmother had died before he was born and his jiji had told him that the pain of losing her outstripped the bond they'd had. Haruki thought that opinion perverse, a monochrome existence to proclaim it better to have never loved than to have loved at all. Now he was beginning to understand. To be flushed with colour and have it taken away was not only about the heart-stricken grief of what was left behind but a loss of vibrancy ahead.

One recent night, he'd pretended to read by the fire but was distracted by the work that Akis and he had done on the back wall of the house, his mind besieged by rotating rocks slotting into place. Meanwhile Yuki filled the table with origami animals. She was trying to impress Petzechroula and as she hurriedly added to the zoo she nicked herself a few times. Haruki didn't know how she could persevere so willingly despite amassing injuries alongside her menagerie when each day at Estia made his heart sing but each evening bruised him. Yuki might have been impervious to the slices but to him, with the impossibility of these eight weeks lasting forever, the summer in Greece was death by a thousand cuts.

He couldn't stop thinking about Akis and Estia. The only way to neuter his brain was when he would fly away in complete withdrawal. Even with this expiration date the present soured. How could he forsake Estia knowing it would go on without him?

He and Akis had fallen into a routine. He would go to the caves with his father on delivery days but would abstain from extended boat trips on the enclosed lake, hanging out on the beach just in case Akis rowed by so that they could wave at one another. On the other days, Akis fetched him from Vatheia. It wasn't far to cycle or walk but the descent to Estia was impossible. There they would spend the mornings working on the house and the afternoons playing in the sea, and all the time expanding a language for everything in their immediacy. The names of tools and cries for assistance, and yells for water and orders to look up as birds took flight were all in their wheelhouse whilst the past and future were rarely touched on. Haruki seldom attempted to describe life in Japan, the foreign world insurmountable for Akis who hadn't even been to Athens. Similarly neither of them broached what would happen come September. When they did talk of the future it was only about what they could do when they sourced other materials and rarely anything beyond the horizon of that.

There were always some subtle add-ons. Scraps of food, gas canisters and a chipped clay pot had been recent additions. Akis was delivering mail and being nourished by the villagers along the coast.

Haruki on the other hand had never been without. He'd never questioned if there would be food nor the means to pay for his tuition, and given as much money as he needed to keep up with his friends. To consider a part-time job was laughable and yet his mother spoke often about the need for a rainy day fund. He didn't understand her cautionary approach when the family had more than enough wealth than to bother with emergency stashes. He wondered if he could live like Akis, unfazed by it all and taking the approach that whilst he could work he could survive. Or would he be on edge about what might lay around the corner?

His absences began to draw suspicion from his mother whilst his father continued to believe the lies that he was wandering Vatheia's surroundings to study its topography. He wasn't sure why he hadn't told them about Akis. He worried that they might forbid it. Now that he had gone to Estia so many times it didn't seem to matter. If he was caught sailing in or out of the bay he would simply introduce them to one another. There was no reason to be ashamed.

He persevered with his lessons whenever Tassos had the energy. He wanted to impress Akis and couldn't learn fast enough, a trickling stream ahead of a dam desperate to expand its banks until it became an entire delta. Tassos was impressed but couldn't understand from where he was picking up so many new words. Haruki fibbed that it was from practice around the village, once again unsure why he leant into the lie.

On the few times that Akis' deliveries coincided with a day off from the caves, Haruki was directionless. He considered borrowing Tassos' boat and rowing to Estia to work on the house alone. Akis had since taught him how to handle a row-boat. The water here was smooth and with little drag but he'd struggled with the weight of the oars and their unnatural pull as they slapped against the sea. He hadn't attempted it unaccompanied but it didn't take long for inflated confidence to grow. Even when his courage gathered steam overnight it was lost by the next morning to the fear of what could go wrong. Besides, he didn't want Tassos to be mad so in the end he spent those days hanging around the village, giving the illusion that he was under the watchful eye of his mother whilst longing to see Akis again.

One morning before setting off for the caves he'd asked Tassos for an impromptu lesson about the Twelve Theoi of Olympus. Tassos appreciated the boy's thirst for knowledge and reeled off the gods of thunder and war and of the sea, the gods of the vine, wisdom and marriage, the gods of the crops, beauty and music, and finally the messenger, the huntress and the inventor.

Haruki massaged his brow. "What about Estia?"

"How do you know her?"

"At school. I remember a list."

"She gave her seat to Dionysus. She was the goddess of peace and of the hearth."

"What does it mean? Hearth?"

Tassos pointed at the fireplace where the flames would later provide warmth and its light a beacon home.

A few weeks passed and it was another of those empty days. Haruki was lazing some distance from Vatheia under the shade of an olive tree. It was peaceful and he was finally reading *Shiosai*. His father was pressuring him to finish the book and it seemed like a good day to dive into it. It wasn't that he hadn't enjoyed it but it had become a running joke between him and Akis that he would bring the book to Estia and return with it untouched. Akis often asked him to describe the plot but Haruki didn't have the vocabulary. Even if he did it was too embarrassing to re-enact the young lovers now that the boy and the character had fully merged in his mind.

Haruki lay on his front surrounded by the cluster of trees whilst reading. In the latest chapter and after many brief encounters, Hatsue, the ship-owner's daughter, and Shinji found themselves alone one night on a beach. A fire burnt between them. They stripped and stood opposite one another, naked and without shame.

Haruki grew hard from the details even though the characters did nothing beyond that, the two agreeing to leave the moment unblemished. It wasn't a sexual encounter but it was sensual. He tried to picture Hatsue's body in the glow of the fire. He pushed himself, his trousers' bulge, against the ground.

He put down the book and searched the landscape. He was alone. He rolled onto his back and his thoughts created a version of the story where the couple moved towards one another. As much as he tried to focus on the girl's breasts it was Shinji that he settled on. His firm body cradling her. The boy lying on top of her. Penetrating her.

Haruki moved his hand inside his underwear and started to tug his shaft. It was Akis' body that he saw. Wading out of the sea. Jogging on the sand. The outline of his buttocks and penis under the wet shorts. Water dripping off his chest. Leaning over him. Lying on top of him.

Every aspect of this moment felt wrong. The guilt of corrupting Akis in his mind, the confusion of why he'd become an object of desire, the violation of their friendship, the fear of being caught masturbating in an open setting, but he couldn't stop and before long he ejaculated. He tried to capture the semen in his hand so that he wouldn't soil his clothes but it was impossible to contain the mess.

He wiped his hand on the dry ground. His face flushed red and yet it was the deepest sexual pleasure he'd ever felt. He usually jerked to memories of girls in his class but never the boys. He'd been naked with them often enough and hadn't viewed them with lust. He told himself not to worry. That this was just the culmination of a novelist at work. The magic trick of a masterful author. He wouldn't have to be weird around Akis and as it was out of his system it wouldn't happen again. He pictured one of the prettiest girls in his class and returned his hand to prove a point but his penis remained limp. He put it down to the typical consequence of having just finished. He would have better success later.

He returned to Vatheia, awkwardly tripping over himself, as unlikely as it was that people would notice a mark or a smell. He bumped into his mother on the outskirts pumping water into a bucket. She barely used the tap at home, commanding Rika to fill pitchers instead.

"Good afternoon, Mother."

"Haruki." She was the only person to still call him that. "Reading again? I've never known you to take so long to finish a book."

"I got distracted. It's a beautiful spot."

"One day I must go with you. There's still time today."

"I thought I would swim this afternoon."

"Tomorrow then? Or are you going with your father to the cave?"

Haruki stumbled over his words. "I need to write more to Jiji. I've let that slip."

"About which course you've picked? Can you tell me or must I wait at the back of the line?"

"I haven't decided yet."

"Whether to tell me?"

"What to study."

"Yuki informed me otherwise. That you'd decided upon arrival."

"Yuki lied." He hesitated. "Do you think Father and Jiji will be disappointed if I choose something other than what they studied?"

"The nail that sticks out is struck."

Haruki was disappointed but unsurprised. There was no peril in selecting psychology but she was resolute that him conforming to one of the two disciplines was a sign of the family's calibre. She had always prioritised status. On their return she would sell this trip as one of merit. Her friends could never know that she was dredging water. He wished that he had a camera to show them.

He rarely challenged her and though the argument could be delayed once more it was unavoidable forever. He couldn't return to Japan and appease her by sticking to friends and a course that suited her better than him. He heard Akis' voice in his head.

"Eftychia," he said.

"Excuse me?"

"What about something that will make me happy?"

His mother scoffed.

He regretted countering her, painfully aware of her histrionics on the few occasions that she'd been rebuked.

"You want a career in a pachinko parlour."

"No. But it's my degree."

Megumi raised her eyebrows, unimpressed with his tone. "Become drunk on life, dream of death."

"I'm not idling my life away."

"Good boy," she said, but only in response to him discerning her idiom.

"But if I go to university why can't it be my own path? How come Otou-san was allowed to do something different to Jiji? Isn't it enough for me to attend Waseda?"

Haruki wanted her to concede but she said nothing. He hated this the most, that whilst his arguments were justified her silence suggested that he had more to prove. He pushed on. "Father would have been miserable if he'd studied ethology instead."

"Instead of geology?"

"Instead of following his passion."

"Running around caves with that man, you mean?"

"They're not running around. It's flooded. They're in a boat." Haruki was unsure why his mother had responded with vitriol or why he'd used semantics to veer her away from it. He would never understand her.

She picked up the pail of water. "Petzechroula is waiting. She wants to make tea for the boy."

Haruki's ears shot up. "What boy?"

"He came with letters for Tassos. A postman at his age? I suppose you'd prefer that, gallivanting across the land on a measly wage. Dirty and sun-scorched. I know, Haruki, you'll tell me he's happy. Such a romantic life. How I must have disappointed you with these horrible comforts and advantages."

He stopped listening. It wasn't like he was asking he if he could skip university altogether but his mother was minded to be relentless. He took the water and marched towards the house. He guessed that Akis had used the delivery as an excuse to see him.

Any thoughts of what had happened under the olive tree were long gone by the time he neared the tower, preoccupied instead by the shouting coming from inside. He recognised Petzechroula and Akis' voices but not together and never with anger as their driving force. Their words were being exchanged like a gunfight, sharp and interrupting.

Haruki forgot the weight of the water as he stood by the front door and picked out what he could: Parents– No– Tell me– Charupi.

He was unsure why his name was mentioned. He locked eyes with his mother. She'd heard it too.

They didn't loiter for long because Petzechroula ducked her head outside. "Tyresia!" Her stance buoyed when she spotted them. She signalled for them to enter.

Haruki tiptoed into the frosty scene.

Akis was gripping the back of a chair. He wore a storm across his face but swallowed whatever he was planning to say next. He nodded politely towards Megumi but was unable to look Haruki in the eye.

"I'm sorry," Haruki said, with nothing to apologise for but too uncomfortable in the silence.

Petzechroula busied herself with boiling the water.

Akis picked up his bag. "Good bye, goddess," he said, and left.

Haruki went after him. "Are you alright?"

"It's nothing."

"You came to see me?"

"I had post."

"Oh. Why did you call her a goddess?"

"What?"

"You said Thea."

Akis cracked a smile and, in spite of himself, laughed. "Theia. She's my grandfather's sister."

"Petzechroula is your aunt?" Haruki regurgitated the news, the words not yet resonating. "You also said something about your parents."

"You understood that?"

"Not really." He paused. "You said my name too."

Akis clenched his teeth. "I have to go."

"Will you come tomorrow?"

He was shamefaced. "I don't know."

Haruki grabbed his hand. "Please."

Akis let his hand rest in Haruki's before pulling away.

"Tomorrow?" Haruki asked, this second time with more force.

Akis deliberated and then nodded.

Haruki didn't follow him along the alley, Akis hadn't wanted him to, but he didn't go inside the house either. He worked through the family tree. Tassos was his cousin, or uncle. Regardless, he had people close by but the intermediate branches had fallen away. Something had happened for him to live removed from them.

He wondered why Akis hadn't said anything. He must have known that they were staying there.

Tyresias approached and looked to him for an explanation. Haruki was unable to give one and simply shrugged before following him inside. This time he could understand the burst of conversation.

"Petzechroula?"

"Akis was here."

"What?"

"Aki."

"Oh."

"He was asking about his parents again."

"About what?"

"His parents."

"His parents?"

"I can't do it any more."

"What?"

Petzechroula turned to face her husband, too late for pretence in front of their guests. "Nothing, you deaf old man. Go away." She shooed him out.

She couldn't have known that Haruki's Greek had improved otherwise she might have held her tongue, but she also muttered under her breath, "And now the boy."

Haruki slipped upstairs, wanting to leave her to fester in peace, now positive that he was somehow involved. But he was even more perturbed by the image of his mother sitting at the table with a look of smug satisfaction.

He camped out in the attic for the rest of the afternoon failing to piece together what had happened. He hoped that Akis would come tomorrow so that he could understand. He remembered a word that Akis had taught him, specific to Mani, that spoke of local hermits. Ksemoni. A life deliberately built away from others. It explained the lone tower houses that were dotted around the region but not why.

Akis had a family, a lifeline, and yet he wanted to be away from them. Haruki pictured him on his beach right now. He would have given anything to be there, even in silence. He remembered holding his hand. It caused a stirring in his body.

He sighed. It was just a reaction of misplaced hormones, like what the book had evoked in him. He was a teenager and there was nothing abnormal about his body betraying him. He just cared about Akis. He wanted to go to Estia and make him laugh. He would even embarrass himself by acting out the book's plot if that could break through. He wanted to tell him that nowhere else and nothing else mattered, and that everything was fine now that they were together.

There was still a glow to the sky. Conversation had struck up downstairs between the men who had recently returned. Haruki was expected to sit with them and pass another night listening to facts about rocks.

It would be foolish to steal Tassos' boat. He could make it to Estia before it turned dark but it was unlikely that he could also get back. He didn't want to wait until morning or risk Akis not coming.

Set on making a break for it he climbed downstairs, ready to say that he wasn't hungry and would instead go for a walk. Not one element of his plan was thought through beyond that.

It was impossible to detect that there had been an argument. The three men were crowded around a map, animatedly dragging their fingers across swathes of blue. It wasn't unusual for them to be detailing the local area but with this much sea they were casting their net wider.

"Good evening, Charupi," said Tassos.

"How was the cave?"

"Fascinating."

"Sit," Toshihiro said, pushing them into Japanese.

"I thought I might go for a walk."

"Haruki," his mother added, her word a command. "Your father has decided something."

Haruki took a chair. The lead-in was ominous, his mother taking pleasure in teasing out whatever came next.

His father spoke excitedly. "Tassos has been telling me about a vertical cave in Antiparos. We've chartered a ship to take us there."

"Where's Antiparos?"

"In the Cyclades, the island cluster farther east. Here. It will take us a week to get there and back without having to rush."

"Well, have a good time."

"I said us. You're coming too. Your mother will stay with Yuki. It's too much with your sister's travel sickness and it would be unfair to leave her here with our hosts."

Haruki digested the words. A week was too long. "I could stay with Yuki, then you and Okaa could go. She hasn't seen the caves at all."

"No," said Megumi. "It will be good for you. Didn't you tell me only today that you wanted more time to consider geology?"

Haruki needed a moment to find his voice. "When?"

"Tomorrow morning," said his father. "We head out at dawn."

14

The Cyclades
13th July 1962

The three men retraced their steps to Piraeus but stopped short at Aegina. There they changed course for the islands famous for their white-washed houses with cerulean domed roofs and the windmills that spoke of a more tempestuous region than the stillness of Mani.

Haruki spent the first leg of the journey confined to his cabin. He was furious with his mother, certain that she'd masterminded the trip. She knew little about his friendship with Akis but can't have liked that it existed. He wavered between annoyance and admiration of her. He would have bet money on her struggling with Vatheia's conditions and jumping at the chance to leave. No running water, using a ladder to climb to her fan-less room, her clothes snagged from manual labour, and still not one complaint. He couldn't understand her resilience but found it fascinating.

On the other hand he had all but given up on studying Akis. They were having too much fun.

He grew restless as it neared the hour that Akis would row into the bay and be met by no one, unable to learn of the sudden change of plan. Haruki had considered running to the beach before sunrise and planting a note but neither could read the other's language. The more distance the ferry gained the more frantic he became. He paced the corridor, unable to calm his mind. Finding it hard to breathe he went up to the deck for air.

As if countering his mood, his father had never acted so jubilant. It was embarrassing to see him at the bow acting like a gallant adventurer, the breeze ruffling his hair as he laughed with Tassos at something in the distance. Haruki had a week of this to endure. It was an expedition that should have been awe-inspiring, bringing to life Tassos' tales of volcanoes, ancient treasuries and marble quarries, and yet Haruki wanted none of it. He retreated to the salon.

The men joined him when the wind became overpowering.

"Have a beer with us," Toshihiro said. "I won't tell your mother."

"You don't even miss her."

"It's only for a week. Mondai nai."

"It is a big deal," Haruki shot back before he stormed off.

He went to the cabin and started on a new letter. He addressed it to Jiji but only out of habit as someone might write *Dear Diary*. None of his pages belonged in his grandfather's hands. He didn't know how to mention the past few days without conjuring up feelings that he didn't want to acknowledge. The book. The olive grove. Instead he focused his frustration on his galling parents and why he'd been dragged to another far-off cave. It read as petulant rather than insightful. Jiji couldn't see this. Haruki would write decoys later.

His father entered the cabin and sat on the lower bunk opposite him. "What's going on, Charupi?"

"Haruki. Nothing. I'm just tired."

"You were rude in front of Tassos."

"You care more about what he thinks than me."

"That's not true. I came to understand why you're angry. I know that's not you."

Haruki sat up indignant. His father had always been absent. Even when he was around his head was in his work and to say that he knew anything about his character was insulting. "Why am I even here?"

"I wanted to spend time with you."

"With Tassos, you mean."

"With you."

"Prove it."

"Isn't this trip proof enough?"

Haruki sneered.

"What?" his father asked.

"It doesn't matter. I was happy in Vatheia."

"I hadn't noticed."

"Of course you hadn't." Haruki knew that it was behaviour better suited for someone Yuki's age but he picked up the letters and stormed out.

Toshihiro is left in the dust cloud of his son's outburst.

He isn't too proud a man to know that he has disappointed him. The boy is quiet, contemplative, and it has always seemed right to leave him be. There has never been an obvious moment to unsettle the waters but something has thrown up in him a storm.

He knows this is a feeble excuse. He knows this from irritation at his own father. He's had to fight to be acknowledged and even then it's for a stocktake of articles rather than for the effort he's put into them. Steering Haruki's future is a stupid contest that he's made worse.

He's been meaning to tell him to choose his own way. What does he care what his son studies? If Haruki wants to carve his own path then there's no value in forcing him down a preordained one. But his father and Megumi have coaxed him out of it time and time again. Haruki hadn't fought back so perhaps it hadn't mattered, easier for the boy to be cajoled and leave things as they are.

Toshihiro looks in the mirror and sees a coward.

Whatever spin he puts on it, whatever excuse for ignoring his son, it falls flat.

He's been so excited about Antiparos that he hasn't stopped to consider his son's feelings. There's nothing in Vatheia for him so he doesn't know why he's glum. He doubts that it's because he feels bad for his mother. He swallows the thought and files it away, somewhere too deep for the murmur to bother him.

He needs to reassure Haruki that breaking the family for a while doesn't matter. He needs to assuage any guilt that is his.

He should go to his son but is drawn to Tassos who is waiting for him on the deck. He looks away from his reflection.

This summer has rejuvenated him. Exploring the cave with Tassos has been the highlight of his career. It has evidently been like a betrayal, finding pleasure away from Japan, and away from his wife, but he was hungry for more and Antiparos was too seductive to refuse. Back in his department, in his stuffy office, there will be the necessary come down. A professional debrief. Dry articles and deadening analyses of the samples he will take with him.

For now he's almost afraid to admit it but everything is just wonderful. Tassos has all but told him the same. It can't last. They've both agreed this.

Academia will kick them into shape.

It was early afternoon when they docked on Tinos where they would stay overnight. The island was a different beast with cars driving to meet arrivals and tavernas along the front whose every table was occupied, with food being eaten in gluttonous consumption.

No sooner had some passengers alighted than they dropped to their knees and crawled from the harbour to the striking Evangelistria church one kilometre farther uphill. A slither of carpet was laid out along the edge of the thoroughfare for these pilgrims who sought answers from the Virgin Mary. Haruki snuck a feel of the worn material. It wasn't much better than dragging his fingers along the asphalt underneath.

The three men sat in a cafe and drank sodas. There was activity here the likes of which Vatheia had never seen. Tourists haggled for religious trinkets and, as peddlers sold caramelised pistachios, taxi drivers blared their horns to move them out of the way.

Haruki lost himself in the hum of the fridges and stared on at the line of the devout who crawled by in near-unbroken perpetuity. It felt rude to look but he couldn't help it. He'd visited plenty of hard-to-reach shrines that required physical exertion on their approach. His favourite was a temple on Mount Takao, a day trip from the capital with its 108 steps that referenced the human tribulations according to Buddhism, but it was nothing on this agonising crawl. He couldn't imagine doing a thing so gruelling. He wanted to ask why they were bothering with such a feat. Their intentions were a mystery that he felt compelled to uncover. It confirmed his suspicion, that if his father had rocks and his grandfather had animals then he had people.

He hadn't spoken to his father since the cabin but he felt daring.

"I'm going to study psychology," he said in Japanese and then in Greek to double down on his pledge.

"Bravo, Charupi," said Tassos. "Although you should consider languages."

"Otou?"

Toshihiro patted his son's shoulder. "A fine choice."

It was what he needed to hear but any relief was short-lived. This wasn't where his battle would be fought. Of the three that he had to convince, his father was the pushover. He'd jumped a prison fence only to find an even higher, unscalable wall behind it.

They settled the bill and took a taxi along a precarious road to a plateau at the top of the island. In every direction were thousands of boulders. Their presence made no sense. It was hard to believe that they'd landed as meteorites or were remnants of a volcanic eruption, and it was unfathomable that they'd been carried here. Tassos told them the mythological explanation was that they'd been the artillery in a war between the Titans and the Giants.

The two geologists walked around inspecting every groove whilst Haruki sat in the shade of a smaller rock wishing that Akis was there to see such a thing. So much had happened since the olive grove that he hadn't thought much about his fantasy. He had, however, staved off any rekindling of arousal, unwilling to consider it as anything other than a blip and not wanting evidence for the contrary.

Encouraged by his father's reaction at the cafe, he started on a letter to his grandfather that he intended on giving him.

The next morning they continued to Paros and from there to the smaller island opposite by way of a dinky ferry that yo-yoed between the two. Haruki was downcast throughout the journey. He'd woken in a panic from a dream in which he'd been waving to Akis from the beach but the boy had merely rowed on.

Despite his gloominess he was impressed by the vertical cave. It was the only one in the whole of the continent. He climbed down between the stalactites that lined the chambers, these mighty waterfalls in frozen motion. He wished again that Akis could be there to share it.

Unsurprisingly he was ready to leave ahead of the others but the cave was high above sea level and he didn't have the heart to walk all the way down to swim. Even after a few days stationed inland, when they passed back through Paros and Tassos guided them to a beach with cliffs formed of clay, Haruki sat away from the sea. The two men scraped sediment and made a putty with the saltwater. They coated themselves from head to toe and sun-dried until the clay lightened and cracked. Throughout, Haruki read his book. Returning to Japan was an act of defiance. The fictional Utajima was based on Kamishima, an island in the Gulf of Ise a few hours from Tokyo. There was a dramatic scene before the culmination, set during a storm in which Shinji had to prove his worth. After that he and Hatsue were given a blessing to marry. Haruki was green-eyed that life could be easily resolved and everyone harmonious. Tassos and Toshihiro splashed about in the sea and rid the clay from their bodies. Haruki cringed. He needed out of here. He could always run away to Kamishima and become a pearl diver.

Before they left the island proper, Haruki walked the back alleys near the port alone. One courtyard was overrun by bamboo. It seemed out of place but he knew from his mother's garden how invasive it could be. One of the shoots had split and hung lopsided. He didn't think twice before snapping off the metre-long strip and scurrying away. He told his father that he took it to show to the others.

The three of them spent the penultimate night back on Tinos. Haruki couldn't believe that they'd be in Vatheia by the next evening. It would be too late to look for Akis but at least he'd be close.

They paid for two rooms in a guest-house in Duo Xoria, a village above the port with views across to Mykonos. They sat underneath a eucalyptus tree that covered the entire square, heavy under its own weight and supported by wooden braces. There they ordered ouzo with an almond flavour local to the island but the two men held a dejected expression and drank in reflective silence until Toshihiro turned in, taking Haruki with him.

They shared a twin room. There was hot water and bed frames with padded mattresses. Toshihiro climbed under his blanket and turned off the light. For a while both were still, neither aware if the other was awake. The small gap between their beds did little to narrow the distance; the extended time together had been in Tassos' company and had done nothing to bridge them.

Toshihiro spoke into the darkness. "Let's not tell them about this."

Haruki pretended at first to be asleep but it was more unsettling to let his father's words hang in the air. "About what?"

"About the room. The shower. The beers. How lovely it all was."

"Alright."

There was a long pause that they'd never needed to fill before. When they spent time together it was in a bathtub gazing towards nature or fixed on igneous rocks, but in the blackened-out room there was nothing to take focus.

"You thought I was speaking about something else."

"Like what?"

"It doesn't matter. Did you have a good week?"

"I told you. I was happy in Vatheia."

"You didn't look like you were having much fun. Disappearing off on your own."

"I just– Antiparos was a long way to come for more rocks. I didn't mean it like that."

"Perhaps you're right. Diros gave me all I needed. Charup– Haruki?"

"Yes?"

"I have been preoccupied. I apologise. Maybe you could show me some of the things you've found around Vatheia when we get back."

"OK. I'm sorry too. I guess I'm jealous really."

"Of me?"

Haruki spoke before he could think, letting the words carve their own truth. "You're in love with your work. I hope that one day I can have that."

He heard his father shuffle in his bed and assumed that he'd turned to face him. Haruki remained on his back, looking up at the ceiling.

"Psychology you said. Tell me why."

"People are fascinating. I want to understand them. Like why Okaa can be so cold and yet adaptable."

"Your mother would be a life-long project. Perhaps we should have visited Dr Freud's clinic in Vienna instead of here."

"He left Austria a long time ago. He died."

"He did? Do you want to be like him? Analysing people and offering treatments."

He hadn't thought about it. He'd only considered studying the mind rather than how it could be applied. "I guess."

"Who else? It can't have just been your mother."

"There's Petzechroula and Tyresias and how they're in love even if they act like they can't stand each other."

"That was like Jiji and Baa-chan. I'm pleased you saw a love like it. It's not so easy to find in Japan."

"And Yuki. How she made friends so easily."

"She's remarkable. I don't know where she gets it from."

Haruki was about to tell his father about Akis but caught himself.

"There's also you and Tassos," he said instead. "You've managed to share a language even if you don't have the words for it. I've never seen you like that with colleagues at Waseda and they speak Japanese."

Toshihiro was silent.

Haruki was worried that he'd spoken out of line and changed the subject. "Do you miss home?"

"I haven't considered it. I suppose I do."

"Will you miss here?"

"How can I miss what isn't mine? This is just a break from real life."

"But the cave—"

"—is simply water and rocks. I will talk to your mother about your studies."

"Thank you. I finished *Shiosai*."

"What did you think?"

"It was lovely. Different to everything else he's written. It made me want to visit there."

Toshihiro chuckled. "You haven't realised, have you? Mishima travelled here, to Greece, two years before it was published. He fell in love with the country and wrote the story based on Greek ideals."

Haruki was grateful that his father couldn't see his widening eyes or the sharpness in the rise and fall of his chest. He had to muffle his quickened breath.

It was why he could map Akis' face onto Shinji's. He'd seen the boy through the novelist's lens, the words jumping out of the page and into his subconscious. Any desire had just been misdirected.

He felt relief long after his father had fallen asleep. He didn't have to worry about anything untoward. He would return tomorrow and Akis would forgive him for disappearing and they could relax for the rest of the summer without worries of case studies or arguments or desire and just have fun.

His father snored, the culprit from the tower house, but Haruki was too riled to sleep. He crept out of the room and onto the square.

It was past midnight and warm. The sky offered a more pleasant breeze than whatever Vatheia was privy to. Tassos sat alone at the same table where they had left him and Haruki would leave him to his peace, his summer of being a tour guide and interpreter too exhausting to be entertaining them at all hours. As Haruki turned back he stepped on a loose tile. Tassos followed the noise.

"Charupi. Come, sit."

It was clear that Tassos was drunk. Not in a jovial way like Haruki had seen of the salarymen in Tokyo's Kabukicho district but cheerless and contemplative.

The man was usually charming, bringing a smile to everyone's face, giving Haruki new words and tirelessly carrying Yuki on his shoulders. Every Maniot seemed to know him and seemed to be his friend. But unlike upstairs where Toshihiro's expression was masked by the darkness, the night's glow revealed Tassos' melancholy.

"Can't sleep?" he asked Haruki.

"No."

"Your father?"

Haruki made a snore sound, not knowing the word.

Tassos exhaled with the intimation of envy. "Vatheia tomorrow. You're happy, I think, to see my cousin."

So Tassos did know. Haruki had spent the week building up the courage to ask. "Why does he live in ksemoni?"

Tassos roared with laughter that stemmed from his belly. "Stop. I'll wake the village. How do you know that word?"

"Akis told me. You knew I was going there?"

"We all did. Me and my parents anyway. Tell me. Is it beautiful?"

"Estia? You haven't been?"

"Maybe one day we'll be invited. Charupi, do you think I'm a fool for leaving?"

Haruki was impressed with how he'd fared with the conversation up till now but didn't understand the question.

Tassos revised it. "Am I crazy to live in Athens?"

Haruki thought of the island in the book and then of Estia. He nodded.

"Oh."

"But I live in Tokyo."

"That's true. Maybe Akis is the smartest of all of us. Is he happy?"

"I think so," Haruki said, but since walking in on the fight and now hearing Tassos speak of the rift he was no longer sure.

"You're a good boy. Forgive me." Tassos knocked back his drink and began to talk. The speech was long and complicated and Haruki understood nothing. He wasn't meant to. Like how Petzechroula talked at Tyresias or how the pilgrims crawled in silent prayer. Or how he himself wrote letters that were never intended to be read. Tassos needed to explain himself towards ears that couldn't hear.

Tassos continued for a while whilst neither of them moved. Haruki stared at the waves as they danced with the moonlight. He didn't try to pick out the words he knew. He wouldn't insult Tassos when this wasn't his intention. But he couldn't ignore the hurt in his voice.

When Tassos finally stopped, Haruki excused himself to bed. He didn't need him to translate. He wouldn't ask, nor would he ever speak of it to anyone.

Alone once more, Tassos picks up the bottle of ouzo and tips it above his glass. He's out of luck. It has all but run dry. He tries to drink anyway but the few remaining drops do nothing to sate him.

15

Estia
20th July 1962

Their return to the tower house was met with little fanfare. Subdued as it was, there was a marked difference between Petzechroula's tender welcome and Megumi's statesmanly greeting. Tyresias had already retired upstairs with a migraine before their arrival; Tassos gave a playful apology, that in his own absence his father had taken the brunt of his mother's shouts. Petzechroula didn't laugh. She went back to dusting surfaces, skipping swathes unlike her usual thorough self. Haruki wondered if she was concerned about Tyresias or mortified about the earlier argument. Worse, he thought, with their visit only halfway through, maybe she was fed up with hosting them.

Questions of how the travellers fared were dealt with swiftly and the men agreed to spend the next day in Vatheia when they could say more. It was enough to see them returned safe even if Tassos looked gaunt, at the tail-end of an exhaustion that was likely the beginning of a fever.

Haruki had other plans. He wanted to ask Petzechroula if she'd seen Akis but his mother sent him upstairs before he could catch her alone.

He woke with a start the next morning and tiptoed out of the house. He beat the sun to the beach. Obsessively, he'd checked that it was a Friday and not one of Akis' delivery days. He didn't know if Akis had learnt about the reason for his vanishing. He hadn't expected him to row into the bay every morning but, overnight, Haruki's mind had run riot as paranoia about Petzechroula's change of disposition spread. Maybe Akis had come a few times and given up. Maybe he no longer cared.

Haruki wouldn't be missed in the village even if he'd promised to spend more time with his father but he couldn't stare at the horizon all day. He hated the idea of surrendering and retreating up the slope still in possession of the souvenirs and the bamboo, and so he waited past the time that Akis usually drew near. Could he make it to Estia on his own? Swimming would see him drowned. He could walk or cycle along the cliff but the final climb was out of the question unless he wanted to break his back trying. Except for giving up, the only other option was Tassos' boat. It wouldn't be missed considering that the men were staying put. All he had to do was get it there and back. He rolled his shoulders and decided that his arms could make the distance. Impetuous, he threw off the canvas and dropped the gifts inside.

The conditions were in his favour. The oars broke the unruffled sea with ease. He forced himself to be moderate, the tortoise a wiser choice than the hare. He was proud as he made headway. He'd never taken the initiative to be self-reliant. He'd never needed to. But as he approached the bay he was full of self-doubt. Akis might be offended that he'd encroached on this place uninvited.

Haruki turned to face the house and stopped sculling. From this distance it seemed untouched but he was sure to find changes. There was no movement but Akis might be behind a wall working away. He noticed the glaring problem. Akis' row-boat wasn't there.

He pulled up to the sandbar but it was unwelcoming in the other boy's absence. It hadn't been the house nor the cluster of trees nor was it the tranquility that had drawn him in. Estia's hearth lay with Akis. Without him the bay snuffed cold.

His forearms ached too much to turn back so he had no choice but to stay. Each footprint in the sand felt like a further intrusion. He looked for innovations and discovered floorboards nailed into a shaded corner that Akis had set aside for a larder.

Tiredness hit him, the adrenaline that carried him here expended, but he needed to get to work before he could lie down. He'd assumed that he would add his offering with Akis' help but maybe it was better as a surprise. He chose a patch by the house and sank a shovel into the ground.

It took an hour and he was parched after he'd finished. He raised water from the cistern that he and Akis had built together. He drank, imagining Akis' lips on the glass as recently as this morning, and promptly fell asleep under the weight of the sun.

He came to, groggy and with Akis above him. Unlike the first time that Akis had woken him, the sun was already edging the cliff.

"Geia sas," said Akis.

Haruki could read neither his expression nor his tone. He rubbed his eyes. "You're here."

"It's my house."

"I know. But you're here."

"So are you."

"Where were you?" It was blunt but only because Haruki didn't know how to say what he really wanted: 'I missed you.'

Akis' explanation was at first complicated, his Greek fast and untranslatable, but they re-found their rhythm and Haruki understood the gist. Akis had learnt about the trip to Antiparos but was under the illusion that they'd arrive this evening. With this in mind he'd brought forward his deliveries from tomorrow to today. He apologised but Haruki stopped him. It was an honest mistake and one which settled his nerves; Akis hadn't been mad nor confused, instead he'd been eager to see him.

The whole time, Haruki had been talking from the ground. He stood to join him. "Hello."

He kissed him on both cheeks to replicate the Greeks. It was the first time to try out the custom and it was unnatural and clumsy. For the intimacy of the touch it was also officious. The boys recoiled and laughed at the bungled act.

Haruki handed him the bag of gifts. "For you."

"From Antiparos?"

"Tinos."

Akis pulled out nougat and a jar of quinces preserved in honey, and finally the copy of *Shiosai*. He looked at a loss.

"And Japan," Haruki added. He was sure that his father wouldn't mind. He could easily buy him another copy. In a way, from what Haruki had learnt, the book belonged here.

Akis thanked him and flicked through the pages. He strained his eyes towards the vertical trails of foreign symbols with such intensity that Haruki wondered if he'd broken the code and was reading.

Haruki turned his own attention to the cover. He hadn't given the design much thought but his father's words were the key to unlocking its mystery. The image was a minimalist depiction of a sunrise, a red semi-circle above five parallel blue lines. That much he had seen before. But what he'd mistaken for the sun and the sea were the two nations' flags.

"I could send you a– with Greek and Japanese," he said.

"A dictionary."

"Or maybe one day you could come to Japan."

Akis sighed and returned the book to the bag.

Haruki knitted his eyebrows. "What?"

"Nothing. Want to see the changes?"

Haruki was encouraging as Akis showed off the floorboards even though he'd already seen them. He was distracted by what had bothered him. Akis was happy here and perhaps he had no intention of ever leaving. Haruki blushed at having suggested that he travel to the other side of the world, something that wasn't possible.

Maybe he didn't have to. "I forgot."

He led Akis past the makings of the terrace like those he'd seen attached to the grander houses on the islands. It was a laborious project but, in the meantime, he wanted Akis to have something no one else did, perhaps not to be found across the entire continent.

Akis couldn't comprehend the object in front of him. At its base was a circular mound of pebbles that tapered to a point. A tube protruded from the centre and stopped at waist-height. He touched it, the stem of an unknown plant, ridged and bone hard.

Haruki had dreamt of constructing this ever since Akis had acquired the clay pot but it was only on finding the bamboo shoot that a suikinkutsu was made possible. His mother had commissioned a water harp for her own garden but that was to be admired rather than toyed with. This one would be different.

It had been gruelling work, digging low enough so that the pot sat upside down in the soil with the bamboo placed on top. Then he'd had to gather enough pebbles.

"Thank you?" Akis said.

Haruki laughed. As a sculpture it had no value but he was excited for Akis to test it out. He directed him to put his ear to the top of the shoot and then he tipped water over the pebbles, slowly at first so that only a few drops hit the ground.

Akis' face lit up.

As the water trickled through the stones and onto the pot, vibrations carried through the bamboo and played a jingling melody. Akis met his eyes with the tacit instruction to go again.

Haruki held his position as more of a tune sounded from beneath the ground. It didn't have to be a deep well for the chamber to reverberate at such a lovely pitch. It rang like a spring day after the rain, a sodden tree above a pond, its leaves weighed down and letting go.

He played with the flow, dribbling the water at a meditative subdual and then upping it to a deafening cacophony. Akis' pleasure exceeded whatever he'd hoped.

After the glass ran dry, Akis fixed a stare on him.

Haruki couldn't decode his solemn expression. "More water?"

Akis straightened his back and turned towards the sea. "Let's go."

Haruki followed this gaze with downtrodden heaviness. There were plenty of hours left in the day but Akis had had enough. "Back to Vatheia."

Akis creased his brow. "Oh."

"What?"

"I meant– I had an idea to go somewhere else."

"I thought–"

"Only if you want to."

"I do."

"You don't want to go to Vatheia?"

"Honestly? No."

"Good."

Akis took them in his boat. Haruki considered the logistics. There was no way around it. He would have to come back from wherever they were going and row Tassos' boat alone. He would have to return to Vatheia before sundown or else everyone would be worried. Or furious. But his arms throbbed with inevitable, delayed muscle pain and for the time being he was pleased to adopt his favoured spot as a passenger.

They rowed in the opposite direction to the village and carried on until Diros. The destination made little sense when the bay at Estia was perfectly fine.

Akis led him across the beach and up the slope towards the cave's mouth. It was deserted. In all of Haruki's visits no one else had been there and, with the older men holding back in Vatheia, Diros belonged to no one but them.

Haruki had come eight or nine times, each less gratifying despite Tassos rowing them to new depths that should have evoked some peril. This time fire raged inside him. He wanted to ask why they were there but Akis hurriedly went ahead and climbed into one of the longboats. Haruki blindly followed.

Akis steered them through the passages with the same assuredness as his cousin. Haruki imagined that he'd come here often during his childhood and was desensitised to the gloom. But they were under-dressed and shivered as they carried along the waterways, the sound of the drips around them eerier than those produced by the water harp. Akis held an earnest expression. His mind seemed to exist elsewhere. Haruki had seen the same disquiet on Petzechroula's face last night. He hadn't noticed the resemblance until now.

In any other circumstance, Akis' consternation, the dim light, the descent towards the earth's core, should have all been unnerving but Haruki trusted him. He thought back to the first day in Mani when he wasn't sure if they would meet again. He'd been so desperate to study his face and now he knew it intimately. He could see it when he closed his eyes. There was still work on understanding what went on inside but he could detail Akis' physique with accuracy. Like one of his father's experiments, he could group every Greek boy across the country and pick him out from a mile away.

Akis secured the boat next to the narrow ridge that Haruki had walked during his first visit. He was more careful this time, making it to the unfinished column without slipping. Given that it had only been a few weeks, the missing section hadn't narrowed although there had likely been microscopic advances from the stalactite above or the stalagmite below. He guessed that Tassos had shown Akis this feature or perhaps they'd discovered it together.

Akis held up his light. It travelled through the gap and created a perfect replica of a shadow on the cave's wall.

"Fifty years," he said. He spread his hand wide as confirmation.

Haruki nodded. Witnessing it filled in would require a jump into the future three times his age. It was almost inconceivable. He would be as old as his grandfather. If things went to plan he would be retired but there was so much to do before then, before he could return and see this minute change. He would have to put so much effort into his life when all the stack had to do was form.

It was exhausting to imagine.

At least there would be flux out there. He could love and achieve and build and grow. He could indulge and debate and wonder. He'd told his father that he was jealous of his discipline but now he pitied him; the cave held nothing compared to what humans could offer.

His father would be furious for him tampering with the formation but Haruki positioned his hand over the column anyway. The rock was fragile and he pressed lightly. His palm hid the gap. He didn't move when Akis placed his own hand on top of his, turning it a fraction so that their fingers interlocked and both of them could touch the pillar.

Maybe fifty years travelled differently in the stillness and semi-darkness of the cave. Haruki didn't know how long they could endure these conditions but now he wanted to stay for the entirety. Maybe he'd been wrong. Maybe as long as Akis was here with him then the cave had everything he needed. The world could wait until the column became whole.

He knew that this was a greedy madness.

He'd acclimatised to the cold but the shiver that passed through him was familiar. It was the same creeping panic that had taken hold every night for the past few weeks: a countdown of the limited number of times that they could be together.

He broke away and returned to the boat. Anxiety pained him but he tried hard not to show it. He focused on slowing his breath but the feel of Akis' hand had left a scorch mark that raised his pulse and countered his efforts.

No. The book had played a trick on him. This was just a continuation of that confusion. He was tired and the cave had further disoriented him. He needed to distance himself from here, disentangle himself from Akis. A softer blow before the summer drew to a close and he would be ripped away.

He returned to his extended essay and drafted the case study in his head, aligning himself as the observer and Akis as his subject, a margin cold and unimpassioned. The facts. Akis was different to any Japanese boy. Headstrong and resourceful. Apathetic to the superficial. He understood how to lose himself in a moment and how to be happy with so little. He had also never been as handsome as right now.

Haruki felt not much better as he attempted to swallow his misguided attraction, cementing it as a childish crush borne from the novel. Still, he was glad that Akis couldn't decipher *Shiosai's* words. He wanted to steal back the book before he ever could. All of what he liked about Akis was what shone from Shinji's character. Simply, this was what had enamoured him. Akis had just been the conduit. Haruki would enter university and find people with similar traits. He would emulate what Akis had modelled. It would be fine to leave him behind.

He felt resolved as Akis rowed them to the central chamber with its multiple offshoots. But not one seemed like a path that Haruki wanted to take. Akis manoeuvred them to the middle of the water. He slid the oars out of their locks and placed them in the hull.

Haruki held his breath.

The boy leant forward and kissed him. It was sudden and tender and over too quickly.

Haruki touched his lips to figure out what had just happened.

It wasn't like it had been his first time. He'd kissed a few girls at school, egged on by friends at dances or through dares, but the pressure had always left it unpleasant and there had never been the heat nor the will to do it again. He'd definitely never wanted to carry on at a love hotel like all his friends were doing. The absence of passion had made it impossible to know how a kiss should feel. He'd considered that he'd been pining for a thing for which he'd had unrealistic expectations of and didn't exist. In truth, masturbation had been perfunctory until the fantasy a week ago. Since then he'd been too afraid to retry it in case his mind returned to Akis. He didn't want to acknowledge this new reality after he'd spent the last week reasoning it away.

But he no longer wanted to be led by fear. Maybe it was easier to feign bravery in the lowlight of the cave but he was certain of one thing here with Akis. This was passion.

Still, he sat for a while, lost as to how to respond. Akis hadn't shown any interest in him before now. He couldn't work out what had allured Akis to him. He was introverted and boring. A weakling, unable to rival the wilds of Akis' character. He was also, as he was learning, disposed to paranoia. He'd assumed that Akis had befriended him as a favour. Perhaps he'd also kissed him as some sort of exotic quirk or for a prank. He had himself confused Akis with the book's protagonist and so maybe Akis was also seeing something else in this moment. It wasn't particularly assuring that the kiss had been concealed inside a cave.

And yet the kiss continued to dance like a firework display on his lips.

Tears rolled down Akis' cheeks. "Say something," he pleaded.

Haruki had never seen him so discomfited.

Haruki couldn't be gay. He'd never considered it. Homosexuality was wrong, the butt end of a joke. Two boys kissing was a ridiculous notion, done only by sinners and those on the fringes of society. He imagined his mother's disgust and felt his own shame.

He reached forward and wiped away Akis' tears.

He looked around the cave and banished his concerns to the shadows. There was no point convincing himself any differently, not even if they had to hide in here for fifty years.

He leant forward and gave himself to passion, kissing the boy with the fury of a thousand suns, the heat of which was sure enough to keep them ablaze even if they tumbled overboard and into the freezing water beneath.

16

Vatheia
20th July 1962

"Tadaima," Haruki said.

Megumi frowned as her son entered the tower house, later than ever before. "Okaeri," she replied anyway, adhering to the social convention from which it would be improper to stray.

"Kalispera," the boy added to his hosts, effortless in switching to Greek. Petzechroula answered in kind, addressing him as her crown, whilst Tassos nursed his temples and spluttered his response, ever feebler as the day had dragged into night.

Haruki took a seat next to his sister who was picking at a stale loaf despite them not having yet given thanks. Megumi tutted at her to stop but, with her son's mind elsewhere, he reached out and ripped off some bread, resulting in a groan of unfairness.

He'd been absent all day and had returned without a hint of remorse. He would spin a tale of walking the coast and reading. Only, no one except her noticed that he was empty-handed, any supposed book as fictional as its contents. Asking would just lead to more lies, and still no support from her husband who resisted every one of her nudges, chiding her with the foregone conclusion that their son was flourishing. And on that, Toshihiro had told her, 'ganbare' to his sense of adventure.

Flourishing. She wanted to swat that word from their vocabulary. How could she protect Haruki when he wasn't willing to be coddled? She caught his eye but he broke away. He may have fooled the others with his innocent act but she recognised the expression that unpacked itself.

Dishonour. Something had happened.

Toshihiro descended from the hatch. "There he is," he told her. "As I said."

"Of course," she replied, smiling through his guilelessness, but by then he'd already turned to Tassos.

She wanted to agree with her husband. To delight in Haruki's newfound sufficiency and his successful adoption of a further language. To be placated that he hadn't fallen afoul of the wilds of the country. Dead in an impossible number of ways that her brain had proven itself, for almost seventeen years, capable of conjuring. Drowned, trapped, suffocated, bitten, kidnapped, at the bottom of the sea or a crevice, his body fish-food or supper for the wolves. But she knew better than that.

Her head had filled with terrible images as soon as she'd learnt that he was hers, many months before he was born. Outside the clinic, before she could even break the news to Toshihiro, her mind had run rampant with what harm could befall him if she was inattentive. Her womb, his crib, a blanket, viruses, all of these things needing to be supervised. More was added to the list as he began to crawl, walk, attend school. It was no longer just physical risks but, for her sensitive boy, there was being bullied or becoming a social outcast. All of these menaces were hers to solve and, until now, enough money thrown at the problems had made them go away. So yes, she wanted to rejoice that he'd survived another day unharmed but she also saw the scars of blisters and fatigue of labour and, though he wasn't injured, that wasn't the same as calling him untarnished.

She swallowed the burning disappointment that Haruki was back too soon for her to tease out the truth of where he'd been, but the sun hadn't quite given up the day and Tyresias only now trundled in, his thunderous voice eliciting a headache that she'd just managed to suppress. Haruki would justify his timing as guided by Petzechroula's crow call but they both knew that it had been a fortuitous accident.

Sirens sounded in Megumi's mind and returned her to Aoyama. These neighbourhood alarms, a remnant from the war, had since been converted into an earthquake warning system and were tested daily at five o'clock, also serving to conclude the work day and to alert children to hurry home. Five. That was a more reasonable hour. Not nine like this evening, a flagrant violation of his curfew and destroying a routine that she'd had no choice but to watch fall apart.

Petzechroula brought a pot to the table. Yet another night of gigantes beans in a measly tomato broth.

Megumi scolded Yuki for her paper cranes taking up space. The girl gathered the birds and squashed them into a pile by her feet so, though they were spring-loaded, they held in place, compact and stifled. Megumi knew that chastising her daughter was just displaced anger.

Whatever her son was discovering, about the world, about himself, she'd learnt something about him too. He was more resilient than she'd credited. But these wings of his that were seeking to take flight would be his downfall if she didn't anchor them.

For weeks she'd monitored him. The days he sulked around the village or went with his father to the cave couldn't have been more at odds with his elation after his alleged solitary trips. She'd had no choice but to follow him. Vigilance served him at first but he quickly became arrogant and, like a mouse with its guard down and forgetting the lurking of a cat, one morning he'd marched to the bay without looking over his shoulder. She'd watched him leave with the boy, and again, and every chance after that.

A second plate of boiled bitter xorta was lowered over her head. The others proceeded to eat but she had no appetite.

Initially, there had been nothing to do but bide the hours, distracting herself from the horrific visions that plagued her until his return. Then he'd turned up with battle-scarred fingers and work-worn limbs, embracing a world that she'd worked hard at keeping him from having to pursue. He was sullying what she'd spent his entire life buffering. He was a shining mirror, glimmering with the surety of a polished future, and she the wool that wrapped its edges. Now he'd not only shrugged her free but had willingly, assuredly, let the edges fleck. She could see it in his stance: he had found rebellion, and rebellion wore him like a chipped frame that he deemed fashionable. Before coming here, her husband had been a pile of fragments that had rusted but now glowed under the Grecian sun, attractive, molten red. Alongside Tassos, her husband – Toshi, pah! – had stretched his palm and played a game of dare with the serrated blades. She wouldn't let their son fall the same way. She needed to bundle him up before he too shattered into an irretrievable mess.

She'd struggled to work out how until one unassuming evening when Tassos had put on a shadow puppet show for Yuki. He'd acted out the story of Icarus and Daedalus in airborne escape. In Megumi's version it was the father that dared the sun first, the boy oblivious to the danger and willing to follow. In her version, who could she be to swoop in and set him on a straight path? A compass, she'd decided later that night unable to sleep, orienting him in the right direction.

The next day she'd taken stock of the delivery boy's argument with his aunt and how Haruki had chased after him. Disregarding Megumi's presence – how the mouth slips – Petzechroula had complained in her cloaked language about the two boys. But the skilful hawk hides its claws; it wasn't only her son who had picked up Greek. Not that she cared for anyone to know.

She'd made a plan there and then to send him to Antiparos and distance them long enough to break the spell. Distress was a thing that no mother should want to provoke in her child but Megumi had no time for such base pleasantries. The idea of herself as a soother alone was as useful as a one-sided die. She was a protector of storms but also the cox on his skiff, navigating the path as he rowed, directing him away from the eye of a hurricane but also allowing him to capsize every so often so as not to tempt rough seas again. She knew when to pull him in and when to push him farther. She would fail if she pampered him without also teaching him his limits. She'd also never seen him so panicked as that night. As the men planned the route, no one else but her had sensed his internal machinery clucking with rabid madness like one of Petzechroula's cooped chicks grabbed by the neck and taken from its clutch.

She would have liked to corner the delivery boy that week and gnarl her teeth but their paths hadn't crossed. It should have been reassuring that he wasn't feral, that he belonged to this family. This was something that had apparently passed by Haruki, whereas she'd spotted the boy collecting supplies from Tassos on their arrival.

Petzechroula served more thinned-out dishes that were less savoury by the day. Megumi would later pacify Yuki with candy. There was nothing else to be done.

As much as it gratified her to have Haruki opposite her now, it had been a strangely enjoyable week with him and her husband out of sight and gradually out of mind. But they'd returned last night and she was disappointed to see him continue to fret.

And then. This morning she'd followed him and watched him steal a boat and row himself out of Vatheia. Everything in that moment had invoked terror. He'd stretched his rope so far from her moorings that she felt the snap. He was no longer tethered to her.

She wasn't sure what it was about this friendship that raised her like a snarling guard dog but she knew that it wasn't right. She understood Haruki better than anyone else could, his father and grandfather too engrossed in their own worlds. He was a timid boy, impressionable and still in the spring-flowering world of following dreams. Built for a narrowed-in life, paddling in the shallows rather than racing towards rocky coves.

"The frog in the well doesn't know of the great ocean," she said out loud. No one around the table took any notice.

He needed the security of the Okazaki name, protected within the confines of a reputation stacked on a solid foundation. He also needed the boys who only kept him in their fold because, by then, to exclude him hadn't been a thing they'd considered. These were the upstarts with influence. They could not only lift him in the world but tread him into the mud should they be done with him. The weak are meat, the strong eat.

She winced as Tyresias chomped open-mouthed on split pea purée, interrupting her husband by spinning off into new or already trodden directions because, if he couldn't hear, it was simpler, and vital, to be heard.

She rarely joined in with their exchanges, and never more than trivial murmurs of acknowledgement about her husband's day. No one asked about hers. What could she offer of consequence? Dogsbody chores that served to fill the hours and keep the glances of villagers away from her. Besides, she wouldn't be so rude as to discount anyone by speaking in Japanese. Her husband didn't share this dilemma, uninterested if people could follow or were enamoured with his rocks.

Megumi cleared her throat and looked at Haruki. "Where did you go today?"

It was so unusual for her to speak that everyone turned. She closed her eyes and smiled to assume culpability before gesturing for the men to continue.

The only person who hadn't looked her way was her son, absorbed in a world from which she was excluded. Unbeknownst to him, he had stained his top with earthy beetroot and was now forking a rusk into impossible pieces that had no place at a table at any time of day. She would savour telling Rika about this. The two women would be aghast as they delighted in the horror of such poverty.

"Haruki."

Nothing. She considered kicking him. Flicking a crumb his way for effect. Leaning over and grabbing his collar.

Yuki elbowed him. "Charupi."

He scowled.

"Okaa wants you."

"Yes, Mother?"

"How was your day?"

"Good, thank you."

"Back to the meadow?"

"It's a grove. But yes."

"To read?"

Haruki nodded without blinking.

"What?" she asked.

"Huh?"

"To read what? You finished *Shiosai* and I don't remember you asking for other books. They're all still in my case."

"Oh. I wanted to read it again."

"In the grove."

"In the grove."

She was too sensible to be offended. She had more important issues to take care of.

Fortune was on her side as early as the next morning when Tassos woke with his fever at its peak. Maybe it was unearned for her plan to come together so easily or perhaps it was a karmic dividend after a month of paying her dues.

She encouraged her husband to take Haruki to the cave. Neither hid their disappointment well, she'd predicted as much, but they fetched their bicycles anyway. She waited until Petzechroula left for her errands before she climbed the ladder, one hand cupped around a glass of water.

She knelt by Tassos' bed and offered him a pill from a pharmacy in Tokyo, the remedy more for her benefit than his.

His body shivered from beneath the blanket. Sweat beads formed on his forehead. "Thank you," he said in Greek and then English and then, realising his mistake, Japanese.

She smiled before making her bid. "Mr Tzanetakis, I would like your help."

Tassos looked at her as if in a fever dream. "You speak English?"

"Proficiently," she replied. "I'm a housewife with time on my hands."

"Does Toshi know?"

She scoffed at the nickname. "No," she replied, before adding, "Mr Tzanetakis. My husband does not know." She'd learnt that it never hurt to be polite.

Tassos sat up with effort.

In other circumstances Megumi would have restrained him and told him to rest. Instead she pulled back his cover, ignored his nakedness and passed him his trousers. "I would like you to take me to the boy's house."

"Who?"

She didn't elaborate.

"I don't think I can— You speak English," he marvelled.

"I would prefer that no one else learnt of this. But perhaps we should discuss some matters in front of your parents and my husband. Now that I can participate."

"Discuss what?"

Megumi tightened her lips, loathed to partake in games about his innocence. Around her the two men had spoken of little else but rocks but she was confident that whatever had transgressed between them would be enough to see Tassos leave his bed.

"Why do you want to go there?" Tassos' muscles seized as he lifted a shirt over his arms.

"Might I share a Japanese proverb with you? Anzuru yori umu ga yasashi. Giving birth to a child is easier than worrying about it."

"I don't understand."

She took his hand and helped him up. "That's the wonderful thing, Mr Tzanetakis. You don't have to."

They came downstairs as Petzechroula entered, surprised to see her son up. Tassos explained something, a fib most likely about being escorted on a walk, the fresh air good for him. Megumi wasn't worried about his condition to row. If her son could manage the distance then so could a practised man in the spills of delirium.

He groaned throughout the journey but it wasn't far to the secluded bay. No one else was there. It hadn't mattered but it was preferable this way.

She left Tassos to recuperate and crossed the sand to inspect the boy's pathetic shack with all its trappings of a teenaged dream. Curiosity had led her here and she didn't expect to find anything that would point to her fears being realised but she'd needed to see this hideout for herself.

Something caught her eye.

A bamboo shoot stood proud.

It had no place here. A suikinkutsu belonged in its motherland, to be cherished and handled with delicacy by those trained to operate it, not frivolously deep-rooted in foreign soil and wasted on the uncouth.

There was a drop of water left in a glass. She put her ear to the shoot and listened as a divine refrain played through, more heavenly than from her own harp in Aoyama. She recoiled.

She wanted to pull the bamboo from the ground and drop it into the sea at an irretrievable depth but it wouldn't suffice to make such an obvious display. Any dismantling needed to be more impactful than that. She returned to the boat empty-handed.

She diverted Tassos to Gerolimenas, the closest village that had electricity. He didn't complain, happy to break the journey in two.

"The telephone please, Mr Tzanetakis."

Tassos pointed feebly towards the corner-shop. "International connections aren't possible."

"Whilst I appreciate your concern, I think you should focus on conserving your energy to get us home. Nito wo oumono ha itto wo moezu."

He gathered some strength. "Another proverb?"

"Indeed. The man who chases after two hares will catch neither."

The village was built around the water. It was hardly thriving but Megumi hadn't seen this many people for some time. She ignored their glances, just as she had taken no notice of the snobs in Tokyo when she'd first arrived there, in her peasant clothes, from the rice fields of her childhood. She brushed the memory of her former life under the carpet that she'd laid down long ago. She hadn't allowed herself to be intimidated there and she definitely wouldn't be cowed here, but the hidden past was never fully swept away and so she had to force herself to keep her head raised high above the steady burble of the onlookers.

She handed more money to the shop owner than he would earn in a month. He directed her to the back wall where she dialled a memorised number.

A woman answered on the third ring. Megumi re-introduced herself and, after a few pleasantries – Mani was suiting them fine, the hospitality lived up to Japanese standards, they were eating well – she gave the nod for what she'd set in motion, back there, at the Embassy.

"The same address?" the secretary asked her.

"Correct. Send it immediately."

"Right away."

'Doumo arigatou gozaimashita," Megumi said before hanging up. She also thanked Tassos for his service as she climbed into his boat. It really did never hurt to be polite.

17

Estia
23rd July 1962

The day after the kiss, and with Tassos ill, Haruki was encouraged by his mother to spend the day with his father. He wanted to sit by the shore and hope for Akis but he couldn't rebuff his father, not after having asked for more during their time in the Cyclades. But it was sacrilegious to the momentousness of the kiss to return to Diros so soon and with someone else. It was also apparent from Toshihiro's listlessness that he didn't want to be there either, wondering often and aloud about Tassos' well-being. Neither ceded for those few eternal virtuous hours in the lifeless cave until enough time passed for them to call off the charade.

Haruki spent a second night replaying the kiss and hoping that Akis would show the next day. They hadn't spoken on their return from Diros to Estia. The silence wasn't, at least to Haruki, borne of embarrassment but of savouring the embrace, clawing at the memory as the protection of the cave slipped away. Then Haruki had needed to hurry to Vatheia, rowing the last stretch on his own. His body was renewed, his mind distracted, and he'd managed easily. But once he'd reached land, every muscle in his body despite the lethargy had urged him to row straight back to the boy. Foolishly, they hadn't arranged to meet again. Haruki wasn't sure, considering what had transpired, and any potential regret of it, whether Akis would come back at all.

This second night, the tower house as colourless as the cave, Haruki panicked. Paranoia created a new narrative that Akis realised the kiss was a mistake and had been keen for Haruki to row away. Haruki stayed up for hours, retracing the echoes of the kiss and retaining the tender memory from within the chamber without pounding the breath out of it; clinging too hard was like ensnaring a bird by wringing its neck and inadvertently choking it of life but neither could he risk letting it free.

The following morning, however, Akis did return. *Doki-doki*, Haruki's stomach sounded with nervous excitement as the boat drew near.

Haruki was unsure how to greet him. If Akis pretended that nothing had happened then they would focus on building the house. That would be good enough. But hadn't Akis made the first move?

Haruki waded into the sea for a quick getaway. "How are you?" he asked, as he climbed aboard.

Akis was stiff-backed and looked at him with disdain. He punched Haruki's shoulder. "How are you?" he repeated, mocking the formality. "Idiot."

It didn't clarify what lay on the other side of the outcrop but at least they were reunited.

"Where were you yesterday?" Akis asked after they turned the corner.

"I had to go to Diros with my father. I'm sorry."

Akis breathed easy. "I had chores anyway." He stroked Haruki's thigh. Relieved, Haruki grabbed Akis' hand and squeezed it.

It was all they could do on arriving to Estia before stripping down, jumping into the sea and grabbing kisses between mouthfuls of saltwater, all the while struggling to keep afloat. They crawled onto the sand and continued groping at one another in and around the house. Akis talked designs each time that they stumbled into a new space. Haruki forgot that the rooms weren't much more than rubble.

Little work was done. At one point Akis climbed a tree and chopped back its branches; Haruki wanted to tell him to be careful but dummied up, not wanting to sound matronly.

They returned to the sand late in the day. An oil tanker sailed by at such a distance that it better resembled a bath toy but they instinctively pulled away from one another. Haruki burnt red. He couldn't look at Akis to learn if he'd reacted the same. Their conversation strained. It was some minutes before they came back together.

During the return to Vatheia they set out definite plans for the next few days. Risking the proximity to the village, Akis leant forward and kissed Haruki good night before they went their separate ways. It carried Haruki through the evening.

According to his mother, when he eventually came downstairs late the next morning, the men had assumed that he'd caught Tassos' fever and, unencumbered by him, had headed early to the cave. In reality Haruki had seen little point in starting the day when Akis was at work.

He returned to the attic and wrote a letter to his grandfather loaded in subtext about what had happened. It was a pointless exercise when his words were clouded by ambiguity. No one would understand. He wasn't sure he did. He started a more honest letter detailing his reasons for studying psychology, but launching himself into tomorrow's business and away from here depressed him.

At midday his mother sent him to fetch Yuki. He tried the classroom and the square and was at the beach, his sister nowhere to be found, when Akis rowed towards him. It was a rare day to see heavy clouds overhead. Choppy undercurrents broke at the shore and warned of a storm brewing past the horizon. The cooler breeze should have brought relief but Akis' grave expression left him unsettled.

"Delivery?" Haruki asked.

Akis rapped his fingers against the oar before pulling a single envelope from the sack. It was in Greek but Haruki could read the name on the top line. *Okazaki Toshihiro.*

"It's just the university," Haruki said trivially, raring to counter this foreboding of bad news.

Neither boy was averse to him opening the letter. Haruki read through without translating then kept his head lowered after he'd finished.

It was the plan in case of an emergency. Rika had called the Embassy in Athens who had then transcribed the message and forwarded it here. Jiji was in a bad way. Not just a sickness but, according to the maid who was a stickler for propriety and wouldn't cause undue distress, Haruki's grandfather was on his deathbed. The prognosis at the time of the call was a week.

Blurry, abject, Haruki read it again. His grandfather had been found unconscious. A suspected stroke made worse after an entire night before being discovered. If the family came quick-speed they could make it.

It was Jiji's wish that this happened.

Haruki wished away these last few minutes. Coming to the bay, opening the letter, reading it, all of these things leading to a fate that shouldn't have been his.

He looked at Akis. He didn't have to tell him. It wouldn't be real if he held off. But every second of procrastination churned his stomach.

"My grandfather. We have to return."

"I'm sorry."

Haruki needed to find his mother even if he didn't want to. He couldn't live with himself otherwise. He hated cursing his jiji but it was selfish of him to demand that they surrender the trip. Even if they hurried and the timings were favourable it would still be days before they were by his side.

He felt the weight of the paper in his hand. He could pretend it had never arrived. He could drop the letter in the sea and wash the ink into oblivion. Akis would be a willing accomplice.

"I don't know what to do."

"Whatever is right."

Haruki raised his eyebrows.

Akis gazed off to the side. "What does your head tell you?"

Haruki didn't want to say.

"Your heart?"

He also knew the answer to that.

Akis tried to say something but couldn't think of how to explain it, complicated and grief-stricken.

Haruki tucked the envelope into his pocket. His father wouldn't be back for a while. A few hours wouldn't make a difference. They made a promise to head to Estia but return by early afternoon when there would be enough time for someone to go to Areopoli or Gerolimenas and make arrangements.

Some way out, with Akis consumed by the tug of the sea, Haruki felt the pull of obligation lessen. He was surprised that the letter hadn't burnt a hole in his pocket. He had to reach down to check that it was still there. He was just grateful to have intercepted it.

He was amazed that his body felt settled and that his mind could work in such sudden denial when this was to be their last day together. Once he was back in Japan, Akis, Estia, the cave would be as faded as his sand drawings lost to the Etesian winds. On the other side of the world, days would soon multiply into weeks. Seasons would become a lifetime. The reality hit him and his heart grew so heavy that he worried it would sink them to the bottom of the ocean.

He worked unproductively on the house for a few hours, a performative display that was as miserable as it was fruitless. A small distance away, Akis swung the axe at a block of wood with force. The coarse sea reflected both of their thrashed spirits.

Haruki didn't want to build or play or lie on the sand. The only thing he wanted wasn't on offer. He walked to the water harp and considered the other things that he'd wanted to do here but wouldn't have the chance.

Akis approached from behind, wrapped his arms around him and kissed his neck. "It'll be alright."

Haruki closed his eyes. He didn't believe him.

Akis returned to chopping wood. Haruki crossed to the shore and sat on the dampened sand. The sky had lost its vibrancy, now a monochromatic grey. Under the sound of the waves he didn't hear Akis draw near until he sat by his side.

Akis reached for his hand, interlocking them. Haruki felt a surge of electricity, strong enough to light up his city from here. But all the draw of Tokyo, all of the things that he'd thought he was unwilling to let go of, all of what he'd craved now waned in comparison. The idea of giving up Akis sent him into a tailspin. The boy's firm clasp of his bookish fingers made no sense and yet it was real. He leant his head on Akis' shoulder.

Neither boy stirred even when they felt the first drops.

"Don't go," Akis said.

Haruki turned to him. "What?"

"Stay here."

"The rain doesn't bother me. We have a few more—"

"I mean *stay*."

"My grandfather—"

"Charupi," said Akis. "Beyond the summer. Don't go to Tokyo."

Haruki was incredulous. It had entered his own head, for fleeting moments, but it was a boyish dream that he'd never expected of Akis. He didn't recognise him. Akis was stubborn and determined, capable and resourceful, but he was also sound of mind. This was a flight of fancy. It was inconsiderate to throw out a thing with such little weight, as if Haruki was a dog given a bone to be appeased.

Insulted, he walked off.

"What?" Akis shouted after him.

"Don't say things you don't mean." Anger brought up words like vomit and relieved his insides. His Greek was the most fluent it had ever been. "It's unfair."

"I do mean it, Charupi."

"It's not right."

"Why?"

"Because."

Akis waited for an answer.

"Because my life is in Japan. Not here." He threw up his hands. "You couldn't understand."

Haruki heard the contempt before he could curb it. He'd insinuated his own life to be bigger. He wanted to force his words back in and pretend that he'd intimated something else.

Too late. He took in Akis' hurt expression.

It was true, Haruki reasoned, but he didn't know how to justify it without insulting him further. Akis' life was this. No doubt it was charming and uncomplicated, his routine unencumbered by nothing more than solidifying foundations already sunk into the ground. But he had so much ahead of him that Akis didn't. A career, a reputation, pleasing the family he already had, creating a family of his own. Impressing others. Earning respect. Leaving a mark.

He wanted to apologise but instead gave Akis time to realise that it was true.

It was Akis' turn to walk away. His gait was purposeful as he headed towards the boat. "I'll take you to Vatheia."

"That's not what I want."

Akis turned to him and huffed. "Not here. Not there. What do you want?"

Haruki knew the answer but it was as unfair to say it as to hold back. It simplified everything by signposting them onto an impossible path. He said it anyway. "You. I want you."

Akis bobbed his head in muted agreement. "This isn't good."

"What can we do?"

"I mean the weather." The sky had listened to their painful goodbye. Rain was past intermittent and hit them with successive drops. "We have to hurry."

The air reached a pitch familiar to Japan's humid season when the heavens would break with interludes that flooded the land and gave it a sweet relief. Akis made a dashed effort to move exposed tools under shelter before preparing the boat.

Haruki adored him all the more for his sincere attempt but with it came his own resistance. "I don't want to," he said, standing in the shallows and refusing to climb in.

"Charupi."

"No."

Akis trudged through the water and took his hands. Haruki dug his feet into the sand.

Akis forced him a step closer, and another.

Haruki submitted but as he reached the boat he started to sob.

Akis turned and let Haruki collapse into his arms.

Darkness lands earlier than dusk dictates and it isn't long before the rain becomes a fully-fledged storm. By the time they're composed and ready to set out, the deluge has stopped any chance of safe return. Resigned to wait it out they give little thought to the two families who will be panicking about Haruki's safety. They both figure that the others will guess he is here. They land on the same decision: let them worry. It will be short-lived considering that they won't be repeating this, split up for the rest of their lives. Tonight the boys are no one else's but another's.

Afternoon mimics night. They build a small fire in front of Estia that loses the battle and does little against the bite of the wind. They huddle together under a blanket inside the tent and watch as sheet lightning strikes the ravaged sea, searching for a rhythm and finding none. The waves wash up farther than seems possible. The belting of the pellets above them is a din and the tempest isn't hurrying towards its peak but, though it won't be going anywhere fast, the boys feel unlikely to be harmed.

The argument that concerned Haruki staying is banished, too long ago for the heat of it to not have dissipated but too far into the future to have consequence. Instead there is only connection as their bodies rise and fall in line with one another, the anticipated breath of spending the night together a shared heartbeat that picks up speed.

Akis has his arm around Haruki and turns to kiss him. Neither of them is experienced. They only have musings of what to do but the other's body reflects their own so that any uncertainty about how to proceed is offset by the knowledge that to replicate their own pleasure is a fine starting point from which to gain traction. Akis helps Haruki out of his clothes and then he too undresses. Their tops are bundled up in a rushed discarding although Haruki folds his shorts, careful to not crease the envelope.

There's no need for haste nor criticism of what they are doing as wrong. Just tame moans and an agreement that they both consent. No other words are needed to be spoken.

They paw at one another, warm in their incandescence, unaided by the fast-extinguishing bonfire and oblivious to the rain that pervades the canvas and lands on them.

They become inseparable. On their sides, one on top of the other, swapping around, rubbing and grinding, and causing a stirring that rivals the pent-up eruptions of two tectonic plates. Their hands and mouths reach for places that they have not yet travelled. Chests, armpits, thighs leading to the curve of buttocks, the delicate, faint-haired skin around their testicles. Their penises. How different they are at first and then grow to resemble one another. The sensation of the other's hand anything but a solo act, finding a beat that fast becomes superior.

What can't be held back in one becomes the finishing point of the other and they cross the line almost simultaneously. The race is over too soon, the meal devoured, the final course relished with gluttony. What has lasted minutes or hours is done. Upon expending themselves there's no returning rush of shame. What they release onto one another, on a stomach, a hip, is left to dry out and marble as a mark of ownership. A branding iron's defacement so that each belongs to the other.

They drift off this way, spent, satisfied, and clear of the heaviness of thoughts if not exactly clear-headed. And, with the thunder overhead soundless, no bolt of lightning is strong enough to perturb closed eyes and invade either boy's halcyon sleep.

18

Vatheia
24th July 1962

Sunlight imbued Haruki's eyelids, waking him to a clear sky white in the pre-dawn glow. Often he didn't hear anything for those initial seconds of consciousness, his other senses only filling in details as the world took shape. He was outside, under the tent. The departed storm had rid the scene of darker hues and left the most sun-struck of mornings. The world was a painted landscape into which he could step. The tide kissed the sand fondly again. A light breeze tipped rainwater off the canvas. Birds flitted back and forth with breakfasts for their young. The fire was washed out, the burnt wood a faint wisp on his nose. Closer, by his side, Akis slept deeply.

Haruki lifted the blanket away to inspect what he already knew. He was naked. His penis was hard. Surprising considering its use throughout the night. He remembered the carnal pleasure but the memory was quickly lost to a mournful recall of what had led to it. Akis deserved to sleep a while longer. He didn't need to rush and find himself in today.

Haruki stared at the sea and forced himself to embrace its calmness. He engaged in the zazen practice that he'd honed with his grandfather. Neither of them could have imagined where it would end up being employed.

On a different day he might have read but there was no need for his mind to be taken elsewhere. There was equally no reason to write, not when his words would only, naturally, trap these moments to paper long after they had been stripped from him.

After a while, having to urinate, he wriggled out of the blanket, dressed in his damp clothes and tiptoed away. He searched for water but stopped short of pulling some from underground.

He walked to the edge of the beach. The sea was tranquil, almost impossible to believe that it had flailed about hours earlier. The boat was intact, the storm not even a distant blot on the landscape. He'd fallen asleep as the rain had continued to fall. He hadn't heard it stop. He'd passed out before then, content.

He undressed so that he was fully naked and strode into the surf. He washed away the sweat and scrubbed at a patch of pubic hair matted with one of their ejaculations. Already his mouth tasted of salt for the seawater not to bother him.

When he looked back, Akis was walking towards him, bleary-eyed and wrapped in the blanket. Haruki recalled the tautness of the body underneath. Erect again, he worried that the rest of him might collapse if not held by the buoyancy of the sea.

Akis loitered at the shore.

Haruki swam to him and shook his hair.

Akis gave a small grunt of being humoured. "Get dressed."

"Not yet." Haruki pushed himself into the blanket to dry off. He kissed Akis as he grappled with finding his way in.

Akis kissed him back, then stopped. "We have to go."

"I know."

"Unless you don't want to." He said it quietly.

Haruki pulled away. Clouds had parted in the sky to reveal a shining day and he found himself caught in the glare of confusion at Akis' offer being made a further time. He'd dismissed the idea as a childish sentiment that hadn't warranted a second thought.

"Stay, Charupi." Akis said to him once more.

Haruki was apparently unable to play make-believe for even a little while, too sensible to shrug off the song and dance of teenage-hood and consider it a viable option. His tastes changed too quickly to commit to any one thing; his favourite novel had switched a hundred different times in the last year alone. How could he say that Estia was where he wanted his life to be? It wasn't like changing course at university or taking up a part time job or moving to a new suburb of the capital and then opting out. Disinheriting his family and his country had a much harder return.

But then there was Akis. It was inconceivable that this could be the end.

Standing separately from him, even by such a small gap, as narrow as the unfinished column in their cave, he realised his nakedness and felt shame. Would he be leaving sex with men behind too? It was something that he'd found without searching for it. A brief, ventured discovery. He already knew the answer. It would be something else left on the tarmac.

"No, Akis. I can't."

"I shouldn't have said it. I'm sorry."

Haruki dressed and strode over to the boat, allowing the apology to hang around the boy's neck.

Out on the water he didn't look back at Estia. Halfway to Vatheia, however, he leant forward and rested his head on Akis' lap. Before they pulled past the cove they distanced themselves for the final time.

He heard the shouting first. Then he saw the crowd of people. There was a flurry of activity, much more than he'd ever seen on the beach prior to this morning. Both of their families, all of them in fact, as well as stragglers-on intrigued by the drama. Petzechroula's voice was the loudest, an unneeded flare, a lighthouse in the daylight. None of Haruki's family made a single noise.

Akis slowed his rowing to suggest that it wasn't too late to turn around. Haruki gave a resigned laugh.

He took in his family's abhorrence, shocked to see him arrive by boat after spending the night away from them. It was easier to manage their consternation when the punishment would come later, whilst Akis had barely stepped onto the sand before his aunt was screaming in his face. Akis joined in, as if the other would submit or be willing to take any notice. Haruki wondered whether he was saying anything revealing about their night or if he was defending him and taking the blame.

"Haruki," said his father, pulling his attention.

"It was a surprise storm. We couldn't get back."

"Back? Back from where? Who is he?"

Haruki laughed and turned to his mother. "Go on."

She paused – he braced himself – and she burst into tears. She threw up her hands as if god had answered her.

"My boy," she wailed loudly enough for everyone to hear. "I'm so glad you're alive." Her outburst was like a charged battery that she'd conserved for the summer and expended in one go. She leant in and hugged him, harder than he knew her strength allowed. "You'll never leave my side again," she whispered into his ear.

Haruki went slack in the continued embrace. Even if he wrestled her clutch his fate was sealed. He was stifled in his insanity, his mother's supposed doting faker than the attack to which Akis was being inflicted. At least Petzechroula's emotions were honest.

Across the sand Tyresias and Tassos were attempting to break up the others. Haruki couldn't take it any longer. It was all immaterial. "Stop," he said in Greek. "It's done." He pulled the letter from his pocket, lowered his voice and switched languages. "Grandfather is ill. We have to leave." It was punishment enough for him and Akis after stowing away overnight; their summer had come to an end.

He handed the note to his father who read it and responded with a low groan. His mother just shook her head. Petzechroula listened to Akis' explanation and didn't strike back up.

His parents didn't discuss it, turning straight to logistics. Tassos offered a plan for the quickest route forward: to pack whilst he orchestrated a boat to take them to Gytheio. From there they could call ahead and plan onwards legs of the journey. Haruki watched them, half envious and half dumbfounded, guided by practicalities and all matter-of-fact. His father and Tassos would be gutted but they didn't show it. Maybe that was what it was to be an adult and not swayed by emotions.

"I hate you," Yuki said to him. It was the first time that he'd taken any notice of her. He didn't know why she said it, perhaps sad to hear about their jiji or sad to be leaving her new friends. Maybe she was mad at something else when neither of these things was his fault.

Villagers gossiped as Tyresias guided Petzechroula towards Vatheia, postponing any further altercation with Akis. The woman made a sudden gasp, a look of horror planting itself across her face.

Haruki was remorseful as his mind gave light to the night before. Whilst the other Vatheians had locked their shutters and hunkered down, the two families in the tower house would have been frantic. He wondered if a search party had braced the storm.

Toshihiro left next holding Yuki's hand and consoling her. Tassos wasn't far behind.

Megumi instructed her son up the slope. "I hope your delay hasn't made the difference."

Haruki didn't have the heart to argue. His feet were heavy as he followed.

"Charupi," Akis shouted from behind him.

Haruki turned and saw his desperation. Akis wasn't leaving the beach, at least not in this direction, not on foot.

He didn't know what he could say to make it easier. His throat was dry, his chest constricted. Now he understood the suffering of which his grandfather had spoken. It would have been better if they'd never met. He now not only had to live separated from Akis but would be consumed by the shadow of a new identity that he would never be allowed. Even if he were to accept it, it would be a cloak worn in caves and never in esteemed company.

"Haruki," said his mother.

Haruki, Charupi. Two such different names. In moving out of the tower house he would take with him a single case and a tag affixed to it; whether destined for Tokyo or Estia, he had only the weight allowance for one.

What could she do if he refused? Handcuff him to her? He thought ahead to Japan. Studying something he didn't want to under his parents' watchful eye. Guilt forever pinned on him for neglecting his grandfather. A social life that was approved, and a partner who if not arranged was vetted. A wealth that meant nothing if it meant bringing pleasure to everyone but himself. If it didn't bring–

Eftychia.

Akis thrived. He swam and ate well. He kept away from pollution and commutes and deadlines. There would also be nights like the previous one. That wasn't worth giving up for anything.

"Haruki," his mother said again, without raising her voice.

He could run to Akis and promise him something, anything, but his mother's eyes burnt into him.

He wanted to make a grand gesture. Something to taunt his family and force them to suffer alongside him. He could kiss the boy in front of them. But Akis wasn't a tool, a thing to be used or damaged each time it was handled. He couldn't.

He turned from Akis and walked towards Vatheia.

He continued into the attic and packed. He found the daruma doll behind the bed, its one eye painted in. His wish had long been granted but he hadn't kept his side of the bargain by inking in the other. In making the request he hadn't been specific enough. The warnings of childhood were distant until they happened, 'be careful what you wish for' such trodden ground that it was easy to scramble over it without taking any notice, and by the time this stretch of earth had turned into a quagmire it was too late to circle its core.

Yuki didn't say another word to him. She dropped her poorly-packed bag through the hatch and then she too disappeared from view.

Haruki expected to be called any minute but until then he took fresh paper and wrote fast. He included everything that had happened and how much it pained him. He didn't read it back or make corrections. The grammar was sloppy, the use of language hyperbolic, the description of last night a study of gentleness in place of crudity. A final sentence of loving the boy.

He left it with the bundle of other letters on his pillow, wrapped in the belt from his graduation robe. His parents would be furious but he found the detail liberating within the hideousness of everything else.

He wrote Akis' name on the front. None of the letters was ever meant for Haruki's family. Not even the first one on the flight when he had scribbled out that he didn't want to study what was expected of him. He knew that now. He just hadn't known to whom they were meant until this moment.

He also knew that it was unfair to include his address in Tokyo so that Akis might come to him when the boy wouldn't have the means. It was a taunt that could never be fulfilled, saved by the mercy that if Akis couldn't read the script then it didn't matter.

A boat was organised to pick them up from Vatheia a few hours later. Tassos would stay behind. Haruki hadn't been downstairs to hear who had set this up, fixing himself in the attic and doing everything in his power to finish the letter and stop himself from running back to the bay.

After strained goodbyes he could hardly breathe as he made his way to the beach for the pick up. He wanted to put pause on nearing the top of slope and learning if Akis was still there or long gone, unable to bear seeing him for one last time and unwilling to bring to light the possibility that he already had.

It was only days later on the touchdown into Tokyo that Haruki had a panic attack. He didn't have the vocabulary nor the mental awareness to normalise it, to catastrophise it as anything less than an apoplectic sense of losing his mind. If he wasn't dying then at a minimum he was folding into himself towards an irredeemable level of lunacy.

The air hostess, used to passengers hyperventilating, helped him to regain his breath and settle his nerves. She assumed that he was scared of flying and talked him through safety statistics. He couldn't find the energy to redirect her to what was fuelling his distress so he dialled down her voice. Facts were of less importance when, as Akis suggested, he needed to listen to both his head and his heart.

He knew how much of a mistake he had made. Not just in leaving, that much he would come to terms with, but that he'd carried out the most heinous of acts by bequeathing Akis the letters. It was cruel to goad him, dangling his words out of reach when he couldn't say them directly.

He wasn't religious but, surprisingly, prayer restored him enough to walk off the plane unaided. For the entire taxi ride to Aoyama he prayed silently to a god, he didn't know which, over and over for one thing: that Petzechroula or Tyresias would not only find the letters first but decide it best to throw them on the fire before Akis could learn of them, his pages burnt down and his words choked of life until they were nothing but embers.

The Sound Of One Hand Clapping

Japan, 1971

19

Kuonji Temple, Mount Minobu
2nd January 1971

Green-blue algae discoloured the barrel pond.

The novice monk removed the mesh covering, netted the scum, plucked the browned pads, scrubbed the stained wooden lining. Whether the chore was an act of grooming or one of defiling remained to him a churning anxiety. An unsolvable meditation on the margin between tampering with nature and making way for healthy regeneration. It was the eighth year that he had been resident at the temple but the same worry, another time around.

The lotus roots had yet to find their way through the murky depths and wouldn't break free until the summer, long after the plum blossom and irises had been and gone. The aquatic plant spoke of its affinity to here, to Kuonji, the head temple of the Nichiren Sect with its sacrosanct and eponymous sutra. Like the monk, the lotus flushed with activity first thing, its dew-bursting pop at morning light a canto unto itself, then quietened as the day drew on and closed up on itself in the evenings. And, like the monk, it flourished under its iron gate, locked away and safe from uninterrupting hands.

"Hanei-bouzu."

Hanei. He'd been ordained this dharma name when he took to the monastery but he'd heard it so infrequently that he often forgot that it belonged to him. There wasn't a compulsory vow of silence in his world of reflective clemency and unchanging daily routine but there was little that needed to be aired. Kuonji Temple was as far up a mountain and as set back from the sea as exactly as it was figuratively. There were no ripples let alone crashing tides, his home buffered by a pine forest and not even beset by the temperance of a sheltered bay where waves should only break so often and so loud.

"Hanei?"

He leant the net against the wall and turned to face the abbot. "My apologies, Tenryu-shinpai."

Kougetsu Tenryu had rarely spoken to Hanei since his ordinance. Their most recent conversation had been over a year ago but the abbot's voice was as commanding as it was mild-mannered and Hanei knew to follow him to his office.

Of all the buildings this was his least favourite. Anywhere within his reach, from the butsudo to the sutra repository, was preferable, each place aiding his purpose in honouring and manifesting the life-state of the Buddha. The office was an administrative hub and only brought home the disappointment that business affairs lay at the heart of the sanctuary.

He looked past Tenryu to the bookshelf. The contents were far removed from those in other offices he'd known but the accumulation shunted his mind to a path he'd once been expected to follow.

Tenryu perfected a neutral expression. It wasn't obvious what this meeting should concern. Hanei–

Hanei. He struggled to think of himself by that name, although in an almost soundless monastery the predicament was mostly side-stepped. He scoured the recent past. He'd done nothing punishable to see him excommunicated but he sat uneasy. Spiritual leaders had a knack of detecting, and admonishing, unseen matters of the soul.

It was rare for the two of them to convene away from ceremony. The frequency of Tenryu's counsel had diminished as the decade drew to a close. At the beginning there had been initiation and instruction but it was now unremarkable for seasons to pass without any communication. At first Hanei had been eager to sit with Tenryu, to have his flailing mind and adrenaline-stricken body reined in. To be apprised and refocused on abiding by the tenets, and fed koans designed specifically for him. He and the other newcomers were free to share these mental conundrums but were reminded of the rules: a koan applied only to its recipient, that it was not meant to be reduced to a root answer but instead mulled over, and that another person's input was a distraction that could weaken its power. A soft rubbing where there should be friction.

Koans revealed their complexity like budding leaves, none an endpoint but each an addition to a thing of beauty. When Hanei thought that a layer was exhausted more petals would grow. He'd been a top-notch student at school, quick to grasp ideas and found it undemanding to regurgitate facts in exams. Here he had struggled without tangible data. Instead of giving up on his personalised riddles he sat in the zendo meditation hall longer than anyone, chanted louder, reflected more. He embraced monastic living and took it upon himself to be responsible for the upkeep of water features around the complex. And yet he was aggravated by the relentless, floundering search for Nirvana. His microcosm of existence should have been serene but instead left him on the verge of collapse. He knew that he was trying overly hard to rush enlightenment and yet it was too terrifying a prospect to stop; he couldn't allow the possibility that this wasn't where he could find it to catch up to him. On the cusp of his third year, chaotic energy had eaten away at not only him but those around him. Tenryu had then sat him down but instead of reassurance had thrown him a new koan: What is a drainpipe when fed a deluge?

Hanei had tried less after that, embracing rather than rushing what came next, resigned to the safety of now. Each passing day in which no one disturbed him became a blessed state of being.

Tenryu broke their silence. "How are you, Hanei?"

"Perfectly fine, thank you."

"I appreciate you cleaning the barrels."

"I like to think that I'm tending to them."

Tenryu paused long enough for Hanei to question himself. Early on, second-guessing had consumed him to the point of inertia. Everything in a temple smacked of a test. He'd caved and asked if this was true. There are no tests except faith, a senior monk had replied, but that too landed like something meant to trip him up.

"Tending to them. Right you are," the abbot continued. "I wanted us to speak about your permanent designation."

Hanei replicated Tenryu's solemn expression.

"Are you surprised?"

Nothing came as a surprise in a monastery. The confines were narrow enough – prayers, chores, contemplation, insight, reflexion, death – that every possibility was matter-of-course.

"I anticipated it but did not expect it," Hanei answered.

Like the given name, he barely recognised his own voice. The same was true when standing in front of a mirror. Twenty-five, no longer a child and yet stunted from adulthood. A vacuous personality carved in the absence of non-religious pursuits. Eight years in which he'd clung to cloistered living, having left behind a messy world that he'd swapped for a frugal one. But it was impossible to fully shirk the past. Nightmares returned despite trying to banish them. Like the lotus flower, every time he thought that he'd broken through he would wither and have to start again. Roots might be concealed but they could not be hacked away in their entirety.

Every other recruit that had arrived around the same time as him had either returned to a lay life or been promoted into the temple as a permanent fixture. It was unbecoming to ask when would be his turn but it had been a wait far longer than expected. In his sixth year, Hanei had cornered the abbot. What am I doing wrong? he'd begged. Predictably Tenryu had replied with another riddle: What is the wanting of a migrating bird? Hanei felt his anger rise. He'd wanted to reply with something facetious, pseudo-Zen: Shitting is the act of a bear in the woods, perhaps. Instead, he stepped away, noticing, observing and delineating his body until he had mastered patience.

Others suggested to him through furtive conversations that they'd been ordained only after meeting the satisfaction of head monks. He didn't know what that meant. He started giving his elders palpable nods and tips of his head as if he possessed newly-acquired wisdom. Then he'd made less-than-subtle murmurs of enlightenment when in their vicinity. It was all ignored.

He tried a range of other tactics. He avoided all contact. He worked hard. Slacked off. Chanted loud and fast. Other times he became so introverted that the dedication to the mystical law barely formed on his lips. *Namu myoho renge kyo.* How could his inherent Buddha nature shine through when he was being held back? Then he kept to himself, heels dug into a state of both waiting and not waiting. Wanting and not wanting. He found genuine acceptance. Finally, with his suffering embraced, petted like a cherished dog, the recent years had passed in pleasant rotation.

And now he was being tantalised with the next step that should seal his future. He calmed his body and brought down his heart rate. Discounting the anxiety that followed the exit of a nightmare, the last time he'd experienced a panic attack had been in Tokyo on the night before high-tailing it here.

"Tell me what is passing through your mind."

"Whether to be honest or not," Hanei said, vying for a stance of cryptic ambivalence, guessing that it would be looked on favourably like some sort of contemplative worthiness. The truth fell out of him anyway. "That to be ordained is to be validated. And to continue to wait is as good as being rejected."

"It is not pass or fail. You will not be thrown out. It just means there is more work to be done."

Hanei wanted to believe that the sect was sincere but cynicism crept in like unwanted knotweed. Where the mulberry there too the bracken. The draw of the city and business opportunities had meant a deficit year on year and a quicker retreat of newcomers. He had proven himself to be an excellent follower, exemplary of persistence and dedication to the cause. As long as he was suppressed he was a lackey. The promise of permanency had been dangled in front of him for so long that he questioned whether he was complicit in enabling it.

What difference? He'd made a pledge to devote his life here, so to stay in one guise or another was inconsequential.

"Would you like to be decreed?" Tenryu asked.

Hanei thought it pointless to argue his case. His preparedness was no one's decision but Tenryu's. "Of course."

"First a task."

Unless carried out on the sly, Hanei hadn't heard of anyone else expected to prove himself with a mission. He had thought ordainment simply a metaphysical readiness, irrespective of time or markable attainments. There should be no extra trials of faith nor endurance. No implemented hoops to jump.

"Climb to the peak of Minobu-san tomorrow."

Hanei's chest tightened. "To the top?"

"You cannot?"

"I can but—"

It would be cold but enough layers would see him to the summit. In all the time here, despite living partway up the mountain, he hadn't seen an altitude higher than the temple. He had only left to the village at the base of the compound a handful of times. Close but where panic still bred.

"Why?" Tenryu pre-empted. "To look out to the sky and give me the answer to a new koan."

Hanei stopped himself from replying that koans were not supposed to hold an answer, especially not to be solved in the space of a three hour hike. In the beginning, gratified and indulged to have received his own, he'd loved the puzzles. He'd lost himself in them. They infiltrated his dreams. Tokyoites could hear of them, could visit a temple or squeeze in a burst of mindfulness on the bookends of a workday, but no one else had the privilege of unfurling a koan as his day's sole pursuit.

Now he hated them. They plagued him. They had no end-point and yet he was expected to give the answer to a new one by the time he'd scaled a mountain. He didn't share his consternation with Tenryu who he assumed was enjoying it far more than he should. Who could argue that monks didn't have a sense of humour?

"What is it?" Hanei asked, alluding to his agreement of the endeavour.

"Is an open door an invitation?"

"Is an open door an invitation," Hanei repeated.

"When you have considered this return to me."

"And?"

Tenryu glanced at him from his paperwork, surprised to be asked; in his mind the conversation had already ended.

"Wrap up. This isn't a punitive exercise. Agreed?"

It was authentic when pursuing Buddhahood to observe one's emotions. Hanei noted rising unfairness, considering that he'd worked harder than anyone. His limbs tingled with a creeping paranoia that tomorrow would be mired in cruelty, that somehow he was being played. After his mother's manipulation and his father's connivance of her scheme, Hanei had fled here to escape being masterminded. He'd turned to the temple because Buddhism not only equalled safety but transparency. Or so he'd assumed.

So to argue that Tenryu's demand wasn't punitive felt at odds with the effort it would take but, already halfway out the door, he didn't feel able to say that he did in fact disagree.

20

Mount Minobu
3rd January 1971

He would start at the bottom. To descend before ascending was an oddity that he didn't want to read into it, the day already set to be encumbered with enough reflection than to heap on extra analysis before he'd begun. Going down to then head up was just a logistical ramification for his starting point. Not everything had to have meaning.

This he desperately wanted to believe.

During those autumn months in Tokyo, sandwiched between there and here, he'd been sincere in wanting to pursue psychology. He'd believed that a discipline chosen by him was enough of a punishment for his parents. Taunting them was a measly consolation but all the same he'd borrowed books about inference and unconscious processes and projection and flicked through the works by Freud and other western thinkers in front of his mother. *Sometimes a cigar is just a penis* someone had inked into the margin of the library's *The Interpretation of Dreams* but it was only a year later when the line returned to him and he understood the joke. Chuckles happened around the temple complex at unsuspecting times, a monk tickled by something, but it was the first time that he'd laughed outright since—

It was three a.m. and pitch black. The forest was asleep. He was used to finding his way around the temple without light even if he wouldn't typically wake for another hour for the alms-giving. That was still a while before the sun crept over the mountain slopes and flooded his valley. He'd embraced this early rise before any other feature of temple life, vitalised by the ceremonial drums that broke in the day better than any alarm clock, and ahead enough from the rest of the country to feel like a different time zone. He'd been comforted by the impression of being abroad.

He walked the back passage from the temple on a downward slope to the village and passed a guest-house. Pilgrims would wake shortly and make their way to the main hall where their gaunt bodies would be ravaged by the taiko reverberations. A self-professed higher experience made possible by their drowsiness, their enchantment perpetuated by the circling of the monks as they recited the gongyo. Hanei would miss this morning's ritual. He muttered the Odaimoku incantation – *Namu myoho renge kyo* – it wasn't its purpose but it helped ground him to now, staving off memories of the past.

It was unsettling to walk Minobu at this time, he a wandering ghost whose sheets only served to beckon the cold whilst others were sandwiched in between theirs. He hoped that the effort of the ascent would thaw him, countering the cooler air higher up.

The bodaitei stairwell of enlightenment cut through the forest, stretching from the village to the temple. It was a tourist attraction in itself, dewy and mossy and a purifying incision between the subpar and the sublime. Despite it being the gateway to the sanctuary, Hanei had rarely climbed it, not needing to, his efforts centred on chanting and gardening within Kuonji's grounds.

He loitered under the imposing gate ahead of the stairs. The sanmon was one of the Three Greats of Japan and another reason he had come here. If he was going to lose himself to Buddhism then he had to commit, which meant the grander the better.

He craned his neck to take in the scale of the staircase that necessitated seven landings. He didn't feel betrayed by his body's apprehension. He'd bounded up a typical 108 steps in his childhood but anyone at any age struggled with these 287. Their magnitude was the other reason that he'd stolen away eight years ago to this particular site. Two trains, a series of buses and a hike later and then this feat. The stairs wouldn't deter people from looking for him but it was symbolic of not wanting to make it easy. In thrifty research the discovery of this long stairwell had sealed his choice. He'd had no other requirements when seeking a hideaway. He hadn't ruled out any religious observations nor specific sects. It just had to be remote and devout. Physically and emotionally severing. He was again satisfied by its approach, from its base off-putting and from its top containing; with an adolescent appetite for the dramatic, poetic motion had seemed a worthy deterrent.

He'd known little about the Nichiren branch other than the Lotus Sutra. He hadn't needed to. He assimilated quickly – *Namu myoho renge kyo* fast tattooed on his mind – and came to understand that it was better he'd arrived open-minded; when others turned up with ideals of what they wanted from the experience the older monks were put-off, preferring a blank not-yet-hardened slate.

He'd since recited the sutra countless times that it now revved on autoplay. The pursuit was supposed to attune his search for enlightenment but happened so automatically that it served as good a purpose in distracting him. Whenever old memories snuck through, the mantra was the faithful hammer and nails that could block up any window until no light pervaded. Tenryu's request of introversion was a forcible torch in a blacked-out room. Hanei had dreaded the time when his mind would betray him, bypassing the chant and turning to the past. Today it seemed.

He yawned. He'd barely slept, too busy fighting off the past to feel relaxed enough to close his eyes. His history had become a static, scratched cassette whose contents no longer resembled the letters stuck onto its label. The original tape had been stamped over by incessant beatings, if not fully erased then at least pillaged to the point of corruption. But every so often something was recovered. Now, for example, as the arched gate above him blended into the theatre on the Acropolis. It tormented him that Greece continued to loom heavy. He couldn't remember the name of the place nor anything about the play. He remembered that there was a man who served importance but he couldn't picture his face. There was something else about that night – *Namu myoho renge kyo* – it was gone.

The past swept his feet from underneath him and he had to lean against one of the gate's pillars to compose himself. He chanted under controlled breath and drove himself back from the cusp of hyperventilation until Greece was a non-thing once more. Refastened to the present, he attended to the beginning of his climb and the more immediate choice of which of the gate's three entrances to step under. Passing through meant leaving behind one of three vices: greed, anger or idiocy.

Day one, Tenryu had stood in this exact spot as if waiting for Hanei like a boatman on the River Styx, although unlike with death there was a way back even if he hadn't believed it at the time. Tenryu had asked him to choose a gate before he had even slung the bag off his shoulder. Whether a test or not, it was a fortunate read of a dropped leaflet on the way here that mentioned the three afflictions, and so he'd been able to fake some preparation rather than just the pensive turning up of a lost soul. Anger, he'd declared. What else? The word barely covered it, swallowed like a dormant volcano concealing a bubbling mess of internalised hatred. Fury had driven him here. He'd had to rid himself of it for the sake of his sanity since forgiveness hadn't worked.

This second time he chose to rescind greed. What he really wanted was to bypass the climb and for Tenryu to give him an answer. But without this as an option he had to work for it. Any revelation about the koan had to be self-attained.

He paced himself as he climbed from one step to the next. He stopped to catch his breath at each platform. Crabs scuttled between cracks in the stairwell. Within view a troop of monkeys played among the trees. Bears were said to roam higher up though he'd never heard of a sighting. Strolling into a predator's den was an open invitation to be its dinner. He considered presenting that to Tenryu and returning to bed.

Back at the temple, briefly, he carried past the weeping cherry trees, the pagoda and Nichiren's mausoleum, relieved not to meet anyone as he crossed the courtyard. He bypassed the rope-way where visitors would later be transported to the summit with views across to Fuji. There they could claim a pressed coin at the souvenir shop or thaw themselves with cans of vending machine coffee.

As he went on, circling dilapidated graveyards and towering red pines, ignoring warning signs of the bear bells to be sounded in emergencies, he set his mind on the koan. It was too basic to conclude that an open door was an invitation if the sole intention was for someone to enter. What was beyond the door also mattered. If nothing, and if there was little harm, then was someone simply free to come and go? Invasion hardly mattered when there was nothing that could be corrupted. But without consent a thing that appeared available was still not. Then again, he'd first crossed to Kuonji without being asked in even if the invitation had been implicit. Anyone was free to see what monastic living was for themselves if willing to leave certain pleasures behind.

What of those foregone things? He felt a rush of adrenaline in considering this. It was always a breakthrough when a koan was dissected and found to hold multiple dimensions. Often what was not being asked was where he needed to set his sights.

So, crossing through an open door was also leaving somewhere behind. Hanei knew that all too well. He wasn't surprised that the koan had guided him to the past. Tenryu knew enough to lead him this way; he was certain that the abbot and his parents had been in contact in the intervening years.

The air turned thinner. The cold sharpened into a blade against his face. Sweat trapped against his body and made him shiver. In his head a reel of film kickstarted but it caught, the frame stuck in place. A snapshot of a boy wrapped in a blanket. And Hanei himself, unencumbered and naked, emerging from the sea.

He pulled his cloak tighter and held the hood over his shaved head. The farther up he went, the idea that there was a sanctuary beneath him became a veiled promise. His fingers tingled. He put it down to the cold although it mirrored a symptom of panic. He had institutionalised himself here for a third of his life, skipping out on things expected in early adulthood. He'd been asked to obey the ten precepts, non-negotiable if he were to stay. Most were easy enough. No swearing, dancing, eating late, dressing up, stealing, earning money, sleeping on a plush bed, killing living creatures, or taking drugs. The tenth, no sexual activity, was what had convinced him to seek out a temple when considering all of his options. He'd needed a reason to remain abstinent. Long enough without touch and his fantasies might subside. He hadn't masturbated since arriving. The idea of it now seemed as foreign as the rest of the world beyond the mountain.

He had closed the door to sex.

Before that he'd had intercourse. Once. Intentional, invited. An olive grove. No. A bay, a storm, a haven, where he had acted on instinct alone.

Memories leapt at him from behind the trees. He blushed but the frost hid his shame. He was surprised to feel blood flowing to his penis. He wanted to return to the temple and neuter himself. In the impossibility of that he sped up, tripping over roots that protruded above the sloping ground.

Few people trekked the mountain. No paths were laid except for sporadically-painted dashes on trees intimating that he was going in the right direction. The altitude was the only real benchmark that he was advancing but he was already spent. Why bother continuing when there was so much pain attached? Another recollection: pilgrims crawling on hands and feet, though the name of the island escaped him. He was encouraged by this pull of lethargy, that to reach the top would be his penance.

His posture had been long trained to suit mindful passivity. The first weeks in Kuonji of sitting cross-legged until he could put heels on top of shins, holding that stance whilst in quiet contemplation, had been painful. Nowadays it didn't hurt. Tenryu rarely guided him via direct instructions but he'd advised him to observe the suffering as it slipped away. Now he could hold the pose for as long as required, outlasting non-resident guests who shuffled and squirmed on tatami, inexperienced with extended sitting and distracted by the golden ornaments or sneaking photos of the painted mural of the dragon occupying the roof.

The slog of the climb awoke muscles that had been in a near decade-long slumber. He remembered building a house, his body flushed with dopamine from the lauded exertion. He picked up the pace and chanted, banishing his recollection to the world below.

The summit held off for another hour. It was anticlimactic to arrive without a definite answer, ruining the panorama of the clouds that raced across the valley beneath him, crashing into the mountain ranges like a sea with vengeance. He had no money to buy something that would warm him. A prayer house no bigger than a shed was filled with hanging pillars of origami birds, their wings and beaks clipped by the elements. There was nothing to indicate who had delivered them nor for whom they'd been made. He assumed that his sister had outgrown them.

He hadn't thought much about her for years, a game he played that he only eventually lost. Accidental reminders that brought faces rushing back were swiftly blocked out again. It was something that he'd adopted during Russian classes, paired with another student and each given a board with distinct faces. They'd had to question one another about descriptive features until they could eliminate the suspects down to one. The idea remained. The cast list of Hanei's own life was mostly knocked down but, confronted by the cranes, Yuki's face remained propped up. She was what, eighteen? He couldn't believe it. He'd skipped so many birthdays and events. He himself would be holding a degree had he stayed. Waseda had offered him an unconditional place but he'd been unable to square off the discord that since his parents had encouraged his new discipline they would have won if he'd attended.

His mother never accepted responsibility for the family's abrupt return to Japan. Rika, who claimed it had been a misguided over-reaction, was fired, only to be re-employed a few months later. For reasons of forgiveness. Too indispensable to let go of. Hanei assumed that she'd been remunerated in her unemployment. The day that she returned was the day he left. It was his punishment to his mother: she could only have one of them. Losing him was a fair trade for him losing accreditation to a university that only wanted him because of his family name. What did it mean if it was insincere? It had been the door to an invitation that he'd held with no regard.

Was Kuonji the same?

His heart sank as the truth dawned on him, inescapable this high up, with the sun bearing down, no longer buffered by the valley beneath it.

A figure appeared in front of him. It was like a conjuring for the abbot to approach from the funicular at this opportune moment. Tenryu didn't have to climb the mountain to reach the peak.

"Hanei-bouzu." Tenryu gave a sympathetic smile. "I see. You've arrived."

Hanei knew that he wasn't referring to Minobu's summit. Reaching a satisfactory endpoint of a koan was less about an answer and more about a look. A new state.

"When you're ready we can return together. I have a ticket for you. There's no need to trek down."

"We both know that I'm not coming back."

"You're welcome here for as long as you require it, Hanei."

"Haruki." He settled into his name like a pair of old boots that still fit him but had slumped.

"Then let us depart, Haruki."

His days in the monastery were over just like that. But instead of descending he wanted to sit and let the freeze consume him. It would be the least cruel option for what came next.

"If I may," Tenryu said. "Your mother told me that you came here after an upsetting time in Greece."

Haruki had been convinced, and now had confirmation, that she'd visited. Most likely in the months after he'd had a pang of conscience and wrote to tell them where he was, that he was safe but also to let him be. As with any monk he was welcome to greet family or to travel home if requested but he'd never wanted to. For months he'd looked away from visitors during dawn ceremonies. He'd also requested to refrain from handing out the talismans that offered safe protection until he felt certain that his family wouldn't be among the congregants.

He wondered what his mother had said to Tenryu apart from not assigning herself blame.

"May I share a story from a colleague?" Tenryu asked. "Another monk who once visited Greece and heard a parable. There are so many things outside of Buddhism that can point us inside. Unless you already know it. The tale of the Prophet Elias?"

Haruki scanned the board of faces but if he'd heard of him it had been long forgotten. He shook his head. He was surprisingly impervious to the cold, though it would soon be unbearable to remain up here. Eight years of committing himself to a life of accepting suffering had come to a head.

"The man was involved in a disaster at sea. He survived but the trauma engulfed him and he couldn't face the water. He took an oar and began to climb. Do you know what this is? he asked the first of the villagers some way up the mountain. Yes, it's an oar, came the reply. He carried on until he crossed paths with a goatherd and asked again. The stranger also recognised the item. Elias continued his ascent and only stopped, ready to build a new life for himself, when the oar was unrecognisable."

"There's safety in fleeing," Haruki answered.

"And a life un-lived. For a man of the sea."

"Was. He was a man of the sea."

"So what is he now?"

Haruki sighed. He'd already come to the same conclusion. An open door could be an invitation inside, away from somewhere else, but this was no longer his space to occupy. He'd succeeded in suppressing his desires but staying would no longer suffice. He pictured the prophet dreading a return to the sea. Shying away from it meant a deprived life. Haruki had already given up eight years.

A series of memories hit in quick succession. His grandfather's studies of animals. Haruki subbed himself in as a wounded animal holding a submissive, freeze position. He wondered if his jiji was alive. For the first time in years he wanted to find out. Then he remembered the book his father had given him. Coincidentally, an Englishman had arrived at the monastery only a few weeks ago with a copy. Haruki had snuck a glance and learnt the translated title, *The Sound of Waves*. The man also told him that on November 25, not even two months earlier, Yukio Mishima had killed himself.

Haruki welled up at the image of two further places that came to mind: his grandfather's residence and Estia. He missed the sea. This was no life without the backdrop of the pealing tide.

He couldn't allow himself to expect too much. Even if he reclaimed his board of faces there was a section that he refused to lift into position. He had turned his back on that part for good. He could never return there.

Resigned to move on, but not knowing where he'd be by nightfall, only that it would be somewhere that wasn't here, he accompanied Tenryu to the temple. He filled the barrel pond with fresh water, gave a last look at the other patches that he'd cultivated, and then, finally, he collected his belongings. These included a pair of shoes that he'd outgrown. Tight and restrictive, he put them on anyway. Both of his big toes stubbed with each step but the pain was not enough to stop him from marching forward.

In A City Of High-Rises

Greece / Japan, 1980

21

Athens
21ˢᵗ October 1980

Apostolis locks the dealership from inside and turns off the light. This is what he has waited for, the singular instance that he cherishes each day. In the dark, before his eyes adjust to the glow of the streetlamp beyond the musty window display, and when the dust disappears from sight and the smell of imported books permeates the air. For a crowning minute he is in no man's land. A non-place between Greece and Japan. Every day he looks forward to this moment when he doesn't exist. If only he could bottle the serenity. It would reach a far higher price than any of the artworks.

The moment passes. He moves to the desk and cashes up again but a day of no sales means no need to recalculate yesterday's sums. He isn't ready to leave but he's expended every other way to drag out the time. There are no remaining tasks, arduous or otherwise. He leans back. Only relics are welcomed into the shop and this seat is no exception. It's a former barber chair, travelled across both great oceans. As befits the shop, it creaks.

"Apostolis-kun?"

He steps into the back office where the decrepit owner of the fool-proof named shop, *Asiatikes Antikes*, is hunched over a slanted desk. A lamp hones in on a row of wooden blocks. Each carving is a different part of a whole print, each stained with a single bold colour. Shavings line the floor. Though the Japanese man leans into the work, his eyes are so bad that thick glasses and dazzling light cannot make up for inaccuracies and no two carvings skew together. Each completed print is a blur of overlapping lines. But, rather than a joke, this defect has resulted in accidental, runaway success. The prints have become collectible for lovers of woodblock art and abstract expressionism, a reinstatement of a lost movement brought forward two centuries. It has unexpectedly funded the business better than any treasures imported from the east and displayed out front. Kenjiro Hasegawa is unaware of why the European market has accredited him a hero. Apostolis only feeds back that he has been deemed talented, creating worthy homages to Hokusai and the other ukiyo-e artists. He would never let him catch wind of the truth. The man wouldn't be proud of the art he has made nor the amount of money it has drawn in. His business has never been about profit.

"Konbanwa, Shachou. Sorry for disturbing you," Apostolis says in perfect Japanese. His accent is exemplary. His speech is second nature, long past having to dredge up words or stumbling over formality. It's not proven but it's likely that for a non-native speaker he's unsurpassed across all of Greece.

"Are you finished?"

"I'm just tidying up. Anything I can do before I go?"

"Actually yes. Unless you're in a rush?" Hasegawa laughs as much as his body allows. He's as old as some of the items here, shrivelled up, his lungs victim to the air that's stagnant from preserving chemicals. He knows after sixteen years of employment that Apostolis is never hurrying off. The boy has always waited to be dismissed. It's very un-Greek and a primary reason for taking him on as his adjunct.

Outside, to Apostolis, autumn is a continuation of summer, just drabber. With nothing to occupy him, the hours will meander with lassitude until tomorrow's opening. He loiters by the door intrigued. Usually he's ushered out of the shop after fetching a glass of whisky for Hasegawa. When his boss is in the fever of creation Apostolis leaves him be, so much so that nearly every aspect of the shop is now at his discretion. Hasegawa is only concerned with the ongoing provenance of each sale; considering that he goes nowhere and has no one to leave an inheritance to, the prices couldn't much matter to him after covering rent and his assistant's salary.

Hasegawa puts down the carving knife. "How was today?"

"There were a few enquiries. The freight company assures me that they will deliver tomorrow."

The Japanese flows without any hesitation. Long gone are the painful days after arriving to Athens and sourcing a Greek-English dictionary along with a second harder-to-come-by English-Japanese version. Gruelling hours lost in multiple binds. Now there is nothing left of stumbling over gaps in his vocabulary. Gone are the years of wanting to forego the entire endeavour when everything ground in his head with pained and clunky translations. He has learnt from his senior not only a language but honorific levels within it.

Hasegawa swats away the information about logistics. He trusts Apostolis' management of the business and has no interest in technicalities. "And how about tonight? I hear there's a new brothel in Metaxourgeio."

Apostolis blushes, which his boss delights in. It didn't take much time before Hasegawa began to throw smut into the conversation. Despite reddening and being unsure how to respond, Apostolis feels proud for being so proficient as to follow the levels of politeness despite the man's vulgarity. Japanese mastery requires the grace of a bird that can navigate the elevations of a mountain range. But the truth is that he has frequented the whorehouses, although the money spent on convincing himself that it could be enjoyable was wasted, especially when his thoughts were turned towards the other men that passed him in the doorways.

He says nothing and Hasegawa continues. "Reject the prostitutes for an infirm man then. You know what they say about climbing Fuji: a wise man goes to the summit once, a fool does it twice. Either it's an honour or you're just a baka. Baka. Vlaka. Ela, malaka. Wonderful how they rhyme. Since you're not going anywhere can you sit for a while? I want to talk to you about something, Apostolis-kun."

Apostolis is thirty-six. He's dressed in stiff clothes fit for a second-hand book dealer and yet his heart soars when the childlike suffix is attached to his name. He has long believed that Hasegawa uses it so as to not advance both their ages.

They are bonded in the way that a professor moulds a student or a bank-roller keeps a geisha. More than that. They eat breakfast and lunch together. Apostolis has even sacrificed an evening meal for an earlier hearty one, an insult to his heritage but in line with the reduced appetite and distaste of the aged for sleeping on a heavy stomach. Rarely do they eat outside. Hasegawa has no predilection towards western cuisine, struggling to even call it that. The few Asian restaurants in the city are an abomination and so it's a luxury but Hasegawa orders a steady stream of non-perishables from Japan. Fresh products would spoil so the dishes are never accordingly quite right but they're better than nothing. Apostolis wouldn't know and likes them well enough as they are. Cooking together pulls focus from their work but keeps them in safe territory. Food is a moratorium that benefits them equally for neither has shared what makes them miserable. A man who remains in his city but speaks a foreign language is clearly holding back from something as is a man who deals in his native products and pines for his country and yet refuses to return.

Apostolis pulls up a chair, now worried about Hasegawa's stern expression. He's almost certain that this is a secure job. It's not like there's a plethora of trilingual speakers banging at the door. But he doesn't know what he'd do if he were to be let go. Just seeing kanji on book spines sends his stomach aflutter. How he can look at something this beautiful every day seems more and more like a blessing than an occupation. To forfeit staring at the characters would be disastrous. He won't give up this shop without a fight. He's about to argue his case when Hasegawa cuts in.

"Don't look so glib. You're more precious to me than any treasure. But I don't deny that you're wasted on an old man's asinine pursuit of bridging the art world."

Apostolis remembers something his aunt used to tell him in church about him being precious. It's amazing how the word spoken in a different language can open the same doorway to the past. He knows all too well that there is never complete escape from retreading what has been. He lives in perpetually frozen time. Unable to look back and unwilling to step forward. He already yearns for the moment at the end of tomorrow, between the here and there, in neither Greece nor Japan. As content as he can imagine himself being.

"I wouldn't want you to leave," Hasegawa says, trailing off like it's an unfinished thought. There's something teasing in his voice.

Apostolis wants to scuttle away and leave it at that but he wouldn't be so impolite. "I'm happy here."

"Do you believe that absence makes the heart grow fonder?"

"I suppose so." It's an idiom utilised in all three languages that he can speak so he assumes that there's a universal truth to it.

"Good. Because I need you to go to Japan for me."

The order comes so sharply that Apostolis is winded. He's glad to be sitting. There have been many conversations about this but always laced in the potency of some unqualified future time and swerved like inclement weather ridden out. This time he senses that Hasegawa has planted him in the eye of the storm.

He settles his gaze on the half-finished sheet in front of his boss. So far it's coated in three layers so that Fuji is snow-capped with a black outline and surrounded by blue and green nature. When red and pink are added it will warm the sky, bring blossom to the trees and shunt the scene forward a season. His throat seizes at the idea of being transported onto the page.

"You're fluent and yet you've always fought off going."

Apostolis finds his voice. "I'm useful here."

"It's not a pleasantry. I require it. I don't trust anyone else with this job. There's something I need brought here and it's too valuable to leave to a courier. Besides, I would like to hear if you think we've done justice to the food. Given my condition, call it stubbornness or imbecility, I wouldn't mind being tormented with an update on my homeland."

Apostolis doesn't move to accede, unwilling to buckle that easily. He thought that he could hold out until the man's death.

"I will pay for the entire thing of course. And I won't torture you by dragging it out, so just under a week should do. One day for the transaction and a second for anything that may go wrong. Plus a couple of days to explore."

"If you need me here then I can make it a long weekend."

"Too late for shirking." Hasegawa pulls out an envelope from a drawer. "I've made you an itinerary and booked a hotel. Apostolis-kun, this isn't a punishment. It's a long-deserved bonus. The flights are paid for so you can't say no."

"I won't be able to pay you back."

"You're supposed to be deferential. Bow and thank me."

"Thank you but—"

"I underpay you here. An all-expenses trip doesn't come close to how much you're owed in lost wages. Don't forget it's also doing me a favour. This piece is worth a lot more."

Apostolis reads the information on the boarding pass. First class. He's never flown before. But it's a forgotten detail when his eyes scan to the departure date that's set for tomorrow. Hasegawa has given him no time to back out.

He wants to refuse, to say it's unfair, but the lateness of the delivery has been on purpose. Hasegawa has no idea of his initial involvement with the Japanese language. Maybe he should disclose his apprehension. Impossible; Hasegawa would just laugh until he wet himself.

In that case. He'll fly in, make the deal, keep his head down and leave. There isn't a reason why it has to be any more complicated. He's doubled in age since that summer. It's implausible that he should cross paths with the Okazaki family. Tokyo has only grown.

He bows deeply. "I will try my best."

"Ganbatte kudasai. Autumn is cooler there so take a jacket. And don't worry about me. I have all the company I need." He picks up the terracotta paint. "Now let an old man be."

Apostolis has never been so dismayed to step out of the shop. His mind turns to packing and then his plants. It might be October but the heat is still clinging on. Despite the browning of the trees it's warm enough to kill off the only things outside of the shop that he's given a piece of his heart to. He could let them suffer. They'd probably get by. His pride shouldn't be their downfall.

He telephones Tassos. He doesn't want to but his cousin is the only person that he can rely on at the last minute.

He arrives soon after the call. They greet each other as estranged families are prone to, with awkward embraces because of convention. Bonded but not close.

"I have to go out of the city for a week." He keeps it vague. "Can you water the plants for me?"

"Of course, Aki– Sorry, Apostolis."

He hands him a set of keys. He will ask for them back. "I have to pack now."

Tassos stands firm. "My father is selling the tower house. It's too difficult there on his own."

Apostolis' stomach is gutted. Crushed like corn being shelled under a donkey mill. It has been so long since he was there that he has no right to share the emotion but a final letting go of Vatheia hits him hard. He doesn't ask but assumes that, even within the practicalities of tower house living, Tyresias' difficulty is emotional rather than concerning the physical upkeep.

"Where to?" he forces himself to ask even though he wants the conversation over.

"Maybe Areopoli. He doesn't know anything beyond Mani."

"We've both made Athens work."

Tassos' glare suggests that they both know that's not quite true. "I'll let you know the address. Or you might want to go before–"

"I'll come when you're ready to tell me about my parents."

It's a stubborn line that he's persevered to not cross for years. He still feels justified even if it's hard to conjure the same level of anger. To be told time and time again that his heritage is out of bounds is both confusing and a betrayal from which he can't move past.

Tassos sighs at the stalemate. Not even Petzechroula's deathbed was enough to reunite them. She died loyal to her brother, to Apostolis' grandfather, despite the hurt she caused the boy. Knowingly, she'd dictated a letter for Tassos to give to him, to seek forgiveness and to apologise. To explain that their fall-out was her penance for earlier undisclosed sins. It hadn't sufficed.

"A drink?" Apostolis manages to say, but his tone is so unpleasant that even he recoils. He won't ask Tassos to leave but it's a polite, superficial level of filotimo. The family has a warped version of what honour and duty means.

"Safe travels, Aki."

22

Tokyo
24th October 1980

Apostolis misses all of the perks of first class. He has no appetite nor is he able to sleep when no headrest is plush enough for his tense body. The pick-up from Narita further reminds him that there have been no expenses spared. This thing that he's due to bring back must be beyond valuable. Saying that, he's been given a converted wad of money equalling just 30,000 drachmas, more affordable than the mission would suggest. Apostolis has scrutinised the itinerary and only Suzuki, the business partner he's due to meet, is named. There's no hint of what he will bring back after the exchange. He can't fathom why Hasegawa has been so closely guarded. His boss has never been shy of egging on conspiracy theories about frauds across the art world but there's been no suggestion that someone might intervene and undercut him.

There are two days to kill until his curiosity is satisfied.

It disorients him to speak Japanese with others beyond Hasegawa and a select group of middle-men at the end of a telephone, as if his acquired language is only now proven to be real, not just a fantastical set of words in a tight-knit industry. One word has always tripped him up however: 'Do' does not mean sand as he was once taught but rather soil or the ground. He's often considered that Hasegawa too threw falsities at him for ease of communication but his teacher has proven himself to be excellent because he is complimented by the taxi driver and then by the hotel receptionist in Nakameguro, with the name Fukuda on his badge, who starts in broken English only for his relief to fall away at Apostolis' proficiency in his mother tongue. Fukuda is also the concierge and can't do enough for him. Apostolis doesn't know how to respond to being fawned over and retreats upstairs.

His room overlooks a man-made tributary, ugly like an open sewer. He assumes that the city can't be plighted with mosquitoes to the same extent as Athens. Bare cherry blossoms loom over the water, their branches reaching out like spindly fingers that almost meet halfway. One tree is a dead stump cracked clean down the middle, the victim of a lightning strike. Hasegawa wanted him to see the city in spring as the buds took to life so Apostolis wonders why the rush. Perhaps there's a serious reason. His boss hasn't disclosed illness, nor his actual age, but he is certainly far older than anyone Apostolis has known.

He's worn out, less by the flight and more from the drive through the metropolis with its sprawling suburb after suburb that has engulfed him. He's no longer anxious about unwanted encounters. The scale of the city wouldn't allow for such a thing. Athens is a snack compared to the behemoth that is Tokyo, a toy for the Godzilla-sized capital. Still he's pleased to use jet-lag and that he doesn't have to meet Suzuki for a few days as excuses to hide away.

At six floors his apartment block in Pagrati is one of the tallest in his Athenian neighbourhood. The influx of high-rises was a push for quick mass-living but no higher than that so as to not obstruct the sky. It had seemed a magnificent feat of architecture but the idea of his city's conurbations and tower blocks is humiliating compared to Tokyo's elevation. This hotel is short at double that height, itself dwarfed by surrounding edifices. A red torii and shrine squeezed into a pocket across the river would loom large back home. Here they better resemble features of a doll's house.

Hasegawa grew up in the nearby district of Omotesando, a wealthy estate at the heart of the city. Outer suburbs are desirable for the Athenians, the core a roughshod place best avoided, but Tokyo is only more precious the closer to its imperial centre. Apostolis meanders the streets there in the late morning. He buys a fried potato korokke at a stall. Hasegawa has described it so perfectly that he already knows how it will taste. He has listened to his boss regale the area and, even with obvious regeneration, so much is laid out as expected that it tricks his mind into nostalgia that isn't his. Some things are the same and some slightly adjusted whilst others are gone altogether. Shop names have been given a lick of paint and where a trolley car shed used to be is now a dog park. He will leave out these details.

He has a shopping list but has been instructed to collect everything on the last day to preserve their freshness. After the croquette he is excited to taste more things he's heard about. The itinerary sets out what he should eat and where. He drops into a ramen place where culture rather than language fails him. The set up is alien. He reddens as a chef leads him back outside past the noren curtains to a ticket machine, defeating the object of simplifying the process and now bothering him with money exchanging hands. It's worth the embarrassment as the broth is divine. Oily and salty, the pork tender, the noodles steaming but not scalding. It's confusing food. Homely and yet made by strangers. He hasn't eaten so well since Vatheia. An image of Petzechroula, who will never cook for him again, spoils his appetite. He pushes the unfinished bowl away.

People don't so much as glance at him than stare with unrestrained curiosity. Hasegawa is an irregularity in Athens but conducts himself with such plume and disregard that the locals have convinced themselves that he's always been a permanent fixture. Here Apostolis is simply misplaced.

He spots the ginkgo trees of Aoyama in the ward north of Omotesando. It's the one neighbourhood that he was determined to avoid. He could have walked in any other direction. To Shibuya's crossroads in the south, west to the fashionable Harajuku or to the foreigner-friendly Roppongi in the east. He would like to think that this has been an accident.

A school-boy in a high necked jacket walks past followed by a girl in a navy sailor outfit. A second boy, older and with floppy hair, catches up to them. Apostolis is sent back eighteen years.

He can't help himself and continues to the house. Just to see it. Then he'll leave. It will be gratifying for history's sake, a part of the past filled in. He walks with purpose. He knows the streets because there have been drunken nights where he has studied a map of the city. Maybe more times than he'd care to admit.

In a city of skyscrapers it's a feat that these houses stand proud, belonging to families with more money than the impetus to sell up and have their land developed. It's grotesque really. No one needs this much space. Hasegawa might have filled in the spectrum of kanji but it was Haruki who had opened his eyes to them. One of the first he drew in the sand was the character for 'house'. It seems somewhat distasteful that one kanji could represent not only Estia and the tower house but also these mansions.

He commands his legs to keep walking but instead slows down. Street signs are non-existent but he has memorised the layout. A few numbered houses point to his destination. He's in disbelief to be standing outside. Hasegawa has spoken of Aoyama's properties but Apostolis has never appreciated just how much money the Okazakis had. Have, if they still live here. His face burns thinking of them in Vatheia. He's glad that Petzechroula cannot learn of this. It's a measly saving grace of her death, one of many that he has accumulated over the past two years, even if they've never come close to offsetting the tragedy of it.

"May I help you?"

A woman stands in front of her door craning her neck towards him. The path from the pavement is long enough that she has to crunch her eyes.

Time has not been kind to Megumi and yet it's patently her. Wrinkles have overtaken her face like an untameable garden. Deep etches surround her lips as if sourness has caved them in. Her hair is grey and frayed and yet she's a paragon of beauty in her kimono.

"I'm sorry to bother you," Apostolis says. He doesn't walk away. Instead he waits as she winds forward the clock to see that he is as grown as his vocabulary.

"For so long I wondered when you would come that I had begun to question if you ever would."

"I was passing by."

"Is that so? Come. Here we don't air our laundry in public."

Apostolis approaches. It seems right to let her digest his appearance. He is a man with a face full of stubble, shadowed by malaise.

"Jouzu desu ne," she says. "You've become proficient. All this to impress my son?"

"I'm here on business."

"A long way to be delivering mail."

"My manager is an art dealer in Athens," he says, but she's right; glorified albeit but he's a postboy once more.

"I see. Well. He doesn't live here of course but I'm certain that he would like to see you. Will you still be in Tokyo tomorrow?"

"Yes." He's succumbing to a plan that he isn't sure he wants to be a part of, least of all because of how accommodating Megumi is being. The possibility of seeing Haruki is giddying.

"Come back at three. That gives me time to prepare."

He has the rest of the day to decide if this is a good idea.

It's too early and he's too hyped to consider sleep but he hides in the hotel room. When hunger forces him out he skips Hasegawa's suggestions and asks Fukuda for a recommendation. The man tells him of a conveyor belt sushi restaurant not far away although up a slope so perhaps he might welcome a taxi. Apostolis will manage. Outside he laughs to himself, remembering Hasegawa's warning that the Japanese will not want him to walk anywhere more than five minutes away. To Fukuda's credit it's a fairly steep slope that takes him back to Vatheia's bay. Feet firm in the concrete jungle, it's the only similarity.

Sushi is the one food that the two men in Athens have had no interest in recreating. Everything else has been a poor imitation but at least Hasegawa could source enough ingredients to make paltry imitations. Sushi on the other hand has been a no-go from the start. Apostolis can see why as he sits at the counter, with the four chefs in the centre working in tandem as if their arms make up one octopus. The men shape fish around chunks of rice whilst customers take premade passing plates and carousels of ginger or call directly for specials. Hot water flows out of taps in front of each seat, accompanied by abundant green tea powder in pots. Waitresses circle the room rolling their fingers down the stacked colour-coded plates to calculate totals. Apostolis could eat nothing but this for the rest of his life and be satisfied. It had been peculiar to him that his boss kept sushi off the itinerary but now it makes sense; Hasegawa hadn't wanted him to experience something this sublime only to lose it again. Apostolis knows this all too well. He's read someone else's feelings about this sentiment enough times.

When the novelty of the belt no longer distracts him from his encounter with Megumi he walks an arcade. Clanging pachinko machines and six-seater bars with poor karaoke aren't enough to drown out his mistrust of her. He has dreamt of Tokyo for so long but his visions were always of being invited and shown around by someone he loved and who loved him back. Now he is just a passer-through, queasy with the thought that somewhere in the city Haruki has learnt that he's here.

Wide awake and not ready to call it a night he reroutes to Hasegawa's guidelines and his final suggestion for the day. For this one activity alone he has been outlined a shaky hand-drawn map that is impressive in its exactness, leading him through a series of back alleys that turn in on themselves and away from all hints of life. There is only a small sign, easily missed, probably impossible to spot without an insider's advantage.

He takes off his shoes and places them in a box that locks when he slides a wooden block out of place. He steps up to the tatami porch and ducks under a blue cloth with the kanji that denotes this as the men's side. A woman sits at a raised counter that oversees both entrances. She snubs him.

"Foreigner. I don't speak English," she says in her native language.

"A ticket and a towel please," Apostolis replies with honorific articulation.

She gives him change. "Do you know how to bathe?"

"Yes," he says, but only in theory, never having carried out the ritual.

"Fine. Enjoy."

Men glance at him in the changing room but keep to themselves. The walls are cigarette-stained, the floor perpetually damp and frayed. A television in the corner displays a black and white game-show with slapstick laughter and bold kanji subtitling its entirety. A hairdryer works in short bursts of ten yen coins. A massage chair with torn leather sits unused in the corner.

Apostolis strips, places his belongings in a second locker and proceeds past the sliding glass door to the sento baths. This is the public communal bathhouse used by a subsection. Rows of low showers and stools are set out front. The back wall is a tiled mosaic of Fuji, sparkling just as Hasegawa remembered it. The dividing wall doesn't reach the ceiling and gossiping can be heard from across the way whilst this side is dedicated to the low groans of washing and soaking. The men are much older than him. Younger men live in newer apartment blocks with private bathrooms and reserve this tradition for posher onsen. Even if they have their own wet rooms Apostolis can see the charm of gathering here. A kafeneio of sorts.

A man eyes Apostolis' hairy body; when he sits at a station and cleans himself the man loses interest. The water in the first tub is blistering. He leaves immediately and plunges into a colder pool. He's surprised by a tub that shoots electric pulses through the water for some sort of muscle relief, then settles in a bath of middling heat where he copies one of the men who has folded his towel into a flannel that he rests on his forehead.

Two men convene nearby and are embroiled in a low chat that he can't hear. They remind him of how his grandfather and Tyresias had once been although here they are much quieter. The comparison is upsetting and he soon leaves. On the street he experiences a second sweat. He showers in his hotel room and lies naked on the bed.

There has been next to no intimacy since leaving Vatheia, at least nothing more than performative and underwhelming. When he first arrived to Athens he'd travelled across the city to a periptero and bought a porn magazine. Occasionally he has taken it out from under his mattress and tried to settle his eyes on the women but instead flicked through to find the men being fellated, their faces bored as their penises stood in various states of arousal. When he has masturbated to these pages the act has often become so grim that he's lost interest mid-way. Any pleasure from a reached orgasm has been fast lost to post-ejaculatory tristesse.

He falls asleep but wakes in the night fully erect. The nudity at the sento did nothing for him but he reaches for his penis all the same. He wants to be stoic, celibate in preparation for seeing Haruki. But carnal needs drive him forward and his grip tightens. Despite his displeasure there's no stopping him. He settles on the image of Haruki as a teenager before the spell will be broken, because tomorrow he will be a man. He nears climax. He pulls his hand away and tries to work out if what he is doing is right. He asks his heart and his head but leaves them to their tug of war and returns to masturbating with its eventual conclusion. And then the darkness swallows him whole, sinking him down, farther, until he is reminded of his loneliness, enveloped by the cavernous mattress.

23

Aoyama
25th October 1980

Shibuya is the only modern feature of the city that Hasegawa has promoted, where more people seem to snake around one another during each bout of the crossing at the infamous traffic lights than take up space in all of Athens. Where the population of Vatheia would fit into a single shopfront. But, rather than being besieged by culture shock, Apostolis is consumed with wanting time to rush ahead. To the meeting. To after it.

Any trepidation that he's felt towards Megumi since 1962 has been cushioned not only by the jet streams of his journey but by her cordiality. Their paths had barely crossed in Mani and yet he took her to be the most savvy of the Okazakis. Memories, dreams and ruminations have corrupted the truth of the past but he's almost certain that he saw her once, watching from a vantage point as he and Haruki rowed out of the bay. Unless she brings it up he'll pretend that he has no knowledge of it.

Understanding that summer has been like translating a fourth language without a teacher. In comparison, Japanese was a far smoother undertaking.

Asiatikes Antikes had recently opened when he dropped in on his quest for dictionaries. With no desire to do anything else with his life, he spent a month translating *Shiosai* at painstaking speed. It became easier as he leant into the rhythm, and he returned after its completion to ask Hasegawa for other novels. Unlimited books were given in exchange for front-of-house support. Apostolis discovered another shared idiom across the languages: two birds, one stone.

Years later, Petzechroula died and a bundle arrived for him in the post. An olive branch of sorts from Tassos. The only Greek was in the cover letter: *If we cannot offer you the distant past then perhaps this will suffice.* Unbeknownst to Tassos, his cousin had a head start in deciphering the contents. Each letter was signed off by Haruki or later Charupi. Apostolis had no idea that he'd written so extensively throughout that summer. He would not speak ill of the dead but thought poorly of his aunt for holding them back; her coddling had left him more alone. He skipped ahead to the final pages. They were addressed to him. Choice kanji jumped out but his damp eyes were unable to take focus. He returned the letters to their package. With some patience he could read them all. More the choice was whether he wanted to. He wanted instead to unlearn Japanese, seal the envelope and return it to its sender. He'd delivered so many letters across his life but it was rare for him to receive something. For the first time he considered his role in handing over the things to people that had ruined them.

Over the next few years he read the letters so many times that certain lines became tattooed on his brain, none so much as the address in Aoyama and the command to go there. Ever since, it had been a possibility to fly to Haruki as requested. But as more years passed it had likely become an invitation that outgrew its welcome. A flight of fancy that was better left untampered. Until now. Any time that Apostolis has pictured them reuniting it has been nothing like this. He figures that the reality makes more sense. Megumi was always going to be the gatekeeper.

His stomach growls but he keeps walking, unable to sit long enough to eat. He'd like the afternoon to arrive already but as sure as the hours dwindle it's here sooner than he wants.

He walks their block multiple times, past a cemetery in which lies Dr Ueno, the owner of the faithful Hachiko. Nearby is a shop selling garden furniture. Stone raccoon-dogs and water features take up the pavement under a yellowed canopy. The awning reminds him of Estia, rusting and unappreciated for over a decade. Any worry that he's had about its disrepair is mitigated by the likelihood that it has only been touched by the elements and not man-handled by trespassers.

A maid answers on his second knock. He assumes that she's been with the family for the long haul, otherwise there are younger and more efficient people to employ. She hobbles as she ushers him along a hallway to a large seating area with couches in the western style. Through a round window, the only native design in this room, is the suggestion of a garden.

Megumi enters and waves off any formality of him needing to stand. She sits at a right angle to him. "I hope this room is to your liking. I wasn't sure if you could manage on the floor. Tatami is uncomfortable for the untrained."

"That's thoughtful, thank you."

"You really understood that? It's enthralling to be able to communicate with you. Tell me how you learnt."

"My boss taught me. He required an interpreter so lessons became part of my payment." He's already decided to leave out the impetus of the book and the subsequent letters.

"Compliments to him. A Japanese boss in Greece?"

"Hasegawa-san. Actually he owned a store not so far from here before moving to Athens."

"Hasegawa Kenjiro? The arts dealer?"

He nods.

"How funny. I bought a print from him once. Remind me to show you. In truth I thought he had died. The shop closed so suddenly and there was no son to pass the business onto so I assumed it folded."

Apostolis feels protective of him. "He also makes his own woodblock prints. They're successful."

"And he lives in Athens?"

"He wanted to share Asian art with the world."

"How delightful that he finds Greece amenable. Tade kuu mushi mo sukizuki."

It must be an idiom that he's never heard before and translates it literally. "Some bugs prefer nettles?"

"It means it's a matter of taste. What a silly thing that we were all there together. It seems fanciful now."

"I think it meant a lot to your husband. May I ask?"

"If he is alive? Yes, and a professor. He's always dreaming of excavations but his travelling days are long behind him. He doesn't stray far now. I won't bore you with that. I'll bring tea."

She leaves the room and returns empty-handed.

"Thank you, Rika," she says to the maid who follows with a tray. Megumi instils silence as she fills both cups. Even though a tea ceremony should be conducted from a kneeling position she possesses a coolness on the couch that doesn't forego the purity of such an important ritual. She offers Apostolis a plate of pink and white mochi balls topped in powdered sugar.

"You can eat adzuki?"

"Yes, thank you." He bites into the chewy texture with its red bean centre, sweet and sticky and foreign but not so strange as to cause him to pull a face. Everything that has touched his mouth in the last few days has been monitored by the locals, amazed that their dishes are palatable to a foreigner. "Delicious. This is a lovely house."

"Thank you."

They look around the room. It's spacious to the point of being cavernous. Sterile like a waiting room but also, if he's being cynical, chosen for its vastness. Apostolis recalls those final moments on the beach when Haruki followed her. Perhaps he was weighing up this house with Estia. Whatever Apostolis could have offered would never have amounted to this. His mind reels back to the day before that: 'You couldn't understand.' His cheeks burn at entertaining the notion that Haruki would have ever chosen him.

Megumi raises her eyebrows upon noticing his flushed face.

"I didn't bring anything for you," he says, an opportune realisation. "I'm afraid I'm jet-lagged and it slipped my mind."

"Nonsense. Your appearance is gift enough. I've waited many years. Jitsu wa, your timing couldn't be better. You must tell me about Vatheia."

Apostolis toys with a mochi ball, uncertain of how to answer. There's no harm in telling her but he doesn't want her to judge him. For years he's felt justified in shunning his family but to say it out loud will confront what he has long assumed: that it has been time wasted. "Petzechroula died a few years ago."

"I am sorry to hear that. I was very fond of her. I'm afraid that I don't remember her husband's name."

"Tyresias. He's alive but Vatheia is struggling. There are only a few residents left." He doesn't know why but the painful confession feels necessary. "It isn't practical for him to live there any longer so he has to leave. Vast numbers of people are abandoning islands and villages for the cities. Vatheia is a ghost town in waiting."

"You left ahead of the curve."

"It's never an easy choice."

"Self-preservation. It seems simple to me."

"Tassos goes often and–"

"Jaa," Megumi says, clapping her hands. "I would like to show you the garden before we go."

She leads him through the house, past an immaculate kitchen and smaller off-shoots that would have suited this encounter better, and then across a tatami room with sliding doors that open to a tidy square of land. Three sides of the house entrap this beautiful garden that brims with red ferns, yellow cypresses and dainty plum blossoms. Cleverly they don't so much as fight for space as they live in harmony. At the centre is a rock pool with a trickling waterfall. A horizontally-sliced bamboo shoot serves as a pivot. As water piles up it spills into the corner of the pond. There's also a water harp planted on black pebbles. It's the first that he's seen since abandoning Estia. He's had countless nightmares about the state his must be in. He wants to cry.

Megumi sighs with dramatic flair. "Forgive the unsightliness of the cloud tree. I'll prune it tomorrow. How humiliating."

Apostolis shakes his head, irritated by the false modesty, but compliments her regardless. "It's exquisite."

"My silly project. I'm glad that I was able to show you. After all, I remember the scenery around Vatheia. I was so envious of the copious space for pumpkins. Shall we?"

Rika helps her change from slippers to wooden sandals.

Apostolis falls into the role of her butler, a step behind as she moves quickly. He regrets not dressing up but even in formal attire he would look hapless in comparison. He and Haruki passed their days together in shorts, never stuffed into a sweater and chinos like he is now. He wonders what Haruki will be wearing. He hasn't asked Megumi what her son's reaction was to this meeting. He could ask now but something stops him.

She leads them through a well-to-do district and it's only a few minutes before she stops at the corner of a T-junction. She hangs back under a flowering dogwood. Apostolis can see the top of the Eiffel-like Tokyo Tower through a gap in the sky-rises, a bold red that offers vibrancy amid the beige and grey of the plastered apartments.

"We shall wait for him here."

There's a stream of passers-by on the opposite side of the road, the majority of them mothers with children. Apostolis traces this to a nursery at the end of the stretch. His heart quickens at the eccentricity of the meeting point. "You did tell him that I'm here?"

Megumi doesn't turn towards him. "Actually, no. I thought it would be nicer as a surprise."

"Maybe it's better to warn him. I can come tomorrow."

"Now is perfect. Awaseru kao ga nai? Or do you have no face to expose?"

"I just– I'm not sure I should–"

"Akis, you worry too much. Haruki used to panic too. After Greece he needed time to reset but he's level-headed now. Do you think you'll recognise him?"

"I think so." Despite the decades that have passed, neither of them could have changed enough to stupefy the other.

"Really?"

He senses that he's being snared in a trap. "Why?"

"Because he is right there."

Apostolis looks out across the street. The only other man is walking alongside a woman, his hands on a pushchair. A girl skips a few steps ahead of them. The couple talk between themselves and then focus on the older of their children. They carry on, oblivious to the two spectators who are only in their line of vision for a matter of seconds. Haruki might be surrounded by a family, and so much else might be different – he dons a suit, his hair is set in a side-parting with the greyscale styling of the salarymen in carbon copy around the city – but the essence of him is undeniable.

The family continues along the road and disappears from sight.

"There he goes with my daughter-in-law and granddaughters," says Megumi. There's a shuddering cruelness within her chirpy tone. "Did I not mention them?"

Apostolis is unable to reply.

"If you would like to say hello then by all means."

He should despise her for thinking that she could be driven by good will but he hates himself more for being gullible.

He could run up to Haruki and introduce himself. It would make for an awkward conversation. That summer in Greece is likely known by the wife but the finer details obscured. What purpose is there in dredging it up? What Apostolis wants, if he is honest with himself, is not on offer. He's uninterested in a version of Haruki that no longer exists if the boy he loves doesn't carry to the present. He casts his head down, relinquishing the foolish notion that a scribbled address and a proclamation of love by a sixteen-year-old had strong enough legs to bear a marathon that could span decades.

His annoyance turns towards Haruki with the crude belief that the boy has betrayed him. That as he has lived in stasis, his own family disintegrating until he has been left with nothing, Haruki was busy getting married and sleeping with a woman and having children.

"Shall I call him back?" Megumi asks. It's a final, fatal stab that she plunges with all the glee in the world.

Apostolis can't find it within himself to engage in battle.

He's back on the beach, standing alone, hoping that Haruki will change his mind. He's watching him follow his mother up the slope.

He can't be that boy again. Exposed. Defeated. Subservient to the decisions of others. He walks away without saying a word, thinking that in doing so he can at least draw the game to a close.

24

Shonan
26th October 1980

Hasegawa-san has only written the name of the colleague and for Apostolis to expect him at ten. It's unusually scheduled on a Sunday but after yesterday it's a blessing. Except for moving up his flight, work is the next best distraction. Apostolis rides the elevator to the lobby and looks around but no one meets his eye. He'll loiter. He's the only foreigner and it will be easier for Suzuki to pick him out.

"Apostolis?" A woman rises from the plush couch. She's a little younger than him with slicked hair and a leather jacket.

"Suzuki-san?"

"Naomi. You seem surprised."

"I'm just–" He doesn't have an end to the explanation. In this industry, women are infrequently traders. Even then he's never come across anyone so young or attractive. He guesses that she's someone's lackey.

"You look exhausted," she says.

He doesn't expect such brashness either and stumbles over his words. "Jet-lag," he says, yet again a helpful excuse. "My boss will be pleased that we located one another so easily."

She creases her eyes at him. "Your boss."

"Hasegawa-san," he says to confirm. "You are here for the exchange?" He only then notices that she's empty-handed.

"Hasegawa-san," she repeats, breaking down the syllables. There's a certain disdain to it.

He considers her informal greeting, a cardinal sin in addressing him by his first name.

"Kuso," she swears, audible enough that Fukuda glances from the reception. "What did my father tell you?"

"Your father?"

"You didn't know?"

She looks to be in her late twenties, early thirties. The timeline fits even if the idea that Hasegawa has a child this young when he's so old sits uneasy. "I had absolutely no idea."

Naomi laughs and repeats his sentence in all its formality. "My father said he taught you well but since he's a boast I was half-expecting you to be able to be all 'Genki desu yo ne' and then I'd have to say 'Wow you're so great at Japanese.' But he actually did a good job. I suppose you do have the correct genitalia for it."

Naomi is either oblivious or doesn't care that her volume is better suited for a Mediterranean disposition. In return Apostolis adopts the Japanese tradition of humility. He looks at Fukuda as if to confirm that he's seeing this and to silently, pleadingly apologise.

He turns the conversation back to business. "I was told to bring something back to Athens. Something too valuable to be couriered."

Naomi curtseys. She is the point of interest.

"Long story," she says. "Or it's not really I suppose. Funny how people say that and then a short version suffices. Yeah so, my father and I haven't spoken for a long time and I think he'd like to make amends before he dies."

Her account leaves out plenty of backstory and Apostolis summarises. "Too frail to travel here so he wants you to go there."

"Or too proud. I guess it is a longer story after all. Am I speaking too fast? Can you follow?"

"The speed, yes, but I'm trying to understand why I'm here."

"To convince me. He gave you money?"

Apostolis nods.

"A bit more than the cost of a flight?"

He nods again. He'd been right to be surprised at the amount, substantial but less than other recent purchases. It's a payment up front. A plea. He isn't sure that he wants anything to do with this but he imagines the awkwardness of returning without Naomi. He feels indebted to Hasegawa to try. "Will you take it?"

She shakes her head. "You have a choice, Apostolis. That's a clunky name by the way. I was trying to guess a nickname on the way here. Posto? Stolis? No. Alright. Apostolis it is. I'm not going to Greece so we can say farewell here and my father can be upset with you. It's then up to you how much you exaggerate about the lengths you went to encourage me. Maybe you can tell him you performed a whole song and dance. Sold what a wonderful surrogate father he's been. That he's amended his ways. Or, since we both have time, perhaps we could spend the day together anyway?"

"What's the point if you won't come to Athens?"

She feigns insult with a little mewl. "Aren't you intrigued to see if you can convince me? I'd like to hang out. I've never met a Greek before."

He can't shake how pointless, how sabotaging this trip has been. Each interaction has been sold under false pretences. Life would have been more pleasant if he'd held his ground and stayed back amidst the dusty books on the corner of Odos Antheion and Odos Platonos, unaware that there were so many daughters dotted around this city that he hadn't known about. He has lived in the shadow of lies for so long that he's been blinded by the truth of them.

There are still too many days before his flight and he has no desire to be anywhere in the vicinity of the Okazakis. He's lost any whetted appetite for tourist destinations and doesn't think that, alone, he can outwit his brain to stave bad thoughts from simmering.

"Are you really weighing up your options?" she asks cuttingly. "Am I that ugly?" She bats her eyes, playing him as if she's worked in a maid cafe for years.

"I have one postulation."

"Big word. Impressive. Well?"

"We get out of the city."

"Done."

He should have been more specific, although tricky without arousing her suspicions, but it's only after she races them through the closing doors of a train that he regrets agreeing to go anywhere. The Yokosuka Line from Shinagawa passes by Kawasaki's industrial zone and Yokohama's port until the sprawl is exchanged for the coast. His worst fears come true when the announcer lists the remaining stations and gives the terminal as Kamakura. The word rushes him back to where Haruki spent his summers.

Naomi sits on the bench but it's a packed carriage and he stands in front of her holding a handrail. "Want a massage?" she asks. "You look tense." She goes to rub his hips but stops short and laughs. "Your face. Haven't you realised? I'm one of the new women that men fear."

He doesn't know this phrase.

"My father didn't include it? Shocking. Go on. What's wrong?"

"It's nothing."

"Ever mysterious." She rolls her eyes. "This will be fun."

She's the only one aboard to speak until now. In the city's grip no one else says a word but as the world opens up and the horizon deepens people relax and soon there are plenty of conversations. Not long after, a space frees up next to her so Apostolis sits. Out of nowhere she starts to talk as if she's in therapy, as if he'd asked.

"I never answer the phone to him but I read all the letters. He tells me that I'm stubborn. He also said that you were a good boy but you never talk about yourself. Maybe he thought I could coax it out of you. Spy for him."

"Would that help bridge the two of you?"

"We could find out."

Apostolis turns back to the scenery.

More people alight where red maples blot out temple complexes but an elderly group steps into the carriage. Naomi and Apostolis give up their seats and sway into one another as the train shuffles forward.

"He must be having fun in Athens considering us together," Apostolis says.

"He doesn't always get his way with me. There's not much I like about him but I admire the lengths he's gone to this time. I wonder what comes next?"

"Death." It's a grim response but at some point this stand-off will come to an end.

"That's dark. I guess you'd like to know why we don't talk. Why I won't see him before he dies?"

"That's between the two of you."

"You're so conventional. I'll tell you anyway. He'll expect that so I'm not betraying him." She slaps him on the shoulder. "Don't be so loyal seeing as he tricked you."

"I'm starting to agree."

"You are?"

"With him, I mean. You're very stubborn."

Naomi beams. He can imagine Hasegawa being driven crazy by her but he doesn't know the whole story and won't take sides.

"Convincing too, I bet," he continues. "In Greek we say you could sell sand to the Bedouin and fridges to the Eskimos."

"It's exhausting being this amazing all the time."

"It must be."

"Must be why I don't have a boyfriend."

"I would've thought if you were that amazing—"

"All the good in the world when I'm also intimidating. But I'm always on the lookout. Maybe I should set my horizons broader."

Apostolis meets her eyes. He's enjoyed her camaraderie but hasn't once considered a romantic connection.

"That wasn't subtle was it?"

"Honestly? Not particularly."

"Lucky escape then. I'm the oniyome devil wife. In fact you're lucky I'm not carrying your wallet."

"You did buy the tickets and choose the location."

"True."

"So no boyfriend and no husband."

"No. Same for you?"

"Sorry?"

Naomi smiles as Apostolis turns inward. He remembers the woman walking alongside Haruki but she's faceless. His attention was spotlighted on Haruki. He wishes that he'd taken in her features, decided if she was attractive. It doesn't matter. She's Haruki's wife. The mother of his children.

"Here's an olive branch," Naomi says. "Get it? Greek reference. You get to make the next decision. See, I'm not completely devoid of compromise. We can either do the tourist route or go to the beach and drink."

"The tourist route sounds more virtuous."

"Right. Oh."

"What?"

"I thought you were going to say, But–"

He doesn't want to go to the beach. Where he lives in Athens is only twenty minutes on the bus in the direction of Alimos and a spectacular beach front. He has avoided the sand for over a decade and isn't interested in breaking that now. "I am hungry though. Maybe we could eat and decide after?"

"Kampeki. I know a place."

From Kamakura Station, Naomi leads him to the third floor of a rickety building where a waitress shouts a greeting. Behind a haze of cigarette smoke and a series of oak booths other women mimic her like howler monkeys.

As soon as they sit, Naomi pushes a button stuck to the side of the booth. "I'll choose for us."

A waitress joins them. The order is long and concludes with two bottles of Kirin beer.

"You're hungry," Apostolis says.

"If my father's paying and you don't want to waste it on a day of getting drunk then I'm going to have to get creative. I've worked it out by the way. You won't keep the money and I wouldn't want him to think that I'm stealing it so it's all going on today. Brilliant right? It's a game we play of who can be the most passive aggressive."

"Sounds like a sad game."

"Not if I win."

"It's only a game if both of you are playing."

Naomi hesitates. It's the first time he's thrown her. "It's only a game if both of us are playing. You got me. I like that. If I had a beer in front of me I'd cheers you."

"You're really not coming to Athens?"

"I told you."

"Not even if he's dying?"

"Is he?"

"He might be. At some point he will."

"I guess."

"You don't care?" Anger rears its head from within his tone.

Naomi stares at him without blinking.

He regrets the accusation. She has no idea how much of a hypocrite saying it makes him. "I'm sorry."

She hits the button again and orders pickled vegetables that she forgot the first time around. The beers arrive soon after. As tradition dictates they pour one another a glass.

Apostolis has lost count of how many days he's been in Japan. But in here, with Naomi and no windows to the outside, it feels devoid of time. Like the dealership at the end of the day. Or inside the caves at Diros.

"Can I tell you something?" he asks, needing to break the silence and his guilt. "I was raised by an aunt and we fell out. It's a long–"

Naomi dares him.

"It's a story. She was dying and I didn't visit. Of course I cared about her. I hate myself every day."

"But you couldn't see her?"

"No. Or I thought I couldn't. Now it all seems so stupid."

"You're just saying that to make me fly to Athens."

"All I know is that I was wrong to accuse you. No one should have to be on good terms with family just because they're related.

I'm just saying that I screwed up and I don't want the same for you."

He sighs in disbelief. "That's more than I ever told your father."

Naomi groans. "You're going to make this hard aren't you?"

"That wasn't my intention."

"Thank you Apostolis." She snaps out of a vacant stare and taps her finger on the table. "We've got to spend cash fast."

The food arrives as she's still brainstorming. They eat soba noodles that they dip into a dark broth with wasabi and spring onions, as well as tempura shrimps on a vat of rice. Hasegawa and Apostolis have previously tried to recreate both dishes; whilst they looked the same as this Apostolis understands why his boss shook his head each time. This is deep, fragrant and delicate. With each meal in Japan he feels more detached from his roots. Where food was fuel. Still, he pines for Petzechroula's cooking.

Naomi talks about her work but it proves impossible to follow. It's something about computing and corporations but is outside of anything that he can picture. An economic boom is coming, she tells him. It's going to happen this decade. Like a soothsayer she's convinced that the eighties will concern greed. There's no choice but to join in with the big dogs. She isn't apologetic about it. It's kind of attractive and for a moment he can imagine being married to her. But the fantasy is cut short when he remembers that it's driven by a revenge that serves no one.

He asks what her co-workers think of her, considering that she's mentioned multiple times as a point of pride that she's the only woman. She looks at him blankly as if it hasn't occurred to her to ask. She's also unafraid to tell him that she earns plenty of money, far more than he does he supposes, and if Hasegawa thinks wielding an inheritance or the promise of money over her will work he's likely to be disappointed. Apostolis guesses that he's not the first person to have been sent to persuade her. It almost becomes a tempting challenge but he doesn't fancy his odds.

After the meal, which ends up not costing anywhere near enough, they board an electric train that runs the length of the Shonan seafront. Apostolis keeps his back to the water until the narrow track turns inland and passes between estates. It's impossible not to look into the gardens. Back along the ocean a sigh slips out.

"Homesick? My father told me that you're not from Athens. Otherwise it's all islands and water?"

"There are mountain villages. But yes I grew up by the sea. I left a long time ago."

"So many words to say you're homesick. You'd never survive here. Cut-throat and envy are the emotions du jour. You're the sensitive type."

"I am?"

"You brood. You've been lost in thought the whole time we've been together. Look away. A memory test. How big are my breasts? I'm kidding. Unless you want to answer that."

He likes her more and more. It's refreshing. There's something Vatheian about her. "You got me. I am homesick." It borders on the truth.

"But you didn't answer the important question."

"What's that?"

She looks down at her cleavage and laughs as he blushes and turns away. "Now you want to look at the sea!"

Lights give them right of way over a pedestrianised shopping street and a food market and then they're back along the water, squashed next to a highway. An island looms in the distance. Mist conceals the famous mountain beyond that. The run is so narrow that it only allows for a single track. Their train pulls into a slip to let another pass in the opposite direction. Apostolis has heard of a similar system on a toothed ascent in the mountains of Kalavryta, not that he has ever visited.

"How does the beach compare to home?" Naomi asks him. The sand is grey, even black in parts, and the surf foamy.

"It's gentler there. Cleaner. Am I allowed to say that?"

"If it's the truth. Warm too? It's always cold here."

"In summer it's like bathwater." His body prickles with the memory of ducking under with ease, the unrivalled joy of being submerged.

"By the way, there's a beautiful guest-house with an onsen not far. Private bathtub on the roof. Kaiseki-ryori. Massages. The works. Maybe we should book into the honeymoon suite. Costs a fortune."

Apostolis turns an ashen colour.

"I'm glad the thought of me naked disgusts you that much. I'm only joking. Sort of. Such a sensitive type."

They come to a station called Hase and Naomi leads them on the tourist route through hydrangea-lined alleys to a compound where at its centre is a massive sitting Buddha. Apostolis is shocked to have forgotten a linked memory until now, expunged when his mind couldn't pin it to a tangible explanation. Decades earlier, Haruki had drawn in the sand a map of his grandfather's summer house. It sat some distance from the capital by the sea. Next to it he'd illustrated what looked like a snowman. They'd lost themselves to laughter whilst trying to work out what he'd meant by it. Haruki had sat like this statue, cross-legged, palms pinched together, making a meditative sound. Unable to work it out, Apostolis told him to stop fooling around because they needed to get back to building the house. Or kissing. One of those things. He can't remember which.

Naomi bats his past away by drawing attention to her own. "My father brought me here after my mother died. I was so young." She says no more and walks off to perch on a low wall.

When she's ready they amble back to the station for Tokyo. Apostolis is tired and they barely speak. He wonders if he should try again to encourage her, for Hasegawa's sake and her own. He's also aware that each of Tassos' interferences made him double down. He's the wrong candidate for such a thing.

The train pulls into Shinagawa late-afternoon.

"That was a bit of a dud," Naomi says on the platform. "I didn't drink my way through our stash. I'm not even holding the money and it's burning a hole in my pocket. How about a love hotel? For a rest stay. Three hours should do it." She speaks purposefully loud so that a few people glance, taken aback by the forward offer. She's only focused on Apostolis. "Do you always blush this much?"

"I should go back to my hotel."

"Alone?"

"Alone. To sleep."

"Tonight then. I'm not letting you off that easily."

"Naomi–"

"Relax. I mean dinner. I called and made a reservation during lunch. I figured we'd have leftover money. And after what you said it'll be perfect."

"What did I say?"

She ignores him. "Seven there or I can pick you up thirty minutes before?"

Apostolis wonders which of the many things he's said that she's referring to but she's not going to tell him. "Give me the address."

"Ha! Got you. Do you like what I did there? I learnt it at business school. It was a false choice. Six-thirty or seven, rather than date or no date."

"Clever."

"I know. Nihombashi Station, south exit. Dress smart." She walks along the platform and leaves him to navigate his own way back. She doesn't give him any more time to change his mind.

Another trick, he's left to realise.

25

Tokyo
26th October 1980

Naomi waits for him outside the station. She looks divine in her thigh-length black dress under the open trench-coat. He's disappointed that he feels nothing; if anyone was going to tempt him it's her. He wonders if that's a compliment that a woman would want to hear but he keeps it to himself.

He bows but she leans forward and kisses him on each cheek. "You said you were homesick. Tonight we're going continental."

His dread is fully realised when she stops outside a restaurant two streets away. The name is in blue and white, the typeface Greek. Οριγκάμι. He assumes that the lack of Japanese conjures exclusivity.

"Your face dropped," she says. "Is this ridiculous? Oh god, it is. You didn't come all the way for Greek food. Let's go somewhere else."

He's known of this place for some time, Origami, a leader in the craze for fusion cooking. He wants to suggest that they move on, that he'd be happy with a hundred yen bowl of street noodles, but he also has a morbid curiosity to go inside.

"It was thoughtful of you," he says.

"Actually it was the only Michelin place with a table." She rubs her thumb and fingers together. "My father will be delighted. Or horrified. By the way—" She spins.

"You look incredible."

"Tell me in Greek."

"You're beautiful but I don't want to fuck you."

She pauses. "Pig. Didn't I tell you I speak Greek?"

His heart skips a beat.

"I don't. Teach me good evening."

"Kalispera."

"Ooh-la-la." She enters and greets the hostess but the word is wasted on the Japanese staff.

Someone else takes their coats and shows them to a table in the corner. Apostolis has his chair pulled out for him and a serviette laid on his lap. This restaurant is dimly lit and chrome, as he assumes fine dining establishments must be, but if it's replicating Greece then it's all wrong. Tables should be covered in paper cloths clipped at the sides, with wooden chairs scraping the floor, a smell of grilled meat, and bountiful portions. Instead everything is sequestered and the sterility leaves him to wonder if the chefs he can see through the crack of wall are actually doing anything.

Naomi picks up the menu. She scans to the bottom and whistles. "Good job my father's paying."

She calls over a waiter and orders the tasting menu adding the drinks pairing.

The only noise from the other diners are coos as they fawn over their plates. Apostolis looks up at the main feature, a metal frame hanging from the ceiling shaped like a folded crane. Two lights are built into its eye sockets. It doesn't seem particularly Greek.

"I heard that the chef went to Greece when she was younger," she tells him. "So it has an honest beginning even if you're the most authentic thing in here. Maybe you can give her your feedback."

"No," he says a little too fast.

He has never felt so unworldly. As a boy he swore that he'd never leave Mani so it's unfathomable to be in a metropolis on the other side of the world, speaking its foreign language and about to spend more money on one meal than three months' worth of pay checks.

The first course arrives and the two waiters lift the cloches with such precision timing as if on either side of a mirror. The food has a relationship to home although Apostolis has to work hard to get there. Miso soup is served in an egg cup which also contains two tough broad beans. Petzechroula would die laughing.

With the next dish comes a shot of tepid tsipouro.

"Excuse me," he says to the waiter. "Could I have some ice?"

"I'm sorry," the man replies as politely as possible for someone that stares through him with disdain. "The chef believes that the warmth complements the pa-su-ti-k-o slice."

"Pasticcio," Apostolis corrects him.

"Excuse me?"

"Nothing." He smiles at Naomi who seems to be enjoying it. He'd love her to come to Athens now more than ever.

A dollop of tzatziki turns out to be the highlight, transfixing and spot-on, but then he's confused by a wafer of red caramel moulded into the shape of an owl. Oregano, rosemary and laurel permeate his nose and bring him hope but whole sprigs are tempura battered. By the seventh course, something cubed and nondescript, easily scooped in one mouthful and yet expected to be eaten slowly, he would forfeit the rest for a decent-sized portion. It's not the Japanese way but he'd tip if it came without a cloche. Double if his seat wasn't eclipsed by the watchful eye of a hovering waiter.

The ever-changing courses make it difficult to speak. Naomi points him towards the head chef as she passes the gap in the window. The petite but imposing woman catches his eye.

Naomi groans. "You're hating this, aren't you?"

"That obvious?"

"Shall we make a run for it? I know a burger place."

"It's fine." He covertly scowls at his shadow. "But it would be nice to relax. Do you like it at least?"

"It's easier to see through it when you're not paying."

He appreciates her cynicism.

"I think I fucked up," she says.

"It's an experience. Don't worry."

"Not about the meal. You were right. The game with my father. Why keep at it? It was justified in the beginning but now it's tedious."

"How do you want it to end?"

Another plate is served but the two diners don't take any notice. One of the waiters scoffs at their lack of a reaction.

"I don't know," says Naomi.

"Holding out until he dies won't make you the winner."

"You know what's the most insane part? After this meal I'd have to pay for my own flight."

Dessert is a sheet of burnt dough smeared with brown paste and a luminescent green blob. A wildflower is stubbornly wedged on top, unwittingly reminiscent of the hardy shrubs of Apostolis' childhood. It's oddly attractive. Somewhat confusing. Mostly bleak.

A waitress coughs to get their attention and speaks with a practised enthusiasm. "Your dessert is named *Charupi's Wild Mani*. You have a flour pancake with locust bean honey and a candied Kalamata olive."

Apostolis is more repulsed by this dish than any other. Its description not only plagiarises a topography that has no right to be appropriated but traps the memory of a boy that has moved on. The chef has bastardised the past. He can't begin to imagine what her family must think.

Annoyingly the carob jam manipulates his senses; if he closes his eyes it could be Petzechroula's offerings. He doesn't know what to do with that. He hears his aunt. 'You need to leave that boy alone– He doesn't belong here– Look at his hands– Don't play innocent with me– He's idealising Mani, and you.'

He swigs an orange liqueur and washes away her voice but it only affords space for his own retorts. 'It's just a summer friendship– Harmless fun– Something to pass the hours.' He's since accepted that Petzechroula had seen that the attraction ran both ways. She'd been wrong about so many things but she'd been right about that.

"Apostolis."

"I'm good. I just need some water."

But Naomi hadn't noticed him zoning out and was instead drawing his attention to the person approaching. "This has nothing to do with me," she whispers.

"Good evening," the chef says.

Apostolis half stands to greet her. "Thank you for having us," he replies, as if the booking had been a personal invitation.

"I heard that you can speak Japanese. Are you Greek?"

"I am. Just here for a few days on business."

"Okazaki Yuki."

"Asteriakos Apostolis."

"Suzuki Naomi," his date adds, her eyes fixed on his obvious squirming. "Delicious meal," she adds.

Yuki dismisses it, uninterested in the opinion of another Japanese diner. There's an arrogance to her. Naomi's first instinct is to loathe it but she reminds herself that as women they need it to survive.

The chef snaps her fingers for a waiter to bring over a chair. She commands the gaze of every other jealous diner but is confident enough to take no notice. "Do you mind if I join you? I hope that I'm not interrupting." She's already seated. "Plenty of Greek businessmen have dined here but I'd prefer your opinion than the labours of a translator who tells me that everything is wonderful. Where are you from?"

"Athens," he lies, ready to kick Naomi under the table.

"I spent a summer in Mani when I was young. In a village called Vatheia. I learnt some of the recipes there."

"That's where you took inspiration for the last dish."

"It left a lasting impression but I've had to scramble to remember the food as I was so young. I always wanted to return. Tell me if I did it justice."

"You did." He stares at her. She's a lighter version of her mother. A touch of her father. He searches for her brother but can't find it.

She hadn't recognised him or flinched at his name. This grown, boastful Yuki wouldn't shy from calling him out if she had an inkling. Had he really become so different?

"Any highlights?"

"The tzatziki. You had the size of the cucumber perfect." He scrambles for something else. "The grilled octopus took me back to my childhood."

"Thank you. This means more to me than any award. The meal is on the house. It's my pleasure to host you."

"That's too kind."

"I insist. Was there anything I can fine-tune? Suggestions for flavours I got wrong?"

She asks so innocently, with a smile as saccharine as the olive spoon sweet, that he doesn't realise the ambush. Naomi clicks her tongue to warn him but he's in too deep.

"The candied owl was an inspiration from the rooster?"

Yuki's smile slips for the slimmest of moments before she composes herself. "I ate one at a festival and I'm positive that it was an owl. It's the patron of the goddess Athena."

He could congratulate her on the research and leave it be but he pushes back. "I've only seen roosters. It's always roosters." He regrets it immediately. Maybe the drink pairing was a mistake.

"I don't know if it matters since it's an homage," says Naomi, whipping out some credible negotiation skills.

"It matters because I curated this menu with care."

Now Apostolis is irritated.

Neither budges as the room turns cold.

He wants to punish her. He could add to his criticism. The food is flavoured but not flavourful, there wasn't enough olive oil to braise the octopus, the orzo should be al dente, the offerings miserly, the price insulting to any Greek. He wants to drag her to Vatheia and sit her at the table and make her eat a bowl of Petzechroula's bean soup and shout, 'This is everything wrong with it,' but it winds him to remember that this isn't possible.

He caves. "It was wonderful. Honestly. If I wasn't homesick before then I am now."

Her face has become acerbic as if she's downed a bottle of the sour plum and quince wine. "You've been very helpful."

She looks to the door as a solo diner enters the restaurant. The older man nods at her, scans the table and meets Apostolis' eyes before continuing to the bar.

"If you'll excuse me," she says. "I hope that you enjoy the rest of your stay."

Once she has gone, Naomi grabs his arm. "I hope you enjoy the rest of your stay," she mocks. "You know she has no intention of changing a thing. If anything she's put out a hit on you. I bet she's furious that she offered to cover the meal."

"Should we pay anyway?"

"God no. I need that money now."

"You're going to fly to Athens?"

"No. But you can tell my father that I did something good with it."

"What's that?"

"Make something up. You'll have to trust me."

"I'm sorry I couldn't convince you."

"You were never going to. But I decided something. Since I'm not telling you about my past it's unfair to expect to find out what that was all about."

Apostolis glances towards Yuki as she greets her father.

He shrugs. "I think this is where we call it a night."

"So I didn't convince you either? I thought this dress might have done it. I was never going to, was I?"

"I'm sorry Naomi."

"I figured. Shame. I think it's why my father sent you. He would've like that, the son he never had. Taking over the business and all."

They ask for the bill but it's covered and so they walk out sheepishly, as if complicit in a robbery that they didn't want any part in.

"Thank you for today," Apostolis says.

"And thank you. Back to my humdrum life."

"Come to Athens and I can repay the favour."

"We could go to a beach. Or you should go anyway when you're back. I don't know what happened there, I'm guessing Mani, but you should. I know, I'm a hypocrite, but you have a better shot at getting over yourself."

"We could both try. Maybe there's a deal to be made."

"Maybe. We could also fuck in a love hotel but some things just aren't meant to be." She pecks him on the lips. "You take care of yourself."

"Wait. Your money." He hands her the envelope.

"You make me feel like an escort." She pockets it before leaving him to face the rest of the night alone.

He's tempted to run up to her and go for another drink. It would be fun but he knows it wouldn't be right. He looks back at the restaurant. He's as irritated by Yuki not remembering him as he is with Megumi for belittling him. Neither has offered a route to the Haruki that he's yearned for.

He couldn't get what he wanted and neither could Hasegawa.

In two days he'll return to Athens empty-handed. He pities his boss who doesn't yet know the outcome and wishes that he could stay here longer so as to keep his hope alive. He'll tell him that Naomi is doing well and that she's thinking it over. He guesses that they'll not hash it out past that. That her words won't be regurgitated or pored over. And that Hasegawa will compartmentalise it and carry on like before until he's no longer alive to be tortured by it.

He guesses that neither of them will speak of this trip again.

26

Tokyo
26th October 1980

Apostolis lingers under the glowing light of a pharmacy and watches as Yuki's father steps out of the restaurant with a bag of food.

He can't help but embrace the excitement of tracking him onto a packed carriage. It's unimaginable that Megumi disclosed his visit so Apostolis doesn't work at concealing himself even if he's easily exposed as the only non-Japanese onboard. He traces the Oedo Line on the map above the doors and guesses that Toshihiro will transfer to the Chuo Line at Shinjuku, homeward-bound for Aoyama-itchome.

Apostolis has nowhere to be, his time in Tokyo unsuccessful but far from over. Otherwise, he's unsure why he's following him. Anthropological research. That's what Haruki had gone with.

When Apostolis first began to decipher the letters he'd questioned his sanity. They read more like a collective effort than a coherent narrative penned by the same person. This, sort of, mind committee sometimes described him as a friend and other times like a hamster ready for dissection. Sometimes Haruki's words were directed at the nameless grandfather and other times spilled onto the page in free association. Once, Apostolis had been reading the letters on his balcony when a gust of wind scattered them and it had been no mean feat to return them to their chronological order.

In one entry Haruki had written that his father was able to pick out any rock from a pile, the nameless grandfather the same with any animal from its troop, and Haruki himself with *the Greek boy from a crowd*.

He gets to test out this theory himself, deliberately losing his target as they transfer at Shinjuku. It's only by chance that he spots Toshihiro on an escalator above head height. Curiously he's headed for street level.

Tourist guides say that this district comes alive at night, with each of the buildings a vertical strip of neon lights advertising J-pop bands and electronics companies. Taxis occupy the six-lane boulevard whilst traffic lights add to the dazzling order. Toshihiro veers towards a pedestrianised area. The man had once been able to cycle the breadth of Laconia but now tired legs make him an easy mark.

As the alleys narrow, Apostolis is accosted by a large American offering him women and beer. He pretends that he can't speak English. Hasegawa had taken delight in forewarning him about here and one other area of the city. 'Apostolis-kun, they must be avoided at all costs and when visiting them no expenses must be spared.' There's Roppongi to the east and right here in Kabukicho.

At a safe distance from Origami, Toshihiro feeds the food into a bin before darting into a pathetic, slim building with grey cladding and a metal fire escape running its height. There's only one gaudy sign for a ramen restaurant on the ground floor. The digital screen is faulty and, as the English romaji letters run horizontally, the left side blinks and the scrolling lags. AME it says for a moment. It's part of the RAMEN offering and incidentally means rain in Japanese. It also, by chance, has meaning in Greek: certainly. Then the display sticks on MEN, which makes more sense: noodles.

He walks into the entranceway to find the restaurant shut. There's otherwise only stairs and an elevator. Toshihiro will likely retreat and cross his path. He might even recognise him from the restaurant but so what? He feels daring and investigates further.

There's a gate at the first landing that can only be opened from the top so he goes back down and calls for the lift. *3* is the only button that can be pressed without a key. He can always apologise in broken English if he's accused of trespassing.

The dinginess continues on this floor through to a second door and a buzzer. The man at the desk looks at him with indifference. "Japanese? English?"

"Japanese is fine," Apostolis answers, burying any pretence of muddiness.

"Two thousand yen includes a towel. Shampoo is free. Oi, you want in or not? Nowhere else caters to your lot. It's this or nothing."

Apostolis holds back, unable to disentangle his confusion. Maybe he was wrong and Toshihiro is downstairs eating a bowl of noodles that would be more sating than his daughter's offering. Or he could be through this way. Maybe this is just another council-run bathhouse.

"My advice?" says the guy, holding a cigarette down to its stub. "Go for it. You got this far. It's safe if you want it to be." He points down at a bowl of multi-coloured foil packets.

The idea of Toshihiro and Tassos occurred to him more than once over the intervening years, evidenced in part by his cousin's singledom, but he's always disregarded it given the unlikelihood of that many homosexual encounters going on around Vatheia. It's unbelievable to picture Toshihiro in a gay bathhouse. He needs to see it with his own eyes, or rather he doesn't; he has no desire to witness the man in any sort of compromising position but it might allow one more part of the confused past to take light.

Just like not rowing too far into the cave's depths, Apostolis has always known his limits, but this time he pushes on. It's only after he's paid and is in the changing room, a towel wrapped around his waist, that something else Haruki wrote in the letters resonates: in this experiment of studying Toshihiro he's no longer a witness but an active participant.

It's not too late to back out. He's spent every day since 1962 shunning situations that could lead to encounters with men; it's not like he hasn't felt the urge pull at him over the years but he's always been disappointed that it would be someone other than Haruki. The few other customers by the lockers, mostly Japanese but some foreigners, keep to themselves. It mimics any nondescript sento until one man reaches for his crotch as he passes towards a lounge area. Apostolis swats his hand away but the man only sneers. Considering that Naomi offered him a couple's onsen only hours earlier, today could have spanned out in myriad ways and makes this one even more peculiar.

It's steam-filled through the doors. Better this way considering the stench of shame that lingers. A few men are spread around a jacuzzi although soaking is far from the only reason for nudity here. Most of the patrons are older but a firm-bodied man looks to be his age. Apostolis' heart-rate shoots up as they lock eyes. He could be interested in someone like him. He moves on.

Beyond is a maze of dark rooms that swallows the light. He hears groans from one cell; the man is alone but leans into the wall whilst being pleasured from the other side. Apostolis is aroused and disgusted at the same time. He's considered that he has a taste for oriental men, Haruki the substitute for his appetite, but it turns out to not be a fetish. Neither is he enamoured with the younger man that walks by with the teenaged physique, hairless and slender, reminding him of the boy curled up in his arms that one night.

A dark-skinned man whistles at him. Apostolis isn't unattractive, especially not here, if the receptionist is right with foreigners able to take their pick. He thinks of the AIDS epidemic gaining traction and described by the Greeks and Japanese as an overseas issue; it's less a wonder than a necessity that any native man comes here for pleasure.

A bin is overloaded with beer cans that spill onto the floor. Enough alcohol might allow him to capitalise on the fact that he's tantalised. He could let someone use his body and make up for lost time but he remembers his original mission. Perhaps Haruki's father was a figment of his imagination, his subconscious leading him to this place, but as soon as he toys with the thought he spots him in the sauna sitting opposite a young Caucasian who is playing with himself. Apostolis hangs up his towel and loiters at the door for long enough to let the heat out and be met with a tut from Toshihiro. He sits alongside him, one row up. The show continues in silence. Apostolis is too stressed to be anything other than flaccid. The younger man grows tired from the lack of reciprocation and leaves to find a willing participant.

Toshihiro turns around. "Japanese? English?" and after a lack of response, "Or neither?"

"Japanese."

"Where are you from?"

"Greece."

"A wonderful country. I'm an old man and you can't be interested in me so maybe we can speak instead? Forget this place for a while and imagine that we're among the olive trees."

"We can do that."

"Come here so that I don't have to crane my neck."

Apostolis moves one level down. They are two strangers squeezed beside one another, on the cusp of intimacy that's heightened by their nakedness.

"What do you do for work?"

"I import art pieces."

"Is that why you learnt Japanese?"

"Yes."

"You must be as rare as the objects you trade. I've forgotten the little Greek I had."

"Where did you go?" Apostolis curses himself for being overhasty. "You said it was wonderful so I assume you've visited."

"The south coast of the Peloponnese. I'm an academic. A geologist. I visited the caves."

"Diros? They do boat tours there now."

"Is that so? That summer had quite an effect on my whole family. I'm married with two children. Judge me if you want but I've made enough sacrifices than to feel self-reproach in coming here."

"I don't judge you."

"And you? Anyone?"

"No one."

"It must be easy then. Or do you bear our shame anyway, for who we are and what we need?"

"I think the only shame is that these places have to exist in the shadows."

"I suppose that's true."

Apostolis can't resist. "Is it strange to mention your family here?"

"It's strange to talk at all."

"Did they like Greece as much as you?"

"We stayed in a poor village in Mani. My wife had lived a life of abundance and was willing to endure one summer. She wasn't always such a snob. She came from a farming town. Her parents were poor and realised that her beauty could snag her a rich husband and a good future. I think Vatheia scared her and she returned to Japan more eager than ever to stand firm in society. I'm disappointed that she didn't learn anything. Don't feel like you have to stay. I assume you didn't come tonight to hear an old man's musings."

"This makes me feel less lonely. Please go on."

Toshihiro chuckles. "Sex doesn't solve loneliness so I suppose you're in luck. Well then. My daughter has flourished. I'm glad she loves her work although I'm embarrassed to tell you what it is. It might infuriate you. It bothers me." He shrugs. "Not that I'm in any position to pass judgement."

"And your son?"

"He was the most affected by that summer."

Apostolis should leave. Haruki's letters were addressed to him but this is the epilogue to a diary that he has no right to read. It proves too irresistible. It also feels like revenge for Megumi taunting him; he imagines her in the house waiting for her husband, unsure why he's late. Or perhaps she knows and overlooks it. Apparently pretence has always been her greatest role.

A man pops his head into the sauna, sees them and leaves.

"Don't take it personally," says Toshihiro.

Apostolis is grateful if anything. "Your son?"

"Oh yes. It's a complicated story but he fell hard in love."

"With a local?"

"With the place. A teenage crush when the brain is still developing and everything becomes life and death. Then we left under false pretences. My wife did something heinous and I supported her because I felt I had no other choice. I'm not explaining myself well."

Apostolis agrees but doesn't show it. "What happened after he returned?"

"He was furious. It's quite amazing how far he went to punish us but he's settled now. Not that he tells me much. I'm not sure anyone in my family is honest with one another but we function. A balancing act of needs and obligations."

Apostolis is desperate to know more. For eighteen years he has locked himself away from the sea in a bookshop. What did Haruki do, and how did he fall back in line when he couldn't? He wants to scream, to claw back those years of not forgiving Petzechroula. To return to a time before Megumi abused her power, before Haruki had been dragged away from him.

"Is he happy?" It's a risky question.

"Is he happy?" Toshihiro mulls it over. "I think so. It's a quiet life and I often wonder if he regrets not making more of himself. But his wife is sweet and his children are delightful. I suppose in a way he's happier than either of us sitting here. Is that the answer you came for, Akis?"

Apostolis' back shoots up.

Toshihiro focuses his gaze on him. "You thought I wouldn't recognise you?"

"You've known all this time?"

"Is it a coincidence that you're here with me tonight?"

"I came to Tokyo on business. I've stayed away until now. But I'm glad to hear that Haruki is happy."

"He was devastated. I don't think he's ever forgotten you but he's doing well. What my wife did to him, to you both, was cruel. But she thought it was for the best."

Apostolis points at the sauna. "And this works for the two of you?" It's a petulant remark but he doesn't care.

"No relationship is perfect or easy. It's been hard for Haruki to carve out a life that works for him. Much like this place works for me."

"A sauna that caters to foreigners. Interesting choice."

"I think you already know the answer to that. My son and I both let Greece go but I cannot leave this wound to heal completely. I wish you a good life, Akis. I hope you can find one."

Toshihiro stands to leave. Their nakedness is long beside the point. "This may sound rather crude but I did come for a reason and the idea of you being here is rather off-putting."

Apostolis brushes past him and returns to the locker-room, not even welcome in the place where men come to escape the contempt of condemning eyes. He's barely dressed before the reality dawns on him that he has been left with nowhere.

27

Tokyo
27th October 1980

A miserable morning follows as expected. He doesn't want to leave the hotel room before check out but he's too consumed by everything that has happened to stay cooped inside with only unpleasant, shouty television for company. Tomorrow's flight can't come soon enough. He wishes that he could return to Athens immediately but the money that could have paid for it has gone to Naomi. His encounter with Toshihiro has left him more unsettled than his time with Megumi or Yuki. He feels incredulous that he's come into some sort of contact with all four members of the family, considering that he'd planned on crossing paths with none. They have all convinced him, in their own ways, that he should never speak to Haruki again.

It's a by-product of Hollywood that sadness should be represented by a loss of appetite because, if it's true, his stomach betrays him by roaring with hunger. He goes downstairs and asks Fukuda for a recommendation following the success of the sushi place. They speak for a while and he learns that the man's first name is Akira. He's interested in whether Greece could be a destination to build a career in hospitality. Apostolis thinks so and sells the country to such an extent that he convinces himself that he'd also like to tour around. Akira thanks him and recommends a breakfast place that does beef bowls. It's an exuberant meal that sits heavy but quietens the rumbling.

The hotelier also directs him to private grounds on the other side of the Sumida River. Apostolis goes there, to the old Edo centre, where canal-ways and shopfronts speak of generations-old businesses. Kiyosumi Garden is a perfect suggestion, away from the sea and residential blocks, and offers somewhere resplendent for him to rest his eyes. He'd considered inviting Naomi and updating her about the rest of the night but is glad to walk around the estate alone. The pond boasts jagged rocks where terrapins crawl over one another and scramble up impossible heights to sunbathe. A crane sits on one of the banks and skates the water before it takes flight. Stepping stones provide a route around the pond that ripples red with the reflection of maple trees. Apostolis takes up residence inside the tea-house that protrudes over the water. A long time ago he had the makings of a place like this.

People come and go from the tatami, drinking tea and eating sugared almonds. The hours slip by before he removes himself.

Inspiration takes hold and he catches a train to Aoyama of all places. He enters the garden centre and has never been so unrestrained in spending money. He purchases everything that he thinks will be sturdy enough to be shipped home. Stone lanterns. A tablet with kanji carved into each side of its square centre. A frog statue with Basho's famous haiku engraved on its back.

The shopkeeper is intrigued that these items will travel so far. Everything until now has been decorative but the man gives him a huge number of clippings that should survive the Mediterranean climate. Apostolis buys more than his one suitcase can manage and the owner walks him three shops along where he purchases a second bag. He asks Apostolis for his address in Greece, promising one day to visit and see how the space is taking shape. Lugging it to the hotel is hard work but Apostolis feels lighter.

He runs out again to a nearby supermarket and manages to cross off each product on Hasegawa's list. Back in the room he miraculously crams everything into the bags, careful not to damage the food that his manager has craved for so long. It will be a feat if the cases hold so he deems it better to leave a few things behind.

He can only bring himself to let go of the bundle of letters, he's unsure why he even brought them, but he tucks them into their rightful place in his carry-on. There's also *O Ixos ton Kymaton*, the novel's Greek title the same as the English, both gentler than the sea roar of the original. Since receiving his first copy, it has been translated multiple times and he's accumulated nine versions and nine bilingual dictionaries. He has no desire to learn more languages but has a penchant for reading the story anew because each time teaches him something different. He considers giving the book to Akira but decides to carry it under his arm.

The evening sneaks up on him and he washes in the small tub in his private wet-room, sitting upright and cross-legged, rather than using the hotel's public bath in the basement when he has no desire for communal bathing. He dries himself and puts on the Japanese-style dressing gown. He pulls the sash tight. The kimono sits well on salarymen that he's seen along the corridors but he looks ridiculous in the mirror, as culpable of appropriating a culture as Yuki with her Mani-themed dessert.

He dials reception and confirms the wake-up call. He doesn't have to leave super early but doesn't want to panic and definitely doesn't want to risk missing the flight. He sets the alarm clock in the room as an extra precaution. He turns on the television and lies on the bed, losing himself in the helter-skelter of a sketch show as he falls asleep.

There's a knock on the door.

He fixes the robe in place before answering.

A businessman occupies his doorway. Apostolis has seen his type countless times, one of a million identical ants in this worker colony of a city. The same gaunt features and stooped from a lifetime of desk work. A tired suit and a tie done up so tight it chokes him. He can see the pain in the man's eyes as he in turn deciphers Apostolis as older than he should be.

Apostolis struggles to recognise Haruki in this costume and deadened expression. This shouldn't have been the destiny of the boy he'd known. He knows instantly that everything Toshihiro said to placate his son's well-being was a sham.

"Aki-mou."

Haruki's voice is rougher, with tints of sadness worn down from a life filled with disappointments. He looks past Apostolis to the suitcases. "You were going to leave. Without—"

Apostolis doesn't respond nor does he move aside. He can't invite him in because there are no words that could rewind the two of them to when it would have been worthwhile. He doesn't want to talk about their lives or their families old or new. He can't hear Haruki explain everything away or attempt to soothe him. He can't tell Haruki that he has lived a half-formed life. No life. That Vatheia is dying. That Estia lays unfinished. He can't hear Haruki wish him happiness.

He wants to cherish the memories because these are all he has left. Any meeting will only sour them. Perhaps Yuki was right. What does it matter if the past is an owl or a rooster if it's just the sweet sentimentality of something that once happened?

"The past is the past," he says. "Both of us have moved on. Be well Haruki." He doesn't give him a chance to respond before closing the door.

He doesn't dare move or breathe, as if by holding still Haruki might forget he's there. But Haruki knocks again. Apostolis can't help but be appeased by this although it's not enough to make him change his mind. He's gratified that he doesn't hear footsteps for some time but is relieved when he finally does.

In the morning, Apostolis brings down his suitcases and pays for the minibar. He thanks Akira and asks him for one final favour besides calling a taxi. He would like him to post something. He has already written an address on the envelope although he's spelt out Megumi's name in hiragana because he doesn't know which kanji she uses.

Before he hands over the bundle he hesitates over a square of hotel-branded paper. He isn't sure what to write and finally settles on something across four neat lines that can prefix the letters. He seals the package and hands it over. It's heavy but Akira refuses money for the postage.

On the way to the airport he tries to forget what he's written since it's too late to re-assess, but the words burrow themselves into his mind long after the plane has taken off.

These are now yours to do with what you wish.
I did what was best for him.
But he came to me.
It was real.

Submission

Cambodia / Japan, 1989

28

Siem Reap
8th June 1989

Thick shards rained down jagged and heavy. Alcohol ran the length of her spine soaking the negligee that he'd bought her from overseas. She wasn't sure what had sparked him to throw the glass but, four beers and a post-orgasm whisky later, some violence was inevitable. For months now their fairy-tale had worn thin and given way to a new convention: his wrath, her retreat.

She was barefoot, crouched by their hotel room's door. She wiped the glass from her eyelashes and tipped her head a swift, sharp fraction. More fragments fell. Past experience intimated that her wig was ruined. Past experience also suggested that she'd buy another. 'Better discarded than salvaged,' she'd told a friend whilst shopping after the last one had been destroyed. 'What's that, Betty?' came the snide reply. 'The relationship?'

No one understood. They weren't there at the beginning.

She wouldn't bother to clean up the mess. Better to just tip the cleaning staff with notes that she'd take from his wallet after he blacked out. For now he stared at the ceiling, his head jerking in arrhythmic turns because intoxication didn't allow him to keep up with the fan despite it rotating sluggishly, circulating the hot air and too weak to deter the flies.

He closed his eyes and gritted his teeth. His paunched stomach rose and fell with his stunted breaths, just like during his night terrors. He'd told her that he used to suffer from panic attacks. *Used to*, he'd emphasised. It was an innocuous lie that she'd never challenged but physiology didn't deceive; he was a frightened boy in a testosterone-fuelled body.

They all were.

Most of her clients were monsters, here to feed off her body and hardly more consenting than the mosquitoes. But he was loving and committed. He'd just gotten lost along the way.

She waited until his breath lulled and his panic subsided before moving again. She wished that she could be the one to ease his suffering. Delayed flights. Bumpy bus rides. Lying to his workplace. Deceiving his wife and children. All of it was for her. A few bruises was a worthy sacrifice.

He mumbled something that she couldn't understand, his words mired in drink. English was their bridge, her Cambodian, his Japanese not understood by the other. She used to jibe him in a kittenish way about his poor pronunciation but she hadn't dared to of late. He also paled in other departments. Not that she was enamoured with it but her own penis was a profitable asset for the tourists and repeat customers. 'Your stubby little cock,' she taunted them. 'All hair and balls,' she mocked them, whilst swinging around her girthy dick. Degrading him in the past had been effective for lightening the mood but not now that he couldn't take a joke. That hurt more than his aggression. She hadn't been able to interpret the change until a shrewd friend had pointed out his psychology: these men were desperate to slip into the little boy, babied fantasy. They wanted the humiliation. The submissive position. But only in moments of arrogance. Not when their egos were wounded.

"Turn off the light," he slurred in a half-raised voice, his anger depleted.

She held still, wanting to take him in and remember how he had once been. At first they'd spent more time outside the room than in it. They'd dined, walked the lake, returned for sex laced with promises, headed out for a nightcap, raced back to the room for more fucking, no, love-making, then fell asleep in one another's arms and delayed the next morning's check-out. Now they had a new routine. He would arrive stressed, demand to stay in, drink, fuck or be fucked, get drunk, shout, strike her, wake hungover, apologise, and slink away.

Nothing was ever without its complications, especially not love. She wanted to burn every T-shirt in the night market with the throwaway slogan 'Me love you long time' and set upon anyone that goaded her to echo the line back to them. Love wasn't just a scant promise but a demonstration of sacrifice. Not that anyone else shared this sentiment. Her friends told her to stop bothering, that there were plenty of calmer businessmen with money. But she couldn't keep herself from running to him each time that he passed through. Not passed. Detoured.

"Betty."

She reached for the switch and flicked it off.

He'd only visited Siem Reap once on business. His Phnom Penh branch had been gifted a tour around the Angkor Wat complex. They'd met by chance and he'd found his reason to return.

He was supposed to be in the capital tonight. He'd received a warning from his manager half a year ago after he was caught AWOL. He'd shrugged it off, that if his shirking hadn't mattered for so long then what difference? He continued to play his employers, boastful when he was with her instead of in Jakarta or PP or HK or any other hub within the APAC region. He played down her apprehension and negated the threat of being fired as casually as the acronyms he threw at her. As if she understood any of what he did or how he got away with it. The only acronym he didn't use was LGBT; their relationship, his orientation, her identity, all of it transcended pigeon-holing.

He hadn't mentioned any problems for a while and she figured that he'd worked it out. She would only be hurting herself to tell him to visit less and so she continued to lap up his trips as greedily as when he licked their cum from her chest. If he was guilty then so was she. It would be easier when he left his wife. He just needed to gather a bit more money and then they were free. A few more years and his fury would be behind them. No wonder he was stressed. She wanted to thank him for all that he'd done. Apologise that her only chore was patience whilst his was burning himself out. A bit of broken glass was getting off lightly when messiness abounded not only inside the room but beyond it.

She knew what would help him unwind tonight, get him back in the mood, but better to let him sleep. She pressed her soles so slowly into the ground that she wondered if this was less about stepping on shards than waking him.

"Come here."

It surprised her. "Bathroom first."

"Betty."

"I'm going to clean up."

"Why?" He'd already forgotten. He whined for her. She could make out his hands trying to grab at her in the darkness. Double-vision set him off by a metre.

She closed the bathroom door before turning on the light above the mirror. Better that he falls asleep and she nestles into his clutch than he slurs an apology and toys with her penis some more. Her clients who wanted to be penetrated or give her head were charged extra but all of them had to keep their hands off her penis post-sex. It devastated her to be reminded of her appendage when she needed to be held like a woman, not wishing to highlight a body that had betrayed her. Only he was allowed to do as he pleased.

The only bills he paid for were hotels and food but never for her time. He didn't like that she was with other men but if he wouldn't detach himself than neither would she. The day he appeared with multiple suitcases would be the last time that another man touched her. This was what her friends hadn't understood. With him she was neither a gimmick nor a commodity. Unlike the men who were racked with self-reproach in the mornings, in sobriety he still wanted her. When he was far from her too. Leaving messages for her, telling her he was bereft without her, sending her money to make up for his absence. Only with him had she not felt like she was for sale. He would whisk her away when the time was right. It was the fantasy that all of her friends had bought into, even the most cynical. None had succeeded so far but she could be the first to give the rest hope.

But by the time she'd become devoted to him, his lovingness and charm had been time-limited and he'd turned a miserable drunk. He cursed his homeland in its totality and blamed its culture for all his woes. She'd lost track of his rants and asked him not to complain in Japanese. When he staved off alcohol he would stay up late, sit against the headboard and scrawl essays that she couldn't decipher. Thrusting hotel pages into his hands worked to de-escalate the violence. She'd stolen one once, slipping out whilst he slept, and photocopied it. A double betrayal when she later gave a client a free night in return for a translation. 'This is not a happy man,' the man had told her. 'I think you should not see him any more.' He'd refused to elaborate. But find her a happy man that had made his way here. She'd ripped up the paper and let him write whenever he'd needed to.

She stripped, stepped into the tub and shook off the remaining shards. She looked at herself in the mirror. She was naked except for the wig. She hesitated before unclipping it to reveal her flattened short hair. Smudged makeup ruined her contours. With nothing adorning her body she resembled a boy. She turned to the side, pushed down her Adam's apple and squeezed together a non-existent cleavage. He'd promised her top surgery. He had the funds but just had to transfer them. The rest was unlikely. She would lose customers, which she didn't mind, but he'd been clear: she would lose him too. She could live with a penis.

She tip-toed to the door and peeked through the crack. The hotel's neon sign flitted through the bedroom curtain. He was asleep. She pretended that he was basked in moonlight on an island in the Mediterranean just like he'd dreamt. She remembered their first encounter. His awkwardness. His coyness in trying to ascertain what every man wanted to know. His earnestness in wanting to spend the night with her regardless. His tenderness.

Her finger was bleeding. It was a minor cut. She ran it under the tap. The harsh light of the morning often saw her contused. 'Better me than his manager,' she'd told the others. 'You're stupid to stick around when no one else would,' they'd replied. 'You'll only have yourself to blame when you wind up dead.' No one knew his hopes and dreams like her. No one saw his potential, nor their addiction to one another, returning even when they'd both tried not to.

Once, when he was in a foul mood and sprawled on the bed, he'd rolled into her, placed his hand between her legs and cupped her testicles. 'One day I'm going to marry you and we're going to move to Greece,' he'd said. 'We're going to live by the sea and build a house together.' He'd been insistent on the specific set-up, and the fantasy had forever played out in his drunkenness. The sex was better, his mood reeled in, and his pledge as bewitching as the bays he described. She found photographs in a picture book. It looked a bit like here. His work hadn't covered Europe and he'd never holidayed there but it was logical, his way to recreate their life away from anything they knew. Perhaps there things were more progressive. 'Fuck me on the Greek sand,' he often said, turning around to her as she penetrated him, with him on all fours. Or, once, with her on her front: 'I'm going to dive into your ass like jumping into the blue lagoon.' That time she'd failed to stifle a laugh and met his fist. Since then she'd agreed with all of his plans even if he rarely remembered them in the morning.

She picked at some final pieces of glass and emptied the handful into the bin. She washed her face and sat on the toilet to squeeze out his semen. She wiped herself down, pulled up her knickers and tucked herself under. He wouldn't like it but without hair or makeup she needed something to anchor herself.

She crept to the bed and lay next to him. Sure enough he rolled into her and his arm flopped over her side. She wrestled him off as he grew erect again, his penis pushing into her back. Impressive, given his state, especially considering the amount of men who blamed her when they couldn't get it up. She allowed one of his hands to slip her panties to the side. Her testicles fell loose but he stopped short of cradling them. That wasn't so unusual as snoring typically followed but this time she heard him sob. It was a perverse thing that she should feel pleased, and that she too should gain an erection from this, but she couldn't deny her happiness as his tears landed on her shoulder.

She was excited to tell the girls about this development. She would ignore the detail of the broken glass. She let him cry for a while, not wanting to break the intimacy of their silence, but it was better that he shared what was on his mind. Better her than his wife. The more secrets she held the less she was the secret. She turned to face him. Her tiny frame was lost in his staunchness. She liked his weight on top of her when they were in missionary position but preferred to be facing away when they were side by side, happy to embrace his warmth but detesting his stench of alcohol. She wiped away his tears.

His hands didn't move to her. If only she had breasts for him to fondle–

She remembered that this was her fantasy.

"What's wrong my handsome boy?"

His body shuddered.

She had an even better idea and put a finger to his lips. "Tell me in the morning."

She rolled over and waited until he fell asleep. He would want to leave at dawn, the intricacies of tonight left unspoken. This time she would force him to confront his sadness. She would have breakfast ready and persuade him to stay a while longer. If she could normalise a routine beyond clandestine evenings then he could see that it was possible. She would suggest that they honeymoon in Greece. Santorini, where she could be photographed in a white wedding dress whilst others would clap and be jealous. Then the two of them would retreat to a hotel room, far cooler and prettier than this one.

His body sagged into the mattress as she wriggled herself away from his clutch. She sat at the end of the bed and stared at his tired suit draped over the chair. He needed out of this life. She would thread it into their morning talk. There was never a good time to break free so why not now? It wasn't like she hadn't said it before. 'Save it for your wife,' she used to say if he complained about work, tarnishing their hours together. Back then at least, she would wave her penis at him and they would laugh it off or fuck it out of their system.

She dressed as silently as she could and threw on a hooded sweater that covered her head.

"Where are you going?"

His voice startled her. "Just a walk."

"I'm too drunk. But not too drunk if you know what I mean."

"I know what you mean."

"You don't want to be with me?"

She put on her shoes. "You sound pathetic." The words slipped out.

He turned to her with a wounded expression.

She never knew how he would respond. She perched on the edge of the bed and stroked his face. "I didn't mean that. My handsome boy."

"Fuck off on your walk." He switched on the sidelight and sat up. He picked up the pad and started to write.

She grabbed her Discman and left.

She went to the 7-Eleven and gathered supplies for a breakfast that she could throw together. Sweet things that would ease him into her ultimatum. She also bought cigarettes and smoked one on the corner. She didn't feel like walking but wanted to give him space. She put on the headphones and pressed play. The Discman had made the others jealous. They were on the receiving end of meals or shopping sprees, usually ludicrous, gauche clothes that the men chose on their behalf, but nothing as special as this. The box had been wrapped in a silk cloth, tied so intricately that she didn't want to undo the folds. He'd since brought her a new CD with every visit. Not that she listened to his offerings. She couldn't stand his enka and J-pop and instead bought bootlegged versions of musicals from the West End and Broadway. They had more interesting melodies and lyrics that she could sound out, if not always offering enough context to spin a coherent plot. She skipped to the songs that she enjoyed the most, garbling over fast-paced lyrics or lamenting alongside the ballads as if under a spotlight.

She liked this particular song, the singer comparing herself to Marilyn Monroe whilst asking her partner to take her dancing. The first track was upbeat but the promise became more veiled across the soundtrack until it was so glib that she was glad to not know what happened on stage. She harmonised but was interrupted by a gruff voice from beyond the headphones.

She looked up to see a man snarling at her. Trained vigilance made her scan for an exit.

He stood between her and the convenience store. Otherwise the street was dark and there was no one else around. She paused the song. She didn't know if she should raise or lower her pitch on answering him, unsure of which would appease him.

She tried to stop herself from trembling. "Sorry?"

"I was talking to you." The twang of an American accent.

"Sorry," she said again, the word not hers to own but hers to bear. She hated having to apologise to men. Hated being deferential. Hated that she had to appease them to survive.

"I asked what you were saying to me?"

She wanted to tell him to move on. "I wasn't," she said meekly and pointed to the Discman.

She could guess why he was loitering. It was how most men crept onto the scene. Someone would likely be on the receiving end of some nasty sex before the night was through; the best they could hope for was that he wasn't rough and that he'd leave with a bit more acceptance of himself rather than expend his shame and become enraged in their presence. She pitied him. Cambodia was a long way from home to be allowed to express himself. Another time she might have tried to placate him or spurred him on but she just wanted to get back to the room. She would tell her friends about him. Compare him to her own man who had come so far. A bit of violence was evolutionary.

She hoped that he was still awake. She would tell him that she loved him. Allow him to do what he wanted with her body. Let him leave without any demands. As long as she could just get back.

The man scanned her body. Her hoodie hung flat against her chest whilst there was a bulge in the fishermen-style trousers where she hadn't re-tucked properly.

"I'm sorry," she said again.

"Fucking tranny." The man snatched her cigarette packet and walked away.

She let go of her held breath. She kept the music turned off and listened for his footsteps, holding still until she was certain that he wasn't coming back.

Fear kept her frozen. She pictured Greece as a safe haven. It must be for it to come up so often in his drunken raves. Japan wouldn't work and they'd agreed that the backpackers here would only continue to sneak photographs of them. She would miss her friends but if Greece was an option then why not? She listened to the rest of the musical and let the finale play out with its wails of a bereaved mother. The melody carried her heart to a settled place but, before the last note, the CD whirred to a halt and the battery gave out. The incomplete belt gave the night an additional miserable tone.

She returned to their room. Her body tingled with the satisfaction of crawling into his nook. Her buttocks would smother his cock so that the tip could work its way in and she could pretend, if they were entangled for long enough, that he could impregnate her. It would help her drift off. Tonight had to be enough.

She only remembered the broken glass when she heard the crunch beneath her feet. The lamp was off but there was enough light from outside to see that the bed was empty. There was a piece of folded paper on the pillow.

"Haruki?"

She listened into the darkness but there was nothing. Not even the typical tumult of sirens and revellers outside. Of all the things, her mind turned to replacing the Discman's batteries in the morning.

"Are you in the bathroom?" she called out.

She turned on the light and whimpered at the sight of him kneeling in front of the toilet door. He was turned towards her with a vacant stare. His face was purple, his tie tight between his neck and the door handle, leaving him suspended and choked of air. Starved of a future that the two of them might have shared and bringing to close any illusion that this fairy-tale of hers could ever have had a happy ending.

29

Phnom Penh
15th June 1989

Despite the stickier-than-home humidity, the scorching heat of a sun so low as if striving to kiss the equator, Kiho hadn't stopped shivering since landing. It was evening now and she was in the hotel's bar, perched at the counter on an unsteady stool that tipped each time she shifted her weight. Slatted walls opened onto the street and carried through the tropical air, insufferable and thick, but the ramped-up heat did nothing to break her frigidity and she pulled her cardigan tight around her.

She was the only woman, or at least the only one who was a paying customer. Not plastered in makeup or on the prowl like all these others, showing skin wherever they could. No one resembled her. Not the darker-skinned women with breasts spilling out of low-cut tops nor the white men lined in a film of sweat whose eyes feasted on them. Nothing was recognisable. Not the Khmer script on the menu nor the music that may have sounded like inoffensive J-pop at first but was dressed in words that she couldn't decipher. And especially not these other women who preyed on their next payday with a self-confidence that she'd never known.

Being here was all wrong.

She'd had this nightmare often, of not being where she should. Pushed onto a stage and under a spotlight with lines unprepared. There were explanations, decent ones, for why she found herself here. A conference, a honeymoon, back-packing, a sabbatical of self-discovery. Even fleeing an abusive partner made sense. Instead she was cast as a widow, forced overseas to collect her dead husband's body, assuming the lead in a play for which she hadn't auditioned. She was here and soon she wouldn't be, but it wasn't as simple as waking from a bad dream.

She was thirsty but a language barrier stopped her from calling the barman. She only knew Japanese. Even water was unavailable without rudimentary English. Aqua? It sounded right but also not. The electronic dictionary in her bag would have the answer but she didn't trust her fingers to stop tingling long enough to hit the keys with accuracy.

There was a fridge in her room. She went to lift her feet but they remained in place, disconnected from the rest of her. She didn't trust them to take her weight.

The barman met her eyes. She looked down at the floor. A moment later he placed a glass of water in front of her. She wanted to cry. She reached for the drink but she'd heard about the unsanitary conditions, that she was sure to get dysentery from the ice. Then again it was a nice hotel. That much she'd afforded herself because if the money was gone then she might as well tap out completely.

She fished for the cubes but had nowhere to drop them and gave up. She wiped her fingers on her skirt. The stool wobbled. She was vertiginous this far off the ground. She hadn't wanted a table even though the hostess had offered her one. 'Me, one,' she'd managed to say at the door, dredging up more English than she thought possible, apologetic in holding up a shaky index finger. She hadn't waited for the answer, shuffling across the room to show herself to the bar.

She didn't want to be down here. Or here at all. In today out tomorrow, that was the plan. She wanted to be a ghost, to not give weight to her stay nor leave any trace, not even an indent on a pillow nor the unfurling of more than the smallest flannel in her bathroom. The stamp in her passport would forever tell a different story.

She couldn't understand why the authorities wouldn't fly his body without her accompanying it. His workplace had refused to offer assistance or pay out any insurance, not when he'd been let go months earlier. 'Hadn't you known this about your own husband?' the man on the call had asked with incredulity when she telephoned to inform him of the situation. She'd kept him on the line by crying, embarrassed to beg him to listen for a while longer, and no longer expecting financial aid but rather compassion. For someone to console her, even a faceless man in Human Relations. He'd been unwilling to offer her as much as an apology; 'Company policy,' he'd said. Sympathy didn't amount to providence. If she hadn't been so scooped out then she'd have been furious. Confused and saddened too. But since the call from the Cambodian police, emotions were just words and any colour or shape to them had been washed away and left in her a frozen core. All she had, all her body knew, was ice.

The bartender coughed to get her attention. He held a small bottle in front of her, cool from the fridge. He tapped the lid to show that it hadn't been tampered with. *Tonic* she read from its label. The barman poured gin into a glass a third of the way, topped it with the mixer and balanced an umbrella on the rim. The paper was torn, the yellow faded.

"Arigatou," she said on autopilot.

"Dou itashimashite."

"Ee?" Her intonation pitched, surprise and hope the first of her emotions to thaw.

He threw up his hands to deal himself out. Her hope nose-dived.

She took a sip and glanced at the Caucasian men nursing beers, cocksure in cat-calling women or sitting alone. They were widow's peak grey or balding, with peeling foreheads and in a uniform of Hawaiian shirts and sandals with white socks. She tried to imagine Haruki in this attire but she only knew him in a suit and–

She shuddered.

A man a few seats along raised his glass to her. She looked away. The last thing she wanted was attention. She would drink up and go back into hiding. In Haruki's absences she'd faced the world with the assuredness of a married woman. His death changed that, at least her impression of herself if not the optics. To feel alone was not the same as to be alone. This is what her life would be now. Dinners for one or nothing at all. Not that her appetite had returned.

She couldn't understand why he was mellow each time that he'd returned from here. Unhygienic food stalls, the stench of sewage, the noise of a million spluttering motorbikes. Something had enamoured him despite his claims to hate travelling. She'd often wondered how his expenses had benefited the business. Apparently he'd made for good morale for these satellite branches. Apparently his expenses had since become hers. She hadn't checked his passport for some time. A simple glimpse would have revealed the truth. After the first year in the role, when he'd been everywhere multiple times, the novelty of flashing her his visas had worn off. Since then he'd simply locked it in his office for safe-keeping. How forthright he'd been when all the time he was so close to being caught. Yet it had been his company that had found him out. If they hadn't he'd still probably be alive and she still wouldn't have known. Why was it that the person being lied to was also dealt the double blow of feeling a fool?

Earlier today, after picking up his passport from the station, she'd checked into the hotel, sat on the bed and flicked through it. So many Cambodian entry stamps. Whoever she was had to be worth it. That was something that she'd figured out on her own. Just one more hit in a series of blows that had followed the first call.

It had been a rude wake-up, the ring of the handset arriving at dawn, more intrusive and cruder than a knock on the door. She'd been confused by the strange Japanese voice on the static-filled line. The caller was merely a tourist, able to speak English and pulled off the street by the police to bridge the conversation. This poor man, she'd kept thinking, feeding her lines about something that had happened somewhere else, all the while wondering why she was being told, and all the time pitying him for having to tell a woman that her husband was dead. It took some minutes to accept that it wasn't a wrong number.

Then a delay.

She'd heard the pressure of foreign voices in the background. The interpreter went off-script and offered his condolences, bracing her for what came next. It had been suicide.

A week passed in her own lifelessness until this morning when she'd flown into the capital. She'd gone straight to the police station that bordered the morgue where he lay in wait ready to be signed off and loaded onto the plane the next afternoon. She'd not used the Japanese-English dictionary that had been a present from him before take-off; she'd only pulled free the plastic tag, separating it from its batteries on the plane, but it had gotten its money's worth in those few hours. Not that there'd been much to say except for one question that loomed over her. She'd needed to know.

She'd typed a string of words. The policeman, who could speak some English, gave her a pitiful look after each entry, but heartstrings weren't tugged nearly as hard when a widow's words were digitised. Boredom and his readiness to break for lunch were better impetuses and he wrote a telephone number followed by a name. *Betty*. She spent the afternoon transcribing sentences into manageably phonetic chunks. She wouldn't stoop so low as to recruit her own go-between, even if the hotel's receptionist had told her that he'd do anything to be of assistance. Not quite anything, she'd considered.

She'd used the telephone in the room which had connected to a bar in Siem Reap, the town where Haruki had killed himself.

"Ar-e you Be-tty?" she'd asked, aware that the gruff man on the other end wasn't but she hadn't prepared an alternative sentence.

A shout into the distance, a lag and then, "It's Betty."

"I am Kiho."

The woman didn't say anything but she didn't hang up.

Kiho ploughed on with her rehearsed lines. A yes was enough to know that Betty would meet her in the bar tomorrow morning. It was why she'd needed to scope it out tonight, the only safety net that she could give herself when the rest of her was in free-fall.

A restless night over, she made her way to the bar once more. The place was nearly empty, with everyone else paired up or in hibernation and biding their time until they could try again. The only other people were the hostess and a woman who sat at a table next to a potted palm tree. She was beautiful. Petite. Oddly not so dissimilar from herself and, coincidentally, wearing a dress that was cut the same and in the same light shade of green. Both of them were wrapped in the same teal shawl. Betty mirrored her so much that she couldn't understand why Haruki had bothered. Unless it was about an emotional connection.

Betty looked up. Her face revealed similar astonishment. Distress too.

Kiho joined her and keyed words into the dictionary, presenting them one at a time. *Kare, He. Taipo, Type. Motteimashita, Had.*

Betty gave a curious nod in return. She bent down and retrieved her own identically-branded dictionary. *Sorry, Gomennasai.*

Betty picked at a cuticle. The skin around her nails was red raw. Kiho was supposed to hate this woman but to see her in pain made it impossible to think of her as the enemy even if Haruki had set them up in competition for a game that neither had won. Not when both had prematurely lost.

The hostess came to take their order. Betty chatted with her in their native language, obviously about more than a drink. It was an unfair advantage and Kiho wondered how she was twisting the narrative to paint herself in a better light. Kiho wanted to offer her side, as if this third person was a judge and she needed her turn to paint Betty as the villain. It was so easy to fall back into hating her. Instead she simply pointed at the plastic menu, at a picture of a glass surrounded by lychees. "Joosoo please," she said, squishing the first word so that it sounded more like its English counterpart.

The two of them alone again, she typed on. *Ni, Two. Kodomo, Children.*

I, Watashi. Know, Shitteiru.
Onnanoko, Girls.
Saw, Mimashita. Photographs, Shashin.

She wanted to be sick. She was glad that she hadn't eaten for days and hadn't stayed past one drink last night.

Anata, You. Kodomo? Children? she asked on.

Betty stared back at her, unsure of how to respond. Her bottom lip fell open. "Oh."

Nani? What?

Nothing. Nanimonai. She was cut off as they were served the drinks. *No, Iie. Children, Kodomo.*

Kiho thanked the waitress. If she should be in on some secret then she didn't understand it. She ignored the ice in the glass and sipped the juice through a straw. She was hit by a burst of alcohol that nested at the bottom. She took a second swig without bothering to stir.

Now that she had met Betty she wasn't sure what she wanted. She had no intention of arguing who'd had the better relationship when she already knew the answer. All that mattered was what to tell her girls, one of them a savvy teenager with plenty of her own questions. They'd grown up with a work-away father so perhaps this had been a good thing, a holding ground for his permanent absence. They knew he'd died but they didn't need to know the finer details. When the insurance claim was rejected, Kiho had dug deeper and discovered that he'd sapped everything including their university funds. She'd never known true anger in her life until that moment. She called the airline, the only people that she could think of, and asked what would happen if she didn't repatriate the body. They suggested that she try the police. It was humiliating to be handed off between different departments, having to explain the situation over and over that, yes, she was considering leaving her husband's body abroad. Finally someone told her that it would be discarded of but by then her anger had settled and she knew what she was duty-bound to do.

Betty placed a convenience store bag on the table. Its contents sat between them, belonging to both and neither.

Kiho felt stupid for wanting privacy before glancing inside but she went ahead and took out each object in turn. First was Haruki's wedding ring, this gold band that made her wonder at what point it was removed from his finger. Then a tie, bought as a birthday present on behalf of the girls two years ago. She remembered–

And dropped it as suddenly. She glared at Betty as if this had been a cruel trick. Tears rolled down the woman's face. Nothing about this was fun for her either.

There was also a book. *The Sound of Waves*. She didn't recognise the title at first, not striking any chord, but the author's name gave it away. She hadn't known Haruki to read Japanese writers in English. She guessed that it had been a chance buy at the airport and, given the timing, loaded with meaning. She thought of their first date, bonding over the setting of the book. She was born on Kamishima. He'd been to Greece as a teen. Her mind shifted to Mishima's suicide. She couldn't decide which of these things held the most sway.

She heard Betty sniff.

Daijoubu? Alright? she typed, aware of the oddness of consoling her. But the image of Betty finding his body burnt into her mind.

Wanted, Hoshii. Us, Watashitachi. Go, Iku. Greece, Grisha.

It was like a knife in her stomach, plunged by Haruki's hand and wounding her from beyond his grave. All she'd ever done was dote on him but it hadn't been enough. He'd talked about Greece with fondness but had shot her down any time that she'd suggested a family holiday there. For all he went on about it, and for all the myths he'd read to the girls at bedtime, he'd always had his reasons for why they couldn't go. She hadn't wanted to buy into a conspiracy but something had prevented him from returning. She'd concluded that it was her, that taking her there would tarnish his memory. She'd asked her mother-in-law but Megumi had cast it off as nothing to worry about with the wave of a hand. When she'd pushed on, asking if Greece was also why Haruki and Yuki hadn't spoken for over a decade, or why he'd refused to go to her restaurant before she'd closed up and set off for Manhattan, she was told that it had endured from a petty squabble about something unrelated.

Nani, What. Kare, He. Iu? Say? she wrote in spite of herself.

Wanted, Hoshii. Live, Ikiru. Sea, Umi. Far, Tooi. Everyone, Minna.

She pictured herself and Haruki on their first date. He'd been excited about her link to Utajima. He'd told her that *Shiosai* was set in Japan but based on Greece.

She picked up the book as if it could somehow reveal something and spotted a folded sheet of paper tucked between two of its pages. She recognised Haruki's handwriting even though the words were ragged. Plenty of kanji were drawn incorrectly, many crossed out.

She didn't read the letter. His words were not meant for her. She deserved more than whatever he'd written. She re-folded the paper, making crisp lines at its seams, and placed it at the bottom of the bag. She followed it with the ring, the tie and the book.

Anata, Your. Ryokou, Travel, she typed before she reached into her wallet to pull out some notes.

Betty held up her hands to refuse.

Kiho shrugged. She placed enough money on the table to cover her own drink alongside the dictionary and the bag. She wouldn't take any of it forward. She stood and crossed over to the reception where she asked for a taxi to begin her journey home.

30

Aoyama
3rd July 1989

The mansion in Aoyama used to be fragrant and alive, with chatter in all quarters and an aroma to rival a flower shop. Now it merely held portraits of ghosts and the lingering, pungent smell of incense from the family shrine. Time had eroded the house's contents and rid it of its inhabitants. Everyone had gone. Everyone but Megumi.

No one visited except out of obligation or because they were being paid to. Leading to his death, Toshihiro had talked to her with the intimacy of a slug. Whenever she dredged his image it was from the tower house that summer with his back turned away. And Yuki hadn't returned to Japan for so long that Mani and Yui talked about their aunt as if she was a mythological creature. When she spoke to her daughter on the phone it was always a rushed affair, Yuki name-dropping filming locations and ingredients so foreign that Megumi barely recognised her voice. She often wondered if it was a personal assistant speaking on her behalf.

A knock at the door disturbed the gloom. Megumi suppressed a yelp from the pain that shot through her left hip as she shuffled along the hallway aided by her walking stick. She had to greet the visitor herself. That was also different.

She peered through the peephole. Kiho. She'd seen her daughter-in-law more times this past week than she'd cared to. Both of them had dressed in black at the funeral but Kiho was in dark grey, not returned to colour but probably not far off it. She restrained herself from tutting. Kiho had every right to wear what she wanted considering what Haruki had done, and yet she was unimpressed. What of sacrifice and of wifely duties even in death? After all, she continued to mourn Toshihiro and he–

She would never wear a vibrant kimono again. Perhaps in time there would be splashes of pink or azure but to denounce her son's memory so soon was reprehensible. Her world had become a dark place. But there was more she could lose.

She opened the door. "Where are the girls?"

"At school. They went back today."

"Already?"

"They need normality."

"They need to grieve."

To think that her granddaughters were able to study or gossip with friends was incomprehensible, but the cremation and wake were in the past and the world had moved on. Not that many people had attended: none of Haruki's colleagues nor Toshihiro's esteemed peers had come, nor had any of the women with whom she'd used to socialise given their support. Only a select few of Kiho's friends had made the effort. Not even Yuki had bothered, contracted into a televised cooking show and was, as the fax had read, *unable to break away*. The two women had passed the bones between their chopsticks to one another, a straight line rather than a circle. Megumi guessed that of all the people that Haruki would've wanted to be there to commiserate him it wasn't them. Then again he'd likely be alive if he'd been allowed to include certain others.

"Can I come in?"

Megumi wanted to barricade the doorway and shoo her away. "Why?"

"We need to talk about Haruki."

"The girls should be here then."

"School is a distraction."

"It's a betrayal."

Kiho closed her eyes and took a considered breath, like one of those anger management strategies that Megumi guessed counsellors taught to the meek and mild. *I am courageous* she could almost hear Kiho say.

"Please."

"Fine. Come in. You are the mother of my granddaughters."

"You make it sound as if we divorced. I didn't do anything wrong."

"No. I suppose not."

Megumi rolled off directions towards the lounge as if Kiho was entering for the first time.

Kiho stopped short on hearing a dripping noise from behind a closed door. "What's that?"

"A gardening project." In truth, it was a leak from an upstairs bathroom that had damaged the ceiling. It needed to be fixed and yet Megumi had delayed because it had been nice to imagine that someone was up there. That was until the sound carried into her sleep and transported her to one of Toshihiro's caves. She'd never been inside Diros but, in her dream, she was there too, watching her husband sneak around under the misguided belief that the shadows had preserved his secret. It would be costly but a plumber had been booked for this afternoon.

She sat opposite Kiho who rested her bag on her lap. Kiho glanced to the round window that opened to the garden, fixing her eyes on the dullness instead of the light that usually shone through. Megumi wanted to distract her but the walk had winded her and she could only sneak a deep, relieving breath, pained as much by her body as by the silence. In the past there had been plenty of noise, chaos even: Rika gossiping as she cleaned, Toshihiro dictating notes, Yuki sighing with displeasure at cock-eyed origami, and Haruki's friends bellowing with arrogance shortly before their parents collected them whilst dropping off invitations to soirees. It used to annoy her to be beset with that much disorder, her family's mess spilling out in unstoppable ways, but their absence was more repugnant.

"I hope I'm not disturbing you."

"You caught me between visitors. I have a few minutes." The most activity she could expect was the daily visit by one of the girls sent by the care service. Miu or Kei or Rei or some such thing. Always a dim girl with a trendy name but never the same twice in a row. Pretty, useless things that were checked out before they'd arrived, making the abhorrent *Eeee* noise when they realised who her daughter was as they organised pills and fixed a bento dinner, or spoke inanely about her handsome son as they half-heartedly dusted around his picture-frame, and with no promise that they'd be back. None of them was a touch on Rika. What good were support staff if she had to direct them? She'd complained but the sub-par service was the only one that she could afford. As the receptionist had explained, there was high demand and they couldn't guarantee consistency. It didn't make much sense to Megumi but little did nowadays. That was evidenced by the almost-empty funeral hall. In a more orderly world it should have been full. She pictured the vacant seats. She shook her head at the dishonour of it.

"You look distracted. I can come back."

"Spit it out, whatever you came here to say."

The girl stuttered.

"Or leave it," Megumi continued. "The mouth is the source of disaster."

Kiho reached into her bag and pulled out an urn. "I thought it could rest here on the shrine until it moves to the family grave."

Megumi cringed at the unsightliness of it. It was the second cheapest that the temple offered. Her boy warranted better but it was all she'd been able to manage given where her funds had been ploughed. She went to take it but didn't trust her hands and instead nodded towards the coffee table.

A husband already in the ground and now her son. The respects paid by Toshihiro's colleagues were about his publications and may as well have referenced a stranger. Only she knew his true character.

The official line was that his heart had given out but the discreet physician had suggested that if they'd had sex in recent years then she should book herself in for a check-up. She thanked him and said that she would do just that because of course they'd been having sex. Because that version stung a little less than the alternative.

Compared to his well-attended funeral, Haruki's had been dire: the priest giving a deceitful obituary of an accidental death, the brutal confrontation of a life cut short, the absence of guests, the narrowing in of margins around a family that nobody cared about. She hadn't noticed at first that everyone had distanced themselves from her. It was immaterial. It was Yuki that troubled her. *Unable to break away.* The excuse loomed heavy and was followed by a flash-forward to her own death where there would be neither the company of ghosts nor the living. She thought of the one proverb that she'd always hated: bad causes, bad result.

Kiho patted her legs. "Well."

Megumi's chest seized. "Must you go?" A husband-less daughter-in-law became one more person to escape her.

"Don't you have another visitor?"

"I have some time." Her granddaughters had to be a strong enough link. She couldn't let Kiho be the authority on that. "The girls will pay their respects when they come to see me. Although with sports clubs and music lessons I'll be lucky to get a look in."

"I have no intention of stopping them from visiting you. I don't want you to think that this cuts ties between us."

"This? What's this? That you couldn't keep my son alive?"

Kiho resigned herself to a defeated sigh and excused herself to the bathroom. Megumi heard her sniffling, low but loud enough to reverberate. She too wanted to step out of the room. She hated it in here. She always had. But others had hated it more.

She glanced at the urn and looked away. Haruki had told her a long time ago of his affair. That he'd lost his job and was broke from funnelling money into flights to Cambodia. He'd been piteous, grovelling at her feet, as pathetic as when he shuffled around the temple's dawn prayers with his head bowed down in hapless chant.

But she'd been thrilled rather than disappointed because this time he'd told no one but her. She'd written a cheque to bankroll him, with the agreement that he could continue this affair as long as he didn't distance himself from her. He'd grown bored of his docile wife and needed a burst of adventure. The novelty of this new obsession would burn out after a while and so she would let it unfold, a better plan than dragging him away from that boy. Let him fly the nest a little, encourage him even, only to learn that the headwinds were too powerful for a delicate soul like his.

It had been later that night when it had occurred to her why he was bothering with the affair. She'd long accepted that the men in her life had sordid needs. She'd further accepted that she would have to be gracious and turn a blind eye. Toshihiro had found his release closer to home, but the child of a frog is a frog and, finally, Haruki too found what he'd been looking for, just farther afield.

She hadn't been able to sleep, thinking of his teenaged mania whilst telling her about this Betty. She hadn't seen him that excitable for decades. If she'd regretted anything it was preventing him from arriving at his happiness sooner. With little chance of switching off she'd moved to her dressing room, retrieved a hat box, and read through the hidden letters. The Greek boy had told her that he lived in Athens but there weren't any more specific details. It had come as a relief that she couldn't have contacted him even if she'd resolved to. That was letting herself off lightly. She could have found a way. Maybe her son wouldn't be dead.

Megumi was parched but unable to find the strength to walk to the kitchen. She wouldn't ask Kiho on her return.

Akis had never slipped far from her mind. He'd sat in here once but he'd left Japan without intervening. His endnote had been disconcerting and yet harmless. Haruki must have found him – how, she didn't know – but the boy had pushed him away. That was admirable. But he'd also been right. What they'd had was the realest of any of them. Itai doshin. Different bodies, one mind. She sometimes dreamt of fighting his corner, casting aside Kiho and welcoming him into the family. It would have been an embarrassment. Still–

She pictured the boys on their beach and remembered Haruki alone on the boat. Only, he wasn't alone. He was rowing towards something. Her faked letter had brought that summer to a close. She'd stolen a lot of happiness. How blunt it had been but it was for his own good. Or so she'd thought. The only good that had followed were her granddaughters. She couldn't risk them disappearing on her. The panicked feeling rushed back. This was her focus now.

Kiho came back from the bathroom, the skin around her eyes red and puffy. "Can I get you anything?"

"No. Sit. I want to apologise for my words just now. I'm angry at the world and you were in the firing line. It's my fault too. Maybe I didn't raise him well enough. I hope this doesn't mean that you're uncomfortable here."

Kiho smiled. "We're all struggling."

"You've always been gracious to me."

"I had no reason not to."

"I haven't been as good to you. Perhaps we could start afresh."

"That means a lot. But–" Kiho threw a disdainful look, one that Megumi respected even if it made the pit in her stomach grow. "I don't think so. I don't buy a word of it. I'm not going to stop the girls from seeing you so you don't have to pacify me."

Megumi finally warmed to her, to see that she had a spark and that she was more astute than she'd credited. Possibly astute. "Tell me about Cambodia."

"Excuse me?"

"This other person. What were your impressions?"

"Of her? Betty?"

"Yes. Her."

"She was– I don't know. In pain."

"But what was she like?"

"What do you mean?"

"Describe her."

"Physically? Short. Thin. She was devastated. I was only with her for ten minutes. I don't know why this matters."

"It doesn't. You're right. You've told me enough."

"You have that smile."

"What smile?"

"Like you think I'm an idiot."

"I think everyone's an idiot." Megumi laughed. Something about Kiho may have been different, some newly-acquired confidence, but she was still naive.

She waved her hand to bring her questions to a close. Looking down at people was one thing but to punish them unnecessarily was no fun. She had always been justified in testing people's worth. Protecting her wealth, her family—

She lifted herself up. Pain shot through her hip again as she hobbled along the hallway. She smacked her walking stick against the floor because even the echoes of her own company were better than nothing. She thought of the house in Vatheia, of the rowdiness, and coveted what Petzechroula had created. She felt better by remembering what the boy had told her. That the village was fading. That she hadn't been the only one whose life had crumbled.

She stopped ahead of the kitchen. The door to the garden was ajar. She peered out onto the patch. Plants had rotted. A maple drooped. The waterfall no longer worked. Algae skimmed the surface of the water harp's pebbles.

"Maybe I could organise a gardener," Kiho said, having crept up on her.

Megumi wanted to slam the door but held still. "I'm planning to get on with it tomorrow. I've been busy with funeral arrangements."

"Or the girls could help this weekend. They'd enjoy it."

"Would they?"

"You'd enjoy bossing them around."

"I'm starting to like you." Maybe Kiho could be worth having around. Maybe there was an ally in her. For now, Megumi instructed her to fill two glasses of water and carry them through to the lounge.

"It's a good idea," she said, back on the couch. "Bring the girls this Saturday." It was her responsibility to sort them out. Kiho would probably do all the wrong things like tell them that life was too short to fulfil familial and financial obligations and that they should instead run off and marry for love.

"How about they stay for the whole weekend?"

Megumi perked up. Something wasn't right. She used to be steps ahead of everyone but Kiho's voice had trilled. She'd been blindsided. "You're moving to Kamishima."

"My mother said that we can live with her for a while and I can help at the shop. The girls have been accepted into schools. It'll be healthy for them to have a fresh start."

"Tade kuu mushi mo sukizuki," Megumi replied with scorn.

"I think it's lovely there. It's a matter of opinion."

"No. It won't do. Your island isn't suitable for girls who've been raised in Tokyo. You'll deprive them."

"They'll be surrounded by nature and a quieter pace. Besides, we can't afford the rent here since there was no pay-out. Tokyo is too expensive even if I find a job that fits around school hours. The girls can take the shinkansen on weekends and we can all visit during holidays. You can also come to us."

"No." Megumi meant that specifically for her own travel but it was as good a sentiment for the entire plan. She'd been to Kamishima once and it had been hideous. An island near Nagoya with a lighthouse and not much else. She knew through Haruki's letters what the island meant to him. It hadn't been a surprise that if he'd found a wife she would come from there, his mind conjuring a character from the book as the next best thing to the boy. That was until he'd taken a step closer by meeting Betty.

It was a day's journey: a bullet train, a local train, and a ferry. Megumi knew that she wouldn't visit and that it would be rare for any of them to come here. Life would always get in the way. "I'll sell the house. Downsize."

Kiho narrowed her eyes.

"Don't look at me like that. Or you and the girls can live here. I have plenty of space."

"That's kind but we wouldn't want to intrude. This house has too many memories for you. You deserve to stay here."

She'd never heard Kiho use that tone before. "That sounds like a threat."

"I may have given you the benefit of the doubt in the past but I finally accepted what Haruki had always told me, that whatever you do there's an ulterior motive. I realised a few days ago that there was no way that he'd funded these past months on his own. The numbers don't add up. It was you, wasn't it? Take my offer, Megumi, because it's the best I'll give you. I won't tell Mani and Yui what you did. Maybe they'll never find out but I assume that they'll figure out your character in time. One more thing. I'm sorry that it's not a proverb but I wanted to offer you a sutra. Esha jouri."

"Those who meet must part."

"I'll see myself out." Kiho didn't bother to glance at the urn before she left.

Megumi heard the front door close. The pitiful sound of being abandoned echoed through the house.

She stared at the untouched glasses of water. Even if the girls came it would be grudgingly. She could make it fun but she didn't know how. She could learn. No. She wouldn't let them visit at all. She would refuse them when they tried. That would teach them. She threw her stick across the room.

She cast her mind to better times when her name carried glory, when a trip overseas conjured envy, and when her family held status that she'd clung to as a facade for happiness. They'd all had to work to survive her: Toshihiro finding a life that balanced obligation with desire, Yuki casting her net wide to find her way, and Haruki depriving himself of every happiness just to bear her. She couldn't remember a time when the four of them were together and smiling.

She recalled that autumn day with the Greek boy as they watched Haruki and his family walk by. Haruki and his wife and children had been together and smiling, hadn't they? Hadn't that been enough?

After all, she didn't believe that anyone could have everything they wanted. There always had to be sacrifice. Maybe she was wrong, maybe happiness could be found in the absence of sacrifice.

"Esha jouri," she said to herself, now that there was no one left to hear it. In the transience of life there could have been more happiness but she'd left it too late. What had Haruki countered her with back then? The Greek word for happiness. It evaded her now. She could find it in the letters but it was futile, too late for her to learn a different way, not now that she had been left to fester alone in the hollowed-out house that had been depleted, all the way down to nothing but her and expensive brickwork.

...to Mani

Greece, 2007

31

Gerolimenas
19th April 2007

Mani faced the sea and ignored the envelope that sat between her and Akis. Or rather, she was making a concerted effort to look anywhere but down at it. It wasn't the same packet that he'd posted to her grandmother twenty-six years ago but something sturdier to better protect the letters inside. She'd presented them to him and revealed her identity in the cave less than an hour ago. She recalled the final entry, his one addition: *I did what was best for him. But he came to me. It was real.* She had come to Greece to ask why, if this was true, had he turned her father away. The sun was low and warm at the tail-end of the spring day but she was chilled that she might now get her answer.

The boutique hotel where they sat was newly-opened after a developer had renovated a collection of tower houses. The patio was roomy with tables and sunbeds. A diving board jutted out past rocks lined with sea urchins and made for safer entry into the water. Nearby, a girl crab-fished in the rock-pools barefoot. Otherwise Gerolimenas was desolate with dilapidated houses dotted around the small beach. Candy-striped moorings protruded from the water, better suited for an impression of Venice rather than somewhere in Greece. Before arriving, Mani had image-searched Vatheia's tower houses as well as Diros' wild caves but she hadn't seen this particular town.

A waiter took their order. Akis suggested tsipouro. Mani had read enough to want to try it but her stomach was doing cartwheels and she instead asked in English for an orange juice.

"Efharisto," she added, thanking the man.

"Bravo," Akis commended her.

She reverted to her mother tongue. "I only had time to learn a few words but it seems like a beautiful language. Although they say that Japanese and Italian have the same melodic tone."

"I've heard that. I don't speak any though."

"You write kanji. That's impressive enough."

"How do you–" He glanced at the bundle. "I must be less of a mystery than you are to me."

She blushed. It was true. Not only had she pried into his life but into a part of it that she guessed most didn't know. "What can I tell you? I live in Tokyo. It's currently the end of cherry blossom season. My company had its hanami party last week." She found herself shifting into something innocuous. A psychologist's habit and, in this case, especially unfair.

"Do you live in Aoyama?" he asked.

"Gotanda. My office is one stop from there, in Meguro. Oh, close to where you– I'm sorry. The hotel paper."

Akis chuckled and she joined in, an awkward reaction that sang to the oddness of their meeting.

"Kampai," he said after the drinks arrived. "Stin ygeia mas. To our health."

"Stin ygeia mas." She took a sip. "Thank you for agreeing to talk to me. It was unfair to just turn up but I didn't know what else to do."

"It made for a memorable tour. When did you arrive?"

"To Greece? Late yesterday. I had to spend the night in Athens. I think if I'd stayed there any longer I would have backed out. It's funny to imagine that Tokyo's still there. I mean, right now, functioning as ever. With all those people just carrying on without me. If that makes sense?"

"I'm the same with Athens and it's only a few hours from here."

"Did you ever go back? To Japan?"

"Just that one time. You said you work?"

"I'm a clinical psychologist. I specialise in trauma."

"Good for you." He made a sound of approval. "So in the end it was neither geology nor ethology that became the family tradition."

She hadn't considered it that way but he was right. She hadn't chosen her profession because of her father. She'd known little about him, only that he was away on business a lot. He'd never complained about his job but he was never effusive about it. A humdrum role with little responsibility mired in even less ambition. She often commiserated that he hadn't lived long enough to attend her graduation ceremony. She wished now more than ever that he had.

"Where are you staying?"

"A hotel in Areopoli."

"That's not far. Not nowadays anyway. Will you be here for a while?"

"I've booked for two nights. After that I'm not sure. My flight's in a week but I didn't know how long I'd need. Until now I've always been a planner." She shrugged away the uncertain future. There was unbound freedom that came with this impulsive trip. Chaos and emancipation two sides of the same coin.

"When did you decide to come here?"

"I'm not sure I did? I haven't explained well. I only just found the letters." She let out a little laugh. "You might not like this next part but I didn't know what my name meant until a few days ago."

"I went to Japan similarly. One day the option was presented to me and the next I was flying."

"In 1980, I think?"

"That's right. It was autumn but I'm not sure of the exact dates. You were either a young girl or a baby."

Instinct told her that this hadn't been a pleasant experience for him. She tried to cast her mind back but she would have been too young. "I was six, maybe seven." She stopped, unsure how far to tread, cautious about suddenly and bluntly disclosing her father's death. "We've met before?"

"Not exactly. Your grandmother took me on a walk and pointed you all out to me." Akis tried to smile but failed. "That makes it sound like I was her lapdog."

Mani was horrified. She wondered what else the letters hadn't captured. The only other person who could tell her about the past was her mother but she'd point blank refused to talk about that time. "I'm so sorry. That must have been—"

"She had her reasons."

"And we were all together?"

"The four of you. It was after school."

His tone was flat. She couldn't work out if he was indifferent to the memory after so long or desperate to stave off any emotion. Still, she couldn't help but be heartened when all she remembered was disjointedness. "My father worked away a lot. It's nice to be reminded that he was sometimes there. You don't want to hear this."

"My mother died when I was born and I don't know anything about my father. I'm glad that I can help you."

"What about Petzechroula and Tyresias? Or Tassos? Not one of them can tell you?" She spoke their names as if they were more to her than characters on a page.

Akis knocked back his drink. "It was spiteful to send your grandmother those letters. I've regretted it for a long time."

Mani half-smiled, half-grimaced. "Don't worry. She made being despised an art-form. She was hard on everyone."

"Was?"

"She died last month."

"I'm sorry to hear that."

"Me too. I loved her all the same. My grandfather passed away many years ago. I found the letters whilst clearing out their house."

"I'm surprised she kept them."

"Me too. Why she hadn't discarded them only intrigued me more."

"You may not want to hear certain things."

"Honesty is the best policy. I decided that on the way here."

"Then we have lots to discuss." Akis shook his head with a devilish grin. "Mani in Mani. Would you believe it? Please stay with me for as long as you need."

"Thank you." She wanted to ask where he lived but she would find out soon enough. She was hopeful that it was still in a certain place.

"San sto spiti sas."

"What does it mean?"

He scrunched his forehead. "I could have sworn that he'd written that down. Time betrays me. It means 'my house is your house.' If I may be presumptuous, I assume that you're here to find out certain things that weren't in the letters?"

She nodded.

"That's your every right. My family refused to tell me about my past. Now it's too late to rectify that and I don't intend on withholding information from you. Except for one thing which isn't my story to tell. But first you must promise to do something for me."

Her eyes widened. "Anything."

"I would like to read the letters. I want to enjoy 1962 once more before we discuss the years beyond them. It's been so long since I lost myself in your father's words. Until I finish them, please don't tell me what has happened to him."

"I understand."

"You do?"

"You want to cherish the past before potentially tarnishing it. It's why what my grandmother did to you was callous. She didn't prepare you."

"You don't think that delaying it makes me a wimp?"

"You could have turned me away outright. It makes you brave."

He sucked in his lips like he wanted to believe her words. "Have you heard of Schrödinger?"

She repeated the name. "It rings a bell. Perhaps from my undergraduate studies. Maybe?"

"He said that if a cat is in a closed box then before you can verify its status it is both alive and dead. There's something cowardly about me not wanting to find out just yet but it's also comforting. That was how it was before I went to Japan. I lived in hope. Before I saw your mother and father and the two of you. Before any possibility of rekindling was dashed. So now I'd like to hold off a little longer. What would a psychologist say about that?"

"They'd want you to be sure it's worth it. Because what if you open the box and the cat is dead?"

"Then at least we can lay it to rest. It's a deal?"

She respected Akis for being upfront, but what he said confused her. *I did what was best for him. But he came to me.* If he'd harboured feelings for her father then why had he rejected him?

She would wait. Her arrival was sprung on him and it was only fair to give him a few days before broaching it. "Deal. But I think I should stay in the hotel. At least for tonight. It's too much to expect you to accommodate me at such short notice."

"Whatever makes you comfortable." He pushed his glass away. "Shall we go? There's something that I'd like you to see before it gets dark."

They settled up and she followed him in her car as the path rose sharply to its crest above Gerolimenas. Since her father's visit, the entire coastline had been joined up and each clifftop bored into for painless descents.

Ten minutes east-bound and Akis took an unsigned exit, this turn even more sharp and obscured than the path leading to the caves. She went after him and was treated to an unspoilt view of the sea over which the sun cast gold ribbons as if the panorama was gifted to her.

There was only one house at the bottom. She was confident that this was where her father had spent his days and one night. Where he'd considered staying. Where he'd forever regretted leaving. If she hadn't bought into his description of the wonderment of this place, putting his words down to adolescent hyperbole, then she did now. This bay. The sunset. It was paradise.

Tiredness sent her mind into free-fall. She wouldn't be alive if he'd stayed. But, logically, so what? She practised existential therapy, that life was without design and what truly mattered was each person's search for meaning. So much unhappiness had followed her father when he'd turned against what he loved. Greece, psychology, men. All of it discouraged through the virtues of others. All of it laced with dishonesty. She pictured him rushing out the final letter, the words scrawled and more manic than any prior entry. He'd only been allowed to fail. Her chosen profession hadn't, to her knowledge, followed a family lineage and instead she'd branched out to do what mattered to her. Maybe it was time to implement this as a new tradition in itself.

She stepped out of the car and felt for the slight bump to her stomach, this second discovery from last week and the other reason for her quick escape. A hurried removal from her husband with whom she hadn't wanted to share the news. A wedding ring slipped off somewhere over Siberia. For now her nausea was settled, the new life inside of her hushed, her preordained future wide open. She had a lot to work out before it was time to leave.

She stared at the completed version of Estia. She pitied her father but also Akis. She could only imagine how that summer had spun him like a tornado. She hoped that there might be someone waiting at the bottom of the path. He deserved that.

He joined her. "Your suitcase?"

"In the car. Thank you, but not tonight." She hated saying it, wanting more than anything to wake here and be greeted by the view. Where a few footsteps would bring her onto the sand. Where she might feel connected to her father.

"It's not a bad start to the day if you change your mind."

"I've seen worse."

Before they reached the house, with no noise coming from it and no smells of home cooking, Akis turned to her with a quizzical expression. "Something occurred to me on the way here. Did you think we'd have to take a boat?"

"I was half-expecting it. When did it change?"

"About twenty years ago. The road is decent the whole way along. A postman drives the route a few times a week. Tourists don't come in droves but they could. And my little bay is still mine alone."

She wasn't surprised by this last part. She hadn't seen his turn-off, her breath catching when she saw his car vanish as if it had dropped off the edge of the world.

"This, as you already know, is Estia."

It was more than she'd dreamt it would be. Two floors. Balconies. A terrace leading to an outside kitchen. A fire pit ahead of the beach. "You did all of this?"

"Half a century of work. And an inheritance I hadn't expected."

"It's incredible."

Akis flushed with pride. "In time I can show you what your father and I worked on together. But there's one part I wanted you to see today. Many things can wait but not this."

She followed him around the house, stepping over a gangway of whitewashed planks that cut across the sand and carried to the sea. He stopped before the final corner, before the side that she hadn't seen from where they'd parked.

"This has been my pet project for the past twenty-seven years."

He stood back as she entered a Japanese garden sensational enough to rival any city park back home. She had grown up fond of her grandmother's garden but it was a small patch in a clustered house and to be admired rather than approached. This one spread far beyond what she could take in. There were likely limitations due to the arid climate but it seemed authentic, as if she'd just left her apartment in Tokyo a few minutes earlier. There was a bamboo run and a forest of maple trees. Azaleas, willows, chrysanthemums and sleeping cherry blossoms laid out around a pond with a red arched bridge and a trickling waterfall. A Zen rock garden to the side, covered in white sand and raked into neat, concentric circles. She noticed obscured lanterns, statues and stepping stones. And through a thicket of pines, adjoining Estia, was a teahouse with a bowed roof whose sliding doors opened to the shade of the trees. There was one other feature that she couldn't ignore any longer.

"Please," Akis said, encouraging her to step forward.

She was careful not to disturb the ring of black pebbles as she approached the water harp.

Her grandmother had never allowed anyone near her own harp, especially not her granddaughters who might damage it. Earlier this week, spent and alone after a day of sorting piles into keepsakes and junk, and after finding out that her father had installed another elsewhere, Mani had decided to change that. In the stillness of the night she'd crept into the garden. She'd pulled away almost immediately. The noise was dense. Unpleasant. The melancholic drawl of a broken organ.

She lowered her ear to her father's bamboo shoot as Akis poured water onto the adjacent ground. Despite being within reach of a suikinkutsu her whole life, it took coming to Greece for her to hear such a beautiful sound.

She was transported to a point in her childhood that she hadn't previously remembered. Her father was home, tucking them in, and animatedly telling stories of myths from around the world. From other places and other times but all under the same stars that connected everyone and everywhere.

As she listened on to the water she felt an explosive rush of gratitude for those evenings. Her father had held so much promise when he'd built the harp here and she'd forgotten that she'd been privy to a remnant of it. Those times he'd read to her proved that the boy he once was hadn't been lost entirely, managing to break free from the undertow every so often. And now she could hear him once more, through the harp that captured his voice, revealing to her his unforgotten song of love and hope.

32

Vatheia
21st April 2007

She didn't stay with Akis that first night nor the second. She'd shut the blinds and hardly left the hotel room, a self-enforced isolation brought on by jet-lag and morning sickness but mostly from a paralysis of whether she should return east and forget the whole thing. She was, perversely, stifled by the fact that she could drive to places that she had read about. Places that Akis was potentially reading about right now. Each time the thought of her father's fate came to her she pushed her face into the pillow.

When she ventured out she didn't go far, queasy in the open and only dashing along Areopoli's arcade for plain bread at the bakery or headache tablets at the pharmacy. She passed out on the second night before sunset, mildly aware of the sound picking up beneath her from tourists meandering the bars and boutiques.

She was surprised to find that her centre of gravity had disbanded. Unlike the umbilical cord that only strengthened inside her, her pull towards Japan had severed. Despite presuming that she would feel remorse for leaving everyone behind, it never arrived. Patients had safety plans in her absence and owning up to her husband could wait. She'd told Daisuke that her mother was ill and that she'd had to hurry home to be by her side. It only dawned on her in the hotel that this was the same lie that had sent shock waves through her family in the past. She didn't have better words for him.

She used the computer in the lobby but ignored her emails and instead searched for the thing that Akis had told her about the cat. She'd forgotten the name of the scientist but it wasn't hard to find. She wasn't sure that he'd entirely grasped the purpose of the experiment but the quandary resonated with her all the same. She could use the box in sessions as a metaphor for avoiding or accepting discomfort. She thought of Akis and the eventual news that awaited him and turned the test on herself. She needed time. Everything beyond the hotel could wait.

On the third morning she woke refreshed but finally felt, there it was, guilt for disappearing on him. She readied herself with a shower at a scalding temperature and went downstairs to ask about extending her stay. She was startled to see Akis enter the foyer.

"Ohayou gozaimasu, Mani. How are you?"

"Good, thank you. I was coming to look for you."

"Then I beat you to it. Kalimera, Manoli," he added to the man at reception.

Manolis held a spellbound expression. The community knew that Akis could speak Japanese but they seldom heard it. "Did you sleep well?" Manolis asked Mani, changing to English.

"Perfect, thank you."

He said something to Akis, switching again and cutting her out of the conversation. After a few exchanged words, Akis translated. "He was commenting on your name. That it's wonderful. He says you must have Maniot blood."

"I'm not sure about that." It was a compliment, albeit unearned, and she beamed. Any apprehension about the day ahead of her thawed. "I was wondering if it's possible to extend for a few more nights?"

Akis jumped in. "Impossible. She's staying with me."

Manolis leant over the counter and swatted his arm. "Malaka, taking away my customers. We're full anyway," he added to Mani.

"You must be special being invited to Estia. Not many people are so lucky."

"Maybe that's because she doesn't call me a malaka." Akis turned to Mani. "That's settled then. I have the day off so I thought we could go for a drive after we drop off your things."

"As long as it's not too much trouble. I'm happy to just be at the house." She wanted to explore the garden and snoop through the rooms. She'd become increasingly intrigued, agitated at times, about his progress with the letters. She didn't know if he'd finished them and she didn't want to distract him until he had. "I don't want to bother you. I'll only be there for a few days at most."

"Stay as long as you like. I would quite like the company," he added in English to take a barb at Manolis.

"What about ksemoni?" she asked, making sure that Akis was alright with the plan *and* to show that she knew the local word.

Both men laughed.

"Exactly," Manolis said. "Keeping that garden from all of us. Who knows what he gets up to down there? You can be our spy."

"Don't believe him," Akis said. "I hold barbecues every summer. I just can't deal with the ramblings of old men."

"You're not so young yourself, Aki."

A couple of guests joined them and exchanged pleasantries before asking for directions to the caves. Mani relished the link she had to Diros that these tourists didn't.

"Why don't you pack and I'll fetch us some breakfast?" Akis suggested to her. "We can drive in convoy to Estia then head off together."

"Perfect. Give me ten minutes."

After driving to the bay, Akis gave her a rushed tour of Estia. He carried her suitcase upstairs and showed her to an end room above the tatami-floored teahouse. The two windows were at right angles that opened to the sea and the garden, their two countries joined with the turn of a head.

Downstairs, he brewed coffee as Mani went outside and stole another glance at the plot, more green than anything within a wide radius.

"I was inspired by Kiyosumi Garden," Akis said, joining her.

"I can't remember the last time I visited there. How did you manage to import so many native plants?"

"From a garden shop in Aoyama at first. I've been chasing down additions ever since. Online ordering and paved roads have made it easier."

"It must take hours to maintain."

"It's my passion. I work at the cave a few days a week, mostly to keep up my Japanese. The council want me to open the garden and teahouse to the public."

"You don't want to?"

"It's my house, not a museum."

"It's more than that."

"It is?"

"Ksemoni." She threw him a smile and he laughed.

They moved to the terrace and ate fresh squares of flaky, creamy bougatsa, more decadent than her usual breakfast of a rushed coffee.

She excused herself to the bathroom. It was the first time to peer around the house unaccompanied and take in the culmination of Akis' life. She hadn't gone far when she stopped in front of a book cabinet. Most of the shelves were filled with titles that she could read about curating a Japanese garden. The bottom shelf caught her attention. She crouched. No longer were the sleeves decorated with kanji but with scripts from around the world. Some she could understand or manage phonetically – *El Rumor del Oleaje, La Voce delle Onde, Le Tumulte des Flots, Mar Inquieto, The Sound of Waves* – whilst others were in writing systems that offered her nothing. Her heart skipped a beat at the final entry. She dislodged the book from its position.

"It's a strange hobby of mine. At last count I was at eighteen."

She span around, the book still in her hands. "I'm sorry."

"That's the one that started the collection. It's priceless. To me at least."

She opened its cover to find a hand-written inscription on the inside sleeve. *Property of Okazaki Toshihiro.*

"I was mortified when I translated your grandfather's name. I had assumed that it was your father's."

"Could I?" she asked. She'd studied *Shiosai* at school but wanted to read the words straight out of this dog-eared version copy whilst imagining who had turned the pages before her.

"Of course. Actually Charupi– Sorry, Haruki."

"I like hearing that nickname."

"He made the whole cabinet."

"Really?"

"Notice how wonky it is. There were a few things he didn't write about. It might have seemed odd at the time, an unfinished house with a bookshelf in the middle of it, but he became enamoured with the saw. He spent the week after he gave me the book doing nothing but this. There weren't many things about construction that came naturally to him but he was so proud that he'd persevered. It was lucky that he didn't seriously injure himself but there were a decent number of splinters by the time he was done."

Mani ran her finger along one of the shelves. Now that she inspected its edges they were nowhere near as neat as she'd expect for a professional job. She'd hardly started on the house and it was already a lot.

She removed herself and walked to the sea. She dipped in her feet. She and the ocean had a frayed history. Long gone was her great-grandfather's summer residence but she could remember him holding her hand on the slow crawl to the shore and her running back and forth as she was chased by the tide. After he'd died, the place was sold and her link to the sea was severed for the first time. Then, in her adolescence, her mother had moved the three of them to Kamishima. She'd missed her grandmother and Tokyo but at least she'd been back by the water. Now, digging her toes into the seabed, she was grounded once more.

When she wandered back she found Akis on the terrace, lost in the letters. He held up his finger without taking his eyes off the page. That one sheet turned into another. Then another. They weren't going anywhere in a hurry.

A while later, with Mani a chapter into *Shiosai* but uninvested, too attuned to the murmurs of acknowledgement from the reader next to her, Akis set down his pages. She didn't ask where he'd gotten to but guessed from the depth: maybe her aunt's first day of school with the grilled fish or maybe the first time her father picked up a saw. He slid them into the pack and suggested that the two of them go for a drive.

After they'd buckled up, Akis slapped the steering wheel with both hands and sighed. "We were so innocent."

They traced the clifftop as she struggled to find an adequate response. She wound down her window and spoke into the breeze in the hope that any unwelcome words should be carried away. "My father was enamoured with you. It's clear from his writing."

Akis smiled.

"It's also clear from my name," she continued. "I bet my grandmother was furious."

"She was a force to be reckoned with. I don't suppose you know that I also met your aunt when I was there."

"You did?"

"I ate at Origami."

"Why? I mean how?"

"It's a long– it's a story." He laughed and shook his head. "For another time. Is she still successful?"

"She moved to Manhattan, I guess not long after that. I barely knew her and she hasn't kept in touch. She offers to host me but she manages multiple restaurants and I'm not sure that the invitation is particularly sincere."

"International acclaim. I'm afraid that my family didn't venture anywhere nearly as far. It seems amazing that I made it to Tokyo. The idea of me being there would have left Petzechroula open-mouthed."

Mani assumed that she was no longer alive. From what Akis had implied, not one of them was. "When did she die?"

"Before that trip. Am I keeping you prisoner? Is it boring to listen to this?"

"I wouldn't want to be anywhere else. Not that I know where we're going."

"You really want me to spoil the surprise?"

It wasn't difficult to guess since there were only a few places in this direction. It was as rural as she'd ever been. And she'd thought that Kamishima held nothing. They passed a goatherd and his flock as they carried on along a slip of pink-tinged daisies that poked through the asphalt. There was nothing else until up ahead, high on a mound, a village took shape.

She'd seen Vatheia online, the grainy photographs always from the same vantage point, but they approached from a different direction. She felt lucky to witness what so few had.

They parked and Akis led her on a route that could only be managed by someone who'd known the village in its former glory. Nature had taken over, with prickly pears and thickets scratching at her legs. Collapsed walls and tree roots pushed through pavements and made her question if what she stepped on had ever been a path. The tower houses sat packaged together, as her father had written, but were now abandoned and ghostly. The church was gone altogether and the square was impossible to cross without the fear of twisting an ankle. There was talk of renovations but arguments lingered between younger co-inheritors. Besides, with its prominence on the cover of tourist brochures, Vatheia was protected and proved a headache for anyone wanting to attempt regeneration.

They drove back, past Estia and onto Areopoli's outskirts where they ate at a taverna. Akis wanted her to try famous dishes: a xoriatiki Greek salad, tzatziki and mashed fava to share, and a chicken merida each. He described growing up in Vatheia with no hint of sadness at its decay. Mani guessed that the letters had returned him to an earlier, more heartening time.

A little way along was a nursing home. Akis suggested that she could wait in the cafe opposite but that she was also free to join him. She followed him through a lounge with a television blasting a game-show and where a group of women played cards, and then into a private room where a man sat by a window. Oxygen tubes carried from his nose to a canister. He was dwarfed by the chair, his body shrivelled like a raisin under a lifetime of sun. Only when Akis touched his arm did he notice them. His pinpricked eyes struggled even from this distance.

"Petzechroula?" Tyresias' voice carried no strength.

"It's Akis." He perched on the bed in front of him.

"Who?"

"Akis. Apostolis."

"Tassos?"

Mani loitered in the doorway before taking the chair in the far corner. Names carried between the men in a jumble of mistaken identities and timelines, including the man's son and someone called Leonidas.

Akis glanced at her with frustration but remained calm. The conversation made no headway and then it stalled. He rubbed Tyresias' hand until he fell asleep.

Outside, away from the stale air, Akis let out a sigh. "I don't know if I'm helping by visiting but I don't want him to be left alone. I worry that I'm confusing him more."

"What you're doing is wonderful." As part of her clinical training she'd completed a placement with older people, many of whom were neglected and left to waste away. Even families with good intentions lost patience and stopped trying.

"He's disoriented but I'm all he has left. Tassos died of cancer not long after I returned from Tokyo. Tyresias remembers him but not me. Otherwise he thinks I'm Leonidas, my grandfather. But then he tells me that he was a good doctor."

"Oh?"

"He delivered post along the coast before I took over. Maybe he's thinking of Tassos who lectured. If I ever thought that I could learn about my past it's too late now."

"Why wouldn't they tell you?"

"I can only imagine that they decided the truth was worse than not knowing. I've come to terms with it. They thought that they were doing the right thing but none of us won in the end. It's why I moved away from them and built Estia. I thought I was punishing them but—" He sighed. "It's why I'm in awe of you coming here. You have the right to know about your father. But maybe there are things you'll wish I'd forgotten. Do you mind if we drive back? I'm quite tired."

"Of course." She was grateful that she was being given an advantage he hadn't. Shying away would only make her a hypocrite in the eyes of any patient that she would later tell to counter their fears.

That evening, they sat on the terrace after the sun had gone down. A light shone through one of the windows but it was too dark to read. A welcome reprieve. Mani was in no rush to retire to bed and hurry the week along. She understood why her father hadn't wanted to separate himself from here.

"Can I tell you something?" she asked Akis without meaning to. She felt relief in just saying that much. "It's about another reason I came here."

"Zehi. By all means."

"My father didn't have the freedom that we all deserve. I think that's why what he chose wasn't what he wanted."

Akis held still.

"It's like what you said. I'd be a coward if I didn't confront this." She took a deep breath. "I have a husband but I don't think I want to stay married to him."

"I see."

"There's more. I recently found out that I'm pregnant. He doesn't know but I want to keep the baby. Just without him."

Silence permeated the air around them. She worried that her words had destroyed the lull of the charmed evening, hitting like a cold spell and bringing as powerful a storm to rival the one her father had endured that night. But her disclosure didn't cause her to shiver nor did it rupture the peacefulness of their setting. Now that she listened more intently, the silence gave way to the ebbing water and distant crickets. And still Akis said nothing.

Somehow she was glad of it. Whenever patients came to her with a dilemma she would never tell them what she thought they should do. She wouldn't even question them at first. In those initial moments she would instead hold her tongue. Space was what people really needed. So she was put at ease when Akis took her hand and held it in his. And she was further placated that this pose held for some time, with no pressure from him for anything but just sitting alongside one another, in a stance that allowed them to stare ahead at the blackened horizon that was also, mercifully, in no rush to carry them through to morning.

33

Estia
24th April 2007

The week sped by and her flight was tomorrow. She had obligations back home but had flirted with the idea of staying a while longer and righting the wrong of her father's forced exit. She'd basked in the simplicity here where hours passed and nothing beyond the horizon mattered. It was easy to be impervious to the stresses of the modern world but it wasn't sustainable; even when she was able to hush her anxieties Akis would either ask if she wanted to buy souvenirs or would tell her that she always had an open invitation to return. She couldn't picture her life in the upcoming months but he was right, she needed to get back to Tokyo and follow through on what she'd decided. She came to a compromise: one final night and then she'd leave at dawn.

She'd found a groove at Estia and would be sad to relinquish it. She woke early and swam, drank coffee and ate sweet tsoureki bread, then marvelled at the garden and pitched in where she could. She read, absorbing few words but taking delight at each turned page, before walking or cycling the coastline and cooling off in the sea once more. Akis disappeared midday to run tours and she served international dishes with local ingredients on his return. They ate whilst he regaled her with tales of his entangled history with the caves or she immersed him into the tribulations of her patients and the complexities of their lives. In the afternoons, only springtime but too blistering to entertain the idea of jumping in the car, they hid in the shade of the teahouse to escape the heat. She took pleasure in guiding Akis through tea ceremonies on the tatami. She'd dreaded her grandmother's officiousness, the drawling time, the boringness of it all, but to see his enthusiasm with every small movement – a turn of the cup, a deliberate placement of a dish – was as enchanting and refreshing as the tea they sipped.

When they read side-by-side she caught herself staring off and having to reel back her thoughts from her husband or her father until her mind dozed like an untroubled watchdog. She tried not to stir, not wanting to break Akis' focus and discourage his own progress.

She rediscovered the scenes with Hatsue and the other pearl divers as one would find a childhood teddy at the back of a cupboard. Her mother had been born on Kamishima but since reading the letters Mani had learnt of the novel's more recalcitrant origins. Both of her parents had encouraged her to read it. It was lore within the family that they'd bonded over the book and it had carried them into a second date. Recent discoveries had detracted from the romance but she clung onto this charmed version.

Reading *Shiosai* also awakened a memory of her father narrating passages of it at bedtime. It was rare for him to read home-grown fiction rather than the Hellenic myths, although the truth of this swam at such a depth that she couldn't dredge its accuracy with conviction. She had no one to ask as her mother wouldn't speak of it and her sister had been too young. Yui barely remembered their father at all. Then, at fifteen, with her father dead and her mother needing a reset, Mani and her sister had been whisked back to Kamishima. It was this sequence of events that she'd regurgitated during her interview for the clinical doctorate as the starting point for wanting to help people in crisis.

A few days earlier, she'd returned solo to Areopoli and used Manolis' computer. It had been the longest that she'd gone without speaking to her mother and sister. There were no emails from them, which was fortunate given that Daisuke could have called the house and worried them. There were, however, a host of increasingly frenzied messages from him. She wrote to apologise. *The signal on the island is bad. My mother requires a great deal of care. I'm shattered at the end of the day. I'll tell you more when I'm back.*

She'd deliberated with how to sign off. He'd done nothing that made her need to leave him. No non-negotiables like the abuse that would force her hand in therapy and intervene in her patients' love lives. He was kind, helpful and hard-working. She just didn't love him. She was sorry for that. She had gone along with the relationship because everyone told her how lucky she was. She had believed it at times and it was no one else's fault but hers. But her indifference when he would travel for work became pleasure when he was away and then irritation when he was there.

She'd struggled within her own therapy to work out what was wrong with her. Why she couldn't love him. It was only when she'd read about her father's kiss inside the cave that she understood what she lacked and what couldn't be coerced out of her. Passion.

She hit the *x* button to leave a kiss at the end of the email, a dishonest but decent manoeuvre. He shouldn't have to fret until her return. He deserved a proper conversation. But she wouldn't be returning as his wife. She wondered if he had an inkling of this. She also had to tell him face-to-face about the pregnancy, a salvaged feature of a war-torn state. She could imagine what her grandmother would have said, her mind in overdrive and plotting how to glue them in place as a couple. Discomfort crept in with the relief that she wasn't alive to have a say.

Remaining in Tokyo made sense for her work and so that Daisuke could be close to the baby. But she missed her mother, and Kamishima not only offered a fresh start but the likelihood of free childcare. Back at Estia, she told Akis about her dilemma. He simply agreed that it was an impossible decision because there was no perfect answer. The best he suggested was to listen to her head and her heart. She groaned. The exercise rarely resolved ambivalence when each played off against the other.

"My garden," he eventually said, "took years to be cultivated. I sacrificed many things for it. I may not have the perfect life but it's a satisfying existence."

Later that afternoon, with Hatsue and Shinji at the lighthouse, and finding herself pining for the same location, Mani had her answer.

Now it was their last afternoon together and Akis was near the end of the letters. She was sure that he was reading slowly to avoid reaching the final pages. Often during their reading sessions he would look up and mutter to no one in particular, "He was spot on."

Mani hadn't witnessed the beginnings of this house. Before she'd arrived she had looked up Estia. Her father may not have known the meaning of the name but a quick search conveyed more information than she cared for. In short, she was the goddess of the hearth and had wanted nothing to do with the pettiness and squabbles of the other Olympians, only concerned with stoking the fires of a homecoming. Mani had also looked up a map of the area. She'd zoomed into different bays between Diros and Vatheia but hadn't been able to find the house. Of course, she'd ignored every alcove that connected to the road.

Or maybe Akis was referring to a passage about the two of them. She imagined her father's own impossible decision. She was also certain that Akis' words held true. *It was real.*

She didn't judge him for his choice but it was a sore point that lingered. *I did what was best for him.*

She tried to smother the flames of rising anger but it was undeniable. If he hadn't turned her father away then–

There would have been fallout. She probably would have hated him. Both of them. But musing about what might have been, how the road could have panned out differently, was a fruitless exercise. She wondered if Akis had figured this out, that she was here because of his endnote. The swift, cold-heartedness of those words. The consequence of them.

She changed into her bathing suit for a final swim and crawled to where the waves swelled but didn't crest.

Afterwards, she towelled off feeling restored. As she approached Akis he threw her an affecting look. The final page was turned over, the hotel's paper on its underside.

She stared back at him. She was about to offer a cup of tea, something to break this impasse, when he spoke.

"Oh, Mani."

She didn't know if he was referring to her or the place. Either could be true, the word carrying a weight to which he was forever shackled.

"Your father is dead, isn't he?"

"He committed suicide in 1989."

"Charupi was the sweetest boy."

"He was deeply unhappy. I don't know what happened. I think that he couldn't find a way out. He didn't know how to manage a life that wasn't his. My mother refuses to tell me any more."

"Our families are both in the business of suppressing the past."

"I wish I could have seen him here. The way you knew him."

"He rowed from Vatheia on his own once to see me."

"I know. After the trip to the islands."

"I was so excited that he had come to find me but I was also furious. It was so dangerous. I trained for years to manage it. He could have easily lost control and drifted out to sea. I don't think he realised how much fight he had in him. It's my biggest regret that I never told him."

"You had another opportunity." Her accusation slipped out, in a harsher tone than she would have liked.

"I don't understand."

She should apologise. Regress to politeness. Meekness. But this was what she was here for. Not that she blamed him. Akis had never been accountable for her father's life. There were plenty of other people at fault, not least her father. Still, she pushed on. "You could have brought him back here. He found you, didn't he? In Tokyo."

Akis' eyes watered. "He did."

"I did what was best for him."

Akis glanced at the headed paper.

"But he came to me."

"Mani," he said. A warning tone.

"It was real. It's not much to memorise. It's there in your own writing. You turned him away. And now he's dead."

Akis bobbed his head. "Entaksi. The truth then. I've warned you enough times. But first I must show you one more thing."

They drove the coastline without speaking but, compared to their earlier ease in one another's company, the silence pained her.

She stared out of the window, feeling justified that attacking him had been a courageous act. She wouldn't apologise when they'd agreed to be honest with one another. But she also realised, as they made more distance, that she'd been caught up in her own emotions and Akis had just found out that her father was no longer alive. Registering this fact made her reproach herself. She wanted to reach out a hand and tell him to turn back. But no amount of condolences would suffice. Besides, she was out of time.

Akis hadn't told her that Diros was their destination but it wasn't long before they arrived at the turn-off for the caves. The entrance was locked, the tours done for the day. He had a key and they slipped in. With the flick of a switch, lights outstripped the dankness of the complex, far easier than back then.

Even in near darkness she was willing to follow him. They climbed into a boat and he took them on a different route to the official one where electricity that was funnelled through thick waterproof cables didn't reach. A battery-powered torch was the best they had from here.

They moored somewhere that looked like a forsaken place where lost souls roamed. Akis told her to be careful but she was the one to help him onto the slippery shelf. He directed her a few paces ahead before shining a light onto a stack that was fully-formed. It met in the middle, tapered to a point from both directions.

She leant in and squinted. It was complete. Half a century of unstoppable nature. She wished that her father could see this. If only he'd waited. If only he'd allowed himself this freedom, if not to stay then to return.

"I loved him so much," Akis said. "I realise that most people would think of it as a childish crush. An infatuation held onto long after it should have passed. So when I was in Japan I went to see him, to see if I still felt the same. But then I saw you and your sister and mother. He had moved on. I couldn't intrude on a family."

"And did you?"

"Did I what?"

"Still love him? When you saw him."

"As much as ever. I've never told anyone this but I used to think that when the column fully formed he would arrive here. That all I had to do was bide my time. I know what people would say. That I was wasting my life on a foolish gambit. But I was certain of it. 'Just a bit longer,' I told myself. 'You'll see. Just wait till he rows back.' Then one evening I stayed behind and it had happened. Without fanfare. Without fireworks. So I thought, 'Patience is a virtue, you've waited this long.' But there was nothing. He never came. That was nine years ago."

He was on the verge of tears but didn't break. Mani guessed that he had stood in this spot and thought it through so many times that he had grown immune to the catharsis of it.

"I really thought that he'd want to see it," he continued. "Or if not that, then possibly this."

He turned the torch so that the light danced around the cave and landed on the dark side of the stack. Carved into it were two names: *Akis*, written in hiragana above the joining point, and *Charupi*, beneath it in a second hand and spelt out in Greek.

Mani was overwhelmed by the sight of her father's hand-writing, taken off the page and planted here. But she was more consumed by the gut reaction that she sometimes experienced in therapy when there was still some way deeper to go below the surface, like an untapped iceberg. It struck a chord in her heart that beat a new, confusing rhythm and undid all of what she'd believed until now.

"You waited for him to come here? I understand that you wanted to protect my family but then you saw him after that. He came to you. It doesn't make sense. Why would you turn him away if you loved him so much?"

"There's more that you don't know, Mani. Not everything that you read was accurate. Your father was honest in all of his writing but I'm afraid that I didn't tell the truth in mine."

Check Out

Japan, 1980

34

Tokyo
27th October 1980

"Wait," he shouts along the corridor.

Haruki stares back in a half-twisted motion but Apostolis doesn't know what to say beyond his instruction that hangs in the air. He has already said too much in that one word. It goes against his decision to move on with his life. But maybe there's a chance that this time will be different. Despite what he's been led to believe by Megumi and Toshihiro, maybe the man that's walking towards him is still the boy he knew.

They loiter at the doorway.

"Is this a good idea?" Apostolis asks.

"You called me back. Or are you going to close the door on me again?"

"I wasn't prepared before."

"You looked like you'd seen a ghost."

"It was a surprise."

"A good one?"

"I don't know. Tell me this is a good idea."

"It's a good idea."

"What are you doing here, Haruki?"

"Fucking hell."

"Excuse me?"

"Your Japanese. It just hit me. It's– When did that happen?"

"It's been nearly twenty years."

The elevator dings and a man enters their floor. He's in a robe, on the way back from the hotel's public bath. Apostolis pulls his own dressing gown tight. He and Haruki nod to the man but neither restarts the conversation until they're left alone.

It's Haruki who speaks first. "I needed to see you."

The break has given Apostolis enough time for his senses to return. "I don't know."

"It's just two friends catching up. I know a bar nearby if you want somewhere public. Businessmen. Straight-laced. Nothing rowdy."

"Alright. Let me get changed."

He goes to close the door but pauses. He can't risk Haruki running off from having second doubts.

He leans his hand against the doorway, deliberating if he should invite him in. Haruki places his own hand on top so that their fingers interlock. Both of them can touch the spine of the wooden frame. It sets Apostolis' mind hurtling back and his heart racing forward. He's worked so hard at dampening the flame of Haruki's touch and doesn't need to rekindle something that will only burn out again.

"Come in," he says anyway.

The room is tidy. He's all ready to make a break and be forgotten from Japan. Or, he was ready. Now he doesn't know.

"What?" he asks Haruki.

"Sorry?"

"You're looking around as if you're searching for clues."

Haruki points at the suitcases. "You're leaving."

"Tomorrow."

"Oh. You managed to get everything in there?"

"Everything?"

"From the garden shop."

"You followed me. How did you– Don't tell me." He doesn't want to know. Maybe it was by chance that Haruki had learnt that he was here. Perhaps both of them had been in Aoyama during an accidental crossover. More likely someone had told him. He scans through the suspects and can't think which of them would have the motive. He offers an inane answer: "There's some fresh food in the mini fridge but otherwise, yes, that's everything."

"For Estia?"

He nods cautiously.

"How is it?"

He doesn't answer. He can't tell him that he hasn't been there in over a decade. His silence says enough.

"Oh, Akis."

"You don't get to pity me. And it's Apostolis."

"What about this?" Haruki picks up O *Ixos ton Kymaton*.

"You can read it?"

"I can't translate it but sure, I can read the author's name. You came to Japan to see me, Akis. I know it."

"It was a coincidence."

"Are you going to tell me that the book was also a coincidence?"

"What do you want me to say?"

"That our summer together mattered more than anything else."

"Haruki."

"Explain the book then."

Apostolis is mindful of being naked under the dressing gown, as if the exposing question has stripped him bare. He picks up his clothes that are draped over the chair and laid out for the morning. There was a time when he would've had no qualms stripping in front of Haruki. He's been naked in front of plenty of Japanese men this week, not to mention Haruki's father. Haruki turns around out of respect but Apostolis crosses to the bathroom. Inside, he takes a deep breath and looks at himself in the mirror. He splashes some water on his face and gets dressed.

When he returns, Haruki is sitting on the edge of the bed, unaware of the fantasies that have involved him from within the sheets.

Apostolis can't grasp that the idea of Haruki has been transplanted by his actual presence. He walks over and puts his hand on his shoulder to prove it. The touch is unimpassioned but carries weight.

Haruki looks up with a curious smile. "What was that?"

"You're here."

Haruki's eyes mist.

Apostolis crouches in front of the minibar. "Do you want a drink? I think we need a drink."

"This is so," Haruki begins to say at the same time. "Sorry. Yes, I would love one."

Apostolis knows that he should put on his shoes and go to a bar where they will be able to have a conversation that is as dry as the business-like environment, and where everyone can assume that they are associates. Where he won't be able to touch him again even though all he wants to do is hold him. But the idea of leaving the room feels as safe as it does perverse. He gives the contents of the fridge a scan. "Beer?"

"Anything stronger?"

He takes a miniature bottle of whisky and pours shots into plastic cups that are oversized for such a drink. Haruki stands and takes one. They clink the cups but the sound is more like a dull thud as the plastic caves inwards on Haruki's.

"Shall we go?" Apostolis asks. He takes Haruki's cup and accidentally touches his fingers.

"What if I don't want to?"

"Haruki."

"Akis."

"I told you. It's Apostolis now."

Haruki shakes his head with a disbelieving smile that suggests it's not.

"Where's this bar?" Apostolis asks, but only because it feels like the honourable thing to do.

Haruki has lines on his forehead that crease and give him a more fixed stare. "I left once. I can't do it again."

"This isn't the same. This is just stepping out of a hotel room. We're going together. Don't over-blow it."

"And then you'll be gone tomorrow. We're repeating history."

"You left me." Apostolis bites his lip to stop himself from saying more. He can hear how they sound. Like teenagers. Their words are spilling out, their frustrations pouncing on one another like untamed beasts. At this rate there will soon be newly-torn wounds over healed scars. Yet it satisfies him to know that Haruki hasn't settled the past either, that these interim years have punished him too. But he's wanted to say so many things and hear so much in return that he almost wishes that this moment wasn't yet here.

"I can't do this," he says. "Despite what you might think I really didn't come to Tokyo for you."

"That's a lie, Akis."

"It's not. I'm here on work. Listen to me. I can speak Japanese. I work in a Japanese company."

"Not a coincidence," Haruki says, talking over him. "None of it is, Akis."

"Get over yourself. And it's Apostolis."

"Alright. Apostolis. Now tell me the truth."

"No. You tell me the truth. You're married. You have children. I saw them. What right do you have to come here? What do you want Haruki?" He remembers asking this exact same question a long time ago. It appears that Haruki does as well by the way that his gaze takes him to a moment in the past. *You. I want you.* This time, he doesn't have to say anything for both of them to know the answer.

Apostolis sighs and divides up a second bottle.

The television has been on mute the whole time. Whatever's been playing has given way to the news. He glances at the scrolling headlines but they all seem inconsequential. There's nothing more important or weighty in any of those stories than what is happening in this room.

He takes in Haruki's appearance. His stubble and wrinkles and greying sides. His poorly-fixed tie. He wants to suggest that he loosens it or removes it entirely but that would sound like he wants him to feel at home. There have been enough places where they've tried to co-exist. Vatheia, Estia, and now a hotel room. Apostolis laughs to himself at the absurdity of this final addition.

"What?"

"Nothing. Everything. Listen, Haruki. I can't do this. I have an early flight. Tell me what you came here to say."

"I just wanted to see you. To hear how you've been."

"I've been fine. It's been a wonderful trip. I tried sushi. Went to some gardens. Is that the sort of thing you were after?"

"You know what I mean."

"If you want to hear how I am how about I give you my address in Athens and we can be pen pals? You were always good at writing letters."

Haruki's face flushes.

"What?"

"You received them?"

"The letters? Was I not supposed to?"

"I don't know. I told you in the last one to come to me. Since you hadn't I figured that you never would. But I never knew for sure. I didn't know if that was because you didn't want to or if you'd never found them."

"I got them. Took me a while to translate them though."

"And then?"

Apostolis looks at him with incredulity. "And then? Says the rich one. Did you think I could just pop over for the weekend? Why didn't you come back to me?"

"I didn't think I'd be welcome. After what I did."

Apostolis lets out an overstretched groan. They can argue the finer points forever. Who should have done what and whose pride got in the way. But the reality is that too many years have been lost in neither of them contacting the other. "It's too late. You have a life now."

"Fuck." Haruki squirms and throws his hands over his face.

Apostolis moves closer to comfort him. He pulls Haruki's hands away to see tears rolling down his cheeks. He wants to feel sorry for him but the crying almost feels like a trap. "Is that how you're going to play it?"

Haruki pushes him away. "Don't do that."

"What?"

"Tell me that I'm not allowed to be sad. I love my girls, I really do. But I've thought about you every day. It was easier when you couldn't understand me. Here's the truth. I screwed up everything. You wouldn't believe what I did to survive after Greece. I came here to tell you that I'm sorry. I wish that I had stayed. I wish that I had curled up in your arms and sat by the fire and built the house rather than waiting two decades to see you in a shitty hotel room."

"This room is fine." Apostolis tries to laugh.

"I sell semi-conductors to overseas companies."

"What?"

"Semi-conductors."

"What are they?"

"Honestly I have no idea. I don't even care enough to find out."

Apostolis gives a half-formed smile. "That's pathetic."

"You're right," Haruki says. "And you're also right that it was selfish of me to come here."

"Yes. It is selfish of you." He feels vindicated. He hasn't been sure what he's been feeling but this is it entirely. It is selfish of Haruki to dump all of this on him and yet it's what he's always wanted to hear. "Well I feel better. How about you?"

"What would?"

"What would what?"

"Make you feel better?"

Apostolis ponders it until he's certain of the answer. "More alcohol."

Haruki laughs.

"And this," Apostolis adds as he leans in and kisses him. He pulls away as quickly. "You have a wife. This isn't right."

"I'm going to leave her. I'll tell her tomorrow. Delay your flight and we can figure out what to do."

Apostolis takes in his words. It's fanciful and extraordinary but no more than when he'd asked him to stay on that summer. Actually it's less outlandish now that they're grown men with autonomy. He truly believes him. Why not? If they could make it work then what's to stop them?

"Really?" he asks.

"Really," says Haruki. "If you want to."

He doesn't need to think about it for a second longer. He kisses him again. This time it endures and he knows that they're not leaving the room.

They move to the bed, grappling at one another's clothes. Apostolis tries to remove the tie but he's had such little experience that he ends up choking him for a moment. He apologises and lets Haruki do that part. He's also, oddly, picturing Akira having directed him upstairs. What must the concierge be thinking about the two of them up here for so long? It's no longer a secret kiss inside a blacked-out cave so if they are going to do this, face the world together, the appraisals of others is a thing that they'll have to contend with.

He's almost fully naked. There's no tender act of slowing down when they've waited so many years to resume what they'd once started.

"Did you think about me when you were with others?" Haruki asks him as he moves his mouth along his back and down to the top of his buttocks.

"There was no one else."

"No one? Not even women?"

"Some women. No one important. You?"

"I was abstinent for ten years," Haruki says. "Until my wife. There was—"

"Ssh." Apostolis doesn't need to know any more. He gives a passing thought about where Haruki's wife thinks he is. And then his thoughts turn to the girls who are probably tucked in bed and unaware that their lives were about to change.

The men are boisterous with one another as if their stauncher bodies can take the roughness. Neither resembles who they once were – there is more hair on both of their chests, Apostolis' back is less toned, Haruki's hairline has begun to recede – but the passion is unchanged. Haruki rolls onto his front and reaches around to rub spit on himself before Apostolis penetrates him. Haruki moans but his pain doesn't slow them down. Before he can change position so that they will face one another, Apostolis orgasms inside him. He withdraws and Haruki turns over and cums within seconds.

They fall back onto the mattress as they regain their breath. Haruki excuses himself to the bathroom and then re-joins Apostolis who's still panting. They lie there for a while before doing a thing that they weren't afforded previously: they crawl under a duvet. Apostolis curls up into Haruki's body and they stare at the television whilst their breaths calm, as if sex before bed could be an everyday occurrence for them. Apostolis could get used to this. He would move halfway across the world for it.

Even when the reality hits, that there are many complications before they could begin to curate a life together, he doesn't panic. He's instead drawn into the fantasy that is fast becoming his future.

"I love you," Haruki says. "I always have. You know that?"

"Yes."

"Tell me you love me. If you do?"

"I do, Haruki. I love you so much."

"Charupi. Call me Charupi."

Apostolis leans up and kisses him. He nibbles his ear and keeps his lips close. "Charupi-mou."

"Tell me your name."

"Akis." He doesn't hesitate. He's lost so much of himself since those days and knows that whatever happens next he'll never be Apostolis again.

They shuffle down until they are horizontal with their heads on the pillows. Akis turns off the television and then the light. There is so much to talk about. How the past years have been waylaid. How they'll wake up tomorrow and start a unified future. But there's a lifetime for conversation and for now the dark and the silence are wonderful enough. Safe within the comfort of plush sheets, they drift off in one another's arms.

In the morning, Akis stirred from a nightmare in which he'd been caught in an earthquake. Tokyo had shaken violently and he'd been running between houses, trying to warn people of the danger but also finding himself a place of safety. Every door was locked. The whole city had been evacuated.

He stretched his body and remembered that it was just a dream. He opened his eyes and rolled towards the centre of the bed. It was empty.

"Charupi?"

He sat up. The door to the bathroom was ajar. Haruki wasn't inside. His clothes were gone. The room's key-card was still in its slot.

Akis washed and dressed and cleaned up the mess from the minibar. Throughout it all, he remained calm. He told himself not to worry. Haruki had just popped out to get them breakfast. He'd be back soon enough and they would figure out a way to postpone the flight without losing any money. It was too early but at some point he'd have to call Hasegawa and explain the delay.

After a while, and with no knock on the door, he was overcome by a feeling of being trapped. He stepped outside to where he could breathe again. The corridor was empty except for a cleaning trolley. He returned to the room and sat at the end of the bed as he watched the minutes on the digital clock flick from one to the next until the hour scrolled back on itself.

His body was heavy and his mind was dull but there was no panic nor tears when the time came for him to check out. He grabbed a piece of hotel paper from the desk before stepping into the corridor, from where he dragged his cases towards the elevator and down to the lobby.

Hestia

Greece, 2022

35

Estia
7th August 2022

Under a blistering sky, Mani's daughter flings her arms around the man whom she has, for her whole life, interchangeably called Jiji, Pappous and Akis.

Hestia then marches to the beach and stations herself on a sunbed before Mani can even retrieve their cases and lock the rental car. It's a whirlwind of an entrance and Mani frets, given Akis' dazed expression, that he might be regretting the open invitation.

She sets down the bags and greets him before turning to acknowledge the bay and, finally, the house. A cursory glance around suggests that nothing has changed in the almost three years since their last visit, a thirteen-year streak interrupted although not out of choice. COVID-19 had landed like a stomach punch, winding her without a chance to brace for its impact. Everything had stopped. Plans had turned to dust and connections severed even if technology kept lines open although, in her opinion, with as much intimacy as two plastic cups joined by a length of string.

Overnight the world had fragmented like a smashed mirror and in its restoration now no longer resembled its former self. Maybe there has been some good in reshaping but she's pessimistic that not many lessons have been learnt.

"Hisashiburi," Akis says.

"It's been too long," she agrees. "How are you?"

"Fine."

"But–"

"Not another word."

"What?"

"Worrying about me. I can see it all over your face."

"I'm– You're right. I'm just happy to be here."

"Good. So relax."

She wants to but she can't help but think ahead two weeks to when they'll leave. It's always upsetting when these annual visits come to an end and she's worried year on year with more levity about whether Akis can cope alone. Not that she'd worried specifically about him and the pandemic.

It's been a surreal day, with proof that the whole world had shut down. Back at Haneda Airport it was still to her a nationwide affliction but that had changed when she'd landed this morning into Athens and seen sanitiser stations and people in masks and was confronted with the true meaning of the word pandemic. She'd had to stop at the baggage carousel to process it.

Hestia had rolled her eyes. Her daughter seemed to cringe at everything. 'What now?'

'It's a lot. The pandemic. It really was everywhere.'

'Duh. Pandimia, Greek origin,' her daughter had replied with authority and condescension.

"You're disappearing on me again," Akis says, bringing Mani back to the present.

"I'm not. I'm just taking it all in."

"You don't have to worry about your patients or the world for two weeks."

"Do I need to worry about you?"

"I told you. Isolation suited me. I was accidentally prepared."

Akis had been retired for a few years when the news broke. He held that his civic duty was to not be a burden on society and he'd spent lockdown tending to the garden. Cut off already, he's been buffered in his settled bay.

"What about now? You're not too lonely?"

"Mani. This is your holiday."

She bites her tongue but she's concerned though about his well-being. Recently on video calls he's been calling her daughter Estia, which isn't uproarious, but that he seemed surprised to see their car roll into the bay is alarming.

"I'll take these up," she says. "Then a drink. Daijoubu?"

"I thought you were coming tomorrow."

"No, today."

"You told me Sunday."

"Today is Sunday."

He shrugs it off. "All the days become the same when you don't work."

It's convincing. From her foray into geriatric populations, those undergoing dementia tests only fail with much worse.

He shuffles behind her as she hauls the cases through the house. He stops at the bottom of the stairs. "You know where your rooms are," he says. Persuasive again.

The house appears to be as she left it in August 2019. Akis too, although she's seen him regularly albeit on a computer screen with a crackly line. He's had Wi-Fi for a few years. She's not sure that Hestia would have boarded the plane if he didn't. No longer is the draw of the beach enough for a fourteen-year-old attached to social media, needing to define every activity's worth in terms of others' feedback. Fourteen. It's a cliché but she can't understand where the time has gone. She curses these recent lost years, stealing her uncontrived daughter and replacing her with a moody teenager without the innocent summers in between. Fourteen. Akis is seventy-nine. She's forty-seven for heaven's sake.

The room is dusty. Cobwebs line the light fixtures and the bed is unmade. She checks next door where Hestia will sleep and it's the same. Only, she can picture her daughter this evening on the bare mattress unencumbered, her two thumbs going quick-time over her phone's screen with the manual dexterity of the ultra-evolved.

She opens the shutters to let out the staleness and shifts her gaze from the Japanese maples in one direction to the beach in the other. She always stays in this end room, the proximity to the garden and the sea bringing her to centre. She breathes in the air. She'll sleep well tonight.

She sees Akis and Hestia on the beach alongside one another although only he is under an umbrella. She'll give them time to reconnect. His spirit is always bolstered by her daughter's presence. But, as if sensing this invasion, Hestia spins around, lifts her sunglasses and glares at her mother before she returns to Akis and continues their conversation. What they discuss Mani doesn't know and not one of the three of them has ever thought to rupture the confidentiality. The age difference has never made an iota to their being, as her grandmother would have said, 'Itai doshin.'

Mani assumes that it's a complaint about her overbearing parenting in the lead-up to this holiday. Packing coursework and career guides on Hestia's behalf. Tarnishing paradise. She's been called an awful mother more than a handful of times of late. Considering that they've navigated a tiny apartment in Odaiba, each the other's sole companion through the prolonged lockdown, it's surprising that they haven't killed one another. A success, she might call it. Besides, considering what she knows through patients with teenagers and teenaged patients with guardians, if Hestia wasn't rebelling at this point she'd be perplexed.

She turns to unpacking, a chore that she does without fail on arrival. The unloading of clothes, hanging dresses in the wardrobe, folding other pieces into drawers is a sham of permanency that will be undone in just over two weeks. Hestia on the other hand will live out of her suitcase and counter her with two arguments: organised mess and time-efficiency. Mani doesn't care. This is an odd pleasure, fixing her stay as if she's been planted like the shishigashira maple whose branches tolerate the sun and nudge into her opened window.

Hestia in Estia. She peers at her daughter as she thinks the mantra. She chants it on the hardest days, rushing her to now, the highlight of her year. It's been her greatest pleasure to watch Hestia crawl across the sand, toddle through the bamboo forest and now hopefully revert to a place of innocence. So many milestones have been broken in this bay. It offsets the horror that the years have also aged her.

She goes to the kitchen but stops at the book cabinet. It's been stripped of most of its gardening manuals. Akis has become a voice of authority on native species, an intriguing word given this location. She often forwards his email address to friends who require his expertise on treating diseased leaves or countering infestations.

During the pandemic, with all sorts of remote activities springing up like some veil of abnormal normality, Akis was bemused to find her sign him up as a keynote speaker for an online symposium on Japanese garden curation. This curiosity – *A Greek man speaking Japanese! A Japanese garden in Greece!* – was the most watched presentation. He was shy at first and there were a few technical hiccups but he'd managed to navigate the camera from where he'd set up at his desk across the terrace. An accidental nudge in the direction of the beach provoked sighs of envy before the garden brought on further gasps of admiration. Despite his time running over, he was basking in the absurdity of the tour when a mention of his teahouse left the comments box full of pleas to see it. With the approval of the moderator to extend, he moved to the end room and, playing to an audience trapped inside their houses, made a promise that anyone was welcome to visit when they were set free. He still prefers his own company but is no longer averse to others intruding. After Mani entered his life, youthful energy became a welcome addition to the bay. He has taken on a part-time landscape gardener and there are also frequent barbecues for friends and ex-colleagues. The grandest are always during Mani's stays.

Except for in the grips of a global catastrophe, she visits every August. In truth it's too hot and she'd prefer to hold off for a month or two but her therapy service has moved towards the continental model and shuts for the entire month. Four weeks of uprooting suits her. A week with her mother, two weeks here and one more, if she and Hestia want, touring Greece or a stopover on the way back. June, July, September, Daisuke can have his pick but they have an unwritten agreement that August belongs to her. He owns an apartment a few metro stations from her in Tokyo so it isn't as if he never sees Hestia, but when her daughter disappears for longer than a weekend Mani's heart languishes until her safe return.

She removes a hard-backed binder from the bookshelf and sits with it in her lap. She remembers that first trip and loses herself in the fallout. Or rather, the divorce was amiable. Upsetting but measured. She was jealous but pleased when Daisuke found someone better suited for him. Not that she cared to ask nor grew envious when mutual friends attended the wedding or told her about the couple's newly-acquired assets. Maybe she'd pried online once or twice but she hadn't been able to decipher the glossy filters and show-reels of happiness and has instead learnt to feel comfortable with not having to know.

She found a nice man herself, on Kamishima no less, who was a polyglot and translated for a publishing house. He was studious and measured and made her happy. But she told him about her discoveries and he was infuriated by the gaps in the story and the unsatisfactory ending. They agreed to disagree; life was not one of his novels with loose ends tied in pretty bows. It was an unexpected sticking point but they couldn't get past this contention. There have been a few men since but none has made it to Estia. Saying that, there is someone new, decent.

She'd had to convince Daisuke for his blessing for her to move to the island before the birth. She'd found a generic primary mental health position and her mother could look after the baby, but it had been more than enough after a few years and Tokyo beckoned once more. Now she heads a service for sexual health issues. A decent number of referrals come from those identifying as LGBT+. She never judges anyone's hesitancy in coming out. The world might appear more accepting of sexual expression but she's never worked with a single person who hasn't been without some resistance. It isn't her place to tell anyone to self-disclose but she's compelled to add that their happiness banks on authenticity.

Her mother wasn't impressed considering the variety of populations that she could have chosen to work with, seeing it as a betrayal rather than an acceptance of Haruki. Kiho was also hurt by her daughter's decision to keep returning to Estia. Mani has tried to move the grudge along, to separate Akis from her father's wanderings, but even she hasn't been bold enough to encourage her mother to spend the summer here with them all. Yui has been a few times with her hearing-impaired husband. They'd bonded over a bumpy bus ride whilst backpacking in the Balkans; twelve hours of typing and flirting over words on a laptop screen later and they were inseparable. She enjoys Akis' company but has no affinity to him nor the place. Everything from the letters left her cold. To her, these events happened to strangers before her time.

Mani opens the binder. Each page is in a plastic wallet. She'd like to read them through but the weeks here are taken over by distractions and so she usually settles on a quiet moment to just hold them. Anyway she has digitised the entirety so that they're always accessible and forever safe.

She returns the folder to its resting place. The botany guides have been emptied but the shelves have been taken over by more copies of *Shiosai*. It's been a united effort by her and Hestia to find a different version each year. There are finite interpretations and so this has been usurped by seeking out an assortment of covers. Akis has lost the stamina to keep translating the book but he appreciates the gesture all the same.

Mani realises that she's left the newest gift-wrapped copy upstairs. A Norwegian edition with a picture of a lighthouse. There's no rush to get it. She reminds herself to take a breath and slow down, to savour each moment in just being here when it's what she's been waiting for, for so long.

Hestia in Estia.

She'll fetch it later.

36

Estia
7th August 2022

In the kitchen she unpacks sachets of sweetened curries and white roués, a box of panko breadcrumbs, ponzu sauce and a host of seasonings. Part of her wants to break free and join the others but she won't risk disturbing the peace. Nor the rejection. She makes a jug of houjicha and puts it in the refrigerator but is concerned by the number of items that are out of date. The cupboards are also run-down. A loss of appetite is typical for someone Akis' age but it's not an excuse for a lack of sustenance. She's already bought a weekly pill box for his various ailments as well as a digital alarm clock programmed to sound twice-daily but there isn't much more that she can do from a distance. Sometime during this stay she will suggest a cleaner who might be able to do a bit of shopping and cooking.

He has friends but she doubts that anyone is closer than an acquaintance, and she guesses that he hasn't met anyone since her father. She knows from work that some people prefer to label themselves with sexual orientations whilst others shy away from them. Her daughter talks so unabashedly of her friends' exploits that she envies them even if she doesn't always believe it all. She just cares that Akis is happy, and if that means dating someone then she would want him to try. Lamentably there are people above his bay who wouldn't be so agreeable.

Some years back, excusable by the waifish abruptness of childhood, Hestia had suggested that he find a boyfriend. Akis laughed it off but an awkwardness lingered over that evening. Mani hadn't remembering telling her by then but was reassured that her daughter had a good head for these things. There were social and environmental problems waiting for her generation but if they could express themselves with confidence and be accepting of others then that was something. Not that Mani knows anything about Hestia's love life either. Gone are the years of divulging crushes and gossiping in front of her. Now there are withdrawn sighs and terms that go over her head along with the favourite line, 'You wouldn't understand.'

Mani can't solve much but she can at least fill up the cupboards and freeze some meals. Tomorrow they'll go on their customary cave tour after which she can detour them to a supermarket. It won't be Akis at the helm of the boat but one of the younger men that can do them the favour of a private ride to a certain corner of the labyrinth. Just a brief stop but one that offers a moment of quiet contemplation.

Long gone are the Japanese-spoken tours although, with Hestia's help, Akis has recorded a final trip that can be downloaded and played in real time. Sometimes after a stressful day, when Mani is homesick for Estia, she listens to it and imagines herself rolling along the soothing tunnels. Otherwise their apartment is filled with Hestia's music; self-appointed to have better taste, her daughter curates the playlists.

That has been something of an oddity in the last few months. In every other way, Mani has been cut out of her daughter's life but each evening, having retreated to her room, Hestia has turned up the volume on one song so loud that it pierces the walls compared to the muffled reverberations of the others. An eclectic mix that Mani ignored at first but her gut told her to listen on. She searched for the corresponding lyrics and realised that she was being offered an insight into her daughter's state of mind. Mostly upbeat, sometimes stressed, a few consecutive days of heartbreak. And worth the price of the streaming service alone. Consequently, she'd asked Hestia on the plane to be respectful of the noise level. But, as an addendum, she'd requested that she didn't stop playing her music altogether. A knowing nod had been enough for Hestia to push her earphones back in and drown her out.

The thing that they argued about the most before the holiday was for Hestia to think about subject choices for her senior high school admission. It was a proviso of coming to Greece that they spend one afternoon discussing her options. Hestia scoffed, telling her mother that she was being just like her great-grandparents and great-great grandfather. Stunned by the comparison, Mani argued back that it wasn't the same, that Hestia wasn't being forced to choose one thing but just something. 'Pressure,' Hestia answered, 'is pressure.' The comment had touched a nerve but there was no getting around it; some family traditions are timeless.

The only person left from that side is Yuki. She's a judge on a cookery show in the States, a cruel format that eliminates people after sapping them of their hopes and dreams. They haven't spoken for years and Mani isn't even sure that Hestia was old enough to hold a conversation when they'd last met. Occasionally she sees her aunt on television or in a magazine. Some feature, her swanning around one of her plush houses – she could almost smell the food in the background – and talking about the importance of her heritage. *I've never forgotten my roots*, one article led. Mani knows better; apart from flying in for guest performances, Yuki hasn't been in Japan for over a decade.

Who is proud of her roots is Hestia: Japanese but with a Greek name. Mani doesn't know how she explains the quirk to others but Hestia is as rare a name back home as Mani and yet it doesn't cause her daughter the chafing that she herself suffered. It helps that it holds no alternative meaning, simply eponymous with the goddess. And the house. Either way it's a beacon that pulls them into safe harbour after whatever rough seas they've weathered that year.

Economic suffering, earthquakes, the nuclear disaster, separation anxiety (both of them), bullying, squabbles, body insecurity. Mani loves watching Hestia forget her woes, skip around the sand, swim without a care, and help with the tea ceremonies that the local women attend with elated curiosity, although the years when she taught origami to the local children have been and gone. Everyone deserves a haven, Mani thinks to herself. She just hopes that Hestia will allow this for herself.

As she finishes unpacking she considers the prospectus upstairs with the different courses. Sciences, the arts, languages. Then maybe university. Hestia is smart and could do anything but she's been apathetic to the state of tedium; apparently if none of her friends has decided yet then what's the big deal?

Akis enters the kitchen and they share another hug.

"It's so good to be here," Mani says.

He agrees but follows her eyes towards the fridge. "I thought you were coming tomorrow. I was going to have a sort out today."

She neglects to mention the state of the bedrooms. She once asked whether he would move into a nursing home if the house became too burdensome. He shut her down with a fierceness that she'd rarely seen: 'I would rather fill my pockets with stones from the Zen garden and walk into the sea.' She'd snapped back that he shouldn't make such grim statements but at the same time she'd understood.

"I made tea."

"You're a guest. What happened to relaxing?"

"It's my pleasure." She pours a glass and carries it out to the terrace for him. She calls to Hestia but there's no reply. More music she guesses. "I'll be back."

She makes her way across the beach and tries to get her daughter's attention but a pair of headphones cut her out. She blocks her sun.

Hestia scowls from behind the ridge of her sunglasses. "You'll give me an uneven tan."

"What with all those expensive snail creams you order from Korea I thought you'd be after pearly skin."

"You're thinking of bleaching cream. In your generation maybe. My skin's glowing."

The way her daughter uses the word – *your* generation, *your* day, *your* way of thinking – feels pointed, as if Mani is the culprit at the centre of all of society's woes.

"I made some iced tea."

"No thanks."

"Come in soon or put on lotion."

"Whatever." Hestia pushes her sunglasses into position.

"I thought we could look at the prospectus later. Get it out of the way."

"Later."

"What does that mean?"

"Later means later." She mutters something else.

"What's that?"

"I said that maybe I don't care. Maybe I don't want to study and have go to university. Your father didn't. If he had then he wouldn't have met grandma and we wouldn't exist."

"Don't try me, Hestia. You don't have to do anything you don't want to. You just have to do something."

"Okazaki Megumi," her daughter says, labouring each syllable.

Mani can deal with huffing or swears but this name gets under her skin. Her quick-witted daughter has an answer for everything and leaves her flustered. Her canniness is proven in her retorts. It's the biggest shame. She wishes that she could see her potential and use it to her advantage. It's particularly vexing that whenever she asks Daisuke to help he replies that she's just being a teenager. Too predictable but there's the fun parent and then there's her.

She must have loitered for a second too long because, although she doesn't say anything, Hestia jumps up from the bed.

"I can't deal with this today." She storms towards Akis, takes a gulp from his cup and disappears into the house. She's quickly out again in a tie-strap crop top and the smallest denim shorts that Mani has ever seen, cut off so that the pockets hang below the frayed ends. Mani watches her push a bicycle up the slope to the top, a sharp getaway made all the more purposeful considering the effort.

Mani collapses into her seat next to Akis. The setup predates Hestia. "Remind me why I was excited to have her."

"Stubbornness runs through your family. Especially the women." His voice is hoarse and his words are stunted but the vocabulary is still impressive. "It's her, what's the word? Right?"

"Prerogative?"

"It's her prerogative to be difficult."

"She opens up to you."

"That's more to wind you up. Let her settle."

She knows that he's correct but hates feeling ganged up on. "I'm sorry we brought this tension. The pandemic wasn't easy on her. I think she needs a break from me."

"I'm not taking it personally. Truth be told, I think that Haruki would have liked her feistiness. Yours too. He'd be proud. Listen. I want to get that other thing out of the way so we can enjoy the next few weeks without sitting on it."

"No, thank you."

"And you thought that your daughter was stubborn. Who else am I going to leave it to? I've booked an appointment on Monday—" He corrects himself with a wink. "Tomorrow afternoon. At the notary."

"I remember you once had a flight sprung on you. I'm not sure that it's fair to do a similar thing to me."

"Tomorrow or Tuesday then. Take your pick."

"Isn't it more a case of yes or no?"

"It's not." Akis smiles. "That's business school for you."

She creases her brow.

"Don't worry. I'm not senile yet."

"I just wish that there had been someone else."

"We all make choices and this is mine. I'm the first to know that inheritance comes from strange places. And you don't have to be sentimental. If you want to sell it, rent it, burn it down—"

"Akis."

"Mani."

"Fine. Tomorrow. But only to cover your options."

She'd never expected to inherit Estia although plenty of people have suggested that it would go her way. Residency restrictions and wanting to be near her mother means that Japan is where she'd prefer to be based even if her work has become so flexible that she could do it from here. Although, she has done what could be described as either shame-faced or sensible by speaking to a financial adviser. For hypothetical reasons. The most prudent choice would be for a management agency to rent it out so that she could still visit. It might not be the most profitable option but she's uninterested in that aspect. She just wants to know that it will be well-kept.

"Anyway," she adds. "Enough of that. It will only sour the mood. Didn't you tell me to relax?"

"True." Akis drinks his tea and says no more.

They're adept at sitting in silence together. She doesn't want to discuss his death. She only met him later in life but he's become such a constant that he's not allowed to go anywhere. Just like the stones of the villa. Then again, a few summers ago the three of them voyaged to the Cyclades following the path that her father, grandfather and Tassos had once taken. They'd stopped at Tinos and saw the boulders that were immovable, just like Estia and Akis had become for her. But this reassuring idea wasn't long-lasting because as early as that evening the line of thought was extinguished by the reality of impermanence. Everything in life eroded even if the changes were too minimal to notice.

"I'm going to finish unpacking."

"Mani, learn something from your daughter."

"What's that?"

"See that big blue thing over there? Live a little."

"And I'm meant to be the one doling out advice." She thinks about what matters. Connection, transcendence, pleasure. She'd be a fool to disregard what he's telling her. "You're right. Maybe we should wait–"

"She'll cool down and come back when she's ready."

She slaps her legs and lifts herself off the chair. "What are we waiting for then?"

"Go ahead. I'll take longer."

She doesn't want to patronise him so she's in her swimsuit and on the sand before he's finished changing.

Now that her toes are touching the waterline she feels the pandemic slip away. She hopes that the only waves to follow will be the ones right in front of her. The tide tickles her. She can't believe that she didn't sprint in as soon as she'd arrived. She's been dreaming of it for the past two years.

She hears the slap of Akis' flip-flops against each plank of the gangway from behind her as he approaches. She wishes that Hestia hadn't disappeared and that she was here to splash around with them. She trusts that her daughter will be careful. She'll go easy on her. Give her a break. There will be more days to hang out together.

Ahead of Mani, the water barely ebbs and flows. She's ready to run forward and dive into the surf. Instead she pauses. She doesn't want this moment to be in the past and so she wills the tide to stand still.

For a moment it looks like it does.

37

Limeni
7th August 2022

Her mother's the worst. She can't get her friends to see it though. Mani Okazaki is the parent they all wish they had. They buy into her niceness and say that she knows how to make them feel heard and understood. They can't believe that she wants to spend time with Hestia, taking the effort to think up activities that would interest her. It's exhausting when no one else gets the manipulation.

She pulls over on the bike and sends a message on the group chat, whose title is some in-joke at the time, to complain about her mother pressuring her. Their replies: *Ignore her. Look where you are. It's paradise. Find a Greek god.* Then a GIF pops up. It takes a few seconds to load. Hercules, bronzed and Disneyfied.

She selects the snake emoji and hovers over the send button. After all, the original paradise wasn't without its own slithering trickster. She deletes it. She's bored of the chain and turns off her data.

She cycles along the paved road where the heat rises like a furnace but, with the breeze on her face and her shoulder-length hair gently taking flight, she embraces the sweetness of it rather than cringing at this clichéd moment of self-restoration. The occasional cars give her a wide berth. She could move to the mule tracks where hardened cyclists brave the bumps for hundreds of miserable kilometres, some sort of lame badge of honour, but she wants speed not authenticity. Distance instead of mindful noticing. Asphalt wins over wildflowers and she pedals faster. It's a halfway house of sorts whilst she's acclimatising. She's had to adapt a lot recently, moving from the two-year detainment with her mother to the mania of Tokyo's wider sprawl, then to jungle trekking with her father and now to Laconia's vast Arcadian-like plain.

She has no destination in mind, only onwards. She passes the turn-off for Gerolimenas and realises that she's actually gone pretty far. The caves are up ahead and she can turn back from there. She won't get lost when there's only one coastal road but she hasn't been this isolated in forever. Like, not lockdown-alone but actually middle-of-nowhere-could-be-a-horror-movie-alone. She looks around but can't feel the terror that would thrill her if it were real; desolate maybe, but this is just a lovely place full of lovelier memories. This is where she's pined for, especially one month earlier when her father had dragged her – 'ungratefully,' as she'd overheard him tell his wife through the adjoining hotel wall – through the Angkor Wat temple complex on the road to Siem Reap. Not that she'd fed this back to her mother. In their debrief, spending time with him had been nothing but the best.

There will be plenty of days to hang out at Estia so it's alright to breakaway for a while. Then she'll wait up after her mother falls asleep and suggest to Akis that the two of them share some tsipouro. She's old enough for a glass or two. A film of sweat covers her forehead and maybe she'll call one of them to pick her up sooner rather than later. She situates herself on the sizeable descent towards Oitylo's sweeping bay. It's a long way down so it's the last place to turn back unaided. The sun is high and, though she's parched and her body is out of sorts with the time of day, all that's waiting for her if she goes back is a prospectus and a lecture. She lifts her feet off the pedals, hovers her hand over the brake and gulps as the road really dips some.

She finds balance and surrenders to the speed. The momentum gives her self-assurance. She can't understand her mother's fuss about the future when there's no rush. At fourteen she doesn't have the first idea of what she wants to do with her life. She's not going to commit to something and then regret it. In her mother's day it was easy. School, marriage (she fucked that one up) and kids (maybe that one too). Everything else was optional. It was her mother's choice to study on, as if she had something to prove, but it was unnecessary given that the rest of her classmates all have stay-at-home mums.

She loses herself in a fit of jealousy by thinking of the incredible summers that her friends are all having, which helps take off the edge from the propulsion of the bike. Internships, volunteering schemes, visiting relatives unaccompanied – unaccompanied! – and art competitions all bulge up their already lengthy resumes. Ayaka even has a piece in a gallery. Each app that Hestia opens details the variety and vibrancy of their lives. She's completely in love with every one of her friends but completely insecure because of them.

What does she have to show for her summer? A stuffy holiday with her father and now a tyrannical one with her mother. She'd asked if she could stay with her great aunt in NYC but her mother refused. Apparently she wouldn't know who they were and, even if she did, her mother had long mislaid any means through which to contact her. There's obviously the beach here. The infamous Japanese garden too which always racks up thousands of likes from around the world. But the attention of her followers will dry up after a day or two if there's no novelty. Sure, random people will comment, have already commented, that they're envious. But there are only so many angles of the southern Peloponnese before her feed's traffic is as barren as the landscape.

She spots the sea, sparkling and luscious, and her self-pity is put on hold. In the back of her mind: sparkling and luscious could make pretty good hashtags. The descent is steep and winding and she flies past hotels with their verandas that hang over the edge of the cliff. A cruise liner crosses in the distance. A yacht is anchored closer to the shore. She spots a host of heads bobbing in the water even nearer. There's no way that she's not joining them. As for getting back from here? She'll figure that one out later.

She stops ahead of the developed stretch at the bottom that, for visitors to Mani, does for sun-seekers what Vatheia does for wannabe historians. #picturepostcardperfection. Limeni is where younger tourists head when they venture south of Kalamata with its bars that rest on the azure water. She's seen this sight plenty of times but it still captivates her. Somehow, though she's already working through a mental thesaurus for words like breath-taking and heaven, she has no desire to capture it for anyone else.

Music blares from the bar-fronts. There's a jumble of traffic, a bottleneck if the region can say it has one. She rests her bike against a wall, unconcerned about its safety. The same too with her phone which she leaves in her shorts after she wriggles out of them and down to her bikini. She dumps her clothes in a corner of a canopied area and climbs the rocks to the sea and lowers herself in. She doesn't want to get her hair wet but she's barely in the water before she thinks *fuck that* and goes under.

She swerves the couples posing for photos. Warm currents run underneath her. Schools of fish come near and dart away when she treads water. She doesn't need to record this moment. It may be the thing that her mother's always preaching, the transcendental mumbo-jumbo that she's always going on about, but she can't disregard her advice this time. She's mindful only of where she is and where she isn't.

She turns onto her back, her face bombarded by the brilliance of the sun, and lets the Mediterranean take her weight. The mildew of the pandemic, the grime of the plane, the stuffiness of the car, the sweat from pedalling. It's all washed away.

Despite her unmistakable Japanese features and her petite physique, her Greek is exceptional and she attunes to the conversations that carry across the surface of the water. She'll study it for sure as one of her options, a cushy ride even if she has to be careful to not slip into slang, already told off once by the examination board for informal speech. She's watched plenty of local news reports and read enough articles to keep up her level – and like the rest of the world, adding scientific terminology to her repertoire

– but actually hearing it in the flesh is enlivening. It's always fun to sleuth on chats, her proximity unassuming. She swims to where a couple are bickering. The man aims his phone at the woman who flashes a smile that lasts as long as the shutter.

After a while her skin begins to raisin and she climbs out, dresses though still damp and takes a seat in one of the bars. Sunbeds are extortionate but a chair is the price of a drink. Plus free water, an underrated asset across Greece that never fails to thrill her. It's served everywhere she sits and is topped up constantly. She's tried to explain it to friends and they just call her a nerd. No one appreciates water like the Greeks. Nor coffee. Which is really what she's dying for.

"Geia sas," the waiter says mindlessly as he approaches. "Oh hi," he adds in English.

"Xairete."

He gives her a curious, appreciative smile. She can see his brain computing her. Here's how it must go: *She sounds great but the thoughtful tourists learn a few words then come unstuck with anything more so should I revert to English, although her pronunciation is pretty good so maybe I should proceed?*

She watches him deliberate, pleased that she's still got a handle on the accent. She's also a bit distracted. He's seriously handsome and she's self-conscious about her state but to brush her hair would be more humiliating than doing nothing.

He opts for Greek. "Would you like a menu?"

"Nah, just a freddo espresso no sugar," she shoots at him.

He throws his head back a little in shock. It's cute. "You're Greek?"

"Half," she lies. She likes perpetuating it. What difference?

She wants to sneak a photo for her friends. Landscapes begone, this is a demigod brought to the modern day. He can't be much older than her. Cropped jet-black hair, adorable smile. Wouldn't need a filter before posting a selfie.

"Which half?"

"Actually a quarter. My grandfather is from here."

"Greece?"

"No. I mean yes but also here here. On the road to Vatheia."

"Wait. The guy with the garden? I went to a barbecue there once. It was pretty insane what he'd done. Sorry, I'm being rude. You're busy."

She's playing with her phone so he must think that she's eager to be left alone but really she's just fidgeting because of nerves. She wants him to stay but she can't be too obvious. She smiles and gives him a little nod before turning back to her screen. She flicks apps open and closed, pretending to look engaged in case he's glancing her way. More deliberately she opens her playlist and scrolls through the thousands of liked songs. *The Waves* by Elisa. She'll blast that one extra loud tonight.

He's back soon with a glass of water and an extra carafe that drips with condensation. "Here you go." He spills a little. "Sorry."

"No problem."

"So you're Maniot?" he asks her.

"I guess. Actually my mum's name is Mani." It feels wrong to use her mother like this, sociopathic even. She'd cringe if her mother could hear the pride in her voice.

"Wow. What's yours then? Gytheia?"

She laughs. "Hestia. Or Estia. Whichever you prefer."

"I love it. I'm Antonios."

"Adonis?" She's misheard and instantly turns red.

He pronounces it again, smiling at the mistake. "I guess you're passing through?"

"Here for two weeks," she says, and quickly throws in, "But I just arrived today."

"Oh yeah? I'm on a break in literally a minute. Can I join you?"

"Uh, sure."

"Great. I'll be back with the coffees."

As soon as he leaves she mutters "Ohmygod" and stealthily checks herself out in her phone's reflection although the sun's glare makes it almost impossible.

He brings their drinks and they talk fluently, nonchalantly, with low-level flirting thrown in. They suss out one another. Both are fourteen. Both are over school. He's helping out in his cousin's bar for the summer but lives in Athens. She's from Tokyo, where she passes the Shibuya crossroads on her school run and hangs out in Akihabara in the afternoons. Neither of these two things are true but he almost falls off his stool with incredulity.

She plays with the plastic sleeve of the straw and ties it into a knot but it gets swept away in the breeze. He chases after it and catches it before it flutters into the sea. He pockets it.

They drink the entire jug of water, him exhausted after running back and forth, her parched after the cycle, both to calm their blushing skin. And then his break is over too soon and he's called to seat people.

Before she leaves she tries to pay.

"I've got it covered," he says. "Or rather, I just won't run it through the till. It was nice to meet you."

"You too. Hey, do you know about the barbecue in two days? At the garden?"

"No but maybe my uncle Manolis has been invited. I think they're friends."

"The door is open," she says, trying to be casual but failing. "What I meant to say, I guess, is that if you've been before—"

"I'll try to stop by," he says, desperate to accept her invitation but caught up in also trying to be cool.

38

Estia
20th August 2022

Both women are asleep and for a slim moment his world is silent.

He's awake before the sun breaks the cliffs and casts him into a new day. Before the cockcrow. Before the heat. And before the dulling of the summer aurora that's wrapped in the wispy sky and, at least to his time-worn eyes, plays out its last dance with the fireflies.

Rising before anyone else gives him precious extra minutes. Every one of them counts. He used to grasp onto the closing time in the antiques shop but now no man's land is situated before sunrise. Even in a subdued place like Mani, his day will be filled with activity. That means momentum. Progression. Time hurtling ahead. Even if he were to test himself and wonder if he's miserable, that time is a brutal sentence, the truth is undeniable: he loves his life. He cherishes the beauty that he's curated within it. Despite the absence of certain things that would have been preferable they no longer leave him yearning.

He creeps through the house, skipping certain floorboards that he once laid and to this day creak. In Japanese castles these would be intruder-detecting nightingale traps, and he steps over them, not only to not wake the others but to steal himself away. Each room contains mess. After two weeks of scattered shoes and discarded makeup there's not much order. It's almost audible, the clutter. He'll find hair ties and snap clips for days after they leave but each discovery will cause a smile and take him that little closer to next August, to when he not only wants the days to begin but when he truly never wants them to end. Not that Estia was built for them. No matter what he might have envisioned that would link him to Haruki he couldn't have foreseen this. It's not a bad outcome though. A granddaughter making use of the beach is perhaps more than he could have asked for. He wishes for nothing but her happiness.

But as he's learnt, eftychia might be a word that flows like syrup, a combination of letters that sound as graceful and honeyed as they read, but happiness is also a fleeting hummingbird; though a hibiscus may entice the creature there's no guarantee that it will appear. The only absolute is that without a purposefully-laid flower there's no nectar from which it could feed. Happiness and wishes, he holds, are the two wings of the bird, groundless without them, but to not inspect the underlying mechanics makes the bird's existence all the more incandescent.

How wings, wishes and happiness work he leaves to the universe. There are plenty of other mysteries he has also never solved and never will. Some by choice but others he's had to swallow like the rough pill of a prescription, decided by others and forced upon him. His unknown parentage. Haruki's lost years. Or, as he's reminded as he catches sight of a recently dusted object in the lounge, whatever happened to the wish doll.

Even with Hasegawa's shoddy drawings, he wasn't able to conceive of a daruma's form until his visit to Japan where he saw plenty. It was only after this trip, after the letters in which he'd learnt about its existence, that he returned to Vatheia to look for Haruki's. It was his first foray inside the tower house for over a decade, a clean-up operation from which he'd amassed little but melancholy. He'd searched the attic in case the daruma had slipped into a crevice but it was as absent as the calls between his aunt and uncle. All of their history had been stripped away and left no trace so that an interloper would have no clue that any of them ever existed. He never found out what happened to the doll mentioned in the letters, if Haruki had taken it or, if left behind, why it had been discarded when the pages had been kept.

There were times when he wanted one of his own, when he wanted to blot in the first eye and wish for miraculous developments. For the column to hurry up and complete. For Haruki to row into the bay. For Petzechroula to hear his apology. Coincidentally, Mani had gifted him one the first time that she entered his life, a token souvenir that was picked up as a mantelpiece decoration rather than an intimation of something more profound. He's never seen to attack it with a pen. He's never needed to. With the garden and the boat tours and Mani's promise to return with a baby, he's never coveted more. 'Hestia in Estia,' he catches himself muttering at odd times, Mani's chant infectious and the concluding chapters of a life that demands nothing more.

Hestia in Estia and Mani in Mani. So many homespun names that he takes credit for, for if not choosing them then for giving them their heritage. Not that he's seen the girl much compared to other years. Since Manolis showed at the barbecue with his nephew she's been preoccupied.

He steps out into the cool dawn and leans into its crispness because in less than an hour it'll be so hot that he'll battle with his senses and wish for the day to be over. His first port of call is the garden, not to do anything at this ungodly hour but to greet whatever has matured overnight or whatever braces for the oncoming grilling in bedewed preparation. He gives the plants a grateful nod. Respect for the environment is one thing that he's appropriated from the Japanese with whole-heartedness. Many years ago, Mani had posted to him a photograph of Hestia's first swimming class. She'd annotated the back with a cute detail, that at the end of the lesson the children had bowed to the teacher, then to one another and finally to the water. He loves this idea so much, and regurgitates the visual so frequently, that he often gets confused as to whether he'd witnessed it himself.

He clears his throat and speaks directly to the trees, reserving the first words of the day for them. He doesn't keep chickens but what he says has been carted across a lifetime, forever scarred into his morning routine: "Sit on your eggs." The sentiment is apposite. Birds, humans, trees, rocks. None of them is infinite yet none of them needs to sprint through a life.

Holding livestock was a long time ago, when his home was elsewhere and his family a different breed. He's reminded that he dreamt of his grandfather last night. They were on the beach, even though Leonidas had never been, watching Mani and Hestia sail away. Fanciful maybe but the message isn't hard to decode and there's no lingering distress to the story, just the tender consolation of a ghost watching overhead.

"A man does not plant trees for his own shade," he says out loud, unaware that he still had this line within him after so long. He turns back from the garden, until now unaware that the premonition would prove so literal.

If dreams are forewarnings, a mix of wish fulfilment and dread, he can rest easy because last week he forced Mani to the notary. He's glad to have been proactive, that his life's work will be left to someone that will handle or dispose of it with care. She will soon return to Japan and he will mope for a few days before getting back to normality. There are things that need fixing that he's still capable of doing but others he'll leave to a handyman. And even if he no longer works in the caves he plans to keep going once or twice a week to check in. But despite the open invitation he will, however, continue to skip the kafeneio scene. Manolis and the others complain and joke about their wives, alive or dead, with an air of misogyny. He knows that it's all in jest and wants to think their throwaway lines tolerable but he can never relax into it. He's never sure how to keep certain conversations going, too busy worrying about an offhand remark that might sting him. Even if there's no intended cruelty behind certain careless phrases he's forever anticipating the potential awkwardness and displaced air if it happens.

He heads back inside and listens for sounds from upstairs. There are no indications of life. Mani has taken over the kitchen and restocked the larder. She's implied more than once that he might not be coping as well as he thinks. It aggravates him and he doesn't want to feel completely redundant so he gets on with breakfast ahead of her. He'll risk the spluttering of the coffee machine. He can't find the filters where they're usually stored and is about to blame her when he spots the packet exactly where it should be. He disregards any sinister reason for missing them, excusing it on the bleary hour.

He spills granules on the floor, again a shaky but innocent accident at the start of the day. He sweeps them into a pile and, frustrated at the mess, finishes setting up the machine and takes himself next door.

In view is the blind daruma on its shelf. There's also the binder in the book cabinet. It's perched at a new angle. He's happy that throughout the visit it's been moved a handful of times. Mostly he's pleased that during the party he'd stumbled on Hestia and the nephew who'd snuck away to have a look.

The coffee maker emits its final groans. He leaves it to steam.

He might glance at the letters after the others leave although kanji don't always strike a chord with him. Skills and memories are seeping away like an outgoing tide that he's impervious to stop. To do anything more than skim the pages depresses him.

He fills a cup and moves to the terrace where he sits under an electric canopy that's semi-extended. The day is barely here, the sky a delicate violet that will give way to its conventional intrepid blue with the slightest turn of a dial. The sun marches across the bay but only his feet are within its reach and his toes prickle. There's nothing for him to do but sit and take it all in. That's pretty remarkable in itself, to have a day with nothing but freedom and merriment ahead of him. Considering the limitations of what would be impossible additions, there's nothing more he wants than this and nowhere else he wants to be than right here. All in all this makes him fortunate. He wonders how many others get mornings like this one. How many people can say the same.

He would, though, like Mani to stop asking if he was managing. He only now remembers taking one of her strategies to bed. For once he didn't think it was aimed at him, not even slyly, but instead had just come up during their late-night chat, his curiosity peeking into the world she inhabited elsewhere.

'When someone dreads or ruminates or hides away and can't see a life ahead of them,' she'd told him over a cup of mountain tea, 'I offer them a confronting exercise. I make them total the amount of days they've spent this way. Then I ask them to estimate how many days they have left to live.'

'That's morbid. What do people say?'

'Usually they land on living until about ninety. It's measured but hopeful.'

'Seems strange for depressed people to suggest so much time.'

She nodded to agree. 'That's the way it is. Then I ask how many of the remaining days they're willing to give to this. Not many, they answer. It's a wake up call.'

In bed, he'd calculated how many days he'd held a grudge against Petzechroula and the others. How much time he'd spent wishing for them to give him more. How much pain he'd suffered since closing himself off. Perhaps he could have benefited from someone like Mani back then. Or probably stubbornness would have won through. Then he'd worked out how many days he'd waited in the caves for Haruki. How many days he could have been doing something else. He'd fallen asleep unable to approximate the number, the arithmetic lulling him unconscious.

In the clarity of daylight he reframes this argument. He may have regretted the family fallout but not anything to do with Haruki. Waiting for him, hoping for him to come, was a deliberate choice. He's been fine to live with the consequences.

He shivers and fetches a blanket. He wraps it around him and returns outside. He watches the sea as he sips the bitter coffee. The air and the caffeine will warm him and then he'll get some gardening in before anyone else stirs.

In the distance a gull swoops low and bobs on the water. Akis watches it duck under before it takes off. As he traces its path he lands on something else. His eyes aren't good enough to make it out but he's sure that there's something materialising from the edge of the bay, distancing itself from the cliff, crossing the horizon.

It's a row-boat but the person has their back to him as they make headway to the shore.

Akis steps onto the sand that hasn't yet cooked and is damp to the touch. His body too remains cold. The sun might scorch his head but he's not yet thawed. He pulls the fleece closer. He shuffles nearer still, confused how this person has managed to row all the way from wherever he might have come. It's far and treacherous yet he has persisted. Maybe there was another guest last night who he hasn't remembered and might have set off earlier for a burst of exercise. Maybe this rower, whoever he is, simply disappeared for a while and is only now naturally heading back. Akis is certain that no one who has been here can leave forever. The pull of Estia's hearth is magnetic after all.

The finer details continue to prove evasive. He stares ahead. Behind him he has to trust that there's a fully formed house, a flourishing garden, two cars, and a driveway that connects to a road above.

Now he can see. It's a young man. Handsome and slight of frame. He isn't far. He's in control of the oars and turns the boat so that he has a full view of the bay. Akis knows this face. If he blinks then maybe he'll be wrong. He can't look away.

The boy stops. He wrestles off his top and stands to strip from his waist down so that he's completely naked. He doesn't hold this position for long as he barrels overboard whilst holding his gaze. His exuberant smile doesn't fade until he's underwater.

Akis watches on. The boy doesn't come up for air.

He's ready to shake his head and make the boat vanish along with this other apparition.

But then the boy reappears and sweeps the hair from his face. He tips his head back, just a little, to greet him. To beckon him in. He mouths something inaudible then waves for Akis to join him. Impatient, the boy splashes around in the water leaving Akis to decide the next move for himself.

There are so many ways that Akis could go. So many options in front of him.

Come here, he initially thinks to say. *Come to me.*

We have to go, he feels compelled to shout instead, reluctantly repeating history with this doleful severing phrase.

Or dreamily: *I could come to you,* he could say. *If you can't come to me.*

He has so many choices. Most are easy, heady. Fulfilling duty, acting on virtuosity, and guided by the appeasing of generational guilt. But only one leads to eftychia. It's an impossible decision when being pulled in so many directions and yet when put this way it's simple.

Akis is spirited by the sun's rays. He takes a breath, lets go of his cover and, heart-led, steps into the tide.

Untested Waters

Austria, 1944

39

Bad Hofgastein
26th March 1944

The top of the Gastein Valley has begun to thaw. Spruces have regained their verdant green. Avalanche fences have lessened their slack from under translucent snow. It's early spring. Cold but bright. The war might be coming to an end.

Propaganda suggests one outcome, hearsay another. For Sophie Neuhold it doesn't much matter. It's a guilty sentiment, punishable even, but if a trumpeter's curtain call from any side can hurry Kurt back to her then so be it. All she wants is for her son to wake up in his bed and for her to sleep a whole night through in hers. Beyond that, everyone else is entitled to whatever they want beneath her village up in the Alps. Trophies, ownership, acquisitions, they're welcome to the rest.

She sits in one of the naturally-sprung thermal lakes but away from the other women. The water is up to her shoulder blades. A few specks of snow land on her nose but these are the exception to a beautiful if overcast day. The slopes are blanketed in a patchwork of melting white that gives rise to the carmine of conifers and larches. She has to close her eyes; for a mind that sees military action at all turns this is an omen of seeping bloodshed. She reminds herself to not fall for superstition. But the image of her son, injured, prevails.

She forces herself to picture a scuffed knee, an inconsequential scratch, the compromise of a scar from a war that she cannot expect to evade entirely.

She simmers in the water but it's not enough. She drops under for a few seconds to boil her brain. It's a reprieve from the iciness of the world and the abrasiveness of dread. Bad Hofgastein's residents are used to being cut off by the thickest of snowfalls so these past years of breaks to the countrywide supply chain have been painless. There are ample amounts of everything required. Logs for fire and snow for water. Furs on coat-hooks and venison in outbuildings. There's a privilege in living in such a remote place, a security that no major power is interested in her unthreatening commune, but Kurt's absence undercuts any relief that this protection brings. Therapeutic waters have no chance when he's out there. Hopefully within reach. Hopefully a place that she has heard of. Or, if he's to avoid action, maybe it's better if she hasn't.

She crunches her toes to get the blood flowing. She won't leave the bath yet because she can't bear to see the frayed posters on the lockers. They're scattered throughout the village, stapled to lampposts and wind-beaten, undermining the promise of how well their boys are doing.

Their boys.

As if Kurt belongs to anyone else. Near enough everyone has given over a son or a husband, a father or a brother, but the safe return of one does not counteract the loss of another. The onus is on her to wish for his well-being. She's a rational woman but when thoughts and prayers are all she has to offer she's backed into having to deliver them. She considers that just thinking him well is vacuous, and she disbelieves in a god that would allow killings to happen in the first place. Yet superstition preserves these acts and gives meaning where there's meaningless. She doesn't believe in the supernatural but she's seen the army men turn up with a role call of the dead. If these harbingers of bad news are real then the least she can do is act like she's also a causal agent.

Other women enter the baths but she keeps her distance. She averts her eyes from their naked frames. She isn't prudish but wraps her arms around her breasts and embraces the warmth of the water as she repositions. Elsewhere she will join them. Shared activities drive conversations through safe territory but out here there's only so much to say of the landscape or weather and, shortly, idle chit-chat will revert to the one topic she wants to avoid.

She thinks of Kurt's favourite dessert, kaiserschmarrn with plum jam and a pot of honey, and runs through the recipe's steps to make it on his return, labouring each point with specificity. It deflects her away from other thoughts. Distraction has become her greatest asset. Ruminating about his potential suffering is so barbarous that she wonders why her mind hates her so. She has to fight to block him out. She doesn't know if the baths help or not. Sometimes they soothe her, other times guilt consumes her for what should be recreational.

To talk about him runs the same risk. Sometimes it brings him closer, other times it tears her heart in two. Female classmates of his check in on her from time to time. The pretty but simple Helena who is earnest in speaking about his bravery comes the most often. Sophie smiles accordingly but each time the girl leaves she lets out a godforsaken wail. Bravery is gallant but in war it gets one killed. There's also Katerina and Eva and Claudia and a host of others. It's no surprise that her house is visited daily. Kurt's a handsome boy and can take his pick. Or none. Whatever he wants. She doesn't care.

Distraction, it appears, is a fool's errand today.

How to switch off has become the golden chalice for the women of the village. They share between one another the successes of their experiments. Focusing on a breath. Concentrating on a fine, fiddly patchwork. Marching through the snow to Badgastein and back, a hardcore campaign that depletes their bones and empties their heads. Sometimes she wants to pick up a pair of skis and go farther to Salzburg where she can bang at the door of a command centre and demand answers. Reality kicks in. She'd be dead before she could make it past the Salzach River. Then there are these thermal pools in the centre of their picturesque village. A perfect place for wellness, a hub of social crossover and why she remained in Bad Hofgastein after becoming a widow. It was agreed by the community to not deprive themselves if soothing their bodies kept their spirits soaring, even if their boys are freezing and malnourished elsewhere. But to embrace the water feels like a misdemeanour.

She's restless. She can't appease her wracked brain. She remembers the washed-out mantra that 'no news is good news' and espouses this. To her, success in war is not about occupying foreign climes but outlasting the shadows that creep up on these nebulous days. She misses Kurt so much that she often dreams that he's returned. In the mornings she's devastated to burst into his empty room. At least he isn't lying there disabled or as a shell of his former self. At least there isn't a medal on a counter-top that speaks of his gallantry as he rots in an unmarked grave outside the borders of his homeland. At least no one has turned up with this gut-wrenching news.

Some of her neighbours have received such unwelcome knocks on their doors. The mother of Jonas Keller just now slides into the water opposite her. Her roughshod eyes construe what she will forever struggle to redress: how can a war rage on if hers has come to an end? There's nothing that Sophie can tell her, especially not that she shares her pain. She can't conjure up the magnitude of Elke's suffering and to pretend to empathise is an insult.

Her body seizes at the idea that she could be next to join this accursed clan. She wants to scream, kick up water, shake the other women out of their passivity. It's little comfort to assume that they all feel the same. If only some leader will concede and this can be over. It hardly matters who waves a white flag. This is where she hates herself the most. A steady stream of rumours have revealed the atrocities of concentration camps. If even a margin of this is true then she's complicit in the extinction of these millions of victims through her greediness of just wanting to protect her precious one.

She considers leaving the bath but a crack in the sky plants a beam of sun on her. She savours this moment as a sign that falls in her favour. Why not when she looks out for all the bad ones?

The evenings are the hardest, when the baths are dark, the air frigid and the hope sparse. She sometimes plays cards, another distraction technique, but refuses homes or gasthauses where there's a wireless playing out summaries. She won't hear what she needs to so why submit herself to the misery? Why do the others listen on, she often wonders. A valiant display of paying attention? A virtuous response to social expectation? She overhears the others talk about the reports plenty as it is. It's enough to be informed without being inundated.

Countering the gloomy nights, the council has organised events to if not instil hope then to offer normality. There have been classes on how to carry out an aufguss, the towel-waving ritual of the saunas. There was a gala at the Badgastein casino but opening up the venue was a gamble that was so inopportune and left such an unpleasant stench that the night ended with more of a squib than a squeal. There have also been a series of lectures in the town hall, where orchestras might otherwise had visited if such an accumulation of musicians was possible. The talks were impressive but intimidating and she regretted attending each one, spending the hours trapped in her seat, undistracted and ungratified.

One speaker did have a lasting effect. He taught at the University of Vienna and was disseminating his research that was as inexplicable as the rest. But he drew in the largest crowd, famous by his association to another scientist. Sophie bet that Kurt knew this other man and attended so that she could tell him about it later. After tedious slides and suppressed yawns the man reluctantly opened up to questions. 'Tell us about Schrödinger,' someone boldly asked. The presenter stifled a disappointing sigh. His enamoured colleague had fled to Dublin but before then he'd captivated many minds, something that the speaker hadn't been able to do. Sophie had perked up at his explanation of the famous thought experiment which seemed to prove the possibility of multiple existences. So far so understandable but then the talk extended to quantum physics and she lost focus. However, the image stuck: this cat in a box, both alive and dead, and the outcome not yet realised. The women in the audience glanced at one another. It was all that they'd needed to hear.

Her hair has crisped, frozen into individual icicles, and she snaps clumps of it with her fingers. She enjoys the childish pleasure and for a second forgets everything else. Women come and go. They're naked and unashamed. The pools aren't segregated but there are so few men anyway. Today there are none. She looks around at the others who are middle-aged like her or older. Each wears her own expression but the prevailing mood is sombre. Some women are old enough, wrinkled enough, to have their husbands at home or dead before they could know of the war. Some are in the midst of a marriage that had no right to be ruptured. Others are in the throes of a romance that has been stalled.

Sophie's husband died of natural causes too young. She's never told anyone as she isn't sure of its appropriateness but there's something comforting about his passing not being at the hands of another man. She won't speak ill of the dead but also thinks that, though he wasn't a bad man, she doesn't miss him. She does however miss the intimacy of another. He was the only person she'd known and she's often wondered if the other appendages she's glanced at would satisfy her the same or differently. Perhaps it follows suit to what her mother used to tell her, that 'once you've seen one you've seen them all.' She's unlikely to find out, the sparsity of men a practical limitation, but she has also grown less curious with time. That is until a strange thing happened a few months earlier.

A woman had climbed into the bath but slipped and brushed against her. It was laughed off but Sophie still remembers the jolt of affection. She was confused as it happened. Water and electricity shouldn't coexist and she'd jumped at the pulse that ran the length of her. She'd never felt such fervour before. Sex, the physical satisfying of her husband, had been his prerogative and her wifely duty. She was taught to not believe in the female orgasm and, as she'd never experienced anything that might amount to it, she didn't doubt that it was myth. But that same evening she couldn't shake the accidental touch and, whilst the rest of the villagers were listening to news reports, she replayed the memory that carried her through to an indescribable climax. It sent her to a new territory, frustrating to not have discovered it for forty years but also wishing that she still hadn't. To experience pleasure in this guise left her in a state of shame and yet she continued to masturbate daily with rigour, a thing of distraction, a rousing of spirits like no other. She didn't believe that a thought could have any bearing on faraway actions but she began to convince herself that even to consider pleasuring herself to the fantasies of women would result in Kurt falling susceptible to danger. She knew it made no sense but the entangled perverseness of it meant that she could tell no one and receive reassurance back.

She makes promises with herself all the time, hoping that there's a slim chance that someone up there is paying attention. That if she cuts out certain things some good will come of it. Some sort of perpetual lent. She prays, skips predictable foods, doesn't listen to music. Just maybe all of these restrictions will allow Kurt safe passage into a life of his own choosing, even if that choice is as wasteful as slothfulness. She has since appended to her list a ban on masturbation. This addition is more demanding than anything that preceded it but she hasn't touched herself since. The visits to the baths remain, though if spring turns to summer and there's still no word then she will happily forsake this too. In a way, to look at women and do nothing is more of a punishment than anything.

There's a sudden commotion as a dressed woman runs towards the crowd. Sophie sits up. Her ears prick as the news widens out like a fan until it reaches her at the farthest edge. A military vehicle has been seen on the road for the first time in months, unsurprising considering the inclement weather and fallen trees. These rare visits seldom bring home the wounded. More often they're a report of casualties. Some women climb out to dry off and dress, returning to their posts but only in the hope that there won't be a rap on their door. At least one of them will be forced to answer and ask the men in, unwelcome as the invitation may be.

A shiver runs through her. She wriggles to recapture the water's temperature and forces herself to picture Kurt right now. Better that he's still in battle and not embroiled in this approach. Maybe he's somewhere similar to here, in a snowy outreach huddled around a hearth, roused in camaraderie and avoiding the action. Or perhaps he's some place hot, deep in the Mediterranean. There's an orange grove, a hazel-eyed girl, a charmed tender exchange from within the depths of war. He's laughing, bonding over a crude joke or acquiring a romantic phrase in a foreign language.

She doesn't leave like the others. Instead she shuts her eyes and lowers herself farther into the water so that the surface reaches her chin. She tries to conjure a narrative where Kurt is taking flight, soaring high rather than folded up like a wounded bird under someone's foot.

The chilly air loses its hold. She takes two deep breaths and calms herself until her body is still. For these next few moments, before whatever will be, she has a choice: serenity or dread.

She drops her mouth below the water, inhales deeply through her nostrils and submerges fully. She can stay like this for about a minute. About sixty seconds in which Kurt's fate is not yet sealed. The world will carry on above her but the waterline is, at least for now, an impenetrable forcefield.

She thinks of Schrödinger but, in this venture of hers, *she* is the one inside the box. As far as she's aware no scientist has ever considered it from the cat's point of view. She might be the first.

She's amazed by where her brain takes her, by what it machinates.

She doesn't want to let go but time is precious and lungs are limited and she can't hold on for much longer. She wishes that this wasn't so but all experiments must come to an end and this one is no exception. A held breath will break when it runs out of air.

She has to come up now.